The Spire
of
Kylet

Books by Connie A. Walker

Young Reader

Timmy and the K'nick K'nocker Ring

Teen and Young Adult

Echoes: A Modern Fairytale
Dark in the Forest: Another Modern Fairytale
Sunshine and Shadows: Another Modern Fairytale

Fantasy

THE WOLKAREAN INSCRIPTION

The Spire of Kylet
The Eyes of Landor
Triumph at Serpent's Head

THE WOLKAREAN ENIGMA – Available Soon

Revelation of Riddles
Sorcerers in Shokareen
Temple of Rulianthabah

Book One of The Wolkarean Inscription

The Spire
of
Kylet

Connie A. Walker

Press Forward Press
Fiction Division
5060 S 710 West
Salt Lake City, UT 84123

This book is a work of fiction.
Any resemblance to persons living or dead is coincidental.

ISBN: 978-1-940802-11-4

Library of Congress Control Number: 2016952699

www.connieawalker.com

Publishing History
Prismatic Publishing, 2010
Press Forward Press, 2018
Press Forward Press, 2021

Cover by Bud Spencer, SUMO Graphics

Printed in the United States of America

Dedicated to my mother, Ruth Christensen.

PROLOGUE

A storm burst above the ancient fortress at Serpent's Head.

High in a tower, Elnid-Kyeh shivered in the cold and damp. He pulled his robe tightly around his shoulders and then added a bit more coal to the braziers heating the room.

Lightning flashed across the clouds, followed by a deep rumble of thunder. Towering waves crashed into the rocky cliffs below.

Elnid-Kyeh spread a map of the northern sky on his worktable. Beside it he placed the list of observations he had made since his patron star, Quorten, changed its course three months earlier.

Using a piece of chalk, he marked the new path on the chart.

According to his latest calculations, Quorten would miss the constellations the Lord and His Servant and the Flying Chariot. That combination would have assured his regaining the monarchy. Now, instead, the star would cross the Royal Crown after going through the Hero's Sword, implying that a rival would appear to challenge his claim to his father's throne.

In frustration, he slammed his fist down on the table.

He was the High King's heir! It was his birthright.

The chalk rolled off the table and fell to the floor.

He ground it to dust with his heel.

A ripple in the air alerted him that someone had entered the door at the base of his tower. Elnid-Kyeh turned an ear in that direction and soon heard the faint click-clack of wooden shoes beginning to climb the stairs.

He hated for his servants to see him when he did not look his best. He stepped over to the mirror on the wall and ran a comb through his silvery white hair. He smiled at his reflection. Although he was over three hundred years old, three hundred and seventy-eight to be exact, his appearance was still youthful and handsome. Even now, his dark blue eyes were clear and alert despite his fatigue.

He made a quick gesture with his hand, eliminating the day-old stubble from his chin and cheeks. Another flip of the wrist cleaned his sorcerer's robes and removed the wrinkles.

He had just completed his grooming when a timid face peered through the doorway.

"Over here, my dear," Elnid-Kyeh said gently in order to put the child at ease. He shoved aside a candleholder and a stack of books to make room on the table for his breakfast.

"Is the storm letting up at all?" he asked.

"No, milord," said the rosy-cheeked youngster. Clumsily she tried to curtsey without dropping the tray she carried.

"I will take it, little one."

The girl bobbed up and down and then backed toward the door. Before she reached it, Elnid-Kyeh began a quiet chant. The child's eyes widened with fear, but he smiled reassuringly at her.

She blushed, making her pink cheeks turn deep crimson. She looked up shyly through beautiful long lashes.

Suddenly, the girl's face filled with pain. She grabbed her chest. Her eyes bulged accusingly and overflowed with silent tears. With a gasp she crumpled to the ground and lay there twitching. Slowly she shriveled up until she resembled a dried cornhusk.

"Such a waste," Elnid-Kyeh mumbled aloud to himself.

He was always upset when he was so tired and hungry that he was forced to drain a person's life-energy too quickly. If he had gone slower, the child would not have died. She would only have needed a few days' rest, and she could have been a "donor" again and again. He tossed a rug over the misshapen body.

"Oh well," he told himself as he took a napkin from the tray and tucked it into the neckline of his robe, "at least my appetite has returned."

He tore off a chunk of bread, slathered it generously with butter and redberry jam, and set it on his plate beside a mound of sliced sausages, onions, and mushrooms covered with cheese sauce. He picked up his fork.

When he had barely finished eating and had tossed his napkin back onto the tray, he felt a tingle from the amulet he wore around his neck. He lightly touched a shimmering crystal that was set in the pendant's center.

The face of his Captain of the Guard—a bear of a man with craggy features and a thin mustache—formed in the air and floated before him.

"Milord," said Lairnus with his fingers in contact with an identical amulet, "Hollenth has returned. He would like to bathe and eat before reporting the details of his mission."

Elnid-Kyeh nodded with impatience. "Did he get it?"

"Yes milord." Lairnus held up a scroll with his free hand. "It cost much less than expected. Only fifty gold links."

"Bring it to me."

Elnid-Kyeh chuckled to himself as he hung the star charts back on the wall and then set the breakfast tray on the floor beside the door so a kitchen servant could retrieve it later.

Fifty gold links!

It was worth ten times that. A hundred times, even.

As soon as Lairnus entered the tower room, Elnid-Kyeh sprang from his chair and snatched the rolled parchment from the captain's hand. While his eyes skimmed down the two columns of information, he pointed at the rug covering the dead girl.

"Remove it. Make sure she is replaced by a look-alike for a few days so her disappearance is not associated with me. This evening bring me two others. Do not choose from among the servants. I would not want them to become suspicious and start leaving."

He spread the scroll out on the workbench and weighted one end with the candleholder and the other end with a book.

"If you have a few troublesome guards you want removed," Elnid-Kyeh continued, "they will do. Otherwise, see if you can catch a couple of poachers in the forest."

"Yes, milord." Lairnus flipped away the rug and threw the girl across his shoulder as if she were a sack of millet. He paused. "Perhaps if your needs are increasing, a raid in one of the southern cities might be in order. We could hold the captives in the dungeon until you're ready for them."

"Excellent! Do that." Elnid-Kyeh waved his hand in dismissal.

Lairnus shifted his load and started down the stairs.

Elnid-Kyeh got a silver bowl from a shelf and set it on the table.

He added a dipperful of water and then, from a small crystal flask, sprinkled the top with five drops of thrice-sanctified oil.

Concentrating on the first name and location written on the scroll, he wove a design in the air with his hands. Softly he chanted the words of a scrying spell.

A prick of light flared up from the water.

The oil swirled, forming shapes that shifted and twined like clouds in a storm.

Colors sharpened.

Shadows deepened.

A picture formed.

Two young girls, one dark and one fair, talked and gestured as they rode their mounts across the prairie, far to the southwest. There, morning had barely started to brighten the eastern horizon.

Patches of wildflowers, their colors dulled in the predawn light, were scattered among waving grasses. Although summer would take several more weeks to reach as far north as Serpent's Head, it had already warmed the plains and teased last year's seeds into growth.

A gentle breeze tangled the girls' hair.

Elnid-Kyeh glared at the vision in the bowl. "Which one of you is it?" he muttered. "Let me see your faces."

The Spire of Kylet

As if she had heard the request, the blond girl reined in her pony and glanced upward with pale, nearly colorless eyes. She brushed a wisp of hair from her face with a hand darkened by sunburn and then leaned forward in the saddle.

She gazed around, squinting, as if she struggled to focus on a distant object.

Her eyes settled squarely on Elnid-Kyeh.

"Coincidence," he told himself with a humorless laugh. "She cannot possibly see through my scrying."

A brief smirk flashed across the girl's lips.

She looked so proud, so triumphant, that a shiver of nervousness snaked down Elnid-Kyeh's back.

Suddenly, the girl pointed her finger straight at him and spoke a word he could not hear.

Fear slashed through Elnid-Kyeh's heart.

He waved his hand over the silver dish.

The picture vanished.

Chapter One

"There!" Katrine of Banur cried jubilantly, pointing upward.

The stars had faded just enough as dawn approached that she could see the dark speck circling in the sky. She rotated her shoulders slowly, trying to decrease the stress she felt. As her weight shifted in the saddle, Stubbs, her plains pony, nickered questioningly. She leaned forward and gave him a reassuring pat on the neck.

"Where?" Polnu asked. "I don't see anything." She glanced first one way then another, her dark eyes opened wide, searching.

"Right there." With a jab of her finger, Katrine pointed to the right spot.

"Oh, bother," Polnu muttered. She let her eyelids droop and her expression go blank as she reached out with her mind. A moment later, she gasped in astonishment. "You're right. It's a golden hawk. How did you ever spot it way up there?"

"Easy," Katrine said with a tap to the corners of her eyes.

"Of course," Polnu said in a joking tone, "your witch sight."

Katrine froze as if she'd been slapped.

It was true her eyes were strange. She couldn't deny that. The irises were so pale they hardly showed up at all. A person had to be very close to her to see the faint, smoky band that surrounded her black pupils.

When she was a youngster, the village children had made fun of her, sticking out their tongues, crossing their eyes, and making rude gestures with their hands. They taunted her and called her Witch Eyes or Devil Girl. No one would play with her. No one, that is, except Polnu—and then later, their friend Rand.

"Oh, curse it," Polnu cried, obviously realizing what she'd said. "I was trying to be funny. I was terrified when I caught my first hawk. I wanted to make you laugh so you wouldn't be as scared as I was. I'm sorry."

"It's all right," Katrine said. She cleared her throat, which had gone tight with remembered pain, and then pushed the hurtful memories from her mind. "Should I do it now or wait to see if the hawk comes down lower?"

The Spire of Kylet

"Now," Polnu answered. "You need to get it before it finds other prey."

Nodding, Katrine reached into her tunic pocket and removed a fat gray pigeon. She had already fitted it with a trapper's harness: a leather device that covered the bird's back, encircled its wings, and laced across its breast. Poking through the rawhide in all directions were thin twine loops. Katrine plucked and pulled at them until they stood straight up. Then she cupped the pigeon in her hands while Polnu attached a length of cord to the harness' underside. At the other end of the cord was a heavy stick, about as long and thick as Katrine's arm.

"Here goes," Katrine said, tossing the bird into the air.

At the same time, Polnu dropped the stick to the ground.

Please let this work, Katrine prayed in silent desperation. Her whole future depended on what happened within the next few minutes. *Please, please, let it work.*

In a flurry of wings and feathers, the pigeon took flight.

When it reached the end of the tether, it faltered. For several seconds it strained against the weight of the drag. Then it spread its wings and drifted down for a brief rest, only to flutter frantically again, trying to climb the sky in a different direction.

Now that the trap had been set, Katrine allowed herself a huge yawn. She'd had to get up quite early this morning in order to finish her chores before she led Stubbs out through the bolthole behind the stables. She had only been able to sneak away because her father was in Drena, the closest neighboring town, on Council business.

Most mornings, he turned the parlor into a classroom, tutoring Katrine and her younger brothers and sister for a couple of hours after breakfast. If the children did poorly, he kept them until noon or made them reassemble after dinner. Taking lessons at home was another thing that alienated Katrine from the village children. They all attended school together, learning from Crennese teachers who could use a bit of magic here and there to help a slow student who was struggling with difficult concepts. Katrine and her siblings had to learn everything the hard way: doing hours of studying, memorizing, and reciting.

"You're sure the hawk will take it?" Katrine asked, refocusing her attention on the current task.

"The brown and red hawks always do." Suddenly Polnu waved her hand excitedly. "Look!"

A golden blur swooped through the sky with incredible speed. When the hawk neared the tethered pigeon, it swung its clawed feet forward. Katrine closed her eyes, but in her mind she heard the pigeon's back snap as the hawk snatched it from the air.

She glanced up.

The pigeon's body dangled lifelessly from the hawk's talons, which were now hopelessly tangled in the twine loops of the harness.

6

"All we can do now is wait," Polnu said, sliding off her horse. "The hawk will tire soon. The dragging stick won't let it go far."

For a moment Katrine watched her friend's smooth, fluid movements. That natural grace came from Polnu's Crennese ancestry, Katrine thought, just as her medium height and delicate bones did. Like all the members of her tribe, Polnu had silky black hair and bottomless dark brown eyes. Her skin was just a shade darker than the copper kettles that hung in the kitchen at home, right after they had been scrubbed with vinegar and salt.

In comparison, Katrine felt huge and clumsy and unattractive.

Swinging a leg over her pony's rump, she hopped to the ground. With a quick flip, she looped her pony's reins around the small branch of a thornbush.

A gust of wind tugged at the long blond braid hanging down Katrine's back. A wisp of hair came loose and caught in her eyelashes. Automatically she brushed it back with her hand and hooked it behind her ear.

Tingling with nervousness and fright and excitement, she wiped her clammy hands on her trousers. She just had to catch the hawk!

If she were to have any hope of being accepted at the Recorders School in Pardish, she needed some kind of advantage. There were never enough seats available for all the applicants. She hoped a painting of the rare hawk would catch Headmaster Miksel's eye and swing the odds in her favor. She had already saved over half the money she would need to join a caravan to the city. She would earn the rest by Midwinter Festival, which was about when her acceptance letter should come.

No matter what happened, however, she was *not* going to spend another year tending her father's herds and working on the farm. And she absolutely, positively *was not* going to get married, manage a husband's household, and have babies. Not now. Not ever.

With her heart thumping eagerly and her teeth clamped on her lower lip, she watched the hawk's progress. As it struggled to fly, it pulled the heavy stick through the grass, flattening a dark trail.

She wished the bird would hurry up and get tired. Although she had finished her household chores before she left the manor, she still had the herd and the fences to check.

She glanced to the east. Dawn was about to break.

She held her breath. This was her favorite time of day.

In a flash of buttery brilliance the sun cleared the horizon. Light flooded the prairie, making small beads of water left on the grass by last night's storm twinkle like tiny jewels.

Wildflowers raised their heads and dotted the landscape with splashes of pink and blue and white and yellow. Sweet perfumes scented the air. Soon bees flitted around, gathering nectar and scattering specks of pollen.

Taking a deep breath, Katrine inhaled the spices of moist earth and growing plants. "On mornings like this," she said with a sigh, "I love the plains."

"Then why do you want to leave?" Polnu asked for the hundredth time. "Pardish, with its great city and Recorders School, can't possibly be as magnificent as this." She made a sweeping gesture to include everything in view.

Katrine stared out over the waving prairie grass to the Daegarn Mountains in the west. "Don't you have any curiosity at all, Polnu? How can you be content to spend forever in this tiny insignificant corner of Kareand?"

"I like it here," Polnu answered with a small shrug.

Katrine shook her head at such simplistic thinking. "But there is so much more to the world than the plains. Just imagine it. Shanree Palace. The twin cities: Pardish and Landor. Boradid Isle and its lost treasures. Wouldn't you just love to travel through the Verdant Mountains and visit Marlett's Cleft, maybe even catch a glimpse of the wildmen of the north?"

"Maybe someday," Polnu admitted, "but all those places are so far away. You would have to travel for weeks, maybe months, to reach any of them."

"But that's part of the adventure."

Suddenly Katrine became stone still. A green and black butterfly landed lightly on her arm. Polnu stepped closer, and they both watched, fascinated by the delicate wings and sleek body, until without warning it twitched and flew away.

"You won't see that when you're cooped up in the city," Polnu said, planting her fists on her hips. "Why do you want to spend your whole life in the back of some stuffy old library studying dusty old books? Or riding around the countryside delivering messages to all kinds of people in all kinds of weather?"

"That's only part of what Recorders do," Katrine said. She couldn't quite keep the exasperation out of her voice. They'd had this conversation dozens of times. "They also keep records of important events so they can document history as it happens. They get to meet people like the Regent and her Council and then write up the stories of their lives and paint their portraits. All Recorders are trained in voice and music and oration. They are welcomed wherever they go, and they get to travel everywhere and see everything. I'll love doing that. It's what I was born for."

"Well, here's your chance. The hawk is growing tired."

Before Katrine could glance upward, Polnu's horse, Shadow, butted her head against Katrine's shoulder and made a demanding whinny. Grinning, Katrine pulled a carrot from her pack. While Shadow crunched it with big white teeth, Katrine was almost overcome by a wave of pure envy.

As much as she loved Stubbs, her little plains pony, she yearned to own a real horse. That was another reason for becoming a Recorder. They were among the few people, besides the Crennese tribes, to ride true horses.

Other than being a Recorder or a Landorian Warrior, there were only two legal ways of obtaining a horse: catch one of the wild steeds that roamed the plains in mighty herds or purchase one at the annual auctions held in the larger cities. Only the Crennese had the skill to do the first, and only the very wealthy could do the second. Most people had to be satisfied with the smaller and less graceful plains ponies.

Katrine patted Stubbs on the neck even if he was a bit ungainly. She pulled out a carrot for him, too. Then she unhooked her saddlebags and slung them over her shoulder.

"You coming?" Polnu called as she followed the dragging stick.

Katrine plucked a blade of prairie grass and, chewing on the stem, trotted along after her friend.

"You seem worried about more than just catching the hawk," Polnu said when Katrine caught up with her. "What's wrong?"

Katrine flicked away the shredded piece of grass and swallowed hard. "I think Father is about to betroth me to someone. He stares at me when he thinks I don't notice, and I heard him say something to Mother about having some new clothes made for me." She blinked to keep tears from welling up in her eyes. Her voice quivered with pent-up emotions. "I'm fifteen, after all, and the High Elder's daughter. If he accepts an offer, I'll never get away from here. You're lucky the Crennese don't force their children into early marriages."

"But surely your father won't give you to someone you don't want," Polnu said soothingly.

"Of course he will," Katrine exclaimed in a burst of anger. "He wanted his first child to be a son, and he won't forgive me for being born a girl."

Although Katrine had made the complaint often enough, Polnu put her arm around Katrine's waist, just as Katrine knew she would. She leaned against her friend, thankful for the offered comfort.

"Maybe it would be different if I was pretty like Jaimi," Katrine said sadly. "But I'm too tall and broad-shouldered, and I have these ugly eyes. I'm sure Father will be so relieved if someone wants to arrange a match for me that he'll give me to the first person who asks."

"Would marriage be so bad? You're very good with your younger brothers and sisters. You'd make a fine mother."

Staring off into the hazy distance, Katrine felt a familiar pressure build up inside her. Her voice dropped into a whisper. "Something's calling me, Polnu, calling me away from here. Sometimes it's so strong I just want to run and run and run, and keep running until my lungs burst or my legs fall off. But where? It must be the Recorders School. Where else could I go?"

Silently Polnu tightened her grip around Katrine's waist, and together they watched the great hawk drop behind a clump of tall, spiky grass.

Seconds passed, and then with a frantic beating of wings, the bird was airborne.

It flew to the end of the tether, faltered, and landed again.

It rested. It regained the air.

"It's tired," Polnu said. "Did you remember the glove?"

Katrine nodded solemnly and began rummaging in one of her packs. She shouldn't have mentioned her father. Thinking about him always put her in a bad mood. No matter how hard she tried to please him and make him proud, she always failed, and he always made sure she knew how disappointed he was.

"Here it is," Katrine said with forced cheer, trying to project optimism. She slid the heavy hawker's glove onto her hand. "I borrowed it from Brac, Father's Chief Herdsman. Of course, I didn't ask him. He wouldn't approve of this any more than Father would."

"Any moment now," Polnu said, winding the long cord onto the stick and taking up the slack.

Like an angel kicked out of heaven, the great hawk dropped to the ground.

"I don't want to hurt you," Katrine murmured, trying to mimic the reassuring tone Brac used to calm the farm animals. "I just want to paint your picture. As soon as I finish, I'll set you free. I promise."

When Katrine was just a few steps away from the hawk, it tried to flee, but its energy was spent. It flopped helplessly. Katrine crouched down in front of it.

Even though the bird's talons were tangled in the mass of twine loops, Katrine worried about the damage the sharp, hooked beak could do to tender, exposed skin.

"Careful," Polnu whispered with a nervous catch in her voice. "Be quick."

Mustering enough energy for one last pose, the bird flared its wings and screeched. Katrine's hand was a flash of lightning. She grabbed the hawk where its legs joined its body. Then straightening her arm, she lifted the huge bird as she stood.

Frantically the hawk swung its head, slashing the air wickedly.

It snatched a bit of glove and tried to rip it apart, but the leather held.

The bird flapped and cried out angrily. Then it settled down and stared at its captor.

A delighted burble burst from Katrine's throat. She felt exalted. If she could trap and hold this mighty master of the sky, there were no limits to what she might accomplish.

She could do—she could be—anything!

"Well done," Polnu said, interrupting Katrine's thoughts. "I've got to go now. I need to collect herbs and roots for my mother before the day gets too hot."

Katrine gave Polnu a quick, one-armed hug. "Thank you. I couldn't have done it alone."

"It was my pleasure. See you later."

As Polnu rode away, Katrine studied the landscape with a critical eye, looking for the best setting for her painting. She finally chose a scrubtree with a twisted branch.

She dumped her saddlebags on the ground and let Stubbs graze beside a trickling stream.

With a small knife from her belt she cut through the loops of the trapper's harness. She secured the bird where she wanted it by flipping a portion of dragline around its feet and then around the branch.

She yanked off the awkward, stiff glove and tossed it aside.

From within her art satchel she pulled out her paintboard and brushes. She assembled a wooden frame and attached a square of bleached canvas to it. Sitting on the ground, she leaned against a rock, balanced the frame on her knees, and began sketching with a fine brush and pale gray paint.

Giving the sun a quick glance, she nearly choked on a horrified gasp. How had it gotten so late? She hadn't even started checking the herds.

She would have to hurry.

No, she told herself. Hurrying caused sloppiness. She'd take the time to do her best and deal with the consequences later.

In the distance she heard the faint yowl of a plains cat. Her heart skipped a beat. However, since Stubbs continued happily chomping on the tender grass growing at the creek's edge, she knew the cat was no threat. Long before the cat got close enough to spring, Stubbs would alert her with rapid stomping and an agitated whinny.

Katrine's brushes flew from the paintboard to the canvas and back again. Gradually golden feathers took shape and flowed across the hawk's breast. They darkened on the bird's back and faded nearly to white at the tips of the tail. Bronze eyes speckled with yellow stared forward from each side of a huge, amber-colored beak.

While the first layers of paint dried, Katrine examined her work and nibbled on the lunch that Rosi, the family's cook, had prepared.

Then she added highlights, accents, and finishing details to the picture. When the final strokes had been applied, she stood and stretched, arching her back and rolling her head from side to side as she admired the results.

She picked up the portrait and turned it toward the hawk. "I think I captured you admirably," she said, smiling at the double meaning. She held the picture so Stubbs could have a look, too. "Don't the plains make a beautiful, subtle background?"

"Ahhccckkk," screeched the hawk, as if reminding her of the promised freedom.

"All right, a deal's a deal," Katrine said with a grin.

After putting the hawker's glove back on, she grasped the bird as she had earlier, pulled out her knife, and sliced the dragline from the hawk's feet. With a fling of her arm, she set the bird free.

When it had winged out of sight, Katrine packed up everything except the painting and reattached the pouches to her saddle.

The picture needed to dry thoroughly before she rolled it up, so she leaned it against the tree trunk and covered it loosely with a cloth.

She leapt onto her pony's back.

The sun had already started to drop in the west.

"Oh, Stubbs, it took so long. We've got to hurry."

Katrine didn't know what the final outcome of her morning's activities would be. Maybe the painting would help her get into the Recorders School, maybe not. But she knew exactly what the consequences would be if her father found out she had wasted the day. He was a stern taskmaster, and his anger was harrowing.

Nudging Stubbs into a trot, she worried about the things she still had to do. It wouldn't take long to check the old section of fencing to see if it had been damaged by last night's storm and to brace it if it had. She didn't need to open the sluice gates to the irrigation troughs because the rain had been heavy enough to water the crops adequately.

The big problem was the herd.

Some of the females hadn't delivered their calves yet.

Father had instructed Brac to round up all the ones who hadn't given birth and keep them in the barn, but a few were stubborn and were hiding. They were particularly vulnerable to plains cats when they were heavy with offspring and slow to run. And when calves were born on the plains, the scent of blood brought predators from miles around, putting the whole herd at risk.

In addition, there was the ravine to check.

Every year when the river ran low, a few herdbeasts braved the steep decline into the gulch. Sometimes one stumbled and injured itself on the rocky trail, becoming stranded and not even making it to the bottom.

If Katrine or a predator didn't find it quickly, it died of thirst and hunger with its head turned longingly toward the stream and thick grasses on the ravine floor.

A few summers ago, after pulling two herdbeasts from the ravine in a single day, Katrine had asked Father why he didn't just build a fence around the gully to keep the animals out.

He had answered that the area was too large and the materials too costly.

Besides, she had added silently to herself, her work was free—or almost. Father did give her a few extra coppers in addition to her pocket money each week to pay for her labors.

Topping a small rise, Katrine saw the ravine in the distance.

Circling above it were three sharp-beaked buzzards.

Damn!

Chapter Two

When Katrine neared the ravine, she heard the frantic wail of a young herdbeast. She pounded on Stubbs's flanks until they reached the gully's edge, and then she leapt from his back.

Peering over the rim, she saw a brown and gray spotted yearling trying to scramble backward on three squat legs. Its fourth was broken and bloody. Scuff marks on the trail showed where the yearling had stumbled and fallen. It had then rolled down the last several feet.

Ten paces from the injured animal, a plains cat crouched, ready to spring. It was over twice the yearling's size and was covered with yellowish-brown fur except where long tufts of black hair decorated its cheeks and hung from its chest like an old man's beard. The beast opened its cavernous mouth, exposing finger-length fangs, and emitted a low growl. Its tail lashed back and forth.

The yearling froze as if it might disappear if it stood still enough.

Katrine reached for the bow she kept fastened to her saddle.

Oh no! It wasn't there!

In her haste to catch the hawk, when she'd snuck out this morning, she had forgotten it.

She grabbed the knife from her belt. She looked at it and groaned. It was too small and the distance too great for the blade to be useful.

Katrine considered dashing down the trail, shouting, hoping to frighten the cat away. She rejected the idea quickly. The cat was more likely to attack her than to let her chase it from a meal. In a flash of morbid imagination, she pictured the cat eating the herdbeast for the main course and having her for dessert.

She shook the image from her mind.

Reaching inside her tunic front, Katrine pulled out a Glainite weapon: a spire. It was a silver, six-sided disk that sprouted blades at each angle once it was thrown.

Do I dare? she wondered doubtfully.

She had only practiced with it a few times.

The plains cat pulled in its hindquarters, preparing to pounce.

Katrine snapped her wrist and flung the weapon. "Don't miss," she whispered. "You're all I have."

As the spire flashed through the air, the sharp, curved blades popped into place. It spun through a beam of sunlight and for one brief moment looked like a blazing star with six bright rays.

The plains cat emitted a highly pitched hunting cry when it sprang forward. The sound turned into a howl of pain and surprise as the weapon sliced its belly open and spilled its innards all over the ground.

Katrine stared in amazement at her luck.

If the cat hadn't jumped into it, the spire would have missed entirely.

Delighted at her good fortune, she forgot to reach for the disk when it completed its elliptical course and returned to her. It wasn't until she heard the whine of the spire's approach, coupled with a click as the blades snapped back into the weapon's interior, that she hopped to the right and stuck out her hand.

The angle of the catch was wrong, and the contact between soft skin and hard metal felt like the sting of a gigantic wasp.

"Snakespit!" Katrine swore under her breath as she flexed her smarting fingers. She bent, picked up the spire, and wiped it on the grass to remove splotches of blood and gore.

"Not bad, Katrine," an amused male voice said from behind her. "Of course, the jump was a bit unusual. Think you could teach me?"

Although Katrine hadn't known Rand was near, she wasn't startled to hear him speak. Over the years she had learned to accept the silent approaches and sudden appearances of her Crennese friends.

She smiled when she turned around.

Like Polnu, Rand was slender and had facial features as delicate and lovely as a fine porcelain doll. Also like Polnu, he was an expert bowman and hunter. But Rand and Polnu were obviously not from the same Crennese tribe. He was a little taller than average, his skin was fairer than Polnu's bronze, and he had brown rather than black hair. His dark brown almond-shaped eyes tipped up at the corners with silent laughter.

"Sorry, Rand," Katrine said lightly, holding the spire behind her back, "that particular move is a well-guarded secret. I couldn't possibly show you how it's done."

"I don't doubt that." Then he pulled back and his smile faded. "Katrine, your eyes!"

Katrine's happy mood evaporated. She flared at him angrily, "Don't you dare call me Witch Girl!"

Rand blinked a few times and shook his head.

"Sorry," he mumbled. "I guess it was the light, but for a second, your eyes seemed to glow. I couldn't even see the black of your pupils. It scared the breath right out of me."

"Grrr," Katrine growled at him, baring her teeth and squinting threateningly.

He gave her an exaggerated look of remorse and spoke in a wheedling, persuasive voice. "Don't be mad at me. You know I can't handle the unexpected as easily as you do." He batted his eyelids and simpered. "Come on. Say you forgive me. Please."

Katrine tried not to giggle, but she couldn't help it. "Oh, all right, you're forgiven." Then she forced herself to be stern. "But don't do it again. Earlier today, Polnu made a joke about my *witch sight*. I get very tired of it."

"I know," Rand said, this time sounding sincere. "I really am sorry." Then he got a glint in his eye. "So, what was that shiny object you were trying to catch with those awkward moves and," he raised his eyebrows with fake reproach, "that unladylike word?"

Without answering, Katrine thought hard. She knew Rand was teasing her in order to change the subject, but he was also providing her with a perfect opportunity.

Eventually, she would have to discuss the spire with a member of the wizard race. It was magical. Even she could feel that. She probably shouldn't have touched it, but when she did, it seemed in some strange way to become a part of her.

At first she had thought about showing the spire to Polnu.

In the end, though, she decided against it. She didn't want to put her friend in a position where she might have to choose between her loyalty to Katrine and her loyalty to her grandmother. Not only was Polnu's grandmother a spire-wielder, but she was also The Glaine, the leader of their tribe. As far as Katrine knew, all spires belonged to the Glainites.

Pursing her lips, Katrine wrinkled her brow. Since Rand wasn't a member of Polnu's tribe, he might be willing to explain the spire's powers without trying to take it from her.

"If I show you, will you promise not to tell anyone?"

"Of course," came Rand's quick reply. "You know you can trust me."

Katrine continued to argue with herself. It wasn't until Rand started to frown and fidget that she made up her mind. Extending her hand, she offered him the weapon.

"Holy Signs!" Rand gasped, jumping back and putting his hands behind him. "Why aren't you dead?"

"What?" yelped Katrine.

"That's a spire. No one is supposed to be able to touch them except the person to whom they've been bound."

Katrine answered with a little shrug, "Maybe it's broken."

Rand was not amused. He spoke with irritated, biting sarcasm. "A spire is not like a water pump or a wagon wheel that you can break. They're pure magic, and Kylet made them all. He was the most powerful sorcerer ever, and he forged weapons, not only with anvil, hammer, and fire, but also with the force of his thoughts and the strength of his magic. No one could break that kind of weapon. Nothing is supposed to break the bond between bearer and spire, either."

Hurt by Rand's tone, Katrine snapped back at him defensively. "That's not true. Glainite parents always give their spires to one of their children before they die. If they didn't, there wouldn't be any spire-wielders left."

"That's true," Rand answered sharply, "but they do a ritual of severing and binding during their Full Moon Festival. Have you had that thing bound to you by moonlight?"

"No."

"Then you should be dead."

"Stop saying that!" Katrine shouted. She took a deep breath, then another, hoping she could speak more calmly. "I found the spire in the ravine."

As soon as the words were out of her mouth, though, she remembered the injured herdbeast.

"Snakespit!" she exclaimed. "I've got to haul that fraggin' yearling up the trail and make it home before sunset. I didn't get my chores done today, and if Father finds out, he'll be in a rage."

"I'll help you," Rand offered, just as if they hadn't been quarreling a moment earlier. "You can tell me about the spire on the way down the trail."

"Thanks," Katrine said. "The yearlings are so hard to move when they've been hurt, and even if I can't save an animal's life, Father still expects me to bring the carcass home so the meat isn't wasted."

"We'll make a litter."

While they cautiously edged their way down the steep path, Katrine told Rand her story.

"I found the spire early this spring, shortly before my fifteenth birth celebration. I was pushing the dead leaves and undergrowth around with the toe of my boot, looking for those tiny, heart-shaped flowers that only grow on the ravine floor. I wanted to wear some in my hair at my party. The tip of my boot caught on something, and I used my knife to dig it out. It was the spire. At first I didn't realize what it was. Then it was too late. I'd already picked it up. It felt good, so I kept it."

"I don't understand," Rand said. He shook his head, puzzled. "Maybe the old stories aren't true. Or maybe they're just exaggerated. My mother said spires would spit fire into eyes or burn off arms to keep the wrong people from touching them. She said the only man who ever threw a spire that didn't belong to him was killed by it. He tossed it, but when the blades popped out, it whipped around in a circle, came up behind him, and sliced his head off."

Not watching where he was going as he spoke, Rand slipped, but Katrine grabbed his arm and steadied him so he didn't fall. After that, conversation ceased as they both stepped more carefully.

A cool sweet breeze, smelling of dampness and clover, rippled through the air, but as they neared the end of the trail, the acrid smell of blood and death overwhelmed the pleasant aroma.

"What are you going to do with the cat's body?" Rand asked while he measured saplings for the base of the litter and then cut them down with his knife.

"Just leave it, I guess." Katrine grabbed a handful of vines and yanked. "If the buzzards don't pick it clean, maybe the odor will keep the herdbeasts away from here for a while." When the vines fell, leaves and bugs tumbled down with them. Katrine brushed debris from her hair.

"This place will soon be swarming with all kinds of vermin," Rand stated. He laid the saplings out in a row, and he and Katrine began weaving them together with the vines she'd collected. "You'll probably have to come back down here sometime this summer. You won't be happy if the area is full of bloat-snipers or spitting lizards."

"You're right," Katrine agreed. "At least buzzards will wait until you're dead. The others would just as soon chomp into the living." She sighed helplessly. "I guess I should bury it, but I don't have time now. I think I'm going to get into enough trouble as it is."

Together Katrine and Rand lifted the injured animal onto the litter. It squealed and squirmed ungratefully.

"I'll meet you here tomorrow," Rand told her. "If there's anything left of the cat, we can bury it together. Around noon?"

"That would be great." Katrine bent her knees and grasped the front of the litter while Rand took the rear. They began to trek upward.

It was a miserable hike. The trail was steep and narrow and slippery from last night's rain. Not only that, but also the young herdbeast was terrified. Its fear seemed to escalate with every step Katrine and Rand took. Finally, its thrashing became so violent it threatened to tip them all over the path's sharp edge.

Rand called a halt. After they lowered the litter to the ground, he touched the yearling's brow and put the sleep on it.

"That's a neat trick," Katrine told him. "I wish I could do that to the twins sometimes."

Rand laughed. "I've never tried it on people."

"Did your parents ever put you to sleep that way when you were little?" Rand's laughter stopped abruptly, and Katrine gave out a little gasp. "Oh, Rand, I'm sorry. That was thoughtless of me."

"It's not your fault," he assured her. "I shouldn't take it so hard. After all, it's been more than ten years. It's just that I still miss them."

Katrine reached across the sleeping herdbeast and touched Rand's arm. "You've never told me what actually happened," she said gently.

"I can't remember much." Rand bent his knees and grabbed hold of the litter, so Katrine turned around and did the same. They began walking again.

She assumed he had said all that he intended. He never discussed his parents' deaths. But after they'd climbed a while, he began speaking quietly, almost as if he talked to himself.

"We were traveling through the foothills, coming out of the Daegarn Mountains. My mother rode in front and held the lead rope to our packhorse. I rode on my father's lap. There was a rumbling sound, and the ground began to shake. Just before the path gave way, my father tossed me onto a little rock ledge above the trail.

"My parents were there one moment, then the path, the horses, and my parents were gone. I don't know how long I crouched on that bit of rock before Leron rode by on a higher trail and heard me crying. The whole side of the hill below my ledge had collapsed, and it took him forever to figure out how to get down to me."

Rand paused and his voice dropped low. "During the nights, animals howled and shrieked and scrambled on the hillside trying to reach me. I was terrified. But that didn't compare to the fear I felt every time Leron tried something new and failed. I was afraid he would give up and leave me there."

"How old were you?" Katrine asked, trying to recall when he had moved into Leron's home. Rand had been her friend almost as long as Polnu had.

"Seven. You'd think I'd remember a lot, wouldn't you? But I don't. Sometimes I can almost remember my mother's face and my father's arms. I know she was beautiful and he was strong. But I can't pull their images into my mind, no matter how hard I try. What has stayed with me the most are the stories they told me and the few charms and spells I had already learned. They had just begun teaching me magic."

Katrine heard him sigh and imagined the sad look on his face. He often wore a melancholy expression.

"Sometimes," Rand continued, "I wonder what my life would've been like if my parents had lived and I'd grown up in a Crennese home. I don't seem to have much magical talent, but I think I could do more if only I had someone to show me how."

"What a tragedy," Katrine said. "You lost not only your parents, but also your birthright and heritage. Your culture. You might have been a master."

"Perhaps," Rand said hesitantly, "but maybe it's better this way. The old Crennese wizards didn't use their magical abilities wisely. I think Manderig made a mistake by creating a race of wizards. There were too many people fighting for power."

Katrine wheezed, trying to catch her breath. "I've got to rest."

They lowered the litter and sat down on the trail.

"I always figured being Crennese was wonderful," Katrine said. "You're all so strong, and smart, and graceful."

"Ha!" Rand exclaimed. "We're the outcasts of Kareand. The magical wars during the Second Great Uprising caused so much havoc, most people still fear and hate us even after all these centuries."

"I don't," Katrine said. "If others do, it's only because they haven't had a chance to get to know any of you."

"That might be true," Rand said thoughtfully. He scooped up a handful of dirt and sifted it between his fingers. "So many Crennese were killed during the war that there are hardly any of us left. And for some reason, Crennese parents seldom have more than one child. Most people will live their entire lives without ever meeting a true Crennese wizard."

"Polnu's people, the Glainites, have thrived."

"Yes," Rand agreed, "but they're not really sorcerers. They do root and herb lore. A few magic spells. Some prophecy and farseeing. But they can't move mountains the way the old wizards could."

An unvoiced signal passed between them, and they stood, lifted the litter, and started up the path again. They hadn't gone far before a rock slipped beneath Katrine's foot, and she lurched forward.

"You all right?" Rand asked as he adjusted his grip.

"Just clumsy," Katrine answered.

When they had the load balanced between them again, they trudged on, and Katrine returned to the thought she'd had about Polnu's tribe. "The first Glaine was a powerful sorceress. That's why Elnid-Kyeh became afraid of her at the end and tried to kill her. If she was the mother of the Glainites, shouldn't her descendants share in her powers?"

"They would have," Rand said, "except she didn't pass her magic on to her children. She was afraid Elnid-Kyeh would capture them and use them for evil. When she did the ritual of sharing with them, she only bestowed the healing, teaching, and social lores."

"But the magic might still be there," Katrine said with barely suppressed excitement. "Maybe it's hidden inside the Glainites like a seed, just waiting for the right environment to let it sprout and grow."

"Holy Signs, I hope not!" Rand exclaimed. "The Glainites have a good life here. If they started exhibiting strong Crennese powers, I think mobs of Nistarians would hunt them down and slaughter them. People won't risk facing a repeat of the Second Great Uprising. Back then, wizards tossed magic around as if they were playing touch-tag with a child's leather ball. The sky turned orange and purple and green from all the wild magic in the air. It destroyed or changed every living thing it touched."

While Rand talked, pictures formed in Katrine's mind, pictures of brilliant colors exploding in the sky. When the colors splashed over people and animals, the creatures shrieked and howled, either dying gruesome deaths or transforming into hideous beasts. When plants were splattered with the wild magic, they twisted into new and dangerous forms: some grew long thorns, others developed grasping vines, still others began oozing poisonous vapors or flesh-eating sap.

These images, Katrine realized, did not come from her imagination. Somehow, Rand was projecting the shadow of his thoughts into her head.

Suddenly the pictures disappeared.

"If life is hard for the wizard race," Rand said, "if we have to struggle to survive, perhaps it is a good thing. Hopefully, we'll never grow strong enough to do that much damage again. The old sorcerers held infinite power. Even the strongest leaders of the other races were wise to fear them."

At the word *leaders,* Katrine immediately thought of her father, High Elder of Banur. If he had lived five hundred years ago, he would not have been intimidated by a bunch of old men wearing robes and swishing crystal-topped staffs around no matter how many colors the sky turned. But then she remembered an incident last winter when she had seen her father frightened.

He and Brac had dragged a strange animal's carcass out onto the prairie, surrounded it with timber, and set it ablaze. The beast had been twice as big as a fully-grown plains cat. It had foul-smelling brown hide and sharp curved tusks. Father had let her watch from a distance.

When they returned home, she noticed deep, ragged grooves in the manor gates. She asked Father about them, and he motioned to the mound smoldering in the distance. That was when fear had flashed across his face. For many nights afterward, Father had stood watch with the guards in the lookout tower at the northeast corner of their estate. Thinking Father was frightened had scared Katrine worse than knowing a creature could gouge finger-deep ruts into a door made of hardened fillantra wood.

When Katrine and Rand reached the rim of the ravine, they collapsed beside the litter, gasping for air and rubbing circulation into their hands. They rested a few minutes then labored to their feet and lifted the yearling onto Stubbs's strong back.

Rand steadied the pony while Katrine swung up behind it.

"It will wake up eventually, won't it?" she asked.

"In the morning."

"Thanks for your help. Now I have to see if I can get home before the sun drops behind the mountains."

"Even with the yearling's added weight, you should make it if you keep a steady pace," Rand assured her.

Katrine bit her lower lip and glanced in the direction of home. "Unfortunately, I have an errand to do first. Polnu helped me catch a hawk today, and I left the painting out to dry. After all that work, I don't want anything to happen to it overnight."

"Tell me where it is, and I'll go get it. My horse is much faster than your pony. I'll catch up with you."

Standing in the stirrups, Katrine stretched so she could plant a light kiss on Rand's cheek. "Thank you."

In the west the sun tinted the clouds with stripes of red and gold as it neared the horizon.

By the time Katrine heard the rhythm of returning hooves, she was within sight of the manor.

"It's exquisite," Rand declared as he rode up beside her. "I almost expected the hawk to fly away when I lifted the cloth."

Beaming proudly, Katrine slipped the rolled up picture into her saddle pouch. "Did you leave the frame there?"

Rand nodded. "After I unhooked the clamps and took the painting off, I didn't know what else to do with it."

"I'll get it tomorrow."

"Do you mind if I ride with you a moment?" Rand asked. "I haven't told you why I came looking for you this afternoon."

"All right." When he didn't continue, Katrine glanced at him and was surprised to see him blushing. "What's wrong?"

Another awkward moment passed before Rand spoke. "Remember, I told you Leron has been seeking a wife for me."

"Of course. Has he found one?"

"He thinks so." Rand studied his horse's black mane. The glow from the setting sun colored his complexion almost burgundy.

"Well," Katrine asked, "who's the fortunate lass?"

Glancing everywhere except at Katrine, he blurted it out. "You. He's dining with your family tonight and expects to make an offer before he comes home."

Stunned, Katrine pulled up on Stubbs's reins. "You're teasing me."

Very slowly, Rand shook his head from side to side. "I tried to explain to him that we're just friends and don't like each other that way, but he wouldn't listen."

"Holy Signs!" Katrine could hardly catch her breath as she watched her world tumble in on top of her.

"Maybe your father already has someone else in mind," Rand suggested hurriedly. "Maybe he'll turn my adoptive father down."

All of a sudden Katrine realized the plains had gotten dark, not because of her personal tragedy, but because the sun had slipped behind the mountains, engulfing the land in long shadows. "Oh snakespit! Father's going to be furious, especially if Leron has already arrived. See you tomorrow."

"Tomorrow."

As Katrine passed through the manor gates, a knot the size of a fist formed in her throat.

She swallowed hard, again and again, but it remained unmovable.

Faint light from curtained windows silhouetted a figure, rigid and motionless, standing in front of the house.

Chapter Three

"Your mother has been frantic," Father snapped at Katrine as soon as she drew near. "The barring of the gates and the evening chants are both late because of you."

As he spoke, servants scurried about lighting torches on top of the high stone wall that surrounded the manor. Others rushed forward and pushed the thick wooden gates closed and slid a heavy metal bar into place.

Although her painting was hidden and the injured animal lay across her lap, Katrine was still frightened that Father would somehow guess that she hadn't fulfilled her responsibilities today.

As he noticed the yearling and stepped forward, Katrine's heart pounded faster and faster. Her hands, slick with perspiration, trembled.

"What happened to this one?"

"The ravine," Katrine answered breathlessly. She paused and cleared her throat. She hoped the dim light masked the fear on her face. She tried to sound casual. "I got there just as a plains cat was about to have him for dinner." Dismounting, she added, "You can see it better if I get out of the way."

"Brac!" Father called.

While Father examined the animal's injuries, Katrine unhooked her saddlebags and slung them across her shoulder, making sure her painting satchel was beneath the others. "If Rand hadn't come along, I don't know if I could've gotten it out. It made quite a fuss. He put the sleep on it, but it'll wake up in the morning." Her nervous babbling was sure to make Father suspicious.

Be calm, she told herself. *Just shut up and be calm.*

"And the cat?" asked Father. He reached for the yearling and lifted it from the pony.

"I killed it."

"Good."

Brac, the Chief Herder, appeared from behind the house, and Father

22

handed him the animal. As Brac strode off toward the barn, Father's eyes narrowed, and he gave Katrine a scrutinizing look.

"What about the females who are late birthing? Did you locate any?"

"No sir," Katrine answered truthfully, "but on the ride back with the yearling I thought of some places I can check in the morning."

"Hmmm," Father murmured. "Did you have any other trouble out there?"

Katrine's heart stopped. He knew she was hiding something. Why had she assumed the yearling's injuries would be enough to distract him? She should have come up with a story to cover the whole day, but she was such a poor liar she knew she would never have gotten away with it.

Don't ask any more questions, Katrine urged wordlessly. *This time just let it go. Please.*

Father's scowl deepened until his green eyes hardly showed between the slits of his eyelids.

Alarmed almost to the point of panic, Katrine portrayed a semblance of composure. She wouldn't squirm. She wouldn't run. She wouldn't blurt out the truth as she had when younger. If she had to bite her tongue in half, she wasn't volunteering anything.

"You deserve to be thrashed," Father said abruptly, "for putting your mother through this worry and for disrupting the evening rituals. If you had been diligent, you would have found the yearling in time to chase it from the ravine instead of having to rescue it. You don't need to make excuses. I know if you were with Rand, you weren't focusing on your work.

"But, be warned, daughter, one of these days you'll come home too late and the gates will already be barred. If they are, no amount of screaming or begging by you, your mother, or the other children will get them opened again before dawn. Do you understand?"

"Yes, Father," Katrine answered with her head lowered. She had to bite her lip to keep from smiling. He hadn't guessed the truth. She was going to be all right.

"Although you deserve to be whipped and sent to your room without supper," Father said, "there will be no punishment this time. Our good neighbor Leron is joining us for the evening meal, and you need to be present and in good form. But do not let this happen again, Katrine, or I swear by the Holy Signs, I'll beat obedience into you or I'll lock you out.

"Now, tend to your pony quickly then clean and dress yourself for dinner. I won't have my eldest daughter appearing at the table in the guise of a stable hand."

"Yes sir."

By the time Katrine was halfway to the stables, her relief at not being caught was replaced by irritation, which was quickly followed by anger.

Father was always criticizing her for looking like a hired man. If it bothered him, why did he treat her like one? Did he think she enjoyed checking the herds, mending fences, birthing calves, hauling stupid yearlings from the ravine, or any of the other loathsome jobs he gave her?

People made fun of her, but not just because she was tall and had strange eyes. They also mocked her because she worked like a man. Her sunburned skin was rough and dry. She wore men's britches, tunics, and boots, and she often smelled of dust, hard work, and animals.

As a daughter of Mer, the High Elder, she should have been wearing fine dresses with lace overskirts and having servants bring her iced drinks and jemnut cakes.

Of course she hated having servants fuss over her. And skirts, whether lace or plain, were not nearly as comfortable as trousers. And staying home all day would be a great bore.

Even so, she should be treated better than she was.

After unsaddling Stubbs, Katrine grabbed a couple of rags and began drying the sweat from his back. She didn't notice Skotlan, her ten-year-old brother, until he reached out and touched her.

"Yeeeow!" she screeched. It took a couple of seconds for her gulping breath and racing heart to return to normal. "How dare you sneak up on me like that?" Then she looked around suspiciously. "Where did you come from, anyway?"

"I was hiding in the empty stall." Skotlan stroked Stubbs' nose, completely unaffected by his sister's temper.

"Hiding? From what?"

"Chants." He rolled his eyes heavenward, positioned his hands as if in prayer, and fell to his knees. "Chants," he repeated, dropping his head so his chin rested on his chest.

Unable to hold onto her foul mood, Katrine burst out laughing. "You'd better not let Father catch you saying that."

Faintly in the distance, Katrine heard the gong that called the household together for evening prayers. A moment later, Mother's soft alto began singing the first mantra. Usually Anton, who was just a year younger than Katrine, led the chants, but his voice had recently begun to crackle and break. He sounded so much like a clucking hen on the high notes that the younger children couldn't help but giggle. Mother had taken over his role for now.

"That's why you always come home late, I'll bet," Skotlan said. "You never get here in time to sing the chants."

"Maybe." Katrine shrugged nonchalantly. "Or," she went on with a bit of her dark mood returning, "maybe it's because I don't ever have any help. Anton's old enough, but the sun makes him swoon, so he says. It's not easy out there, especially when a yearling gets trapped in the ravine and I have to kill a plains cat to save it, like I did today. Then, after that, I have to carry the stupid herdbeast up that steep, fraggin' trail."

Wonderment, respect, and a touch of horror washed over Skotlan's face. "Did you really kill a plains cat today?"

"Yes," Katrine answered, gratified by her brother's reaction. "I almost missed, though. Then the cat would've ripped the yearling to pieces. Me, too, probably. It was scary, I can tell you that."

"What happened?"

In silent pantomime, Katrine slashed across her stomach with a pretend knife. "When the cat saw its insides spilling all over, it just up and died of embarrassment."

"Aw, come on. Tell me the truth."

"I'll tell you something else." Katrine returned to the task of drying off her pony. "If I don't hurry, Father is going to do something worse than threaten to lock me out."

Skotlan paled. "He wouldn't do that." Then with his voice quaking, he whispered, "He wouldn't, would he?"

Tossing the rags aside, Katrine nodded. "He said he would if I stay out after sunset again. I think he meant it." She gave Skotlan a bucket, and he took it with a tremulous hand.

"He won't do it, 'Trine. I won't let him."

"Nevertheless, I've made him angry, and he's going to be even angrier if we're late for dinner. Run and get Stubbs some water, will you? I'll tell you about the plains cat later."

Quickly they completed the work in the stable. Fresh straw was scattered on the stall floor, Stubbs's coat was brushed and shiny, the tack was cleaned and hanging on the wall, and the pony had grain and water. With Skotlan chattering away while they worked, Katrine's mood had changed to a more peaceful, happy one. He always had that effect on her.

When they were finished, Katrine grabbed her saddlebags and a small pail then followed Skotlan toward the house.

"Leron's here," Skotlan said, skipping backward so he could watch Katrine as they talked.

"Already?" Katrine stopped at the well to fill the bucket with water since she didn't have time to use the bathhouse.

Skotlan rushed ahead and pulled open the door to the backstairs for her. "He rode in a few minutes before you. Anton says Leron and Father want you to marry Rand."

"Where did he hear that? Leron only discussed it with Rand yesterday."

"I don't know." Skotlan shrugged, unconcerned. "Anton says Father will betroth you to Rand for the Crennese bloodline."

Halting halfway up the stairs, Katrine shook her head defiantly. "Father's Nistarian, Mother's Boradid, and Rand's Crennese, so if he and I had a baby and the latent Wolkarean blood popped up, I would become the mother of the Warrior of Four Bloods. Is that it?"

"I think so. There aren't many Boradids left, you know. Or Crennese, either."

"So Father wants to marry me off to Rand just to fulfill that stupid old prophecy. It doesn't matter that no Wolkareans have been born for over three hundred years, or that Rand and I aren't in love with each other."

Skotlan nodded. "Anton heard Father and a councilman talking. They said signs in the stars say it's almost time for the Warrior of Four Bloods to show up, and the councilman said maybe they should hurry things along. I don't remember it all, but Anton said they talked about you."

"Well, they'll just have to hurry things along without me," Katrine said with a haughty toss of her head. "Getting sorcerers' blood into the family line is not in my plans. Neither is having babies, Wolkarean or otherwise."

"They might not ask you," Skotlan said with real concern. "What if Father just tells you? Then what will you do?"

Katrine felt her cheeks and hands grow cold. Lightly she ran her fingers through a fringe of her brother's disheveled auburn hair, brushing it back from his broad, plain face.

"I don't know," she said, working to keep her voice steady. "All I know for sure is that I'm not marrying anyone from Banur. I'm not! Not ever."

Before she could be tempted to tell Skotlan her plans about attending the Recorders School, she changed the subject. "I've got to hurry, or Father will be furious. You're clean enough for dinner. Well, almost." She brushed a little dust and straw from the knees of his trousers. "Go down and listen for me. Please."

A wicked, delighted gleam danced through Skotlan's eyes. "Sure." With much dramatization, he tiptoed down the stairs and out of sight.

After a quick wash, Katrine selected an ankle length skirt of soft rose tones, a cream colored blouse with pink flowers embroidered around the neckline, and white leather slippers. She undid her single braid, brushed her long blond hair until it gleamed, and tied it with a ribbon, letting it hang loose down her back in soft waves. When she was finished, she tried to be objective as she looked in the mirror.

She wasn't pretty—she knew that. Still, she wasn't actually homely. Although her eyes were pale, they were large, set wide apart, and framed by long brown lashes. Her chin was a bit too square, and her nose a bit too small, but her lips were full and naturally red. Although her skin was much too tan for ladies of her mother's status, it was clear and unblemished.

She could not compete with her sister, Jaimi, who was truly beautiful, but she need not be ashamed of her appearance.

With those thoughts, she dashed off to join Skotlan in the secret alcove at the upper end of the audience chamber, where Father would be entertaining Leron prior to their meal.

The audience chamber was seldom used now that the Council of Elders met in the new town hall, but it was still a splendid room. Elegant tapestries and paintings were attractively arranged on the walls. At the front of the hall was a collection of finely wrought swords and shields and several colorful banners.

This was the one area of the house from which the children were banned.

It was only by accident that Skotlan had stumbled onto the little alcove hidden behind one of the chamber's dark wall hangings.

It happened two years ago on the third consecutive day of pouring spring rains. When the children became bored with staying indoors, they decided to pass the time with a game of hide-and-seek. Usually, they didn't venture into the servants' passages, but all the good hiding places had already been used, so Skotlan darted into a narrow corridor off the kitchen. Even though he soon became disoriented, he kept going. When he found himself in a concealed alcove off the audience chamber, he immediately recognized its potential for eavesdropping on the adults. He hadn't told anyone about it except Katrine.

Later, by questioning the servants, they learned that in olden times hired soldiers had stood in the recess when the master of the house held formal council with friends or enemies.

As Katrine ran through the kitchen, she snatched a small loaf of bread from the cooling rack. Joining Skotlan, she handed him half and then leaned forward to listen.

Chapter Four

"Why do you let her roam around the plains like a ragamuffin?" Leron asked in a critical tone.

"She has chores," Father answered calmly.

"Female children need mothering and housekeeping skills, not animal husbandry and farming." Leron's tone was insulting and patronizing.

Katrine waited for Father to take offense. He didn't.

He must really want this betrothal, she thought with dismay.

Although she couldn't see them, she knew Father and Leron were seated in the plush velvet chairs situated on either side of a small round table near the alcove.

A clinking sound was followed by the melodious gurgle of liquid.

There was a moment of silence then the faint smacking of lips.

"Excellent," Leron mumbled. "A Glainite wine?"

"One of their best. More?"

"Just a little, thank you."

Chewing nervously on her lower lip, Katrine wondered if she had missed anything important, but she didn't dare ask Skotlan. Not here. Not now. Discovery by Father would be catastrophic, and his ears were as sharp as a plains cat's.

"Well, Mer," Leron said, sounding much more mellow than he had earlier, "I'm sure you know why I'm here. On behalf of my son, Rand, I would like to make a formal offer of marriage for your daughter, Katrine. She is of an appropriate age, and Rand is fond of her. Since our lands adjoin, their home could be built between our estates." He chuckled. When he went on, his voice had a merry lilt. "It would be nice to have them and the grandbabies close by, don't you think?"

Babies? With Rand? Katrine was appalled at the idea.

"If you'll match the size of the plot of land I've set aside for them," Leron continued, "and provide them with three dozen herdbeasts and two carriage ponies, I'll forgo the traditional dowry in gold coin. Now, that's a good offer, generous, even if I say so myself."

No, no, no, no. Vigorously, Katrine tried to project her thoughts into her father's mind just as Rand had sent his thoughts into hers.

"Here, let me refill your glass," Father said.

"If you insist."

Prickles of anxiety skipped up and down Katrine's spine.

Say no, say no.

When Mer finally spoke, his words came slowly, as if he were testing each one before verbalizing it. "Katrine is an unusual child. She has always had more energy, curiosity, and enthusiasm than any of my other children. I had her weeding her mother's vegetable garden almost as soon as she could walk, just to keep her busy and out of mischief.

"When she was old enough to understand instructions and to recognize dangers, I sent her out on the plains to watch the herdbeasts. She is a hard worker and has a great love of the outdoors. Several summers ago, Rand himself taught her to use a bow, and she is better than all of my hired men except for Brac and his eldest son. She is not a common girl, and I fear a common marriage will not suit her."

Joy swelled up in Katrine's chest. She felt as if she might burst with pure happiness at this unexpected sensitivity from her father. As he continued speaking, however, she felt as if he jabbed a red-hot poker into her heart.

"Now, if you want a wife for your son who is everything that Katrine is not, you should consider my second daughter, Jaimi. She is a quiet, gentle girl with a loving temperament and a festive spirit. She is exquisitely beautiful and has all the manners and grace necessary to be the mistress of a great and distinguished house such as yours."

"She's a mere baby," Leron sputtered indignantly.

"She's almost thirteen: a little too young to wed, but certainly old enough to betroth. And she's a prize worth waiting for."

"Rand is seventeen, nearly eighteen," Leron declared, slapping the tabletop. "I've already lost a wife and two children, and my second wife has failed to conceive despite everything the Glainite healers have done. If I hadn't adopted Rand, I would have no one to give my family's land lore. I'm an old man. Before I die I need to see if Rand can pass the knowledge of my father's fathers on to his own children."

"Sometimes even blood heirs can't accept or pass on the family's skill lore," Father said with gentle kindness. "If Rand can't do it, then what?"

"He must." Leron's soft tone exposed the depth of his longing. "All that we are, all that we have learned over the generations, must not be lost. You have many children, Mer. You know your line will be preserved and your family's lore continued. I have only Rand."

As if a new thought had just occurred to him, Leron's voice quivered with suspicion. "Is it because he is Crennese and adopted? I know there is some prejudice—"

"Of course not," Father interrupted. "If that were the case, I wouldn't offer you Jaimi."

"Then I don't understand. As you say, Katrine is different, but it is not a difference that's likely to attract many suitors. I don't think you'll find anyone else willing to take her unless you offer a large dowry in gold."

Katrine began to tremble. Tears welled up in her eyes. Leron wanted her for Rand, not because they would be a good match for each other and not because they could possibly make each other happy, but because he saw them both as defective: Rand because of his Crennese heritage, her because she was too tall and had ugly eyes.

She clamped her arms around herself and dug her fingers into the flesh of her upper arms in an effort to stop shaking.

"Let me be frank," Father said somberly. "Katrine is simply not ready for marriage. I accept the blame. I've allowed her too many years of freedom on the plains, roaming around like an untamed animal. She is unpredictable. I cannot arrange a union for her until I know she will comply faithfully and honorably with my wishes. As High Elder, I refuse to risk my family's reputation on a betrothal I can't guarantee."

Katrine bit down on her fist to keep from gasping aloud.

How could Father humiliate her like that? Did he really think of her as an animal, like a wild horse that had to be broken before it could be trained?

So what if she did refuse to marry Rand?

Would that bring such a terrible disgrace onto the family? Didn't she have the right to have feelings and opinions about her own future?

Hot tears of shame burned her cheeks as she edged past Skotlan and shuffled through the dark, narrow corridor.

When they reached the kitchen, serving girls were bustling around, adding final touches to the dinner preparations. Dodging elbows, hot platters, and flashing cutlery, Katrine and Skotlan ducked and sidled their way around the harried workers.

Rosi, the cook, who was usually a jovial soul, scolded them for getting in the way and shooed them out, not even noticing Katrine's tears.

As soon as they were in the hall, Skotlan pulled a wrinkled handkerchief from his pocket.

"Better wipe your eyes and nose—and pinch your cheeks a little." When Katrine had complied, he looked her over approvingly. "It's a good thing you're so tan. You don't blotch up nearly as bad as Jaimi does when she cries."

With forced smiles, they entered the dining hall as soon as they heard the dinner bell ring. Father and Leron joined them a few minutes later.

Throughout dinner, conversation proceeded as usual.

All eight children were present, including the infant twins. After asking Leron about his wife, Rand, and the condition of his fruit orchards, Mother turned her attention to each of the children. She asked first one question and then another about their activities.

When her turn came, Katrine answered with indifference. The demeaning comments she had heard from her father and Leron still echoed in her ears.

Excitedly Skotlan answered for her. He told everyone that she had killed one of the dreaded plains cats. Although the news brought gasps of fearful delight from the other children, a look passed between Father and Leron that made Katrine wish she could sink into the ground.

Woodenly she turned her lips upward when Leron told an old joke, and again when the twins started babbling toothlessly.

All the while, Jaimi batted her eyelashes and tossed her bright red curls, brazenly flirting with their guest. It made Katrine sick to her stomach to watch.

Toward the end of the meal, as one group of servants cleared away bowls and plates and cutlery and another group passed out redberry cobbler for dessert, there was finally a lull.

Katrine seized the opportunity to make a feeble excuse of exhaustion and, at a nod from her father, fled to the safety of her room.

Behind her locked door, she stopped trying to hold back the tears. She fell onto her bed and buried her face in the pillow.

Did her father absolutely hate her?

Every time she thought he expressed a little understanding or concern for her, he turned around and made another comment that demonstrated his dissatisfaction and disappointment.

Maybe if she became a famous Recorder, he would love her.

She wiped her face dry with the backs of her hands and then moved from the bed to the table below the window. She retrieved the hawk's portrait from her art satchel, attached it to her extra frame, and sealed the color.

Then she sorted through the best of her artwork, trying to decide which other pictures to send with her application to the Recorders School.

The best painting she'd ever done—well, second only to the hawk—was of Jaimi gazing thoughtfully into the distance with sunlight glinting off her vibrant red hair.

The Headmaster was sure to like that one.

She considered a couple of paintings of wildflowers, but she finally rejected them. Next, she looked at one of a herdbeast and its calf, then some autumn-colored trees by the river, followed by several homey scenes from around the manor. They were nice, but not exciting enough.

Jaimi and the hawk. Were two enough?

She thumbed through a pile of sketches and pulled out a charcoal drawing of a young plains cat swatting playfully at a puff weed. She had hidden downwind and sketched it while the mother cat was hunting, one of the most frightening and dangerous things she had ever done. But it was worth it. The scene was every bit as unusual and eye-catching as the hawk.

She continued searching until she found a drawing of the heart-shaped

31

pinks she'd worn in her hair at her last birth celebration. The picture was nothing dramatic, just a little bunch of flowers she had captured on impulse right before she went to bed that night. But every time she looked at them, they made her smile. She added the drawing to the others. Two paintings, two sketches? That should be adequate.

When she had finished her letter to the Headmaster, she sat on the side of her bed and counted her money. If she remembered right, each time Father hired a runner to take a letter to the Regency in Pardish, it cost at least two full silvers, maybe even two and a half. That was more expensive than she could afford.

She would have to wait for the large traders' market that would be held in Banur sometime before autumn. If she arranged delivery with a caravan master, he wouldn't charge her more than five or six coppers and maybe a few iron flecks.

At the very most, it might cost a half-silver.

That would leave her with seven full silvers, one half-silver, nine coppers, and six iron flecks to apply toward her passage to the Recorders School.

Then she could escape.

Chapter Five

Sluggish and grumpy, Katrine woke the next morning at her usual predawn hour. For a few minutes she thought she might pretend to be sick so she could sleep a little longer, but she quickly rejected the idea. The last time she had been ill, Mother had kept her in bed the entire day. The squealing, squabbling, and shouting of her seven younger brothers and sisters had nearly driven her crazy.

Nothing was worth that.

By the time Anton and Skotlan were up and dressed, Katrine had completed her household chores. By the time they had finished with theirs, she had eaten breakfast and was on her way to the parlor, which served as their classroom. She was reviewing the day's lessons when her father herded in her younger brothers.

Anton, with his nose in the air, came in first. Behind him, Skotlan had his arm draped over Raeph's shoulders, whispering something in his ear. They giggled. Anton spun around, scowling, as if they were laughing at him. Maybe they were.

Katrine winked at Raeph as he sat next to her, and he gave her a wide grin that revealed two missing teeth. He'd just turned seven, and this was his first day of studying with the older children. Mother would continue tutoring him in reading and arithmetic along with Bramt, who was four.

As usual, Jaimi arrived several minutes later than everyone else. Katrine was certain that if *she* ever showed up late, Father would yell at her until his face went purple.

But he never yelled at Jaimi. In fact, hardly anyone ever said a cross word to her. It was because she was so pretty. Even Katrine could not stay angry when Jaimi opened her clear green eyes wide, tossed her flaming curls over her shoulder, and flashed her whimsical little smile.

After Jaimi got herself and her papers arranged to her satisfaction, she looked up at Father expectantly.

"Today," Father began, "we're going to review our history lessons for

Raeph. Skotlan, we'll start with you. Please describe the events that led to the establishment of Kareand's four races."

Turning in his chair, Skotlan faced his younger brother. "A long time ago, nobody lived in Kareand. They all lived beyond the Edge of the World in Shokareen. The people were called—?" He crinkled his brow and flipped his lower lip with a finger. "Just a minute, I'll remember."

"Shokareenites?" suggested Jaimi. "Shokarinians? Shokalots?" She shrugged and looked up with a helplessly beautiful grin. "Shoka-something."

"Shokai," Anton said in a superior tone. "Two syllables. Shoh-keye. How could anyone forget something that simple?"

"I knew it was something like that," Jaimi said, tossing her head so her hair swirled around her face like a red mist. "I just couldn't remember it exactly."

"Thank you for the enlightenment, Anton," Father said with a disapproving frown. He didn't like it when the older children mocked the younger.

Katrine pursed her lips so she wouldn't grin. Anton was such a pompous idiot. Wouldn't he ever learn? In his effort to show off for Father, he had only succeeded in irritating him.

Father turned back to Skotlan. "Continue," he said.

"The Shokai loved war," Skotlan told Raeph. "They liked battles and killing and destroying things. They hardly ever stopped fighting until almost everyone was dead. Then, as soon as there were lots of people again, they went right back at it. Powerful sorcerers lived there, too, but they usually didn't join the fights. When they did, the wars got worse."

"Worse in what way?" Father asked.

"Magic filled the air," Skotlan answered. "And it didn't just kill people." His voice dropped, becoming dramatic and ominous. "It twisted them up on the inside and the outside. Their eyes boiled, and their fingers and toes turned black and dropped off. They got open sores that oozed green slime. Their skin peeled away in big strips. All of their hair fell out."

Although Jaimi had heard the tale many times, her eyes grew large as Skotlan described the gory details. Her hand clutched tightly to one long, red tress. Katrine glanced over at Father, but he didn't seem concerned.

Skotlan made small hand movements that became more and more exaggerated. "The sorcerers wove evil spells. They picked a target." His gaze danced around the room. "They threw their power!"

He tossed a handful of air straight at Jaimi.

She shrieked.

Raeph giggled, and Katrine smothered a laugh with her hand.

Narrowing his eyes, Father gave Skotlan a stern look, but Katrine thought there was a hint of amusement underneath it.

"I was just demonstrating," Skotlan said innocently.

"I know what you were *just* doing. Go on."

Mischief still played across Skotlan's face. "Then one day, the magicians got together and decided the Shokai had to stop killing each other or there wouldn't be anyone left. They wrote laws, and if people broke them, the wizards turned them into toads."

"Is that true?" Raeph asked Father.

Anton cut in before Father could answer. "No, Skotlan just made it up."

"How do you know?" Skotlan demanded. "It's the kind of thing sorcerers did back then."

"That's right," said Katrine, supporting her favorite brother. "You weren't there, Anton. You don't know."

"Neither do you," Anton fired back at her.

"Returning to the lesson," Father said calmly, "the sorcerers enforced peace, and Shokareen entered its Golden Era."

"Sounds boring to me," muttered Skotlan.

Father raised his eyebrows.

With a grin, Skotlan resumed. "It didn't stay boring very long. Not after Haldrid learned to change shape."

Father asked Jaimi, "How did he learn to do that?"

Her cute little mouth puckered up while she thought. "Didn't he go somewhere dark and pray to a demon?"

"Exactly," Father said, and Jaimi beamed with delight. "Haldrid went into a deep cave and prayed to the darkness. A demon answered and gave him the secret."

"I knew the right answer," Jaimi whispered to Raeph. He smiled at her admiringly.

"What happened next, Skotlan?" Father asked.

Again Skotlan dropped his voice, affecting a menacing tone. "Haldrid said he would share the demon's power with anyone who helped him kill the sorcerers. He organized a religion that worshipped the demon, and the members went to war and fought against everyone who didn't belong. They made weapons, created armies, mixed potions, and recited spells. The priests made human sacrifices. They cut the hearts out of young girls," he whirled around and pointed his finger at Jaimi, "especially if they had red hair."

"Father," she screeched. "Make him stop."

"That's enough, Skotlan." When Skotlan opened his mouth, Father gave him a warning look, and Skotlan's mouth snapped shut again. Father turned to Anton. "Why don't you take over?"

Inwardly, Katrine groaned. She hated listening to Anton.

He stood up, and a sunbeam flashed through the window and stroked his golden brown hair, bringing out the red highlights. He clasped his hands behind his back, imitating Father, and cleared his throat.

"Not everyone fought on Haldrid's side," Anton said. "Some people joined the sorcerers. Soon, everyone on the whole continent was engaged in the war. Even children took up weapons and fought beside their parents.

The Spire of Kylet

"As the years passed, entire cities were demolished. Blood flowed through the streets and turned the ground red. Bodies rotted in the open or were eaten by beasts because no one had time to bury the dead or even to build funeral pyres.

"The demon's priests killed the wizards, and Haldrid's followers fought and killed almost everyone else. Eventually there was only one good sorcerer left. His name was Manderig, and he was afraid human life in Shokareen was going to be completely destroyed. He traveled in secret and gathered everyone he could find who did not want to fight anymore.

"He led the people to the northern tip of the continent. He told them they had to leave their homes and travel to a new location if they wanted to survive. Then he divided them into three groups to represent three of the four elements: land, water and fire."

Katrine covered a yawn with her hand, not because the story was boring but because Anton's presentation was. He talked in a monotone whenever he recited, sounding like a tedious old man.

"Manderig named one group the Nistarians," Anton droned on, "and he gave them land lore, which is the ability to nurture animals and plants and help them thrive. He called the second group Boradids. He gave them water lore so they could understand the seas and rivers and could harvest all manner of marine life. The third group he named the Crennese. He gave them fire lore, or sorcery, which could heal the sick, open the minds of the ignorant, and even move mountains if necessary."

"Excellent," said Father, "but when you speak of the lores, what do you mean exactly?"

Anton's face went blank. He always struggled when Father asked him a question. He was good at memorizing, but he had difficulty when asked to clarify or interpret.

He began haltingly. "Since I haven't been given your or Mother's lore yet, I'm not sure I can explain." His brow furrowed as he tried to find the right words. "My understanding is that the lores create a bond between a person and the knowledge amassed by his ancestors."

"That is certainly part of it," Father agreed, "but it's more than that. You don't have to go through a ritual of sharing to have access to much of your blood heritage. You are Nistarian through me and Boradid through your mother, so you are already in tune with the land and water lores. All you have to do is find the powers within you. Our ancestors gained most of their insights and skills through quiet meditation.

"If I pass on my lore to one of you," Father said, glancing at each of the children in turn, "you will receive the knowledge our family has accumulated over the generations. You will also develop a special sensitivity to our farmlands and animals. However, even without the gift, you can tap into the wisdom of your lores by seeking understanding within the stillness of your heart."

A scowl formed on Anton's face. Katrine immediately understood why. Father had interrupted his recitation, and then he hadn't even taken the hint and identified to whom he intended to give the family estates and land lore. At fourteen years old, Anton was old enough for a sharing ritual, but Father hadn't offered it to him.

It serves him right, Katrine thought.

Anton hated the ranch, the gardens, and the herdbeasts. He was always making up excuses to get out of his chores. He said his hands were too tender. He burned too easily in the sun. He got leg cramps if he rode too long in the saddle.

He didn't want to work the ranch. He only wanted the land lore for the power and the status.

"I've strayed from the lesson, I'm afraid," Father said. "Katrine, tell us about the fourth race."

Usually when Father called on her, Katrine felt a flutter of nervousness in her stomach and had to take a moment to compose herself. This time, though, he had asked about her favorite subject, and she spoke right up.

"After Manderig told the people about the first three races, they asked him why there wasn't a group to represent the fourth element. So he talked to them for a long time about the nature of air.

"He explained that it is very powerful when it comes in the form of wind storms and cyclones. At those times, it can be dangerous and destructive. At other times, it is gentle enough to cool your brow, freshen your laundry, or fan a campfire.

"He said the two most significant things about air are that it is everywhere and that it is required to sustain life. The members of the fourth group were to be as important as air because they would ensure peace. He said that without peace, as without air, people died."

"But," Father said, "Anton told us Manderig divided the people into three groups. How could there be a fourth?"

"Actually," Katrine said, "there was one man left. He was a strong, wise man named Zeroon. Manderig touched him and put some kind of mark on his body. He told everyone that Zeroon was the first Wolkarean and the rest would be born to the people of the other three races.

"Any child who was born with the mark of Zeroon was supposed to be taken to him at the age of twelve. Manderig said Zeroon now had a special power to recognize and deal with evil, and he would train the children to be soldiers of peace. They would make sure Kareand never suffered internal warfare like Shokareen did. All the people with the mark of Zeroon became known as Wolkarean Warriors."

"What did the mark look like?" asked Father.

Quickly, without waiting to be acknowledged, Jaimi blurted out, "Terina's mother says it was a great big slash of red, like a scar, right across their foreheads. I'd hate that, myself. It would be so ugly." To make sure everyone realized she definitely was not ugly, Jaimi batted her eyelashes and tossed her hair.

"Actually," Anton said, flashing a self-important smirk, "we don't know anymore what the mark was. The Wolkareans disappeared hundreds of years ago when Shanree Palace fell. No new Wolkarean children have been born since then."

"So are the Wolkareans gone forever?" Father asked.

Katrine thought he was talking to her. She opened her mouth to answer, but Anton cut her off.

"Not according to prophecy," Anton said. "Someday they're supposed to come back."

"Katrine," Father said, this time looking squarely at her, "tell us about Kylet."

"Kylet was the last Wolkarean Warlord," she said. "After the High King and his elder two sons were assassinated by Elnid-Kyeh, the third son, Kylet feared for the safety of the Three Sister Wives. So Kylet smuggled them out of Shanree Palace under the guard of the Wolkarean Elite. To give them time to escape, he stayed and fought Elnid-Kyeh's soldiers all by himself.

"Before Kylet died, he wrote something on one of the palace walls in his own blood, so the legends say. It's called the Wolkarean Inscription. It's a message for the Warrior of Four Bloods, who is supposed to appear when the Wolkareans return, which will be when Kareand is in grave danger. When Kylet finished writing the Inscription, he left Shanree Palace and the Island of Renath and went off to die. When he crossed the western bridge, all four bridges to the city fell at the same time. That was a symbol of the collapse of the fourth race."

"Personally," Anton said, "I think we've proven we don't need them. The Landorian Warriors have been able to keep us safe and secure without Wolkareans."

"At least, so far," Father said. He returned to Katrine. "Do you have any theories about the sign of Zeroon? What it might have looked like?"

For a moment, Katrine was startled by the question. No one remembered how the Wolkareans were marked. *Except for maybe Terina's mother and Jaimi,* she thought with a mental giggle.

But she had given this a lot of consideration.

"I think the mark must have been something small and almost unnoticeable, like a birthmark or a mole," Katrine said slowly. "In the story of Cavena and Trenton, the Warrior Trenton stayed in a village in the Verdant Mountains for almost a year before he was recognized. Even though no Wolkareans had ever been born in that village, the people knew about them. They knew Wolkareans traveled the countryside, watched for wrongdoers, enforced laws, handed out judgments, and kept the peace.

"It wasn't until Trenton killed a giant in a battle that lasted for three days that the villagers realized what he was. For all we know, the Wolkareans have already returned, but because we've forgotten how they were marked, we don't know how to identify them."

"Don't be stupid," Anton sneered at her. "If they were marked at all, someone would have noticed. The Recorders have all the histories. They must know what the sign was. Besides, Manderig changed the Wolkareans so they couldn't be ambushed and slaughtered. You can't hide an immortal."

"Still, Katrine has a point," Father said, surprising Katrine and making Anton flush angrily. "Many people think we're teetering on the brink of a major calamity right now. There is civil unrest in the big cities and a growing number of renegades on the caravan routes. Some people see these as signs that the Wolkareans need to return.

"In fact," Father continued, "if the disaster is close, the Wolkareans must already be young adults or older. Otherwise, they'd be too immature to defend the land. But as you and Katrine have mentioned, Anton, the common people have forgotten what the mark looks like. If Wolkarean children are being born, the parents don't recognize them and aren't sending them to Landor to be trained as Warriors."

"If that's true," Katrine said loudly without thinking, "the Warrior of Four Bloods must already be an adult since he's supposed to lead the Wolkareans."

"That's right, Katrine. If we're truly approaching Kareand's time of greatest need, the Warrior of Four Bloods must exist somewhere."

Then Father turned his attention to Jaimi. "Can you tell us how the Kareandeens got to this continent?"

Jaimi chewed on a strand of hair as she concentrated. "Didn't Manderig build magical ships for them or something? They sailed around the Edge of the World, I think."

"Can anyone help Jaimi out?" Father asked.

Just as Anton opened his mouth to answer, Raeph yelled, swinging his arms in the air, as he bounced up and down on his chair. "I know! I know!"

When Father nodded at the younger child, Anton turned away. He clamped his mouth shut, folded his arms across his chest, and clenched his hands into fists.

Raeph grinned, delighted to have an opportunity to recite. "Manderig told 'em how to build some big boats. Then he gave 'em something like a compass, but it was called—it was called—"

As the intensity of Raeph's bouncing increased, Katrine whispered out of the corner of her mouth, "Enchanted . . ."

"Oh yeah," Raeph said. "It was called the Enchanted Beacon! It showed 'em how to sail around the islands at the Edge of the World without smashing on the rocks. Big storms almost sunk 'em a couple of times, but they made it safe."

"Very good," Father said, tousling Raeph's hair.

"They landed on the northeastern coast," Anton said, scowling at his younger brother, "up by Marlett's Cleft."

The Spire of Kylet

"That's correct," Father said.

Once a week, after the children had finished with their regular lessons, Father included half an hour of music.

Today, Jaimi and Raeph performed an old ballad, with Raeph singing the melody and Jaimi the harmony. Their voices blended beautifully.

Then Anton played an original composition on his flute.

The session ended with Skotlan and Katrine accompanying themselves on lyre and drum while they sang a popular folk song. They began well, but by the end they were humming the tune because they couldn't remember the rest of the lyrics.

Father just shook his head and sighed.

After making the assignments for the next day (geography and social politics), Father dismissed class. Without a word, Katrine rushed up to her room, threw her papers on the table below her window, grabbed her bow and quiver, and dashed downstairs again. As she hurried, she puzzled over a couple of questions that had occurred to her earlier while Father talked about the Wolkareans.

Did he actually believe the Warrior of Four Bloods had already been born? If so, did that mean he wouldn't force her to marry someone of Crennese descent? Was it possible that he would support her decision to become a Recorder?

Chapter Six

Holding Katrine's luncheon pouch behind her with one hand, Rosi, the cook, wagged a pudgy finger at Katrine with the other.

"Yesterday you didn't eat very much. Did I give you something you don't like?"

With a grin, Katrine pretended to lunge left, and when Rosi shifted her weight, jumped right instead. She grabbed the bag and held it jubilantly above her head.

Rosi put her fists on her ample waist and laughed.

Katrine told her, "You don't know *how* to cook something I don't like. I was busy yesterday, but I'll eat today. I promise."

"You'd better." Rosi turned to the stove and stirred a pot of yellowberry preserves, which bubbled aromatically. "I don't want your mother saying I'm not feeding you."

"As fast as I'm growing? No chance of that." Katrine gave Rosi a hug, and then headed for the dining hall, as she always did, to say good morning to her mother before she left.

Mother sat at the head of a long table. The twins in their tall toddler's chairs were on her right side and Bramt was on her left. She wore a simple blue work dress, which looked lovely with her auburn hair and creamy complexion. Her face was so youthful that she was often thought to be Katrine's elder sister.

"Good morning, Mother," Katrine said. "I'm going to check the herds now. Do you need anything before I go?"

"I need Bramt and the twins to finish breakfast so we can get on with the day, but I'm afraid that's not something you can help me with." Mother laughed a soft tinkling sound. "I can't seem to help either. I guess they'll eat if they get hungry enough."

"Not if it's mush," Bramt grumbled as he scooped up a glob of cooked cereal with his spoon then plopped it back into the bowl.

"It's good for you, dear," Mother said automatically. "You'll be careful out there, won't you, Katrine? We've heard more and more stories about highwaymen on the roads and vicious animals swimming across the Meriad River from the east."

"All the more reason for me to watch the herds and keep the fences mended," Katrine said with a twinge of conscience for yesterday's dalliance.

"I worry about you out on the plains alone all day."

"I'm always careful, Mother, but I'll be extra careful today if you're worried. Besides, Rand is meeting me later, so I'll have company for part of the afternoon."

"Thank you, dear." Mother tried unsuccessfully to sneak a spoonful of cereal into Mauree's mouth, but Mauree pursed her lips and shook her head. Gwenna reached over, awkwardly took the utensil from Mother, and dribbled mush over her chin as she tried to feed herself.

Mauree screamed with outrage and then began babbling nonsense syllables that sounded very much like cursing to Katrine. Within seconds, the twins were engaged in a howling game of tug of war over possession of the spoon. Mother intervened by providing a second spoon, and the twins quieted down and happily began flipping cereal all over each other.

Katrine turned to leave, but Mother called her back.

"With Leron here last night and your going to bed early," Mother said, "I didn't get a chance to tell you the news. I got a letter from your aunt and uncle in Branston. They're sending Heni out for the rest of the summer. She'll be here in a few days."

"Oh no, Mother," Katrine howled. "Not Heni."

"Yes, dear, Heni," Mother said firmly. "And you're to do everything in your power to make her visit a pleasant one. I'll put Jaimi in with the twins and give Heni Jaimi's room, so you'll be able to keep your privacy, but you can't ignore her completely. She's only a year older than you, and if you try hard enough, I'm sure you two can become friends."

"But she hates everything about me," Katrine wailed. "She's afraid of horses, even little plains ponies. She can't draw a bow or throw a knife. She even hates art. Really, she's much more like Jaimi. Can't Jaimi entertain her? They can talk about lace skirts, and parties, and sugar confections, and—and—boys. Besides I have my chores and my studies and the plains to worry about. I won't have time to—"

"You will make time," Mother said in her no-more-arguing voice. "I'm sure you'll find ample excuses to keep yourself busy, but I also expect you to spend some time with your cousin. Uncle Charel is your father's dearest brother, and his daughter deserves your kindness while she's here."

There was nothing for Katrine to do except capitulate. Mother could be just as strict as Father, although in a much gentler, kinder way.

"I'll be nice," Katrine grumbled.

As she rode Stubbs out through the courtyard gates, she muttered to him under her breath. "It's not fair. I didn't think the summer could get any worse.

We have this awful heat that keeps alternating with thunderstorms, making the air almost too muggy to breathe. And the plains cats are particularly mean-tempered this year. So, now, what do I get to top everything else? Heni!"

Katrine's first chore was to check the log fence that surrounded the vegetable garden south of the manor. If it wasn't properly maintained, the herdbeasts would get inside and strip the plants bare.

A couple of sections had tipped over.

Working on the closest segment first, Katrine straightened the posts, repacked the ground, and then gathered some big rocks to reinforce the bases.

She continued complaining to Stubbs. "I wonder what Heni will find to criticize about me this year," she said as she wedged a small stone between two larger ones. "Well, that's easy. Everything. She doesn't like one single thing about me. Never has. Never will."

She had moved on to the second section and was shoving a log back into place, when she felt a jab in her palm. Turning over her hand, she glared at a long, dark splinter embedded in her skin.

"Damn," she muttered. "I'd better watch what I'm doing or I won't live long enough to see Heni arrive or leave." Katrine smiled to herself and began picking the sliver out. "That's what I need to concentrate on—Heni's leaving. No matter how awful life becomes, everything feels brighter and more hopeful as soon as I get to say goodbye to Heni."

As Katrine swung up onto her pony's back, her attention was attracted to a movement among the shadows of some fruit trees that clustered on the far side of the garden. Anton and a shabby old man ambled aimlessly around the trunks. For a moment Katrine tried to identify the stranger, thinking surely Anton wasn't acquainted with anyone she didn't know.

But her head began to ache, and she had trouble focusing her eyes.

She nudged Stubbs with her heels.

It wasn't her business, anyway.

* * *

"She did it to me again, Hollenth," Anton said angrily. "She's always trying to make me look foolish in front of Father."

"Why?" the old man asked. "Is she cruel?"

"No," Anton snarled, "she's sly."

"Sly? How so?"

"She wants Father to give her the land lore so she doesn't have to marry Rand and become the mother of the Warrior of Four Bloods. As the land and lore heir, she would get to choose who she married and when."

"I'm just an old wanderer," the man said, "without any education. I've never been too clear about the Warrior of Four Bloods mythology. Maybe you could explain it to me."

The Spire of Kylet

Reaching above his head, Anton broke a twig from the apple tree. He plucked off the leaves while he talked.

"Oh, it's just some ancient legend. No one believes in it anymore except maybe my father and a few other high-and-mighty councilmen."

"I'd like to hear the story anyway."

Anton shrugged indifferently. "The legend says that someday a terrible evil will wage war on Kareand. To combat it, a Warrior will be born who carries all four bloodlines that Manderig created: Nistarian, Boradid, Crennese, and Wolkarean. The Warrior of Four Bloods will command an army of Wolkarean Warriors, even though they disappeared centuries ago, and lead the people of Kareand to victory. He's supposed to have some special powers that will give him an advantage regardless of the odds."

"What kind of powers?"

"No one knows for sure. Back when Shanree Palace fell, Kylet wrote a message on one of the walls. Most people think it's for the Warrior of Four Bloods and will tell him how to use his powers to win the war."

"And this has to do with your sister because—?"

"Well, we're Nistarian and Boradid. So, if she marries a man who's Crennese, and if she has a Wolkarean baby, then he would have to be the Warrior of Four Bloods."

"I see. And she doesn't want to do that?"

"Of course not. She wants the land lore so she can be the ruler around here. You can bet if she got it, she'd never share it with the rest of us. Especially not with me, even though I am the eldest son."

The old man paused and leaned against a tree trunk, wheezing while he caught his breath. "But why do you want the lore? You've told me you don't like the farm work or the animals."

Anton glanced up shrewdly. "I wouldn't work the ranch myself. Father doesn't. He just tells other people what to do. If I had the income, I'd go to Boradid Isle and search for the records about the lost water lore."

"Others have tried and failed."

"I know, but I would succeed."

"Then what?"

As Anton considered all the possibilities, he felt an intense hunger grow inside of him, a hunger for power and eminence and wealth. "People like my mother would pay a great deal to learn about their Boradid heritage. I might sell it to them. Or maybe I'd keep it for myself. I could have all that knowledge to use any way I wanted." He grinned in anticipation. "No matter what I did with it, I'd become rich and important."

Putting his hand on Anton's shoulder, Hollenth murmured, "Worthy goals, indeed."

"Then I could burn this place to ground if I wanted." He shrugged and shook his head. "But I probably wouldn't. I'd share the land lore with one of my younger brothers, either Raeph or Bramt. Not Skotlan, he's just a toady for Katrine. They could run the farm and send me the money. I'd live in Pardish or Botul. Maybe Cajetta. Somewhere exciting."

"You're an ambitious young man," Hollenth said with an encouraging smile. "It's a shame your father doesn't see that fine quality in you."

"My father is a fool."

* * *

Heat waves lined the horizon as Katrine went to get the painting frame Rand had left behind the day before. She disassembled it and stuffed it into her pack.

Mopping her brow with a handkerchief, she headed for the ravine. The day was unseasonably hot, and even though she dreaded going down the precipitous path, she would be happy for a respite from the heat. She tethered Stubbs to a bush and then sat at the upper edge of the trail to wait. Cool air oozed from the gorge, but today it had an unwholesome feel. Despite the temperature, she shivered.

Before long, two majestic steeds pranced into view. Rand rode one, and Polnu rode the other. Oh, how Katrine longed for a real horse. Someday she would own one. She was sure of it.

"I met Rand and invited myself along," Polnu said as she dismounted. "Hope you don't mind."

"I'm delighted," Katrine told her, "but did he tell you what we're going to do?"

"Bury a dead plains cat. Is there more?"

"Isn't that enough?" Katrine looked questioningly at Rand. When he shook his head slightly, she interpreted it to mean that he had kept his word and hadn't told anyone about the spire.

Polnu laughed. "Come on, let's get it over with."

Rand and Katrine took short-handled shovels from their packs.

In single file, the trio started inching along the trail. It was drier than yesterday, but they still had to step carefully. Every now and then, a little cascade of dirt and pebbles rattled down the slope from someone's footfalls.

After going about a quarter of the way, Katrine stopped. Something was wrong. She strained to see into the shadows of the trees and bushes that grew beside the stream. Turning her head to one side, she listened a moment.

"What's wrong?" Rand asked from the end of the line.

"Don't you hear it?" Katrine whispered.

"What?" Rand asked, lowering his voice too. "I don't hear anything."

"That's the point," Polnu said, catching on quickly. "It's totally silent down there."

Katrine pointed at the dead plains cat. "No scavengers on the carcass. It's as if something has scared the birds and the animals into taking cover."

"I don't sense any magic," Polnu said.

"Still, there's something." Katrine's whisper took on a harsh quality. A mixture of excitement and dread tightened her throat, and she concentrated on the sensations, trying to identify the cause. "I can feel it."

Polnu glanced around apprehensively. "What do you feel?"

"Freezing cold and searing heat." A violent shudder rocked Katrine's body, and she rubbed her arms briskly with her hands to drive off the pins-and-needles that prickled her skin. "It's burning and freezing me at the same time."

"I think we'd better turn around," Polnu said, grasping Katrine's shoulder. "Suddenly I'm very frightened."

"Me too," Rand admitted in a hushed voice.

Shaking off Polnu's hand, Katrine took an uncertain step forward. "The heat. The cold. Feel it? Fire and ice. Wave upon wave." Pressure built inside her head, threatening to blow her apart. She couldn't bear it much longer. Her lips twisted awkwardly as she tried to force more words from her mouth. "I've got to find it!"

In a frenzy, she bolted down the trail.

Her foot slipped on a rock.

Time slowed down.

She flung her arms out as she fell.

Her head turned to the side.

Below, something rustled behind a bush.

A face, or was it two, disappeared into the shadows.

Katrine saw Polnu's hand reach for her, but it was too late.

Pain exploded inside Katrine's skull.

Everything went black.

* * *

Katrine blinked her eyes to eliminate the extra Rands and Polnus wobbling before her. She lay on a patch of scratchy plains grass several paces from the top of the ravine.

"Are you all right?" Polnu asked.

"I think so." But when Katrine tried to sit up, the world spun around her fitfully. "Maybe not," she said and eased herself back down. She was suddenly glad that breakfast had been so long ago. If there had been anything in her stomach, she would have vomited. "What happened?"

Gently, Polnu washed Katrine's face with a damp cloth. "You were running down the trail and slipped. You banged your head on a rock. You've got a nasty lump and some bad scrapes, but thank the Powers, you didn't break any bones."

"I was running? On the trail? Why?"

"Frankly," Polnu said, "I was hoping you would tell us."

Katrine tried to remember, but her head hurt so much that thinking was

46

difficult. She could feel her face scrunch up from the pain.

"Don't worry about it right now," Polnu said, patting Katrine's hand.

"Can you stand?" Rand asked.

"I think so. If you steady me." Rand took one of Katrine's arms and Polnu the other. Katrine reeled to her feet. Then she clutched at empty air and crumpled to her knees, almost pulling her friends down with her as she fell.

"We had better get her home," Rand said. "She can ride with me. She would fall off of Stubbs."

Working together, Rand and Polnu pushed until Katrine was astride Nightrunner. Then Rand swung up behind her. Before Polnu mounted, she gathered up the pony's reins.

Leaning against Rand, Katrine allowed herself to be carried until they neared the manor.

She considered what was waiting for her there. "Please," she begged, "don't take me home like this. Mother will put me to bed, and the little ones will swarm all over me. Let's go over to the river instead. I'll feel better if I can rest in the shade for a while. Then I can spend a few hours checking on the herd and go home at the regular time."

"What do you think, Polnu?" Rand asked. "You know more healing than I do."

"I guess it'll be all right. Some shade is bound to help, and I'd like to clean those cuts better. If she doesn't improve, we can take her home then."

As soon as Katrine was lying under the sinella trees beside the languid waters of the Ildec Minor, she perked up. Polnu washed her scrapes and smeared them with a strong herbal-scented salve from her medicine pouch.

Relaxed and doctored, Katrine offered to share her lunch with her friends. As it turned out, Rand had some dried meat and biscuits with him, and Polnu had three waterpears and a chunk of cheese, so they combined everything and made a picnic.

As they ate, the river murmured softly to itself and a gentle breeze ruffled the grass around them. Occasionally, a butterfly hiccupped through the air. A bird trilled a few joyful notes.

Katrine lay on her back with one arm curled beneath her head, looking through the green canopy of leaves to an azure sky beyond. "Remember when we were little," she said. "We came out here nearly every day to play Wolkareans and Shokai."

"It was great," Rand said as he sat cross-legged between the two girls. "We rushed around with stick swords, chasing tillee birds and mudhoppers, pretending they were Shokai shapechangers."

"We never caught very many," Polnu said with a grin in her voice. She lay on her stomach, her chin resting on her folded arms. "I don't suppose we were very good Wolkareans."

"You," Rand said, tapping Katrine's hand, "liked to sit in the shade and make sketches of us as if you were a Master Recorder." Then his voice became thoughtful. "I remember one day in particular. I was pretending to be a Shokai priest weaving a spell—"

"And it actually started to work," Katrine finished for him.

"The next thing I knew," Rand said, poking Katrine's hand again, "you were pounding me with your fists, and Polnu was screaming in the background."

"I remember that day," Polnu said, raising her head to glance over at her two friends. "I described it to my mother, and she got really angry. She said you could've accidentally conjured up anything, even a demon or a plague. And then, when Katrine and I interrupted you, the power could have gone wild and killed us all. I've never seen her so angry, before or since."

"When I told my father," Rand said, "he slapped me and called me a stupid, reckless child. It's the only time he's ever struck me. If I remember right, we never played that game again."

"What about you, 'Trine?" Polnu asked. "How did your parents react?"

"Actually, I never mentioned it." Katrine rolled over onto her stomach, picked up a stick, and made random scratches in the dirt. "They take Wolkareans, Shokai, and sorcery very seriously at my house. I imagine Father would've given me a switching if he'd known." Then she smiled impishly. "It might have been worth it. I loved those games."

"But now they're over," said Rand sadly.

"Now we're facing adult responsibilities," Polnu said, sounding almost as mournful as Rand.

"But what kind?" mused Katrine. "That's what worries me."

Rand sighed and flopped down on his stomach too. "All I know is that my father expects me to marry, have children, and pass on his land lore. I love my adoptive father and want to please him, but—?" He let the sentence dwindle away.

"But it's not enough," Katrine said, turning her head to look at him.

"That's right. Tending orchards and raising children, well, I guess that's important, but surely there's more to life."

"I think we'd all like to do something significant," Polnu said, "to feel like we've made a difference in the world."

"You two will," Rand said. A glossy brown beetle waddled through the grass, and Rand put his hand, palm down, in its path. "You'll be The Glaine, Polnu, after your grandmother and mother pass on. And you, Katrine, you'll be a Recorder, traveling all over Kareand. Me, I'll be nothing. Stuck in this mud-hole till I die."

"I don't know if I'll ever get to be a Recorder," Katrine said as she watched the beetle traverse the hills and valleys of Rand's fingers, "but I'll become a caravan driver or a trader before I'll live my whole life in Banur."

"I wish I could say that," Polnu said. She propped her elbows on the ground and rested her chin in her cupped hands. Her eyes followed the beetle's progress until it reached the far side of Rand's hand and trundled off into the grass again.

She sighed softly. "Rand's right. I'll have to be The Glaine eventually. If I had a choice, though, before I settled down and became all grown-up and serious, I'd go looking for the lost Crennese tribes. One of our farseers said the children of the Sister Wives yearn to come home, but they don't know the way. Sometimes at night, I sense them beyond the Daegarn Mountains in the west somewhere."

"Me too," Rand said, jolting upward in surprise. "It feels like they're calling for someone to come show them what direction to take. Sometimes I wake up thinking I must be going crazy. I never imagined anyone else could feel it."

Katrine sat up, tossed the stick she'd been drawing with into the river and watched it float away. She wrapped her arms around her bent knees. "Since you both have the same impulse, maybe it's your destiny to go looking for the tribes together."

"Ha!" said Rand and Polnu in unison.

Chapter Seven

For the next few days the household was in a flurry.

Rooms were aired, rugs were beaten, furniture was rearranged, bedding, linens, and curtains were all freshly laundered, and everything that could be cleaned had been washed, dusted, or polished.

Mother even hired a couple of neighbor girls to come over and help.

Although Katrine assured Mother that she wouldn't let Heni set foot in her room, Mother insisted it receive the same thorough cleansing as the rest of the house.

On the anticipated day, Katrine wasn't allowed to escape onto the plains until after her cousin arrived. She sat in the parlor watching Mother arrange flowers in a large vase.

Katrine's stomach twisted with dread.

Suddenly, Raeph burst into the room and shouted, "A carriage is coming. Heni's here."

"Go tell the other children," Mother said as she poked the last few stems into place. "And you, Katrine, remove the frown from your face. It is most unbecoming."

"I'd rather fight a dozen plains cats than spend one minute with Heni," Katrine said sullenly.

"I'm sure you would," Mother said, and then added firmly, "but she's here, and you will behave yourself."

Wheels clattered on the cobblestones, and an elegant carriage pulled into the courtyard. Katrine noticed it was the same one Uncle Charel had sent Heni in two years ago. He'd probably purchased it just for her. When it stopped, a heavily muscled man jumped down from his place beside the driver, opened the door, and positioned a footstool.

A small black slipper with an ornate gold buckle appeared, followed by lace dotted with little pink roses and bows along the bottom of a pale blue skirt.

Heni stepped out and glanced around.

Mother was there to embrace her.

As Katrine lagged behind her siblings, she eyed her cousin judiciously. Although she hated to admit it, Heni was quite pretty. She was petite with a little oval face and milky-white skin. Her eyes were brown and fringed with long dark eyelashes. Her hair, the same brown as her eyes, was done up in curls and ribbons. She was sixteen years old, but her lips curved in a little-girl pout.

She had been on the road for at least two weeks, yet her fashionable gown showed no travel wrinkles or dust.

Katrine snickered silently. *I'll bet she made her driver stop at the public bathhouse in town so she could change into something fresh.*

Heni was oohing and aahing over the twins when Katrine took a deep breath, steeled her nerves, and stepped forward. "Hello, Heni."

"Oh, Katrine, let me look at you," Heni gushed with exaggerated pleasure. "My, my, you've grown."

Here it comes, Katrine thought.

Her hands slowly clenched into fists. She held them behind her back to prevent them from doing something foolish, like punching her cousin in the nose or strangling her.

Either one would have been satisfying.

"You're so tall. Where in Kareand will your parents find a man to be your husband?" Heni thoughtfully tapped a delicate finger on her pretty little mouth. "Oh, I know! The northern mountains are full of ogres and giants."

Although Heni's words stung, Katrine kept her face blank. She would never give her cousin the satisfaction of knowing her comment hurt. Katrine had never said it out loud—not to Rand, not to Polnu, not to anyone in her family—but part of the reason she wanted to leave Banur was because she knew she would never marry. Even though she had been horrified when she thought Father was going to betroth her *now* that didn't mean she *never* wanted to wed.

For one brief second, when Rand told her that his father was going to suggest a betrothal, her heart had thumped ecstatically. Then reality had set in. Rand was like a brother to her. She could no more marry him than she could marry Skotlan.

Leron had been right when he said no one would want her. Even when he offered a match with Rand, he hadn't really wanted her. He'd only requested the betrothal because he was desperate for grandchildren and had assumed her father would be equally desperate to get rid of her.

That her father had turned him down was still puzzling.

"Perhaps I choose not to wed," Katrine said to her cousin with as much dignity as she could muster.

"Sensible," Heni said, "if that's all you can expect."

Yes, I am sensible, Katrine thought. *I have to be.*

Just then, Jaimi rushed out of the house and threw her arms around Heni's waist. "I'm so glad you're here. You look absolutely beautiful. I just love your dress and the way you've done your hair. Will you teach me how to braid ribbons like that into my hair?"

"Of course." Heni patted Jaimi on the head as if she were a pet. "Where do you want me, Aunt Evi? With Katrine again?"

Even though Katrine knew this wasn't the plan, her heart missed a beat until her mother answered.

"No, dear. You're too grown up now to have to share a room. Jaimi is going to move in with the twins, and you'll have her room all to yourself."

"How thoughtful, thank you." Heni looked Katrine up and down. "I suppose we could both use the privacy, we're so nearly the same age. Of course, that's all we have in common, thank the Powers. Come on, Jaimi, if you wash your hands, I'll let you unpack for me." She pointed at two small travel cases on the carriage floor. "Grab those for me, will you?"

Smiling as if she'd been given a gift, Jaimi picked up the bags and scurried toward the house behind Heni. Mother paused to stroke Katrine's cheek and give her a smile before she and the little ones left to follow.

Heaving a sigh of relief, Katrine sauntered over to where Heni's guard was unstrapping a large trunk from the rear of the carriage. "Any new scars, Sal?" she asked.

"Two," he answered, laughing, while he pulled her into a hug.

Sal was older than Father and had served Heni for as long as Katrine could remember. He was totally bald, and his face was lined with wrinkles from years of doing a difficult, thankless job. His arms and shoulders bulged with hard muscles, and he moved with the deadly quickness of a fighter.

Years ago, after eight-year-old Heni hit Katrine in the face with a stick, making a jagged cut from nostril to lip, Sal began showing Katrine his battle scars. Today, he pointed above his left eyebrow. "This one happened last winter when I wouldn't take her shopping on the waterfront at night. She hit me with a broom." He touched a freshly healed cut on his arm. "Here, she threw an earthenware pot at me right before we left Branston because I wouldn't let her bring any more luggage with her."

Katrine tsked sympathetically. "Too bad you can't just drop her down a hole somewhere." Unconsciously, she ran her finger along the pale, pink scar under her nose.

"I might be tempted if I didn't love her father like a brother. We sailed together as youths, and I owe him my life."

Ferrill, the driver, winked at Katrine from his seat at the front of the carriage. "I know what we should do. We'll convince Heni's parents that her hair went blond and she finally grew up. Then we'll take you back with us in her place."

Katrine blushed.

Ferrill wasn't much older than she was, and although he was short, he was extremely handsome with that striking combination of black hair and blue,

blue eyes. His teasing always embarrassed her.

"How were the roads?" Katrine asked in order to switch the focus from her. "Any trouble?"

"Not for us." Ferrill swished a handkerchief over his perspiring forehead and then hopped to the ground. "But we sure heard some disturbing tales. There was talk about enormous dog-like beasts attacking caravans, and marauders who didn't just assault lone travelers but attacked farmsteads as well. In the taverns, people sat with a mug of ale in one hand and a club or a knife in the other. Everyone was suspicious of strangers."

Sal hefted Heni's trunk onto one shoulder and started for the house. He paused so he could add his comments. "All the trouble we heard about was east of Plains Springs," Sal told her, "but I'd best report to your father anyway. Never know where disturbances will develop next."

"Father's gone to town on Council business," Katrine said, darting ahead so she could hold the front door open for him, "but he'll be back by suppertime. You'll both stay and dine with us, won't you?"

"I'll be staying for more than supper," said Ferrill. "Your father has hired me on for the rest of the summer, and I'm grateful. I hated working for the tanner the last time we came. Besides, it'll be more convenient if Miss Heni needs me to take her somewhere." He took hold of the ponies' harness and started leading them toward the barn.

"And you, Sal?" Katrine asked.

"Well, I'll be here for supper since I must speak with your father," Sal answered. Then his rugged face broke into a grin, and his cheeks reddened. "After that, you know, I have my lady friend in town. She's promised to keep me occupied until we start back for Branston."

* * *

For the first few weeks of Heni's visit, Katrine managed to avoid her except at meals and during morning classes.

Then after breakfast one day, Mother told Katrine that she wanted her to accompany Jaimi and Heni into town. "A trader's caravan arrived yesterday. You girls might find some good buys. Even if you don't, it's always fun to see the exotic wares from the north."

"But the herds," Katrine said automatically, "it's almost time to gather them for market. I really ought—" Her mouth snapped shut as she remembered the paintings and application that she needed to send to the Recorders School in Pardish.

"Your father is taking Anton with him today to tally the herdbeasts and mark the ones he plans to sell next month. There's no need for you to be out there as well."

Katrine didn't want to change her mind too quickly, or Mother might suspect something. She didn't know what to say, and she paused overly long.

The Spire of Kylet

A frown formed on Mother's face. "Sometimes you need to engage in more feminine activities, Katrine. Shopping is a woman's right."

Katrine nodded her acquiescence.

Inside, though, she was brimming with delight. The large trader's market wasn't due for another month, but now she wouldn't have to wait that long to send off her pictures.

What a bit of luck!

Sometimes the Fates were unusually kind.

"This is an opportunity for you to create some pleasant memories with Jaimi and Heni," Mother went on. "Maybe you girls can learn to appreciate each other."

"I'll try," Katrine said dubiously. She might be glad to go to the trader's market for her own purposes, but enjoying time with her sister and cousin was expecting a little too much.

Although Mother tolerated Katrine's tunics and trousers at home because of her chores, when going to town, she insisted that Katrine dress like a lady.

Up the stairs Katrine ran to change her clothes.

She chose a pale green bodice that had a matching skirt that wasn't too fancy. It was full enough for easy striding, but not so full as to be heavy and cumbersome. Beneath the underskirt she tied a cord around her waist, and from it she hung the package she had prepared for mailing.

Although it banged against her leg when she walked, she thrilled to the rhythmic reminder that soon her pictures would be on their way to Headmaster Miksel, bringing her one day closer to leaving home.

Mother accompanied the three girls to the carriage. "Now, I want you to stay together," she told them. "There are always a few sneak thieves traveling with caravans, so keep alert for cutpurses and pickpockets. Don't let people know how much money you have, and don't mix with strangers. If you have any problems, find a peacekeeper or a caravan guard. I'm trusting you to be careful and to watch out for each other."

"We will," they all assured her. Mother passed out hugs and a silver coin to each girl before they climbed into the carriage.

Ferrill snapped the reins, and they were off.

Although Banur was small when compared to the older cities along the banks of the Great Meriad, it was one of the largest towns on the Ildec River. Traders arrived off and on all year, but there were only three or four big caravans that ever bothered to travel this far southwest.

When one of the large trading companies arrived, the town assumed the air of a carnival. Bright, colorful tents and other temporary structures were erected outside the northern gates of the city so the merchants could show off their goods.

Minstrels, jugglers, food vendors, and flimflam artists wandered around outside the tents, performing, selling, and sometimes begging—doing whatever they could—to gain a few coppers from the crowds.

At first Katrine felt uncomfortable in the company of her sister and cousin, but soon she was caught up in the atmosphere of excitement and enthusiasm that radiated from every direction.

The girls wandered in and out of the displays, laughing and chatting about the merchandise, the strangely dressed traders, the many enticing odors coming from the cook tents, and anything else that caught their attention. For a while Katrine even forgot how much she hated Heni.

"See all that jewelry," Jaimi cried, pointing through a break in the crowd to the inside of a spacious tent. "Let's go in and shop around."

"Yes," Heni said quickly. "Some of it looks interesting."

When the girls had worked their way through throngs of merrymakers who seemed to lurch in groups to block their progress, Heni appraised the tent's interior with a glance.

"Look at the odd junk on the table in the back," she said disapprovingly. "I'll bet they have a lot of worthless trash mixed in with the finer things. We'll need to be cautious."

Then she and Jaimi began searching through racks of necklaces and bracelets, some made of bright beads and shiny metal links and others made of small shells and silken cords.

Katrine, however, was drawn to the table that Heni had pointed out. It was cluttered with tools, books, weapons, and strange, unidentifiable devices.

An old leather-bound tome caught Katrine's attention.

She noticed it, even though it was dirty and scuffed, because the elegant designs that had been tooled on the front were still visible. Around the outer edge of the cover was a border made up of vines and flowers swirling around an occasional bird or butterfly. Within the border were the Old Crennese symbols for the four elements: a sun to represent fire, a horizontal line with a triangle above it for land, two stacked wavy lines for water, and a double curlicue for air.

There was no title etched on either the cover or the spine.

Katrine thumbed through the first several pages and recognized some old ballads and poems written in outdated and stylized Nistarian script. In the back, however, was a section that used an alphabet she didn't recognize, an alphabet full of loops and dots and crosses and squares.

The book would make a nice birth celebration gift for Father. If she could afford it, she would buy it.

After haggling over the price for several minutes, Katrine finally convinced the seller that a book written in such an uncommon language had limited appeal, and he sold it to her for only four coppers. Katrine could have danced for joy. She had brought a half-silver and five coppers with her. She should be able to put the silver Mother had given her with her stash for the trip to Pardish.

Shortly after Katrine bought the book, Heni and Jaimi completed their purchases too.

When they emerged from the tent, Katrine had to blink her eyes against the brilliance of the day. It was nearing noon, and the sunlight seemed overly bright with no shade or shadows to dull its glare.

"I'm hungry," Jaimi said.

Heni pointed to a small tent decorated with purple and green streamers. "There's a food vendor from Cajetta. Let's go there. They make the most wonderful delicacies from dried or cured fish."

The two girls headed in that direction, then stopped when they noticed Katrine wasn't moving with them.

"I'll be right back," Katrine said quickly. "I have to use the—the uh—public convenience."

Heni and Jaimi smirked.

"Don't fall in," Heni said with a chuckle.

Katrine ignored her. She pointed at a curly-headed young girl dressed all in bright yellow. "Oh, Jaimi, isn't that your friend Terina and her family? It looks like they're going into the tent Heni was talking about."

Jaimi beamed with delight. "Come on," she said, pulling Heni by the hand. "I'll introduce you. You'll just love Terina."

At least now I don't have to worry about them while I'm gone, Katrine thought. *Terina and her mother will want to know everything Heni can tell them about fashions in the north. They'll be gabbing for hours.*

Stretching on her toes, Katrine surveyed up and down the promenade. She had caught a glimpse of the Caravan Master earlier in the day, recognizing him by his traditionally colorful uniform, but now she couldn't spot him anywhere. She let the flow of bodies carry her until she saw an official looking man standing near the doorway of a temporary wooden structure.

"Excuse me, sir," Katrine said, trying her best to be polite, "could you direct me to the Caravan Master's tent?"

The man looked her over as if she were a plump chicken he might take home for his dinner. "Aren't you a little young to be seeking a grown man's tent? You might not like what you find." Leering, he moved suggestively closer. "I'm nearer your age and certainly better looking than the Caravan Master, how about you and me—?"

Drawing herself up straight, Katrine glared at the man with her eyes opened wide with anger. "I must arrange for the delivery of a parcel," she barked, "so watch your dirty mind. If you don't know where the tent is, just admit it."

Hastily, the man stepped backward.

"No offense intended, miss. Go straight ahead until you come to a tall pole flying a red banner. Turn left. His tent is the third one. Yellow with black stripes. You can't miss it."

"Thank you," Katrine said stiffly and then hurried on her way.

Why had the man revised his manners so quickly? she wondered. Perhaps other girls he had addressed that way had responded with giggling and flirting. She must have caught him off guard by confronting his rudeness. Well, teasing and playing coy were things she simply didn't understand and probably never would.

Increasing her pace, she pulled the cord from beneath the band of her skirt and fumbled with the knot while holding the book between her arm and body so she could use both hands. When the cord came loose, she let the bundle drop to the ground. Bending, she snatched it up.

The Caravan Master asked no question when Katrine found him. He took the package, wrote a receipt, and charged her six coppers and a fleck.

When Katrine turned to leave, she felt let down.

There should have been some kind of fanfare, trumpets at least, for dispatching her pictures and application.

Instead, it felt rather disappointing.

Chapter Eight

Early the next morning, Katrine carefully cleaned the leather binding of the book she had purchased and then flipped through the pages.

After the Nistarian poems and ballads, there were a few verses written in Crennish. She was familiar with some of the words, and she considered translating the rest, but it felt too much like her school lessons, so she didn't bother.

Before she put the book away, she took a moment to glance at the section in the back again. She had never seen such strange script. Father would get hours of pleasure figuring it out. Decrypting obscure languages was his favorite pastime.

She dressed lazily and sauntered down to breakfast well after her usual hour. At dinner last night, Father had told the children there would be no classes this morning. Katrine had been so excited about the prospect of sleeping in that she had done her household chores before going to bed.

When she sat down at the kitchen table next to Skotlan, who had almost finished his breakfast, Rosi greeted her with a plate of fried sausages and two hot muffins dripping with honey and slivered nuts. She set a glass of milk on the table next to the plate.

"When you're finished eating," Rosi said, hustling around the kitchen and doing a dozen things at once, "your father would like to see you in his study."

Skotlan put a steadying hand on Katrine's arm. Having to go to Father's study was never a pleasant prospect. It was the place of chastisement and punishment.

Crinkling her brow, Katrine asked, "Am I in trouble? I don't remember doing anything—"

"He didn't seem angry," Rosi said. "In fact, he has someone with him. I think he wants to introduce you, but I'm just guessing."

Katrine gulped down her food without really tasting it. She hated not knowing what to expect from Father. If he was going to yell at her, she preferred to get it over as quickly as possible. When she had swallowed the last of the milk, she brushed crumbs from her lap and hurried from the kitchen.

"Come in, Katrine," Father said. "I want you to meet someone."

The man with Father was a distinguished elderly gentleman with a finely lined face, thinning white hair, and bushy gray eyebrows. His lips parted in a friendly smile, making a red curve between his clipped gray moustache and short gray beard.

What struck Katrine, though, and almost sent her reeling, was that he wore the maroon, gold-trimmed robe of a Master Recorder. It took all of her self-discipline not to swoon.

"Master Neyac, this is my daughter, Katrine," Father said. "Katrine, please meet Master Recorder Neyac."

Even though her legs felt rubbery, Katrine managed to bob a small, awkward curtsy. "I'm honored, Master Neyac."

When Neyac stood, Katrine was surprised to discover that he was much shorter than she was. Nevertheless, his dark eyes twinkled, and he bowed gallantly to her. "The honor is mine."

With the formalities completed, Katrine didn't know what to do with herself. She fidgeted and tried not to stare as if she were a foolish child gaping at an enchanted, mystical creature. Yet, anyone who reached Master Recorder's status actually was a magical being—he was a giant of intellect, talent, education, and wisdom.

"Won't you join us?" Neyac said, taking Katrine's well-calloused hand in his own and guiding her to a nearby chair. "Your father has just been telling me about you."

"About me?" Katrine stammered, giving her father a confused look. "Why?"

"Your father says you are quite talented with paints. We Recorders are always looking for gifted young people. I can't stay long today because I'm traveling with a caravan and it'll be leaving soon. I'm going to Nallee to fetch my new apprentice, but I'll be back this way before fall. I'd like to see some of your artwork then, when we have time to talk about tints and techniques, if you don't mind."

For several seconds, Katrine just sat with her mouth agape. Father had never indicated that he thought she had talent. Did he know she wanted to become a Recorder? She hadn't told anyone except Rand and Polnu. Not even Skotlan.

"I think my daughter has forgotten her manners," Father said with controlled irritation. "Katrine, Master Neyac asked if you would show him some of your paintings on his return trip."

Turning her head to stare, Katrine felt as if she were seeing a stranger instead of her father. He appeared as alien as if he had suddenly sprouted horns or wings. She didn't know how to react. As he met her baffled gaze with deepening furrows between his brows, she pulled herself together. She knew what that look meant.

"I'd love to show you my pictures," Katrine said quickly. "They're not as good as ones done by Recorders, but they're the best I can manage." With her mouth going dry, she added, "I like to paint. The Glainites taught me how to make and mix my colors."

"What other things do you enjoy," Neyac asked.

"Other things?" From the corner of her eye, Katrine could see Father watching her. She had to say something. Anything. "I—uh—I like to ride my pony on the plains, though I'd really rather have a real horse. Unfortunately the Glainites won't trade or sell the ones they catch, and they're the only people around here who know how. Of course, if I were rich I could buy one, but I'm not." She sounded like an idiot and could feel her face burning. She bit her lip and tried not to let tears well up in her eyes, as they usually did when she felt strong emotions—like humiliation.

"You've mentioned the Glainites twice," Master Neyac said, as if he hadn't noticed her escalating discomfort. "Tell me about them."

Katrine wished she could have a heart seizure and die. She knew she wasn't making a good impression. Maybe if Father weren't there watching her, judging her, it would be easier. But he wasn't going to leave, and she couldn't jump up and run away.

Inhaling deeply, she plunged into a long narrative about Polnu and her family. When she ran out of things to say, she was desperate to flee. Thankfully, Neyac had no more questions.

Throughout the remainder of the day, Katrine agonized over her poor performance. She had never met a Master Recorder before and had been caught completely off guard. Whenever Recorders passed through Banur, they always stopped to see Father because he was High Elder. They brought him up-to-date on the news of the land and sometimes carried communiqués from other Councils or even from Regent Laria.

Often they stayed for dinner and entertained the children with dramatic tellings of the old legends, or showed off their sketches, or sang songs they had composed. But they had all been Journeymen. She hadn't even known the Masters still traveled beyond Pardish.

She would have to be better prepared when Neyac returned. She couldn't afford to make a fool of herself twice. But which pictures could she show him? She'd sent her best off to Headmaster Miksel, and none of the others seemed good enough.

She had done a copy from memory of the golden hawk because she could hardly bear to give the picture away. Sometimes she felt it was equal to the original; other times she thought the colors were inferior. She must find time to paint something new. If she could impress Master Neyac, he might say a few words on her behalf when he reached Pardish with his apprentice.

* * *

Not long after Neyac's visit, Father received an order for fifty herdbeasts and sent Katrine and a couple of hired men out to gather them. Knowing the habits of the animals, Katrine crossed the shallow Ildec Minor to the south of Banur. There was a little hollow along the western bank that was almost as cool as the ravine.

As anticipated, she found a dozen herdbeasts grazing there, protected from the heat by the shadows of large sinella trees. Delighted that she had located so many at one time, she rounded them up and headed for home.

She would have part of the afternoon free to work on her art!

She was keeping her tiny herd in a tight grouping and was making good time when she noticed several buzzards circling in the distance. Below them, she saw a telltale swirling dome of dust where some animal, probably from her father's herd, battled with a plains cat for its life.

She was already tired from the heat and was tempted to leave the dying animal to its fate, but at the last minute she found she couldn't do it. Even if the herdbeast was already dead, she couldn't let the cat escape. If she did, it would kill again and again. One of these times, it might attack her or Stubbs. She clicked her reins and turned toward the struggle.

"I hate these fraggin' herdbeasts," she muttered to Stubbs. "How did they survive before I was born to take care of them?"

A hot dry wind swept across the plains from the south, hurling bits of dirt and debris into the air, obstructing Katrine's view.

She had already leapt from Stubbs's back when she realized with a shock that it wasn't a herdbeast thrashing about in the plain cat's grasp.

It was a person!

Katrine caught a glimpse of a red beaded armband, the symbol of a Glainite Master.

Because of the strong gusting breeze, Katrine didn't dare trying to aim an arrow, and she didn't have enough experience to throw the spire.

That left only her knife.

Without another thought, Katrine grabbed her dagger and ran, screaming as loudly as she could. When she hit the plains cat, her knife caught its shoulder, and her weight knocked it off balance.

Whirling around, the cat turned into a fury of claws and teeth.

Katrine's quick reflexes kept her throat from being ripped out by the huge jaws, but a swipe of sharp-tooled paws set her back on fire. She cursed herself for being as stupid and helpless as a yearling.

She was going to die.

Wildly she jabbed with her knife, determined to hack up the cat as much as possible before it killed her. She made one long slash all the way down its ribs. For a second, the cat was motionless with shock. Katrine's dagger found its way into the beast's neck again and again.

With a gurgle, the plains cat inhaled its own blood, quivered, toppled over, and was still.

Gasping, trying franticly to fill her lungs so she could breathe, Katrine realized she was trapped beneath the weight of the dead beast. Inch by inch, she squirmed and wriggled her way free.

The Glainite, covered with dirt and gore, lay face down a few feet away.

"Holy snakespit," Katrine whispered to herself. This wasn't just any Glainite Master. It was Polnu's grandmother. Bainu. The Glaine. The revered leader of their tribe.

Stumbling over to Stubbs, Katrine dug around in her saddlebags until she found some clean rags. Using water from her drinking skin, she dampened them and began washing grime from Bainu's face. The ancient eyelids flickered open, and a smile of recognition flitted across her pale lips.

"Do you have your medicine pouch with you?" Katrine asked.

"No," came the faint reply. "It was tied to the saddle. My horse managed to escape when the plains cat attacked us."

Without medicine and with limited water, the best Katrine could do was bind up the worst of Bainu's injuries.

When that was done, Katrine pulled up her own tunic and wrapped rags around her torso from underarms to waist. Hopefully that would keep bugs out of the claw marks on her back and slow the bleeding.

Because she had chosen to gather herdbeasts near the southern end of the river, Katrine was closer to Glaine's Stand than she was to her own home. She chewed on her lower lip and tried to figure out how to get Bainu back to her people.

A dry tree had fallen to the ground not far away. By jumping up and down on one branch and then another, Katrine was able to break off two that were about the same length. After she stripped away the twigs with her knife, she fastened the branches to either side of her saddle. Then she used her knife to poke holes in an old blanket she always carried. She laced it onto the branches with pieces of cord.

"When I move you," Katrine said to the old woman, "I'm afraid it's going to hurt."

"You saved my life," Bainu whispered. "You have my gratitude. Any pain I experience will remind me that I have not yet gone to greet my ancestors."

Katrine led the pony around so the sling was as close to The Glaine as possible. With feet apart, she bent deeply at the knees and lifted. Two tiny steps were all it took.

Glancing over her shoulder, she noticed the herdbeasts had already begun drifting back toward the river. She sighed and gathered up her pony's reins.

Then she had to decide whether she should walk or ride.

If she rode, the burden of carrying a rider and dragging the litter might become too much for the sturdy little pony. On the other hand, if she walked, it would take longer, and there was the risk that she might become too weak to continue. She decided to walk. If she had to, she could ride later. Also, on foot, she was more likely to spot bumps and dips that she might miss on horseback. She was sure Bainu would benefit from as smooth a trip as possible.

Within minutes, perspiration was dripping into Katrine's eyes and running down her back, nearly blinding her and setting her numerous abrasions on fire. The wind increased and pelted her with grit, drying out her mouth and nose, making breathing difficult. Often she stopped to rest the pony for a few minutes while she gave them all a sip from her water skin. Each time she filled her cupped hand for Stubbs, he slurped the liquid up and whinnied for more.

Several times after taking a break, Katrine considered mounting and letting the pony carry her. Always she decided against it, wanting to preserve his strength as long as possible.

The sun was halfway to the horizon when they approached some Glainites working in their crop fields. Leaning on Stubbs, Katrine could hardly keep moving.

She tripped and was struggling to pick herself up when she noticed people running toward her. The first man to arrive cried out in dismay when he saw The Glaine. Immediately, he dispatched a runner to inform Renee, Polnu's mother.

At the sight of assistance, the last of Katrine's strength evaporated and the world disappeared.

* * *

When Katrine regained consciousness, she was sitting on a chair in the large central area of Polnu's home. Someone had draped a cloth over her back and tied the ends in a loose knot under her chin, probably to keep her bloody back from ruining the cushion behind her.

Renee was busily tending The Glaine, who lay on a cot across the room.

Unlike Nistarian homes, with their separate chambers for almost every function, Glainite dwellings had a central room that was used for cooking, eating, socializing, entertaining, and working. Only the sleeping rooms and bathhouse were separate, and most Glainite homes, like this one, had extra couches and beds in the central area for guests.

"Is she going to be all right?" Katrine asked in a hoarse croak. Her throat was dry and sore and felt as if it were caked with dirt. She swallowed several times with no relief.

"Here," Polnu said, "this'll help." She handed Katrine a cup of warm broth pungent with herbs and spices. As Katrine sipped, the dusty taste in her mouth was washed clean.

"Her injuries are serious," Renee said as she dabbed a raw spot on Bainu's shoulder with a cloth, "but she is strong for her years, and I think she cast several healing spells on the way here. She'll recover."

Renee gave Bainu a potion to drink, and within minutes, the old woman was snoring quietly, a slender smile curving her lips.

"Now it's your turn." Renee slipped an arm around Katrine and helped her to a bench beside the table. Katrine almost cried out from the pain. Only pride kept her silent.

"Lean forward," Renee said, "and let me see your back."

Katrine felt Polnu's mother lift the hem of her tunic and then make a tsk-tsking sound.

"You're more than a little hurt yourself." Renee took away Katrine's cup, added some powder from a jar she'd had on a shelf, stirred the liquid, and handed the cup back. "Drink," she commanded.

Obediently, Katrine took a deep swallow.

Renee slit the sides of Katrine's tunic with a knife and then tugged gently at the fabric. "Polnu!" she called.

"I'm here, Mother," said Polnu, entering with a jug of water and setting it beside the stove.

"Katrine's tunic is blood-stuck to her back and so are the strips of cloth she used to bind the wounds. All of it will need to be soaked off." Renee busied herself at a sideboard, gathering bits of this and that. With mortar and pestle she ground everything together. "See what you can do while I mix an antiseptic. I've given her leiti."

After pouring heated water from a kettle on the stove into a basin, Polnu told Katrine, "You can sit or lie face down. Even with the leiti, this is going to sting a little."

"No," Katrine said feebly. "I'm fine. It's almost sunset. I've got to get home. Father will be angry if I'm late."

Without taking her eyes from the task she was performing, Renee answered. "Sillem, my lifemate, has already gone to tell your parents what has happened. You're in no condition to travel, let alone ride your pony all the way back to your home."

"You don't understand. Father is very strict."

"And Sillem is very persuasive. He'll assure your father you're safe here with us. You might be able to return to your family tomorrow. We'll know in the morning." Renee dumped the concoction she had mixed into the basin Polnu held.

"But—"

"No more!" Polnu said. "Do you want to lie down or to sit?"

"Neither. I'm all right. Really."

"It is forbidden to speak an untruth in front of The Glaine," Polnu said piously, then giggled, "even when she's asleep. Now get down on that mat. If you don't have a preference, I do. It'll be easier for me if you're lying flat."

When the medicated water reached the first of Katrine's injuries, she gasped out loud. "You said it would sting a little. I thought you couldn't fib in front of The Glaine."

Polnu shrugged. "It stings worse for some people than others. You might be more sensitive than most."

"What was—?" Katrine's tongue felt thick, and she found talking increasingly difficult. "What was The Glaine doing out on the plains by herself?" she finally managed to ask. "I thought she always traveled with attendants."

"Usually," Polnu said, "but not if she's communicating with the spirits of the ancestors. She always goes alone and often stays out all day when she's meditating." Polnu cut away Katrine's tunic at the shoulders.

Katrine was getting very sleepy, but she was aware enough to wonder what she was going to wear home if Renee and Polnu kept cutting up her clothing.

Polnu applied liquid to the rags wrapped around Katrine's middle. "I wonder why Grandmother's horse didn't come back," she said. "If it had, the tribe would have started a search immediately."

"Maybe a plains cat got it," Katrine mumbled, trying hard not to slur her words. It wasn't easy.

As soon as the cloth strips were loosened, Polnu and Renee peeled them away from the skin. Before they even began tending the wounds, Katrine decided her eyelids were too heavy to be kept open. She slid sideways into sleep.

Chapter Nine

A beam of sunlight tickled Katrine's eyelids, rousing her from a foggy half-slumber. She was in Polnu's bedchamber. The door was slightly ajar, and she heard hushed voices coming from the next room. Part of her mind told her to wake up and pay attention to what was being said, but the part that told her to go back to sleep was stronger.

When wakefulness came to her again, the light was dimmer and the murmuring voices became shockingly identifiable. Katrine jerked into a sitting position. Pain seared across her back.

"When will she wake?" her father asked.

"Soon," Renee said, "but she will still be weak from fatigue and blood loss. In addition, some people are overly sensitive to leiti, and Katrine is one. What I gave her yesterday should merely have dulled her aches. Instead, it put her right to sleep."

"I've heard of people dying from leiti," said Mother.

"It can be dangerous," Renee agreed, "if not used correctly, but I am a Master. Also, Polnu and I took turns watching over Katrine and Bainu throughout the night. Katrine has been in a deep slumber, no more than that. With rest and care she will be fine."

"You should be proud of her, Elder Mer," the deep voice of Sillem, Polnu's father, said. "Last night, two of our villagers prepared the cat's skin for tanning. It was an extremely large animal."

With great effort, Katrine swung her legs around and struggled to her feet. Her clothing was nowhere in sight, although her saddlebags were on the floor next to her cot.

A faded blue tunic and brown trousers were spread out on a bench at the foot of the bed. A long woven belt lay across them. Katrine assumed they were for her since all she was wearing were her pantalees and several rows of bandages. Apparently Renee or Polnu had cut away her breast-band in order to treat her back.

Pulling the tunic over her head, Katrine wondered where it had come from.

It couldn't belong to Polnu. Her shoulders were much narrower than Katrine's, and the tunic fit. Maybe it belonged to Polnu's father. He was a metal craftsman, and even though he usually worked on things like household utensils and jewelry, he also did the blacksmithing for the tribe, giving him a muscular upper body.

Although every movement hurt, Katrine managed to dress herself.

Polnu's brush was beside the basin on the washstand. Katrine worked the bristles through the worst of the tangles in her hair and then divided it into thirds so she could braid it. Glancing around, however, she realized she had nothing to tie around the end. With a sigh, she hooked the side tresses behind her ears and let the back hang loose. After splashing her face with cool water, Katrine felt her head clear. She took a few teetering steps and pushed the door open.

Since she'd heard only the voices of Polnu's parents and her own, she assumed they were the only people present. She was quite surprised to discover many tribal members lounging about.

The room went silent. Then the Glainites stood and touched right hands to left hips. Those who wore blades touched the pommel of their weapons; those without simply touched the area on the hip where a pommel would have rested.

Awestruck by this show of respect, Katrine returned the gesture. The Glainites bowed or nodded to her parents and then left. Renee and Sillem accompanied their guests out the door.

Only then did Mother rush over and help Katrine to a chair, clucking and fretting the whole time. Katrine absolutely hated having people fuss over her. It always made her feel weak and helpless—as if she couldn't take care of herself. She attempted to deflect her mother by saying, "It's late. Shouldn't we be getting home?"

Father answered from across the room. "Renee and Sillem have invited you to stay with them for a while. The tribe would like to hold a celebration in your honor."

Hardly able to contain her excitement, Katrine beamed. It would be a great adventure! Last night had been the first time she'd ever been away from home for an entire night, and it hardly counted since she had been unconscious during the whole experience. She'd love spending the extra time with Polnu and, she thought happily, Heni wasn't here.

"May I?"

"Is it something you would enjoy?" asked Mother.

Suddenly Katrine was afraid she might sway Father negatively if she was too enthusiastic. "I think so," she said, keeping her voice neutral.

When Polnu's parents reentered the room, Father had a question for them. "You said you'd like her to stay for several days. How long were you considering?"

Sillem answered. "There is a festival we sometimes observe at the full moon. It begins when the moon rises and then continues throughout the night. The next day, we sleep. This morning, The Glaine's first words were that we would hold a Festival of the Full Moon for Katrine. We would like her to stay with us until it is over. We would accompany her to your gates before the sun sets on the day of the sleeping."

Mother stood beside Katrine, stroking her hair, but her eyes were locked on Father. He returned her gaze. "It's a week until the full moon," he said.

"A long time to be away from home," said Mother.

"We would take care of her as we do our own daughter," Renee interjected in a reassuring tone. "She risked her life for our beloved leader. We owe her a debt that's not easily repaid."

"It has been a long time since anyone performed so great a service for the Glainites," said Sillem. "Perhaps not since the time of the first Glaine, when so many laid down their lives to protect her and her unborn child from Elnid-Kyeh."

"She's fifteen," Father said to Mother, "and we've done all we could to raise her well. We can't cling to her forever."

Tipping her head forward, Mother nodded slightly. "Old enough to betroth, almost old enough to wed. Still, I hate to let go. How can we bear to let go?"

Having Mother and Father discuss her in front of Polnu's parents embarrassed Katrine. They sounded as if they were planning to bury her, rather than letting her spend a few days with trusted friends. Renee and Sillem must have experienced something similar, for they both stood.

"Perhaps," Renee said, "there are considerations of which we are unaware. We'll leave you alone so you can talk privately."

"No," Father said. He got to his feet and crossed the room to Katrine's side. "There is nothing left to discuss."

With a sinking heart, Katrine stood up. Controlling her disappointment, she said, "I'll get my things."

For the first time since she was a little girl, Father gathered Katrine into his arms, very carefully, as if mindful of her injuries. "I think your destiny is beginning to assert itself," he said quietly. "We can't interfere. We wouldn't even if we could. You may stay."

Mother also embraced Katrine, and there were tears in her eyes. "If you want to come home early, dear, you can. You know that." Her voice dropped to a whisper. "We're so proud of you, and we love you very much."

"I'll be home in a week," Katrine said cheerfully, trying to lighten the mood, which felt too somber, and because of that, somewhat frightening. "It's not really that long."

Mother paused to stroke Katrine's cheek before taking Father's arm. "The sun is getting low," she said. "We promised the other children we'd be home before dark."

"We'll go." They started out, but Father stopped at the threshold. "We're proud of you, Katrine," he said.

Then they were gone.

Katrine let her parents' words nestle in a special portion of her heart. *At least this once*, she thought, *I didn't disappoint my father.*

* * *

Four days after being clawed by the plains cat, Katrine woke feeling almost normal. The potions and healing spells that Renee had used on her back made the wounds close rapidly, and unless she turned too quickly, she felt very little discomfort.

All in all, she was at peace with the world.

Not having to do her chores would have been enough to put her in a jovial mood, but she was also missing a full week of Heni's visit. Plus, the Glainites were treating her like royalty. She felt well rested, well fed, and completely pampered.

On top of everything else, the past few days had been overcast with sporadic rain showers, cooling the air significantly and giving it a light, clean scent.

Today, Renee had loaned Katrine her art supplies, and Katrine wandered through the village looking for subjects. In the shade of a large fillantra tree, three giggly girls were taking flowers from a basket and braiding them into garlands.

When Katrine asked if she could sketch them, they looked up and smiled, flashing white teeth and dimples. After she finished the drawing and showed them the result, they blushed brightly and giggled even louder than before.

Many of the youths, those near Katrine and Polnu's age, were engaged in competitions of skill and daring. Katrine watched Polnu unsaddle a young man in a contest involving riders on horseback and oddly shaped lances with wide bludgeons on the ends. Shortly thereafter, someone toppled Polnu over. After her defeat, Polnu joined Katrine in her wanderings.

"Why don't you try one of the games?" Polnu suggested.

"Me?" Katrine exclaimed. "How? You've got people running around carrying things, and jumping over obstacles, and climbing poles, and sliding down boards. I've no idea what they're doing."

"I guess some of them are a little complicated." Then Polnu pointed to her left, where two men were hanging gourds by long strings from the branches of a tree. "That's archery. Each contestant gets eight arrows. You see how many swinging targets you can hit within ten drum beats. That's not complicated."

After watching the first few contenders, Katrine decided she could do at least as well as they did, even though ten beats of the drum wasn't much time. She handed Polnu the drawing she'd done and Renee's art satchel, then joined the line of hopefuls.

The Spire of Kylet

When her turn came, she took the arrows and planted them tip down in the dirt in two tight lines as she had seen the others do.

The judge yelled, "Now."

Katrine grabbed the first arrow, pulled the string back, and released it. Without even waiting to see if she hit the target, she nocked the second and let it fly. Then the third. The fourth. Just as the drummer sounded the last beat, she released the final arrow. Only then did she notice how well she'd done. Each of the eight gourds had an arrow protruding from it, and everyone was congratulating her.

The judge held up a neck strap beaded in yellow, orange, and black. He fastened it around her neck.

"Thank you," Katrine told him, "but what's it for?"

"The contest ends when someone makes a perfect score," the judge told her. "You are the winner."

As people drifted toward other activities, Katrine turned to Polnu. "I don't understand. There might have been others who could have done as well as I did, but they didn't get to try just because I was in front of them in the line. That doesn't seem quite fair."

"Don't let it bother you," Polnu told her, handing back the art satchel and picture. "There are plenty of other challenges. In fact, one is beginning in the meadow. Come on. You might find it interesting."

Interesting? thought Katrine. *Fascinating! They're throwing spires.*

Katrine and Polnu found a shady spot, sat, and watched a stocky Glainite with a scar on his chin send his spire whirling at a life-sized straw figure at the other end of the field. The spire struck, and the "head" flew off.

"Spires are weapons of war," Polnu said. "As Glainites, we use our bows and spears and knives for hunting and defense. But Kylet designed spires to be employed against evil people. That's why the target is shaped like a human, to remind the wielder never to toss a spire frivolously."

Uncomfortably, Katrine bit her lip.

Would the Glainites be offended to find out she had used a spire to kill a plains cat? They would probably be horrified to know she had one at all. Ever since the incident with Rand, she had been nervous about carrying the weapon inside her tunic front—afraid someone might see it and try to take it from her. Now it was wrapped in a cloth and buried at the bottom of her saddlebags.

For quite some time, Katrine watched, spellbound, as one person after another flung a spire so it slashed through the distant object. Sometimes, the spires did elaborate twists and turns along the way, somehow controlled by the thrower.

Finally, she realized she was missing an opportunity. She quickly got out paper and charcoal and then began sketching the next competitor and his straw target. Neyac would surely be impressed. He had seemed interested in the tribe, and she knew of no other pictures of this type outside the village.

By the end of the day, Katrine had finished another three drawings. Adding them to the one of the giggly girls, she had four new and unique pictures to show Neyac when he returned in the fall. If she had enough time when she got home, she would reproduce the best with her paints.

As the sun began to set, Polnu said, "It's time to get ready to go over to the Hall of Chiefs for the banquet."

After a quick trip to the bathhouse, Polnu handed Katrine a long violet shift and matching belt, both trimmed with yellow and white beadwork. "This'll look good with your new neck band," Polnu said.

To Katrine's surprise the shift fit as if it had been made for her. "This is lovely," Katrine said, "and it fits. Whose is it?"

"Yours," Polnu answered. "Mayla, our best dressmaker, measured you for it while you were sleeping off the leiti."

"You'll have to be sure to introduce us so I can thank her."

After Katrine had fastened the belt, Polnu braided Katrine's hair for her. She styled it in the Glainite fashion, making four long blond plaits that she coiled around each other in a knot at the back of the neck. Polnu inserted a large purple flower above Katrine's left ear.

Staring in Polnu's hand mirror, Katrine was stunned. She didn't look like herself at all. She was sleek and stylish—and almost pretty.

Then Polnu put on her own gown of bright yellow trimmed with red and black. She wore a crimson flower in her dark hair. A yellow beaded band, symbolizing her position as a student of the healing arts, encircled her left arm.

The Hall of Chiefs was a large, centrally located structure. Tables and chairs had been set up to accommodate everyone in the village. The walls were draped with garlands made of flowers, prairie grass, and ribbons. Bowls of additional flowers were arranged on each table, making the whole building smell like a garden.

When Katrine and Polnu arrived, people were already selecting seats. Katrine started to follow Polnu to where the young people were congregating, but an elderly man wearing the red armband of a Glainite Master intercepted her.

He took her to the head table and showed her where to sit.

Mouthwatering scents drifted in from the communal ovens.

When Bainu entered the Hall, supported on one side by Renee and the other by Sillem, the tribe all stood and touched right hands to left hips in respect. Although The Glaine moved slowly, as if she were not completely healed, she looked regal in an all white shift and belt. Her gray hair was twisted in a complicated knot on the top of her head. The only color she wore was the scarlet armband of a Master; above the red she wore a similarly designed band of white beads on bleached leather to indicate she was also The Glaine.

Everyone turned toward the head table as The Glaine took her spot at its center. When she sat, people began sitting down while continuing to watch her expectantly.

With all eyes gazing forward, Katrine felt a moment of panic.

She was used to being invisible. Anyway, that's what she called the feeling she frequently had that her parents never saw her except when she was in trouble.

Her stomach began to hurt, and her tongue felt thick and heavy.

She hoped she would not be expected to say anything. She was not a good public speaker.

As soon as everyone had regained their seats, Bainu stood, steadying herself with a hand on the edge of the table.

"When Glaine settled this land," Bainu said, "after the crown city of Renath fell to Elnid-Kyeh, she had with her an assortment of family, friends, and Wolkarean Warriors.

"It was a time of treachery and deceit and lost innocence. Glaine knew the time was near for her to deliver her first child, and she chose to stop and establish Glaine's Stand rather than to continue fleeing with the Sister Wives. Even so, she was afraid her evil husband, Elnid-Kyeh, might have placed spies among her courtiers.

"So, using her magical powers, she devised a series of tests that she required everyone over the age of twelve who wished to stay with her to take. She called them the Tests of Truth. Glaine wove powerful spells into the challenges so anyone with evil intentions toward her or her child would surely fail. Four men and two women died."

Bainu looked around the room and shrugged her narrow shoulders. "Perhaps not all who died were Elnid-Kyeh's spies, but they all surely wished Glaine ill. Had she not protected herself, it is possible she would have once again fallen under the power of her husband and been spirited away to Serpent's Head. There, he would have stripped away her lore and her magic. What would have been left of her, we cannot know, but she knew.

"Those who passed the tests were adopted into a new tribe, the Glainites, through the first ritual of joining. Since then, the tests have been modified and used on various occasions, most frequently when one of our members has wished to mate outside the tribe.

"Manderig asked the Crennese to keep their bloodline pure. He did not want their sorcerous powers to creep into the blood of those who were unprepared to deal with their mixed natures. Even though the Glainites do not possess the strong magic of the other Crennese tribes, we have honored Manderig's request by only allowing individuals to join us if they proved worthy and were willing to accept our heritage as their own."

Bainu turned and addressed Katrine directly. "The Masters and I have discussed this, and we would like to invite you to take the Tests of Truth. We shall always count you as a friend, but we would be honored to count you also as part of our family."

Even though she had felt it coming, Katrine was momentarily overcome with shock. The legends told of the Glainite Tribal Joining, which had to be conducted by the light of a full moon. It was more than just adopting someone and sharing one's skill lore, as Leron had done with Rand. No one outside the tribe really understood what happened, but all accounts agreed that a new member of the tribe experienced a significant transformation.

Blithely, Katrine wondered how her parents would react if she went home with dark hair and eyes.

Swallowing a lump that had suddenly formed in her throat, Katrine asked, "What do I have to do?"

"For three days," Bainu explained, "you will be given a specific task. Each one requires physical stamina, cleverness, and courage. The last one also requires a pure heart and an honorable soul. If you succeed at all three tasks, you will be accepted as a member of the tribe during the Festival of the Full Moon."

"And if I fail?"

"In your case there can be no true failure during the first two days. If you don't succeed within a reasonable amount of time, we will help you. You won't be allowed to continue and you won't be admitted into the tribe, but you will come to no harm.

"During the third test, we are limited in what we can do for you. It is a test of spirit and will be of your own making. If after you hear the details you doubt your ability to endure it, I recommend you decline. Watchers will ensure the safety of the body, but the spirit? Who knows? Who can protect you from yourself?"

Closing her eyes, Katrine considered.

On one hand, the decision seemed easy. Accepting a challenge developed by the original Glaine was almost too tempting to resist, especially since Bainu implied there was really no danger. Well, no physical danger. Not even with the third task. What would a spiritual test be like? she wondered. Facing her fears maybe? She did that every time she fought a plains cat.

On the other hand, she didn't have much information. Her knowledge of the Glainite culture was superficial. She'd be foolish to assume she could draw rational conclusions based on her scanty knowledge.

Still, others had succeeded in the past.

She wished she could take a walk with Polnu and ask her advice, or even have a night to sleep on it, but she sensed neither would be allowed. This was a decision to be made on the spot. If she couldn't depend on her reasoning, she would have to trust her instincts.

Squaring her shoulders, she answered in a voice that sounded bolder than she felt. "I want to try."

Chapter Ten

Before daybreak the next morning, Katrine was roused from sleep by a group of Glainites, their faces covered and all wearing red armbands. They provided her with loose fitting trousers, a lightweight tunic, and soft boots to wear. As soon as she had dressed, she was given breakfast and then taken on horseback to the Pink Desert, south of Glaine's Stand.

Just as the sun was rising, Katrine was instructed to dismount.

One of the masked figures handed her a small bundle.

"Our village lies directly to the north of this spot," the woman said. "The bundle contains a knife, a rope, and a scarf. These things and what the land will provide are enough to get you safely across the desert before dusk. We must warn you, however, that there are dangers even in the barrenness of the desert. Be cautious. You will be watched, but you will not see the watchers."

Then a man spoke. "We are aware of the injuries you sustained on The Glaine's behalf, but Renee has assured us you have healed adequately for this ordeal. If for any reason you want to stop the test, wave the scarf. Someone will come. You must enter Glaine's Stand before the sun disappears behind the Daegarn Mountains. If you do not, we will come and take you back."

Each of the masked figures saluted her by touching right hand to left hip. Without another word they rode away, one of them leading Stubbs by his reins.

For quite some time, Katrine stood motionless.

She had never been to the Pink Desert before. Farther to the south, she knew, there was a wide expanse of ocean and a chain of islands called the Edge of the World. Often during childhood, she had dreamed of traveling to the southern tip of Kareand to gaze out over the waters. She wondered if it was possible to see beyond the islands and catch a glimpse of Shokareen.

Someday she would go there and look, but not today. Not now.

Thoughtfully she examined each item the Glainites had given her.

Why these particular things?

The scarf was easy. She could tie it around her head to keep the sun off her face and neck, which she did. The knife might be necessary for defense, but what was she supposed to do with a rope?

More than anything else, she needed water to drink. She could probably forgo food for a day, but not water. Not on the desert.

She turned in a slow circle to make sure she wasn't missing something, like a small well, but she saw nothing helpful.

She started to walk.

The sun was coming up in the east, so if she kept her shadow on her left side, she would be going north. That was important to remember because there were no other landmarks to show her the way.

Because the desert was new to her, she gazed around in fascination. Although the landscape was mostly sand, it wasn't empty the way she'd always imagined. There were plants, rocks of various sizes, and even an occasional clump of coarse, dry grass.

Here, the spindlebushes were shaped differently than the ones on the plains. These were stark with long thorny spikes and few leaves. The scrubtrees were squat and stunted, their trunks gnarled and rough.

Scattered here and there were clusters of strange looking round plants. They were bluish-green and had fuzzy crowns of bright pink or yellow. Katrine had seen drawings of them in one of Father's books. They were called kaktus? Or kakti? Something like that.

She could hardly believe all this vegetation grew out of the glistening pink sand. It was eerily beautiful and delightfully strange.

Then she saw a small rodent scurry from beneath a spindlebush to grab a beetle that peered from under a rock. In a breath, the little animal seized its prey, darted back under the bush, and burrowed into the sand.

Katrine resolved to watch more carefully.

Since all animals required moisture to live, maybe one of the rodents would lead her to water. But no. Every time she saw one, it came from under a spindlebush. Then after darting around, doing whatever it came out to do, it would disappear under a spindlebush again.

Maybe they only drink at night, she thought. *Or maybe they get enough fluid from the insects. But there must be other animals. The rodents eat the insects. Something must eat the rodents.*

She kept her gaze moving, trying to watch all directions so she would not miss anything.

As the sun climbed the eastern sky, heat waves began to distort the horizon. The sand caught the sun's rays and reflected them as if by a billion tiny mirrors. The light stabbed at Katrine's eyes, making them water until she could hardly see. Her skin grew hot and tight and tingly. Her mouth was dry. Her head began to ache.

Gradually, the desert transformed, no longer thrilling Katrine with its novelty. Everything seemed alien and forbidding and unreal. Pink sand shimmered through ever changing shapes and hues.

One moment, Katrine felt as if she were walking through a rose-colored fairyland.

The next, she felt as if she were mired in a field of puddled blood.

Plants cast unnatural shadows. Ghost cities wavered in the air. Some unidentified beast howled in the distance.

Katrine's heart began to pound frantically.

This wasn't her prairie, where she knew every trail and every plant and every creature. Here, she was a stranger. Her eyes darted from side to side, upward and downward, scanning for threats. Everywhere she looked she saw danger—in the sky, behind the plants, from the sand.

Her hands shook. Her legs trembled. She couldn't breathe.

For the first time in her life, she knew terror.

A shadow swooped across the ground, and Katrine looked up to see a high-flying bird of prey with a wingspan wider than a man's extended arms. When it opened its beak and screeched, her nerve broke.

She ran.

Desperately and without direction, she ran. Her short boots filled with sand. She kept running. She tripped over a rock, snagged the leg of her trousers on a spindlebush thorn and heard the fabric tear. She stumbled to her feet and ran some more.

The hot desert air burned her lungs.

She ran until a stitch in her side doubled her over. Her quivering knees buckled. She collapsed to the ground, gasping like a fish pulled from the water and suffocating on the shore.

A minute passed.

Then another. And another.

She was still alive.

No gigantic birds attacked her. No strange creatures popped out of the sand to bite her. No terrifying plants sprang up to engulf her. Her panic subsided. Her rampaging heart slowed to normal.

She sucked on the insides of her cheeks to stimulate enough saliva so she could swallow. She dumped the sand from her boots.

Sitting with her legs drawn up and her arms wrapped around them, she tried to look at the desert from a fresh point of view. If she were to succeed at this task, she had to stop reacting to her fears and start thinking clearly and objectively.

The Glainite Master said she had everything she needed for survival, including assistance if she decided to quit. Well, she wasn't going to quit! She had never been a quitter, and she wasn't going to start now.

So she would have to develop some kind of plan.

Since the desert supported plant and animal life, there was water somewhere. She needed to take care of that problem first. The little rodents all lived under spindlebushes. That was the place to begin.

Too exhausted to stand, she crawled to the nearest bush and scooped sand away from its base.

Deep beneath the plant, where the ground was cool, she found roots with bulging nodules on them. Some oozed a sticky liquid and showed signs of having been chewed on by tiny teeth. Using the knife, Katrine cut one of the lumps off. She held it up to the light and studied it. If the rodents chewed on them, they probably weren't poisonous to humans either.

Cautiously, she dabbed sap on the back of her hand and then rubbed it in. She waited to see if she broke out with a rash or got nauseated. Not only did she feel no ill effects, but also her skin lost its tight, burning feeling.

Still she hesitated a moment longer. If she made herself too sick to continue, she would fail the test. On the other hand, if she didn't find water or a substitute, would she care?

Lightly she touched the raw end of the nodule with the tip of her tongue. The taste was sour, but not unpleasantly so, and it seemed to cool her mouth. She held the nodule to her lips, squeezed it gently, and sucked out the tart juice. The charred feeling in her throat vanished completely and her energy returned.

Sighing gratefully, she stuffed her pockets with as many nodules as would fit and then climbed to her feet.

She checked her shadow to orient herself, making sure it was again directly on her left, and began walking. She had gotten off course when she panicked, but once she reached the edge of the plains, she knew she could reorient and find Glaine's Stand.

Whenever her mouth felt dry, she sucked on a spindlebush nodule. After a while, however, she began to feel sick to her stomach. She grew queasy, her vision blurred, and she had trouble with her balance.

Was she drunk? She'd had a spoonful of fermented spirits a few times when she had been ill, but that was all, so she wasn't sure.

No, she didn't think she was drunk.

The sensations reminded her of when she had been trying to shake off the effects of the leiti the day after she'd been clawed. With a shock, she realized she had discovered the source of the Glainite medicine.

But now what?

If she couldn't use the nodules for moisture, she had to find water.

Katrine had inherited the Boradid water lore from her mother, but the knowledge of how to use it had been lost during the First Great Uprising when most of the Boradids had been slaughtered. Yet, Father said it was possible to access the principles through meditation even without proper training.

Desperate enough to try anything, Katrine sat down in a tiny patch of shade to search inside herself.

She thought about water. She imagined its scent, its touch, its very wetness. When she finally found the part of her inner being that knew water on the most basic level, she nearly laughed at how easy it was to recognize.

Almost anyone could smell an approaching rainstorm on a hot day.

The scent of moisture, both above and beneath the ground, was just as distinctive.

If there were water anywhere nearby, she would find it.

She walked slowly in a circle.

When she smelled water, she went that direction until she lost the scent, and then circled again to get another clue. It took a few tries, but eventually she knew without a doubt that she was standing over water.

She knelt down and began digging with her hands.

It was not an easy task.

Sand kept slipping back into the hole, and she had to expand the diameter repeatedly so the shifting sands wouldn't refill the cavity. She had gone down maybe four feet when she hit dampness. At first she was ecstatic, but the moisture in the sand made it more solid, making it harder to dig. She used the knife, plunging it into the compact sand to loosen it.

Before long, the hole was too deep for Katrine to throw the sand out.

She tied the rope to a scrubtree and pulled on it to make sure it would support her weight and then eased herself down into the well. She piled sand onto the scarf, tied it to the end of the rope, pulled herself up, and then hauled the sand after her.

It seemed forever before water began pooling around her feet.

Her fingertips were scraped raw.

She broke a fingernail past the quick, and it had bled so badly she ripped a strip off the bottom of her tunic to bandage it. She kept digging.

She was afraid if she didn't make the well deep enough, each time she climbed out, she'd tumble back so much dry sand that she'd bury the water again.

Finally, the water reached above her ankles.

She knelt and splashed it over her hot face and shoulders, then waited for several minutes to let the debris settle. She cupped her hands to drink. Violently, she spat.

The water was full of grit. It was like trying to drink mud.

Katrine was frantic. Her thirst was worse than ever.

She was kneeling in water, but it was undrinkable. If only she had something to strain it with.

She shook as much sand as she could from the scarf and wiped her face and neck. She was just about to tie the scarf back around her head when she started to laugh. That's why the Glainites had included it!

Gently, she laid the scarf on the water. She gathered the corners in one hand and carefully pushed an indentation in the middle of the fabric with the other. Slowly water seeped through the cloth and gathered in the depression. Water without sand.

When about a cup's worth of liquid had accumulated, Katrine took two corners of the scarf in each hand. She bent forward carefully, lowered her head to the water, and slurped it up. It had an earthy taste and was still a bit gritty, but she'd never been more thankful for a drink in her life.

When her thirst was sated, she pulled herself from the well. The heat of the sun blasted her, and she wondered what to do with the water now that she'd found it. She couldn't take time to search and dig whenever she needed a drink.

In fact, having taken this much time might cause her to fail the test. If she were to have any chance of winning at all, she would have to carry water with her.

She tied the scarf into a basket shape, attached it to the end of the rope, and lowered it into the well. What came out was a dripping scarf. She wiped her face and the back of her neck with it.

How was she supposed to carry water with so few tools? It was impossible.

To make matters worse, now that her thirst was gone, she realized she was quite hungry. Maybe eating would clear her mind so that she could find some sort of creative solution.

Just as she had previously drawn on the powers of her mother's heritage, she now opened herself to her father's line. The collective knowledge of the Nistarians dealt with things that lived on land. She searched her inner being to see if there was anything growing in the desert that people could eat.

There was! The round kaktus-plants.

A deep sigh whistled through her lips.

Even if she didn't make it to Glaine's Stand by sunset, she would have the satisfaction of knowing she had found a way to survive without assistance.

Cutting into the kaktus was a challenge.

The skin was tough and covered with sharp little thorns. After a moment of pondering, Katrine sat with the plant between her feet, letting the soles of her boots hold it steady while protecting her from getting pricked. She sawed off the fuzzy crest with the knife.

Once she removed the top, she sliced wedges from the interior. The plant's flesh was yellow and firm with a surprisingly sweet flavor that reminded Katrine of wild flowers and herbs. She ate until she felt comfortably full. Then she scooped out the rest of the fruit and stashed it in her tunic pockets with the spindlebush nodules.

Although the kaktus was a blessing, Katrine didn't think it could supply everything she needed to continue walking for the rest of the afternoon. The hottest part of the day was still ahead of her, and regardless of the food, she had to have water to keep going.

Damn. Damn. Double and triple damn.

In frustration, she kicked the kaktus.

It rolled a short ways then stopped.

Amazing.

The shell was round and empty, and the top fit back on like a lid. Giggling with relief, she cut a piece of rope and tied the scarf securely over the opening in the kaktus.

She lowered herself into the well for the last time.

After immersing her 'bucket,' she waited a few minutes. When she unfastened the scarf, the shell was over half full of water. With a relieved shriek, she hopped up and down, churning the water and splashing herself as high as her knees.

She climbed from the well and gathered her things together.

Refreshed by food and drink, she walked at a brisk pace, hoping to make up the time she had lost. Because the sun now descended in the west, she was mindful to keep her shadow on the right.

The heat was merciless.

So was the sand.

Katrine found that treading on a surface that continuously shifted and stirred was exhausting. Lifting her feet became an ordeal.

Her pace slowed.

Perspiration dripped down her back and made her healing wounds itch. Twisting like a contortionist she'd once seen performing with a troupe of acrobats, she scratched down her spine, not quite reaching the spots that itched the most.

At one point, she almost panicked again when, not watching where she was going, she nearly stepped on two venomous sandserpents that were sunning themselves on a flat rock. Luckily, they warned her by rearing their heads and hissing. She froze. One darted toward her. Reacting instinctively, she grabbed a rock and smashed its head. Its companion disappeared, slithering quickly across the sand.

As Katrine hurried away, she worried with each step that the snake might sneak up on her and bite her out of vengeance. For quite a while she was hypervigilant, trying to watch everywhere at once, knife in hand, ready to fight for her life.

But her fear faded with her growing exhaustion. She was too tired to do anything but move one foot in front of the other.

Her legs ached.

Her skin burned.

Her head throbbed.

Occasionally, she stopped to bathe her face and neck, but she didn't have much water to spare and couldn't waste it. She wished she had some leiti to easy her misery.

"I do," she mumbled to herself.

She took a couple of spindlebush nodules from her pocket and sucked the juice until her hurts subsided. She split another and rubbed the sticky liquid all over the exposed parts of her body.

Tired, but now without pain, she pushed forward.

The sun was nearing the Daegarn Mountains when she spied the first few blades of real prairie grass. They were unbelievably beautiful. She wanted to fall to her knees and kiss them.

But she didn't.

She couldn't spare the time.

Trudging on, little by little, she became aware of the smell of flowers and rich soil. A gentle breeze ruffled her hair. Her heart wanted to sing with joy. She was back on the plains. She was home.

Up ahead was Glaine's Stand.

The last of the water was gone. The kaktus flesh had been eaten long ago. The numbing effects of the spindlebush medication was but a faint memory.

Six horsemen rode toward her.

Katrine waved them away.

Focused only on staying erect and moving forward, Katrine stumbled victoriously into the village.

Chapter Eleven

Because of what she had endured the day before, Katrine was nervous when she went to Bainu's house and said she was ready for the next test. Even though she'd had a good night's sleep and had been served a fine breakfast, her body ached all over.

She dreaded the challenge that was waiting for her, and she wanted it over.

"Good," Bainu said when Katrine asked to get started. "The Masters would have come for you soon. But since you came to me first, you can start now, which gives you an advantage because this task must also be completed before sundown."

After leaving Katrine briefly, The Glaine returned with six masked riders. One of them held Stubbs by the reins. Without a word Katrine mounted and followed the Masters out of the village. They rode to the east, the easy pace set by Stubbs.

The plains swelled into rolling hills that were dotted with boulders and small clusters of trees. The nearer they drew to the banks of the Ildec Major, the more the trees looked like part of a forest and the rocks like part of a crumbled mountain.

"This is far enough," one Master said, "dismount."

Unable to believe she'd heard correctly, Katrine's mouth dropped open. "It's impossible," she said, sliding from Stubbs' back. "I couldn't get from here to Glaine's Stand by sunset if I flew. Not even if I started flying right now."

The Master took the reins from her. "Yes, you could. But you won't fly. Today you'll catch a wild horse and ride it back to the village. You must capture it using only the strength of your body and the cleverness of your mind. There's a herd that comes here every day to water."

Handing Katrine a leather pouch and her own knife, the Master continued, "This is not a test of survival as was the one yesterday. You'll be watched and kept safe throughout the day, and the bag I just gave you contains food and drink. By sunset, you must ride your new horse into the village. If you don't, we'll come for you and the tests will be over."

Then the Masters rode away, taking Stubbs with them.

While Katrine followed them with her eyes, she wondered sarcastically how many of them had captured their horses with just cleverness and physical strength. But after a moment, she acknowledged to herself that they probably all had. Polnu had been required to catch her horse as part of her tribal youth rituals. After she succeeded, Rand decided he had to catch one too as a matter of pride, even though Leron was wealthy enough to have purchased one for him at auction.

Without much hope, Katrine wandered in and out of the trees, looking at the wildflowers. How was she supposed to attract a horse if one didn't just happen to walk by?

Then a new thought struck her. If there were horses, there were plains cats. The predators liked their prey large.

Before worrying about a steed, Katrine decided she ought to see to her own safety. Although the Glainites said they would protect her, she couldn't see anyone anywhere. She'd better not count on them.

Cutting and tearing at the bottom of her tunic, she removed a long strip of fabric. Before Rand taught her to use a bow, she had used a sling. She gathered a pile of stones and took several practice shots at a tree. After a few misses, she started hitting the mark more often than not.

That was good enough.

She couldn't kill a plains cat with a few rocks, but she might be able to scare one off. She put the rest of the stones she'd gathered into her tunic pockets.

Next she searched until she found two tall straight saplings, which she cut down with her knife. She stripped away leaves and twigs and whittled the ends into sharp points. These should be sturdy enough to kill if necessary. Armed with spears and sling, she felt safer and more confident. Still, she'd have felt better if she'd had her bow and quiver.

With nothing else to do, Katrine began exploring.

A few times, the passageway she had been following between boulders turned into a dead-end chamber. Just as she was leaving the third one, she heard the distant screech of a plains cat. Rapidly she retraced her steps, thinking how foolish she had been to risk getting trapped.

A large assortment of trees grew along the banks of the Ildec Major, including Katrine's favorite variety of apple. They were hard and tart this time of year, still she'd always enjoyed them anyway. She picked several and slipped them into the leather bag with her lunch.

Because of the shade and gurgling water, Katrine felt cooler than she had out on the plains. Flowers made little patches of color on the ground, and birds of unfamiliar species flitted overhead, making colored patches in the air. Longingly, Katrine wished for her art satchel. Maybe when her life returned to normal, she could come back here to paint.

The Spire of Kylet

Lulled by the peace and beauty surrounding her, Katrine was startled when she heard the thunder of hooves growing nearer and nearer. If she hadn't jumped behind a large tree and pressed her back hard against the rough bark, she might have been trampled.

Dozens of elegant, dazzling horses galloped through the trees to the river. They were so numerous and so close to her that she could have reached out and touched them if she had dared. She held her breath, hoping they wouldn't notice her.

There were no words in her to express how much she wanted to own one of these gorgeous creatures. If she managed to catch one, she would treasure it forever. Riding it would be ecstasy, like riding the wind. Never would Father have to remind her to feed and brush it. Mucking out its stall would be an honor she would share with no one.

But how was she supposed to catch a horse and convince it to let her ride?

She was thinking so hard that she jumped a foot in the air when she heard the wild scream of a plains cat. The horses milled around nervously, as if they weren't sure which direction to go for safety.

Snatching up her weapons, Katrine ran toward the sound. She had been waging war with the plains cats for so long she could not ignore a challenge now.

She scrambled up a tall cluster of rocks, hoping to get high enough to spot her enemy. If she didn't get rid of the cat quickly, the horses might panic and disappear, taking all her hopes of completing the Tests of Truth with them.

Again the cat's roar sliced the air. This time the vibrations shook the very boulder on which Katrine stood.

A terrified whinny followed.

Inching on her stomach, Katrine followed the horse's cry. When she reached the edge of the huge stone, she peered down into one of the dead-end chambers. The bulk of an adult plains cat blocked a narrow doorway, trapping a gray and black stallion inside. The horse reared and thrashed with his front hooves while pressing his hindquarters into the rocks as far as they would go.

With all the malicious patience for which felines were known, the plains cat yawned, displaying its long sharp teeth, and then lay down as if ready to take a nap. Only an occasional flick of the tail indicated it hadn't fallen asleep.

Painstakingly, Katrine scooted sideways across the rocks. Her puny spears would be of no use against such a monster. She had to use her brains and pray that she was smarter than the cat.

That was her horse down there!

When she was perched above and behind the plains cat, she set the spears down gingerly and pulled the sling from her pocket. She twirled it above her head. The stone caught the cat on the tip of the nose.

A lucky shot, Katrine told herself.

The cat sprang to its feet.

Quickly, Katrine pelted it with a bevy of smaller rocks.

The cat jumped backward.

Mind racing and heart thumping, Katrine proposed and rejected a dozen ideas. Then, near the edge of the boulder, she noticed a spot where the rock was splintered. She kicked it with her heel and created a small avalanche. Slabs of rock and bits of gravel ricocheted off each other as they fell clattering and rattling to the ground.

Leaping from side to side, from front to back, the cat tried to avoid the rockslide. Then a big chunk dropped right on its rump. The cat howled, turned tail, and ran.

Before the horse recovered from his fright, Katrine grabbed her weapons and replaced the cat as captor. She sat on a low outcrop at the chamber's mouth. From that vantage point she could watch the passageway between boulders as well as her captive. Each time the horse stepped forward, Katrine waved a spear and shouted until he stepped back again.

Although technically the plains cat had done the catching, Katrine was willing to take the credit. After all, she had saved the horse's life by ridding it of the murderous hunter. That gave her some rights.

Slow moving minutes added up to an hour, and she still had no idea how to proceed. The young horse showed signs of restlessness.

For want of something better to do, Katrine opened the luncheon pouch and spread out the food on a rock next to her. Absently she bit into one of the crisp green apples she had picked. As her teeth crunched through the flesh and a small trickle of tart liquid dribbled down her chin, the horse stopped pacing and eyed her, snuffling the air.

"Want one?" Katrine asked. "Of course, you do." She tossed the rest of the apple near the horse's hooves. With a snort, he turned his back and stepped near the wall.

"Have it your way," Katrine murmured.

Mischievously, she pulled out her knife and cut another apple in two. "Hmmm, hmmm. That smells good." She ate half then threw the rest of it near the one already on the ground.

The stallion glanced down.

He tossed his head, swirling his black mane much the same way Jaimi swirled her hair when she was acting haughty and disdainful.

All at once, Katrine realized she was hungry. The Glainites had packed a meat pie, a fruit pie, some crunchy vegetable stalks, and a handful of shelled nuts for her lunch. Everything was delicious and she ate it all. Every now and then she tossed another apple to the horse.

By mid-afternoon, the chamber simmered, and the apples on the ground smelled like the fermented cider Father enjoyed making in the fall. Katrine's braid hung heavily down her back, and droplets of perspiration trickled between her shoulder blades down to her waist.

The Spire of Kylet

When she took the skin of water from the pouch and pulled the stopper from the neck, the horse eyed her. His nostrils flared.

"You're as thirsty as I am, aren't you?"

She crept across the rocks, looking for something she could use as a makeshift-watering trough. The horse leapt forward. Instantly, Katrine jumped in his path, waving her arms and yelling. He hesitated, spun on his hind legs and returned to his former position.

Angrily he thrashed with his front hooves.

"No need to have a tantrum," Katrine told him. "I'm as hot and tired as you are. But I'm not leaving without you, so you might as well get used to the idea that you're not leaving without me."

Looking around, she found a nice sized stone with a large chip out of the middle. Bracing it with smaller rocks, she positioned it as near the horse as she could. She filled the hollow with water and then went back to her seat near the chamber door.

At first the horse ignored the water, reminding Katrine of a child in a pout who doesn't want to give up his anger even when he's gotten his way. Eventually, however, thirst overcame petulance, and the horse drank all that was available. He eyed her a moment, as if chastising her for the miserly allotment, then began pushing an apple around with his nose. Suddenly, large white teeth snapped, and in one gulp the fruit was gone.

So, Katrine thought, *he's willing to eat my apples. Well, I'm certainly happy to let him, but I don't see how that helps our situation any.*

Some people might be able to vault onto the horse's back and hang on until the horse was tired of bucking and twisting, but not Katrine. She had never been on a real horse except for the rare occasions when she had shared a ride with Rand or Polnu. Although she had ridden her little pony bareback a few times, she was used to saddle and reins. Even if she managed to leap onto the stallion's back, he would toss her to the ground between her first and second breaths.

There had to be a way to get acquainted first.

If only she could concentrate like she had on the desert, maybe there was an answer in the Nistarian lore. But she was afraid to close her eyes and think—if she did, the horse might escape or the plains cat might return and catch her unawares.

The stone chamber became an oven and Katrine the hunk of meat that was being roasted. She expected at any moment to hear her skin start to sizzle and pop.

How do horses say hello? Katrine asked herself wearily, trying to make her throbbing head function.

As she considered, the stallion took a step forward and snorted. Katrine threw him another apple.

Through half-closed eyelids, she watched the gray stallion eat. At the same time, she envisioned all the other horses she had ever seen: Rand and Polnu's

86

mounts, her pony, the others in Father's stables. In her mind they seemed to drift toward each other until they were nose to nose.

Rubbing noses? No, that wasn't right.

With a jolt she figured it out.

She splashed a little water on her face and neck and dried them with the hem of her tunic. She repacked her luncheon pouch and sheathed her knife.

Moving cautiously, she eased herself off the rock slowly so she wouldn't startle the horse. She placed her hands behind her back, leaned forward a little, and blew gently through her nose.

Pricking his ears, the stallion glanced at her.

Again, Katrine exhaled a long steady breath, flaring her nostrils and keeping the rest of her body motionless.

Step by step the horse approached.

When his face was a few inches from hers, Katrine blew another deep exhalation through her nose.

The horse sniffed her breath.

He tossed his head and shook his thick black mane.

Katrine held her ground.

The stallion lowered his head and blew a big puff of air up Katrine's nose. Imitating the snuffling sound he'd made, she sniffed his breath.

That is how horses introduce themselves, she thought.

In as non-threatening a way as possible, she lifted her hand and placed her palm on his neck. Although the muscles tightened, he didn't move away. He nickered.

"So, sweet thing," Katrine whispered softly, "how do we make the transition from getting to know each other to riding?"

At the sound of her voice, the stallion shied and skipped away.

Katrine turned her back on him and sauntered forward a few steps. After a moment, there was a clump-clump behind her.

She walked on, keeping her body between the horse and the entryway.

He followed her.

They made one complete circuit and started another.

After the second time around, Katrine stopped and faced the stallion. He dipped his head, as if searching the ground for another apple, and ignored her. When she began walking again, he trailed behind.

With tiny, slow steps, she maneuvered the horse toward the place she'd left her luncheon pouch. She pulled out the last apple and rolled it to him.

She tied the bag to her belt.

The time had come to try riding.

Even if she courted the horse from now till winter's first frost, eventually it would all come down to her attempting to get on his back and taking her chances. The chamber was in shadows now, which meant afternoon was waning. If she waited much longer, she would never make it to Glaine's Stand in time.

Then, all this effort would have been for nothing.

A puff of breath warmed her cheek, and she barely stopped herself from jumping out of her skin. The horse had come up right beside her, and she hadn't even noticed. Without thinking, she raised a palm to his nose and let him smell it. With her other hand, she stroked his neck.

While she distracted him with her petting, she edged onto a rock about a foot and a half high. Since she had no saddle and didn't know how to leap up like Rand and Polnu did, she needed to stand on something in order to mount.

Now or never, she told herself firmly.

Just as she was pulling together her courage, the scream of a plains cat cut through the silence.

For a tiny moment the horse froze, and at the same time, Katrine jumped. At a second wail from the plains cat, the stallion bolted.

As he zigzagged through the boulders, Katrine clung to him with all her might. She wove her fingers into his mane, and clamped her legs around his middle. His speed was so terrifying she closed her eyes and prayed to all the gods she could think of that he wouldn't careen into something and kill them both.

When he cleared the rocks, he ran along the river, dodging trees and leaping over logs.

At last, they emerged from the forest onto the prairie. In front of them a sea of grass rippled in the breeze like a gigantic ocean. The horse stopped, craned his neck, and looked back at Katrine with one big brown eye, as if he had just noticed her weight.

"Holy Signs," she gasped, "what a thunderous ride!"

Gently, she disentangled her white-knuckled fingers from his mane. "Are you going to buck me off now?" she whispered, stroking his glistening neck. "I wish you wouldn't. I'd like us to become partners. Please."

The horse stood as still as a statue for a long moment, then he jerked his head up and down, as if nodding, and whinnied. Katrine leaned forward and rubbed her cheek on his neck. An indescribable joy flowed through her. This was her horse now, and they belonged to each other.

"I'm going to name you Thunder Cloud," she said. "You are gray and black like a storm, and you run as if your legs are made of cyclones."

With some subtle coaxing and exaggerated shifting of her weight, Katrine got Thunder Cloud headed south toward Glaine's Stand. As the rocking of her body matched his smooth gallop, she felt a bond develop between the two of them. She no longer bounced awkwardly on his back, and he did not fight her delicate commands.

The sun was almost touching the Daegarn Mountains when they rode into the village.

As cheers from the tribe escalated, Thunder Cloud put back his ears and fidgeted nervously, but Katrine crooned an old lullaby to him.

"Shh, little one, shh. All is well.
Love surrounds you like the night.
I'll care for you with all my might.
Surrender now to slumber's spell.
Shh, little one, shh."

Responding to the soothing tone of Katrine's voice, Thunder Cloud relaxed and let her take him to the corral.

Chapter Twelve

During the third day of the Tests of Truths, Katrine felt as restless as a caged plains cat. Early in the morning, Bainu had informed her that the final task would not be explained until after the evening meal, and Katrine hated waiting. All her life she had made a point of dealing with unpleasantness as quickly as possible. To her, putting things off was like trying to nap at the base of a cliff with a teetering boulder above her head.

Throughout the morning and afternoon, even though she kept busy by riding Thunder Cloud and painting, she had difficulty not growling at everyone she met. She wasn't actually nervous. She didn't know enough about the upcoming test to be frightened. She just wanted it over and the results decided.

When at last it was time for dinner, Katrine was surprised to learn she was dining with the tribal Masters in the Hall of Chiefs. She wasn't going to enjoy being the only young person among all those adults, Katrine thought as she walked to the Hall with Renee and Sillem.

Throughout the meal, smatterings of conversations popped up here and there, but in general the mood was subdued. Even the servers entered and left silently. By the time people were pushing back their plates, an ominous tension had filled the room.

Katrine felt very apprehensive.

Bainu stood. "This is the last task in the Tests of Truth, Katrine. Tonight you will ride your new horse to Echo Hall and spend the night there. Watchers will go with you, but you will not see them. Although they will protect your body from harm, they can do nothing to defend your heart and your spirit from what you will see and hear there."

Katrine's blood froze. She stopped breathing. Surely there had been a mistake. Echo Hall was in the foothills of the Daegarn Mountains, and it was haunted.

The townspeople of Banur told endless stories about the people who had gone there. Some hoped to gain inspiration, others wanted to speak with their ancestors, and a few simply wanted to prove their courage. When they returned home, they told terrifying accounts of unnatural occurrences: ghostly visions, disembodied voices, and demonic shrieks. Some people came back mad. Some never came back at all.

Bainu's lips turned up in a slight smile. It was not a mocking expression, but an understanding one. "Although I can tell by your face that you have heard of Echo Hall, I doubt you have heard the truth, or at least not all of it. It is true that Echo Hall is a place of power. The spirits of the dead enter this world more easily there than any other place in Kareand, but it is not true that spirits can harm the living, not in a physical way.

"When Glaine and her two Sister Wives fled from Elnid-Kyeh, they paused here on their journey. Glaine's time to give birth was near, and she could go no farther. The Sister Wives, the wives of her husband's brothers, were afraid to leave her. They were also afraid to stay. Finally Glaine told them that, for safety's sake, they must divide their company in hopes that some might survive.

"Before the Sister Wives separated, the three of them went into Echo Hall to use their powers to see what they could learn about the future. The spirits of Manderig and Kylet both appeared to them, offering comfort and guidance.

"Kylet assured them that, even though they would soon be parted from each other, someday their children's children would reunite. He said that when the ancient enemy of peace came to Kareand, a Warrior of Four Bloods would be born to lead the people into battle. At that time, the children of Jallyna and Terishe will join the descendants of Glaine to defend the land. The Glainites teach their children the sword and the bow, and a select few the spire, in preparation for that day.

"It was Manderig who told Glaine that she must not pass her magical powers on to her children. If she did, he told her, Elnid-Kyeh would find her children and corrupt them. He prophesied that when Shanree Palace is rebuilt and a descendant of Danied-Ohln and Terishe sits again upon the throne, the strong Crennese powers will return to the Glainites.

"I'm telling you this, Katrine, so you will know that not only horrors come to those who visit Echo Hall. I have spent many nights there. You can gain wisdom and maybe a glimpse of the future if you're not afraid to take what the spirits offer you."

But I am afraid, Katrine thought to herself. *There aren't any friendly spirits waiting to bring me messages. I'm not Bainu or Glaine or anyone important. But if I give into fear now, how will I ever face real danger again? What is it that Father says? "Once you turn coward, the next time it's easy."*

All the Glainite faces were focused on Katrine, watching her intently. She was sure they were looking for defects in her that would mean she was unfit to join the tribe.

Father also says, "Courage is doing what you need to do even when you're frightened."

"All right," Katrine said. At least the waiting was over, and like everything else, stalling wasn't going to make it any easier. "I want to do this, so I might as well get started."

"Good." Bainu clasped Katrine's hand encouragingly. "You might not enjoy all you experience, but I think your night will be enlightening. Perhaps you will get a hint of your destiny."

"Is there something I can do to convince the spirits to communicate with me instead of just trying to scare me to death?"

"Have faith," Bainu answered. "Trust yourself and the spirits, and all will be well."

No masked riders accompanied Katrine as they had before.

The Glaine and the Masters saw her to her horse. A woman handed her a bedroll, a torch and a flint box. Another offered her a pouch containing food and water. Katrine didn't think she'd get hungry in the night, but she accepted the bag anyway.

She rode out of the village alone.

It wasn't dark yet, and she knew the way.

Like most of the children of Banur, Katrine had secretly prowled around Echo Hall when it was bright with sunshine. A few times, she had tarried until late afternoon shadows spread out from the mountains to fill the glade with darkness. Each time, she had sensed something eerie, as if a sinister force watched her. Each time, she had ridden her little pony as fast as possible out onto the plains, not relaxing until she was within the safe walls of home.

Tonight, Katrine advanced on the grove as twilight neared. She kept repeating what Bainu had said. "It is not true the spirits can harm the living. It is not true the spirits can harm the living."

When Katrine reached Echo Hall, the first thing she did was to start gathering firewood.

She couldn't tether Thunder Cloud and wouldn't have even if she could. If she panicked and needed to leave in a hurry, she didn't want him hobbled. Besides, Polnu told her that once the large horses found human partners, they were extremely loyal and wouldn't wander.

Even after her campfire was burning and filling the glade with a cheerful light, Katrine gathered more dried branches and twigs. She wanted enough fuel to last her throughout the night, not for heat since the summer nights were warm, but for protection against predators and her fears.

Although she tried to suppress it, she was deeply afraid.

Her gaze darted around in all directions. Her hands shook when she used them. Tears threatened to spill down her cheeks. She even tried to remember some of the chants her parents had taught her, chants that tempered the darkness and warded away evil. But Skotlan had been right when he accused her of missing the evening chants on purpose. Now she wished she had paid more attention.

At last, Katrine unrolled her blanket, spread it on the ground, and sat near Thunder Cloud's legs. He put his ears back and shifted his weight, but he didn't move away.

A breath of air rustled the leaves on the trees and blew smoke into Katrine's eyes. The fire crackled. Sparks danced upward until they were lost in the night. Crickets chirped. An owl hooted mournfully.

Then quietly, gently, slowly, the breeze began to murmur as if it were speaking in a foreign tongue. The gusts strengthened until they became a wind that whipped dust and sand and twigs all about. The unrecognizable language grew louder and more urgent.

Katrine jumped up, startling Thunder Cloud, and searched the darkness. She could see nothing beyond the circle of light cast by her fire. She turned, pressed her body against the comforting warmth of her horse, and buried her face in his scratchy mane.

"There is no need to fear, little sister," said a melodious feminine voice from behind her.

Spinning around, Katrine found herself staring into a pair of almond-shaped dark eyes. They belonged to a beautiful woman with a flowing mass of blue-black hair. She was transparent, and she looked so much like Polnu that Katrine assumed that the woman was the ghost of one of her best friend's ancestors. Beside her were two other attractive female spirits.

Suddenly, without knowing how, Katrine recognized them.

They were the Three Sister Wives.

Glaine, the youngest, was the one in the middle.

Jallyna stood on the right.

Terishe, the eldest, was on the left.

Glaine was nearly as tall as Katrine, though narrower of frame. She wore a long arcane gown of pale green silk that hung gracefully from her left shoulder and draped low across her well-rounded breasts and under her right arm. On her head was a circlet of gold with one large, blue-green emerald at midpoint. She was lovely, but her eyes were sad. She appeared to be in her mid-twenties, although the histories said she had lived to be nearly one hundred.

Jallyna was easily recognizable by her thick, auburn hair, which hung in ringlets to her waist. Recorders had commented on the color many times because it was so rarely seen in those of Crennese blood. She was shorter than Glaine and thinner, with a figure that had more angles than curves. Her ivory skin was lightly dusted with freckles, her lips perfectly shaped, and her eyes large and dark. Her circlet of gold held an oval sapphire. Its vibrant blue matched the color of her simple gown, a narrow shift with skinny little shoulder straps.

Eldest of the Wives, Terishe was the shortest and the plumpest. A wholesome innocence glowed on her face, as if she were a little girl and not a grown woman. Her gown was rose colored and had an off-the-shoulders lace ruffle that hung to her elbows like a cape. Her light brown hair, the same color as her eyes, was coiled on top of her head with one long curl flowing over her right shoulder. The gem in her golden circlet was a round, blood red ruby.

Seeing them together, their eyes slanted upward at the corners, Katrine realized the Three Sister Wives were Crennese, all of the wizard blood.

Yes, she thought, Bainu had hinted at it.

She mentioned that they had used their powers to divine the future.

"We have long awaited your coming, little sister," Terishe said, reaching out with her soft, round arms. "You have nothing to fear from us. We have come to give you our blessing, for on this night you will discover your destiny."

"Destiny?" mumbled Katrine. "You mean like if I'm going to become a Recorder or whom I'm going to marry and where I'm going to live?"

"Not quite," Terishe said, then stopped and glanced at the other two ghosts as if she weren't quite sure how to explain.

"You're confusing her," Jallyna said, her prickly tone matching the sharp angles of her body. "She's just begun the journey, and the path is veiled to her. Right now she is merely a hope and a promise."

"I know," Terishe said, "but tomorrow—"

Glaine interrupted. "Jallyna's right. We must be careful. Without thinking, we might say or do something to influence Fate and possibly change the future we all hope for."

In a small voice, Katrine asked, "Why are you here? Do you need to tell me something? Do you have a message for me?"

With a glance Terishe and Jallyna deferred to Glaine.

"We are here," Glaine said, "to be with you and to protect you from those who might wish you to fail tonight or try to harm you. We are also here to leave you our blessing, as Terishe has said. Soon you will embark on an adventure that will determine the course of your life, and we wish you to know you do not travel into the unknown alone."

"As for the message," Jallyna said, "we want you to know your coming was foreseen, and your path set, before you were born."

"But that does not mean you cannot choose," said Glaine quickly. "If you decide to follow a different course, someone else will come forward to complete your task."

Katrine was sure her face looked as blank as her mind felt. She hadn't understood a bit of what was just said. The words sounded like normal speech, but they didn't make any sense.

Terishe snapped peevishly, "Now who's confusing her?" She held out her hands to Katrine as she had before. "Let us keep you company this night, little sister, to comfort you, to allay your fears, and to keep your free will safe."

Katrine was tired, physically and emotionally.

If they wanted to tell her something why didn't they just say it? Were all these insinuations supposed to be clues? Did she have to guess what the message was?

If so, why didn't they at least tell her the rules?

Her lower lip began to tremble and tears snuck past her eyelids and dripped down her cheeks.

"Well, you're not comforting me." Katrine hid her face in her hands, embarrassed that she couldn't control her emotions. "Bainu said the spirits couldn't hurt me, so I knew, even if I was afraid, I could hold out until morning. But now you say someone might want to harm me and make me fail. And I don't know how anyone's free will can be unsafe. Now I'm really scared."

A warm, soothing touch cupped Katrine's hands. She opened her eyes to see Glaine's insubstantial hands covering her own.

"You are young, little sister," Glaine said tenderly, "and we must seem strange. But although we are clumsy with our words, our hearts overflow with affection for you. If you wish, we will sit with you in silence so we do not upset you further."

Sniffling, Katrine wiped the wetness from her face with the collar of her tunic. "I'm sorry. I usually don't cry this easily. But so much has happened lately, I don't know what to expect anymore."

"Let's sit down," suggested Jallyna, "and you can tell us what is troubling you."

Katrine fed wood to the fire and then sat cross-legged on her bedroll.

The Sister Wives folded their legs beneath them and sat on the ground across from her.

Katrine almost cried out to them to be mindful of their beautiful gowns, but she caught herself before she said anything so foolish. Spirits wore spirit clothing. Their hems weren't going to get dirty or snag on a broken twig or a jagged rock.

At first Katrine was hesitant to tell the ghosts about herself. She hardly ever revealed anything personal to adults. She didn't even know where to start.

"Take your time," Terishe said, "we have all night."

"Maybe," Glaine said, "you could start by telling us about some of the things you enjoy."

Jallyna nodded her head.

All three of them wore expressions so kindly and so interested that Katrine had to respond.

She began slowly, telling them about her love of painting and the joy she felt whenever she was able to capture a moment in time permanently on paper or canvas. This led naturally into her desire of becoming a Recorder and the disastrous interaction she'd had with Neyac, the first Master Recorder she'd ever met. Soon the words were pouring out.

The Spire of Kylet

She told them about her siblings, especially Skotlan who brought so much fun into her life. She described how her cousin was always mocking and criticizing her, and how she (Katrine) seemed to become more awkward and clumsy whenever they were together.

She talked about her loneliness and isolation, about always feeling she was different from her family and friends, and about the sensation that something was calling her away from her home. She wasn't even aware of some of her feelings until she had put them into words.

When she could think of nothing to add, she felt more peaceful than she had in a long time.

"Indeed, you have had much on your mind to trouble your serenity," Glaine said sympathetically.

Katrine stood and stretched. She picked up a stick and stirred the fire to perk up the flames. Then she sat back down on her bedroll.

She was just getting comfortable when a sudden gust of wind blew out the fire, leaving only a glimmer of red embers and a trail of smoke.

A loud *whoosh* preceded a bright fountain of sparks.

The campfire flared up again, higher than before.

Thunder crashed, and at the same time, a bolt of lightning struck the ground no more than ten paces in front of Katrine. When she had blinked away the afterimages, she was amazed to see a handsome young man with deep blue eyes and silver hair standing in the spot where the lightning had hit. He smiled with perfectly straight white teeth and extended his hand to Glaine.

"My beloved wife," the man said, "and my dear sisters, I sensed your presence." He bowed to Jallyna and Terishe. "What brings you from the realm of spirits back to the world of the living?"

Floating to their feet, the Sister Wives inserted themselves in front of Katrine.

"This child?" he asked, pointing at Katrine. His brows pulled together, and two furrows wrinkled his forehead. "I have seen her before, I think. If she interests you, perhaps I should learn more about her. Come here, girl!"

To her horror, Katrine climbed to her feet and took a few involuntary steps toward the man. She tried with all her might to stop herself, but she couldn't.

The Sister Wives joined arms and blocked her way.

"You shall not touch her," Glaine cried.

"We are united," said Terishe. "We will not let you harm her."

Flipping his hand up, palm forward, the man hurled a ball of flames at the women.

The Sister Wives made a similar gesture, and a golden shield appeared before them. The burning orb bounced off it and shot back toward the man. He made a fist. The fireball disappeared.

"Children's tricks," the man sneered. He vanished, only to reappear at Katrine's side. He grabbed her by the wrist.

96

She experienced a moment of pure panic.
He was not just another spirit.
He was flesh and bone and alive.

Chapter Thirteen

"Let me go," Katrine yelled as she struggled to free herself from the man's iron-fisted grasp.

Suddenly, a beam of moonlight arced through the night.

When it reached the man holding Katrine, it slashed his arm. Howling in pain, he loosened his grip.

Katrine ran and hid behind a tree. She gulped noisily, trying to catch her breath, and then peered around the trunk.

A second man had joined the others.

He was tall and broad and wore a glittering mail vest over a black leather uniform. His helmet was plumed with bright feathers, and long brown hair was knotted at the nape of his neck and trailed down his back. His eyes were the color of smoke. In one hand he bore a shield with the signs of the four elements decorating its center. An enormous broadsword hung in a sheath across his back.

Reaching up, he caught the moonbeam after six curved blades snapped back into its hexagonal interior.

"Your time has come, Elnid-Kyeh," the second man shouted. He flicked his wrist and sent the spire soaring through the air again. "Prepare to die at the hand of a Wolkarean Warrior as has been prophesied since the fall of Renath."

Katrine's heart almost stopped as she recognized the tall Warrior. She had read descriptions of him in her textbooks. Besides, Father owned an old history book that actually contained a sketch that was supposedly copied from the man's portrait in the Regency at Pardish. This was Kylet, the last Wolkarean to serve as Warlord before all of the Wolkareans disappeared.

Crimson rivulets oozed between Elnid-Kyeh's fingers where he held his wounded arm. When the spire whizzed toward him again, he let go, made some quick gestures, and mumbled a few words. As if it had been hit with a club, the spire dropped down. Before it crashed into the ground, it tore a long gash across Elnid-Kyeh's leg.

Kylet snapped his fingers, and the spire sprang up and spun back to him.

Even as his clothing became saturated with blood, Elnid-Kyeh smirked contemptuously. "You could not vanquish me in life, Kylet, and you cannot defeat me now. I do not fear the Wolkareans. I lived as the King's son for twenty-eight years, and none of you guessed my true nature. The Wolkareans have always been the weakest of the four races."

Kylet caught the spire and threw it for the third time.

With a mocking curl to his lips, Elnid-Kyeh glanced toward Katrine. "Keep the child for now. I can collect her later if I choose."

Before the spire reached him again, he was gone.

Kylet turned his face to the skies. "Face me, Elnid-Kyeh. I know what you are. Face me."

* * *

Elnid-Kyeh swore profusely, something he seldom did, but he was frustrated beyond endurance. His Healer would need to use strong spells to close the wounds in his arm and leg, binding them until the flesh renewed itself. But that was nothing. No more than inconvenience.

He was enraged because he had been so debilitated that he could not gather enough energy to teleport himself and the girl to Serpent's Head.

It was that damnable spire.

It had a power, a magic, all its own. It had sapped his strength until he felt as weak as a baby. It had begun sucking away his energy as it neared his body both times.

Angrily, Elnid-Kyeh summoned his spies.

They must redouble their efforts at gathering Kylet's magical weapons, and this time they were to bring him a spire, whatever the cost.

Also, he must know more about the girl.

He remembered her now. Her name was on the scroll he had purchased. He had crossed it off.

His man, Hollenth, had reported that, according to her brother, she was completely devoid of intellect and talent except in caring for her father's land and herds. The brother had also said she was shallow, self-centered, and filled with petty jealousies.

Yet, the Sister Wives had communed with her in Echo Hall, and Kylet had come to her aid and appointed himself her protector.

Why?

* * *

"I fail, again." Kylet's voice broke with heart-wrenching sorrow. "I am doomed always to fail."

Peering around the tree, Katrine was almost as afraid of the towering

Warrior as she'd been of Elnid-Kyeh.

Glaine took Kylet in her arms. "It is not your destiny, but don't be downhearted. He will fall soon. Then we can rest."

Kylet bent and kissed Glaine's lips. Her arms slipped around his neck, and the kiss lingered so long that Katrine had to look away. She was startled to see Elnid-Kyeh's wife and the last Wolkarean Warlord locked in an embrace. Obviously, they were in love with each other.

Father had never mentioned *that* in any of the history lessons.

With his arm around Glaine's ephemeral waist, Kylet addressed Katrine. "Beloved daughter, you can come out now. He is gone, and you are safe."

Hesitantly, Katrine slipped from behind the tree but stood with her back pressed against it. "Why did you call me daughter?" she asked in a meek voice.

"Because," Kylet answered, "you are the child of my soul. I have seen you again and again in my dreams, and you are exactly what I would want my daughter to be."

Before she could stop them, tears streamed down Katrine's face.

Perplexed, Kylet asked, "Why are you crying?"

"I don't know." Katrine sniffled and wiped her cheeks with the back of her hand. "Maybe because you said I was what you wanted in a daughter. My father is always disappointed in me. He doesn't even like me."

A small chuckle seemed to slip unintentionally from Kylet. "Do not judge your father too harshly, Katrine. You are young and know nothing of your future path. Everything your father has demanded of you has been for a purpose and for your good.

"At the time of your birth, he had a glimpse of your destiny, and he has spent his days trying to make sure you'll be strong enough to carry the load you will be given. He has almost burst with pride every time you have demonstrated a new skill that you will need."

"Then why doesn't he ever tell me?"

Cocking an eyebrow at her skeptically, Kylet asked, "Has he never told you?"

Feeling the blood rush to her face, Katrine remembered her father's parting words as he left her in Polnu's home, when he said he was proud of her. "Not very often," she said sheepishly. "Mostly he just tells me what I've done wrong."

"Well, he is mortal after all. Even though he cares deeply for you, he has been afraid too gentle a hand would make you weak. He knows you cannot afford weakness."

Not meeting Kylet's eyes, Katrine scuffed at the dirt with the toe of her boot. "Did you come all the way from the afterlife to tell me that? Or did you come to keep me from going with him?" She hooked her thumb toward the space Elnid-Kyeh had occupied. Before Kylet could answer, she went on. "Was that the real Elnid-Kyeh? Didn't he die hundreds of years ago?"

"No, yes, yes, no," Kylet said. When Katrine glanced up, confused, Kylet grinned, which made him look much nicer and less intimidating.

"You asked me four separate questions," he said, not even trying to hide his amusement. "No, I didn't come all the way from the world of spirits to tell you your father cares for you, although I found pleasure in doing so. Yes, I wanted to prevent you from going with Elnid-Kyeh, but in all fairness, I must admit, the Three Sisters could have done it without my aid. Yes, that was Elnid-Kyeh. No, he didn't die hundreds of years ago."

This time when he laughed, Katrine laughed with him. He wasn't so frightening when he was all smiles and good humor.

"Thank you," Katrine said graciously, "for answering my questions."

"You are most welcome," Kylet said with a bow. Then his mood became more sober. "But I did come for a purpose, daughter of my heart. Please sit. We have much to discuss, and the night is passing quickly."

Kylet led Glaine over to a fallen log that was charred at one end where it had once, long ago, been struck by lightning. He sat and settled her down next to him with his arm around her waist. Katrine, Jallyna, and Terishe sat on the ground as they had earlier.

"Soon," Kylet said, "you will find yourself on a journey far from your home. As you travel, your path will cross that of a young man named Asher. He is a Warrior from Landor, but not a Wolkarean. As yet, no Wolkareans have returned to that great training ground. Captain Asher needs the information I will give you so he can get it to Warlord Leeds. At a time when you are alone and can speak confidentially, I want you to deliver my message to him."

Katrine couldn't think of anything to say, so she just nodded.

"I want you to tell him that the enemy who will bring war to Kareand is Elnid-Kyeh, and he is a changeling."

A shiver sneaked up Katrine's back as the warm summer night took on a sudden chill. "A changeling?" she whispered.

"Three hundred and seventy-eight years ago, when the third son of High King Drannen-Toln was born," Kylet said, leaning forward, "the midwife killed the baby and his mother. Then she replaced the baby with a Shokai infant. His father named him Elnid-Kyeh. Secretly, Shokai priests watched over the boy and trained him in their evil traditions. He is an adept sorcerer of the black arts, and he is getting ready to open the way for his brethren from Shokareen to come and destroy the people of this land. The time draws near, and preparations for defense must be made with haste."

"Why are you telling this to me?" Katrine asked. Such an important communication shouldn't be entrusted to a simple herd-girl from an insignificant town in the southwestern reaches of Kareand far from the seats of power. A message like this should be given directly to the Warlord or the Regent—or maybe even to her father.

"First of all," Kylet said, "you are here in Echo Hall, where the veil between the land of the living and the land of the dead is thinnest. Second, your journey will cross paths with Asher, who is in a position to make sure the information gets to the Warlord. Third," Kylet stopped himself. "No, the third one you must find out in your own time."

"But I'm not going on a trip," Katrine said. She turned her hands up in a hopeless gesture and shook her head vigorously. "Our family never goes anywhere."

"For you, then, this will be a first."

"But—"

"Wait and see. If you do not go on a journey and if you do not meet a Warrior named Asher, I will not expect you to deliver my message. Is that fair?"

"Yes." Suddenly Katrine felt very silly. She was acting as empty-headed as her sister, Jaimi. Kylet was a sorcerer and a ghost. If he said she was going on a trip, she probably ought to go home and start packing. "I'll deliver your message if I can."

"Good. Now, I suggest you get some sleep. The Three Sisters and I will watch over you and keep you safe."

That was the second time he had referred to the Sister Wives as the Three Sisters, thought Katrine. After giving them a good studious look, she felt like thumping her head in consternation. Had the Recorders written about their true relationship and she had missed it? Another history lesson she had breezed through? Or had the information been lost over the generations?

"You are sisters, aren't you?" Katrine asked as she settled on her bedroll, lying on her side. "Real sisters, not just the wives of three brothers."

"Yes," Glaine answered. "We are sisters."

"But how did you come to marry the princes of Shanree?" Katrine glanced at Kylet and gave him what she hoped was a beguiling grin. "A mystery like this is bound to keep me awake all night unless I have some kind of explanation."

Kylet quirked an eyebrow at her, letting her know that he recognized an excuse when he heard one but that he was going to let it pass.

"Our father was king of a city high in the Crenn Mountains," Terishe said, her eyes downcast. "One year, most of our herdbeasts died because of heavy snows. Then the summer was cold, so our crops did not flourish."

"We were dying of famine," Jallyna said bluntly. "Our father, being proud, hesitated to ask the High King for help. But when our mother became weak and ill, then died, he realized he had to take action. He traveled to Renath to speak with Drannen-Toln, to ask, to beg if necessary, for assistance."

"When he got there," Glaine said, taking up the tale, "he discovered the High King wanted to arrange a marriage for his eldest son with a daughter of Crennese blood. The High King was a greedy and foolish old man. He wanted the wizard blood to make himself even richer and more powerful than he already was."

"Perhaps our father was also foolish," Terishe said with a sigh, "to offer us to the king. But he was afraid for us, fearing we would waste away as our mother had. He thought if the High King wanted Crennese daughters-in-law, well, the King had three sons and our father had three daughters."

"Actually," Jallyna said, exhibiting a certain pride, "Father considered that an omen. He was certain that marrying the royal sons was our joint destiny. More than one child is rare in Crennese families. Having three daughters was a miracle. Father proposed an exchange. If the High King provided food and warm clothing and other necessities for our city, Father would betroth us to his sons."

"He sold you?" Katrine asked, feeling sick to her stomach. She had been horrified when she thought her father might betroth her to someone, but if he had, it would have been to someone she knew, someone from Banur, not a stranger far from her home.

"Sold is too strong a word," Glaine said, though something in her tone made Katrine think she might have used the term a time or two herself. "Father clearly thought the matches would be good for us, better than he could arrange among the few remaining impoverished Crennese kingships. One of your Nistarian myths is that the wizard blood naturally leads to prosperity and abundance, but the sorcerous gifts are varied, and some are small and weak. We do not have the land and water lores, and one cannot eat magic. Our father sought to protect us from want."

While Katrine threw a few more sticks onto the fire, Terishe and Jallyna nodded agreement.

With a wistful expression, Jallyna twisted a lock of her deep auburn hair with graceful fingers. "It was not all bad. Brannald-Din, the second son, and I immediately liked each other. Given enough time, I am certain our bond of friendship would have developed into a truly deep love." Her face saddened as she went on. "We married and had children. We were happy until Elnid-Kyeh interfered in our lives."

"Likewise, Danied-Ohln and I." Terishe's sorrowful dark eyes filled with tears that spilled down her pudgy cheeks. She forced a wan smile to form on her lips.

"I was so immature," Terishe said. "Even though I recognized the goodness in my husband, I was not always kind to him. When our son fell from the eastern bridge at Renath Island and disappeared into the waters below, I blamed Danied and punished him cruelly for being away at the time. Still, he comforted me with loving words and tenderness." Primly, she dabbed at her eyes with an ethereal handkerchief. "I loved my husband, and I like to think that in time I would have matured enough to become the kind of wife he deserved."

When it was clear that Terishe had said all she was going to say, Katrine's attention automatically switched to Glaine.

The older sisters had talked about the relationships they'd had with their husbands, and Katrine was curious to hear what Glaine would say about her marriage to Elnid-Kyeh. But the youngest ghost stared at her hands and remained silent.

Finally, Kylet kissed her and stroked her cheek and whispered in her ear until she looked up.

"I don't like talking about Elnid-Kyeh" Glaine finally said. "He always frightened me with his sullen moods and curt words. He felt no joy and allowed me none. His only passions were for studying and solitude and political intrigue. But I had promised my father I would try to be happy in marriage, so I ignored my instincts when they shouted of my husband's evil nature."

Her hand wandered over to rest on Kylet's knee. He covered it with a hand of his own.

"Even when I realized I had feelings for the High King's Warlord, I could not face the disgrace of leaving my husband. If I had been stronger, perhaps Elnid-Kyeh could have been stopped before he gained his full Shokai sorcerer's power. It was several years later, when I unexpectedly found myself with child, that I knew I could stay with him no longer."

Lowering her eyes, Glaine's transparent face took on a reddish hue. Surprised by the blush, Katrine found herself wondering who the father of Glaine's child might truly have been. She didn't ask.

"Do not blame yourself, sweet Glaine," Kylet said gently. "We all failed. I had been trained to recognize the Shokai even in their shape changing, but I refused to believe the truth of my own gifted vision. I thought my heart had betrayed me into thinking the third royal son was not what he should be, so I did nothing. You carry no more blame than the rest of us. Not a single member of the Wolkarean Elite accused Elnid-Kyeh, nor even hinted at a suspicion. Perhaps he was too strong from the beginning."

Glaine looked tenderly at her lover and then shifted her gaze to Katrine. "We failed, and your generation must right our wrongs. Now we have told you our history, and it is time for you to get some rest."

Out of the corner of her eye, Katrine saw Kylet make a slight gesture with his hand. Her eyes closed.

As slumber encompassed her, she wondered fleetingly if this was how the yearling had felt when Rand put the sleep on it.

Chapter Fourteen

When Katrine returned to Glaine's Stand the next morning, Polnu rushed to greet her. "Are you all right?"

"Of course," Katrine said. "Why do you ask?"

Polnu looked away, her face full of unspoken worry.

Katrine slid off her horse. "What's wrong? Tell me." Katrine kept a hand on Thunder Cloud's neck, stroking and patting him. His size and warmth were comforting, and she feared that she would need the support. She had expected to return to the village amid cheers and celebration. Not this tension—whatever it was.

"The watchers returned at daybreak," Polnu said, "and they were very upset. They told Grandmother they couldn't remember anything that happened at Echo Hall last night. That's unheard of. Watchers always witness the visions when someone is there taking the final test. The Masters are all meeting right now, trying to decide what to do."

They had reached the corral where the Glainites kept their horses, and Katrine grabbed a rag from a box and began rubbing Thunder Cloud down.

"Deciding what to do about what?" Katrine asked, relieved that the problem was no more serious than a few tribal spies who had fallen asleep on the job.

Polnu grabbed Katrine and turned her around so their eyes could meet. Her expression had changed from worry to exasperation.

"About you!" She poked Katrine in the chest with her finger. "About whether or not you actually passed the Tests of Truth. The watchers thought they'd been put under some kind of spell. One suggested you might have had a Crennese friend like Rand bewitch them so you wouldn't really have to spend the night in Echo Hall. Some even suspect it was me."

"What!" Katrine could hardly believe her ears. Frustrated, she tossed the rag she'd been using onto the ground. "I had dinner in the Hall of Chiefs. After we finished eating, Bainu described the final test, the Masters accompanied me to my horse, and I rode straight to Echo Hall. At what point was I supposed to be in contact with Rand? Or you?"

Polnu shrugged her shoulders and raised her hands, palms up, in an "I-can't-even-guess" kind of gesture.

The more Katrine thought about it, the angrier she became. She set Thunder Cloud loose in the corral and rounded on Polnu. "Where are they meeting?"

"In the Hall of Chiefs. What are you going to do?"

"I'm going to report to Bainu as I have at the completion of each of the tasks. If the Masters think I've cheated, let them tell me to my face." Shoulders squared and chin high, she marched off to confront her accusers.

By the time she reached the Hall of Chiefs, Katrine was angrier than she had ever been in her entire life. After all she had gone through—being cooked alive on the desert, risking death by that huge plains cat in order to catch her horse, consorting with ghosts all night—how dare they think she was a coward and a cheater!

She pushed open the door and entered without knocking. She stood glaring at everyone in the room.

"I spent the night in Echo Hall," Katrine said to The Glaine, her outrage bubbling to the surface, making her voice harsh and loud, "but you don't believe it. Is that right?"

"It's not that we don't believe," Bainu said mildly, "it's that we don't understand what happened. Come in and sit down. Help us understand."

The gentleness of Bainu's tone disarmed Katrine for a moment, but she didn't move. Hostility poured off the rest of the Masters like a flash flood. They didn't believe her, and they didn't want to. They had already made up their minds. She felt like telling them all to go to the Seventh Level of Hell.

She bet none of them had ever had a visit from Kylet or the Three Sister Wives. Or even Elnid-Kyeh.

She could really tell them a thing or two, the judgmental hypocrites. If she did, wouldn't their eyes bug out? She could really put them in their place.

However, should she?

Kylet had told her, even when she met the Warrior, she wasn't supposed to deliver his message until they could speak privately. She didn't know why, but there had to be a reason.

"I don't think I'm supposed to talk about it," she said.

"A convenient excuse," mumbled one of the Masters. Katrine tried to spot him, but she couldn't tell which one he was.

Another, bolder, man stood. His antagonism was apparent. "I was there, and I saw and heard nothing after the building of the fire. I'm Crennese and I know the feel of magic. It was present, and it kept me from watching as I had been assigned."

"Maybe there was magic," Katrine said, trying not to sound too defensive or to lose control of her temper. "Those who visited me were of the wizard blood. But I don't have any magic of my own, and I didn't ask for any to be used on my behalf."

Grumbles of disbelief came from all directions.

Polnu's mother stood up. "Why don't you describe your experiences to us?" she suggested. "I was one of the watchers, as I have been in the past, and always before I shared in the visions. Maybe if you tell us who visited you and why, we'll be able to understand the reason we were excluded."

Katrine's mind swirled in a maelstrom of confusion.

What part of the night's revelations had her visitors been trying to protect by not letting the watchers watch? Was there anything she could safely share?

Except for The Glaine and Polnu's parents, Katrine didn't sense any great open-mindedness. Everyone else already thought she was a cheater. No matter what she told them now, they would probably assume she was a liar too. She could tell by looking at the faces that almost everyone wanted to kick her right out of Glaine's Stand. They certainly didn't want her to be a member of the tribe. She felt like crying.

She had been so excited about being here in the village the day of the competitions. When she'd won the archery contest, she'd almost felt like she belonged, like maybe she could get the acceptance from the Glainites that she didn't get at home.

She'd been daydreaming.

There was no way out of this mess. She was sure Kylet was responsible for the watchers' plight, and even though she didn't understand why he'd put her in this position, she accepted it.

If the Glainites rejected her, so be it.

"I don't know why my visitors didn't want you to observe," Katrine told Renee, "but if it was important enough for them to magically hamper you, they must have had their reasons. I need to respect that."

"What's to be done then?" a skinny female cried out. "Watchers must confirm the completion of each task, and we can't. Now what?"

Without warning, a possible compromise popped into Katrine's mind.

"I'll tell The Glaine." Katrine used Bainu's title to remind the group that the old woman held ultimate authority within the tribe. "I don't think they'll mind if she knows." She gave Bainu a beseeching look. "May I tell you, and only you?"

"As you wish. When and where?"

Biting down on her lip, Katrine assessed the Hall. Large windows were spaced along the walls, and three doors opened in the back, one to the kitchen, one to a storage room, and the other to the outside. There was no possibility of privacy here.

"Now," she answered, "but somewhere else. Out in the open where we can see if anyone tries to overhear."

Several Glainites jumped to their feet, all of them trying to yell louder than the others. Katrine only caught snippets.

"How dare you imply . . ."

"Masters are not so petty as . . ."

" . . . you think we would spy . . ."

" . . . gone too far now . . ."

"That's enough," Bainu said, and although her voice stayed low, it silenced the clamor. "Katrine, what is your reasoning?"

"It's just that if the spirits didn't want the watchers to see or hear, they probably don't want anyone else to either. People can overhear things by accident as well as by design."

"She is right," Bainu said, raising her palm to forestall further comments. "We'll ride to a place I know. The task of the Masters will be to assure we are not followed by the curious. When we return, I will share what I can." Halfway to the door, she paused. "Tonight is the full moon, and there is much to keep the tribe busy, especially if we are to have a tribal joining, as I believe we will. Rumors and hostility help no one. Peace and harmony benefit all. Please cultivate the proper atmosphere while we are gone."

Before leaving, Bainu suggested that Katrine try Stubbs' saddle and bridle on Thunder Cloud. Although the great horse put his ears back, stomped all four feet, and managed to look insulted in the process, he did not actually refuse to be accoutered. Katrine petted him, stroked his neck, and rubbed her face on his mane, all the while praising him for his tolerance.

A questioning whinny came from Stubbs, and Katrine took a moment to hug him and scratch his forelock, the way she always did. He looked at her with soulful eyes, as if he was trying to figure out what he'd done wrong to make her choose to ride someone else.

"I still love you," Katrine whispered to him.

While Katrine was busy with her horse and pony, Bainu packed a lunch and gathered her art supplies. She handed the bundles to Katrine to stow in her saddlebags.

"I have a lovely little spot in mind," Bainu said, swinging astride a bay gelding. "It's perfect for promoting inner tranquility and for inspiring the urge to paint."

They rode in a southeasterly direction until they came to a hill that was slightly higher than its neighbors. At the hill's pinnacle was one colossal tree, its huge branches stretching so high and wide they seemed to support the sky.

Surrounding the trunk in haphazard clumps were hundreds of delicate flowers of all different colors. The effect was so dazzling that Katrine could hardly take it in.

In the middle of the garden was a single stone bench.

"My grandmother cleared the trees, except for this giant, and then transplanted the flowers," Bainu said as she and Katrine followed a spiral of large flat stones. "My mother added the bench. My contribution was cobbling the path. My grandmother called this place Glaine's Rest, because here she could lay down the burdens and responsibilities of leadership. When Renee becomes The Glaine, I'm sure she'll appreciate it as much as I do. Unless someone has stumbled onto this place by accident, Renee and I are the only ones who know it's here. And now you."

"It's absolutely beautiful. And no one can approach without our seeing. That's good."

Bainu perched on the edge of the bench, and Katrine sat at her feet. She took a moment to inhale, tasting the sweet summer air that was filled with a dozen floral flavors. She exhaled slowly. Muscles she hadn't known were tight gradually relaxed.

She began her story and found that it flowed easily.

Every now and then she paused, giving Bainu the chance to comment, but she always just said, "Go on."

When Katrine finished, Bainu sighed as if she'd been holding her breath. "That explains much, doesn't it? Elnid-Kyeh was—is—a Shokai and the Wolkareans failed to recognize him. It seems impossible. No wonder the Warriors were taken from us."

Minutes passed as she sat lost in thought. Then she began speaking. "For three centuries, there have been rumors that Elnid-Kyeh was still alive, wandering Serpent's Head and plotting to recapture his father's kingdom, but few believed it was possible. As the High King's son, we thought Elnid-Kyeh was a Nistarian with no magic to prolong his life. As a Shokai sorcerer, of course, it makes sense. But why you, Katrine? Why did Kylet give the message to you?"

"I asked him that. All he said was that I'll be in the right place at the right time to deliver his message to the Warrior."

"I suppose so," Bainu said, lapsing into silence again.

As the seconds crept by, Katrine started to feel a bit restless, but she didn't want to interrupt The Glaine's contemplation. She began watching the clouds, looking for familiar shapes. Two pulled apart, creating an image reminiscent of lovers separating after a kiss.

Katrine thought of Kylet and Glaine, whose love spanned the centuries and refused to end even with death. She considered Heni's taunt about her parents not being able to find her a husband. It was true. No one was ever going to love her the way Kylet loved Glaine.

Suddenly Bainu's voice, tinged with an ominous, heavy quality, made Katrine jump. "You have indeed been given an important task, Katrine. Perhaps that is why the object you carry in your saddle pouch has let you live."

For a moment, Katrine was stunned senseless.

"Will you let me see it? It has been calling to me ever since our battle with the plains cat."

Shamefaced, Katrine retrieved the spire from the saddlebag where she had hidden it after showing it to Rand. She sat down and with trembling fingers removed the rags she had wrapped it in.

Reluctantly, she handed it over.

"Holy Signs," Bainu gasped. "Kylet's spire. Few people without my powers would even dare touch it." Her fingertips lightly traced the four designs engraved in the middle like the points of a compass: land, fire, water, air. "He always decorated his personal items with the signs of the elements, just as Manderig did in ancient times."

"It can't be Kylet's spire," Katrine said. "He had it with him. I told you that was how he wounded Elnid-Kyeh." Katrine's face was burning, and she wished the ground would open up and swallow her. She should have given Bainu the weapon as soon as she found it. But now, if it actually turned out to be Kylet's spire—a priceless treasure—that made the situation go from bad to worse.

Still, Bainu did not look angry. In fact, a slender smile curled the corners of her lips upward.

"All things exist on two planes," she explained, "the physical and the spiritual. The insubstantial cannot touch the material. That is why the spirits in Echo Hall cannot injure the living."

"But I saw Kylet's spire cut Elnid-Kyeh. Twice. If you're holding the real spire, what was Kylet using?"

"Power is neither spirit nor matter. It just is. Kylet must have fashioned his ghostly strength into the image of a spire, perhaps because it is what he had done while mortal. It was that force, not metal blades, that split Elnid-Kyeh's flesh." As Bainu paused, her wrinkles became etched even deeper across her forehead and around her mouth.

"I didn't know spirits could control such power," she said thoughtfully. "But Kylet was very strong in life, and he died with a task uncompleted. Maybe that makes a difference. Surely his hatred must have multiplied with his new knowledge of Elnid-Kyeh's origin." She shrugged as if the behavior of ghosts was something to accept, not question. "There is much we mortals cannot understand."

Although her hands were gnarled with age, Bainu caressed the weapon with a lover's touch. "Spires are enchanted, and Kylet made them all. He was a Wolkarean, but both of his parents were Crennese, and he retained his wizard's heritage. He infused magic into every weapon he forged, but always a little more into the ones for his personal use. Or maybe that is a myth. Perhaps it was the constant contact with him that made his weapons appear to have minds of their own."

Much to Katrine's surprise, Bainu handed the weapon back to her. There was wistfulness in her eyes, but no wavering in her voice. "I believe if Kylet's spire has chosen you, I have no right to take it away. Nor do I think I could. But I am happy to have touched it and sampled its power. Ever since I was a child I've dreamed of holding Kylet's spire. There is only one other wish that comes close to this desire, and that is before my death to behold with my own eyes the—"

Bainu went silent. Her breath became shallow, and she studied Katrine as if looking at a stranger. Little by little her expression changed, showing confusion, hope, doubt, anticipation.

Alarmed by the vacillations on Bainu's face, Katrine shifted position uncomfortably. *Have I sprouted antlers or turned purple or something?*

Quietly, barely breathing the words, Bainu whispered, "Tonight I think I shall have my second wish."

"What wish is that?"

A shudder rippled through Bainu's body, and then her face regained its familiar composed appearance. "Not now, child. All things come in their season. Why don't we have a bite to eat and then do some painting? The view of the Ildec Major is beautiful from up here."

Sensing there was no point in arguing, Katrine climbed to her feet. She opened her saddlebags, pulled out the bundle containing their lunch, and handed it to Bainu. Then she got out the canvas and frames, paintboards and brushes.

Her stomach felt odd, and her heartbeat echoed in her ears. She accepted the bread and cheese that Bainu handed her and nibbled on it while she thought. She came to no conclusions, had no great insights.

After they finished their meal, Katrine followed Bainu's lead and painted until afternoon waned. When Bainu said it was time to leave, she called her horse, filled her saddlebags again, and mounted.

The farther they got from the peaceful hilltop, the more uneasy Katrine became. But The Glaine was humming a little tune, beaming like a child who anticipated a birth celebration.

When they arrived at Glaine's Stand, several Masters strode forward to intercept them.

"You may tell the others that Katrine did indeed spend the night in Echo Hall. Tonight, we shall have a tribal joining. I can share no more."

Bainu waved a hand of dismissal.

Before the Masters turned to leave, Katrine glanced at them. They didn't look happy.

Chapter Fifteen

At sunset the tribe all gathered in a field outside the village to watch the moon rise. Tables were piled high with food and drink, and several small fires burned cheerfully. People clustered in small groups, eating and chatting as they lounged on blankets or pillows or chairs from their homes.

When the moon rose, it was as white and brilliant as winter sunlight on snow. As it peered over the eastern hills, a hush fell across the field. Then the tribe began singing.

Harmonies filled with awe at the marvels of life joined together and infused the night. They extolled Glaine and the Sister Wives, mourned for the fall of Renath, and gave thanks to Manderig for bringing the people to Kareand in ancient times.

A young boy with a voice like a tender breeze sang a solo about life on the prairie: the seasons, the herds of wild horses, the frightening plains cats, and the sanctuary of Glaine's Stand. When Katrine whispered to Polnu that it was one of the most beautiful things she had ever heard, Polnu told her the child had composed it himself.

When the moon was high, but not yet overhead, several youngsters who had come of age since the last Festival of the Full Moon were taken by their parents and blessed with the family's lore in the Ritual of Sharing. Katrine understood enough Old Crennish to catch a phrase here and there and to be touched by the gentleness and concern expressed in the chants.

As the moon neared its zenith, Bainu stood.

"Tonight we will have a Tribal Joining," she said, "but first there are things that must be understood. For Katrine to truly become one of us, she must be accepted totally and with no masked distrust or doubt. We must be united in our giving as she must be sure in her receiving.

"Katrine saved my life, and for this she was invited into the tribe according to the Tests of Truth. She has completed each task successfully. Usually as part of the joining, we ask the initiate to share his or her experiences in Echo Hall, for we can gain a great understanding of our new member through the occurrences in that sacred place. We cannot do that with Katrine."

For a moment, The Glaine paused, apparently allotting time for the tribe to absorb her words and giving them the opportunity to ask questions or offer comments. All remained silent.

Bainu nodded to the crowd and continued. "Katrine has described her experiences to me. For her to share them with the tribe at this time would create a grave danger to her, perhaps to us all. I can only tell you she received a glimpse of her destiny. In time the truth will be made known.

"Now, Katrine, I must ask you to search your heart to make sure you are at peace with all members of the tribe, as I must ask them to search their hearts to assure they are at peace with you. If there is anything amiss, now is the time to speak."

Bearing in mind the Masters who had been angry with her earlier in the day, Katrine clambered to her feet. "I'm afraid this morning I offended some of the Masters." She stared at the ground and fidgeted with embarrassment. "I'm not always tactful, especially when my temper is involved. I didn't mean to be disrespectful. I'm sorry."

A brief moment of silence followed before a man stood up. He was the one who had been so hostile in the Hall of Chiefs. "It is not easy to break with tradition, but if Bainu says you must not disclose your experiences in Echo Hall, we accept that. Even when we do not understand, we trust The Glaine." He glanced around as if checking for contradiction. Many Glainites nodded in agreement. "I apologize to you for taking offense when none was intended." He sat again.

Studying the ocean of faces that surrounded her, Katrine searched for any signs of indecisiveness or animosity. All she saw was friendly encouragement. She sighed with relief. "I think everything is all right now."

"I agree," said Bainu. "Stand here with me, Katrine. Masters form a circle around us. Tribal members form a circle around the Masters. The moon is high, and it is time to begin."

Holding Katrine's hands, Bainu began chanting in Old Crennish. The refrain was taken up by the Masters, and then by the rest of the tribe.

At first, Katrine strained to understand the words, but she only caught one here and there. So she closed her eyes and relaxed, letting the singsong quality of the chant take her where it would.

The rhythm of the voices stirred her senses, and a quivering sensation grew in her stomach. The chant rose and fell and rose again. Melodies drifted on the wind.

As surely as she had felt the sun's heat while in the desert, she felt moonlight flow across her skin. It stroked and caressed her, sending tingles skipping up and down her nerves.

Patterns danced on her eyelids. They were full of unusual shapes, brilliant colors, and crashing movements. They were beautiful. They were horrific.

Katrine felt her body swim through a sea of unrelenting sound.

The Spire of Kylet

The pulsating beat of the chants changed. The pitch crept higher, the cadence faster, the volume louder.

Power crackled all around her.

The air was gone. She couldn't breathe.

The chant rose to a crescendo.

In one huge gulping breath, it was over.

When Katrine opened her eyes, she was still in the field outside of Glaine's Stand. Bainu held her hands, and the Masters and tribal members encircled them.

Everything was exactly as it had been, and yet everything was different.

The night was alive with colors, odors, textures, and sounds she had never noticed before. The prairie, which had appeared silver in the moonlight, was now laced with blues and greens and purples. The night hummed with insects, sang with gurgling waters, and creaked with shifting timbers. The familiar scents of grass and flowers combined with the musky odors of animals sleeping in their lairs and the acrid tang of night predators consuming their kills.

Thrumming under, over, and through it all was a wonderful sensation of unity and rightness.

Katrine was conscious of each individual Glainite, and at the same time, of the tribe as a single entity, embracing and supporting her. Beyond the village was the rest of Kareand, and beyond that were wide seas, scattered islands, other landmasses, the moon, the blackness of space, and all the stars of the universe. She was part of them, and they were part of her. One moment, she felt enormous, as if her essence could contain the cosmos. The next, she felt like a speck of nothingness within a gigantic and incomprehensible totality.

"Is this what it's like to be Crennese?" she asked Bainu. "There is so much awareness, so much feeling."

"Yes, child, and it is a mixed blessing indeed."

Suddenly, Sillem, Polnu's father, broke the circle. With a laugh, he grabbed Katrine, hugging her and calling her "daughter." Then Polnu and Renee embraced her. After that, she was passed, laughing and crying, from person to person as she was welcomed into her adopted family. She had never been hugged, kissed, and petted so much in her life.

When things had settled down, several individuals brought out musical instruments. There were flutes, lyres, tiny bells, three different kinds of drums, and gourd horns.

As the musicians played, the tribe danced.

First was the Women's Walk. Polnu demonstrated the steps, and Katrine happily linked hands between her and Renee. In a long line, the women and girls wove in and out among the men and boys, doing a little slide-hop-step-step while shaking their shoulders and wiggling their hips.

Next came The Hunt. Men holding arrowless bows crept stealthily through the crowd. Others, dressed in animal costumes, jumped and twirled in the air, their only accompaniment a deep rumble of drums. The hunters snapped their bowstrings, and the animals leapt up then fell to the ground.

Many other dances followed. Some Katrine watched in wonderment. Some she joined.

When the moon finally hung low in the sky, everyone settled down and slept in the field, knowing no evil could harm them while the tribe's power was so strongly united.

* * *

As morning sunlight heated the field, Katrine woke and moved into Polnu's house. Once again, unfamiliar sensations tried to pound their way into her awareness.

She paused in front of a looking glass and was startled by her reflection. She didn't know what she had expected—maybe some outward symbol of the internal change.

There was none.

Her hair retained its sun-bleached whiteness. Her pale eyes had taken on no new color. She was still too tall and too broad-shouldered. Only her skin appeared different, slightly darker from her desert sunburn. Also, perhaps, her lips were more inclined to turn up instead of down.

Although Polnu's family dozed, Katrine could not. She wandered through the silent village and ended up at the corral. In an outbuilding she found an assortment of brushes and rags. While she groomed Thunder Cloud, Stubbs looked at her so longingly that she felt guilty for neglecting him. As soon as she finished with her horse, she brushed and groomed her pony as well.

Then she upended a bucket and sat in the shade of a fillantra tree, staring at nothing.

Not much later, Bainu joined her. "Feeling let down?"

"Not really," Katrine answered.

Bainu gave her a sidelong look, and Katrine slowly nodded. "Maybe a little let down," she said. "The days have passed too quickly and so much has happened. How can I go home and tend the herds, and watch my brothers and sisters squabble, and eat and sleep and study as I always have?" She sighed wistfully. "I'm different, but the world around me has stayed the same. I don't feel like I belong here anymore. Maybe I never did." She sighed again. "I suppose I'm just restless."

"Come with me," Bainu said. "We'll take a walk."

Stopping long enough to give Thunder Cloud and Stubbs each a hug, Katrine let Bainu lead her away.

"Do you know what is making you restless?"

"No," Katrine answered with a shrug. "I feel odd. My body and my brain are filled with apprehension. It's like when you're supposed to be doing something, but you've forgotten what it is, and questions in the back of your mind niggle at you so much that you know you'll never relax until you remember." She kicked a small rock and sent it careening. "I'm not making sense, am I?"

"More than you know." Bainu hooked her arm under Katrine's and clasped her hand. "Perhaps part of your discomfort comes from having received a new lore that you know so little about." Leisurely, they ambled beyond the boundaries of the village. "The Glainites might not have the full Crennese lore, but we can still do magic, especially the Healers. Renee used medicinal incantations on you, first on your injured back and again on your terrible sunburn. She used them on me, as I used them on myself."

When they reached a little knoll overlooking the village, Bainu eased herself to the ground and patted a spot next to her. Plopping down, Katrine lay on her side with her head supported by her hand.

"You need to learn about enchantment," Bainu said.

"Why?" Katrine asked with surprise as she sat up.

"You're a Glainite now," Bainu answered, "and it's part of your new heritage. Besides, I sense that someday you will need it." She pressed a finger gently against Katrine's lips. "Please, no questions. I need to teach you what I can, and I'd like to do it before more people awaken and want my attention."

Katrine felt a momentary fright. Although magic had always fascinated her, she had never wanted the responsibility of wielding it.

"All spell-weaving must be done with respect for the power behind it," Bainu said. "Magic is both a wondrous gift and a tremendous burden. Never use it casually, to amuse or to show off."

"Yes ma'am," Katrine said automatically. Actually, she told herself a second later, she couldn't imagine doing magic casually under any circumstances. In fact, she couldn't imagine doing it at all.

As if she had heard Katrine's thoughts, Bainu patted her cheek. "Don't fret. All will be well." Then her voice and demeanor took on the characteristics of a schoolmaster. "Spells are cast using energy, words, and gestures. First, you must learn to gather power with your thoughts. Picture a yellow glow that imbues everything. Rocks, plants, air, animals, water."

She touched the middle of Katrine's forehead. "Pull the glow into your mind, right here. Don't try to take it from anything specific. It's everywhere. Open yourself to it."

Squinting a little, Katrine thought she could actually see a faint halo outlining the objects around her. She stretched her mind and pulled. Something stung her forehead.

"A bee," she cried, swatting the air.

"That was power's sting. After you develop a finer touch, it won't burn. I didn't expect you to try before I finished explaining." Bainu's voice was amused, and Katrine blushed. "Nor did I expect you to be quite so adept. I must caution you. Once power is collected, it must be discharged. You did fine this time. When you reacted to the sting, you instinctively released the energy and let it dissipate. There was no danger because you had collected so little.

"But if something distracts you while you hold a great deal of power, or if you misspeak a word or forget a hand movement, the magic might go wild. It could destroy you or conjure something you hadn't intended. You must be careful and concentrate. Now, we'll practice. Pull energy into yourself for a slow count of three, then relax your mind and let the power flow away."

This time, the sensation didn't sting. Rather, it felt like a fly landing on her skin.

"Very good. Now, pull harder. Still to a slow count of three, but take in as much as you can."

Envisioning herself inhaling the yellow glow through her forehead, Katrine accompanied the pull with three deep breaths. Her brain tried to explode.

"Holy Signs," gasped Bainu. "Let it drain."

The grass around them went limp and started to brown.

Bainu cried, "Slowly. Drain it slowly."

Like droplets in a water clock marking the seconds, Katrine imagined the energy trickling away. It took forever. When the last had emptied, Katrine wrapped her arms around her throbbing head. "What did I do wrong?"

Grasping Katrine's hand and looking deeply into her eyes, Bainu said, "My dear, never drink a river when a single swallow will do."

"But you said to take in as much as I could."

"My mistake. I failed to recognize the size of the vessel you were filling."

Katrine's brows pinched together, and she bit her lower lip. "This is complicated. And painful."

"We'll try a few spells," Bainu suggested, "just the words and gestures. Then we'll practice gathering energy again, focusing this time on quantity. Experience and practice will help you judge how much you need each time. Right now, how would you like to learn the incantation for invisibility?"

"Invisibility?" exclaimed Katrine. "Is that why I could never spot the Watchers?" Bainu nodded. "But what about their horses? Did you put spells on them too?"

"I didn't need to. This particular invisibility spell extends to most things the bewitched person is touching: clothing, weapons, food, tools, and horses. It usually doesn't affect large things like buildings or carriages or furniture, but you can modify it to include or exclude whatever you think is appropriate. Ready?"

"Ready," Katrine said hesitantly.

One by one, Bainu taught Katrine all the spells she knew.

She taught her healing spells for herself, different ones for others, and how to bind the magic to the body's life force so it continued working without constant attention. She showed her an incantation for capturing a

117

conversation, another for listening to someone's thoughts, and how to induce sleep and to force wakefulness.

There were simple hexes to influence a person's health and behaviors, charms for good luck, wards for protection, and cautions about when and when not to use them. The last spell Bainu showed Katrine was one to protect herself from being enchanted by someone else, but unfortunately, there was no way to bind it so that it became a permanent shield.

Then they practiced with Bainu resting her hand on Katrine's knee so she could monitor the amount of energy Katrine collected.

"That's enough," Bainu said gently. "Now maintain that level while you say the guide words and make the hand movements. With the last gesture, release the power."

Surprising herself, Katrine made a pebble bounce a few feet then stop. "I did it."

"Yes, you did. Let's try the invisibility spell now."

"*From bright and keen to sight unseen,*" Katrine recited while making a few sweeping gestures. She looked down and groaned. Her torso and legs were gone, but there were her feet, as big as life. "Ooops."

With a laugh, Bainu demonstrated the hand movements again.

Katrine's next attempt was perfect.

"There are many enchantments I don't know," Bainu said somberly. "There are spells for unleashing unnatural storms, for going from one place to another instantaneously, for controlling others and breaking them to your will. There are many dark and evil spells I don't want to know and numerous ones just waiting to be created."

She reached into a pocket of her tunic, pulled out a bound booklet, and handed it to Katrine. "This tome was begun in ancient times, shortly after the settlement of Kareand. It's called the Book of White Spells. The Recorders have made many translations, but I would like to give you this, the original. One of the duplicates would be easier for you to read, but you will probably get more from this volume than anyone who has handled it in the past."

"Why is that?"

"Someday you'll know. If I prove wrong, bring it back, and I'll give you a Nistarian copy."

Katrine glanced at Bainu quizzically, but when the older woman said nothing more, she opened the scruffy leather cover and turned a few pages. The edges were ragged with age, and in places the writing had almost faded away. A musty smell drifted up and tickled Katrine's nostrils. She rubbed her nose with a finger.

"Although incantations are included inside, the Book of White Spells is more a history and a philosophy than a book of magic. It has passed from generation to generation with many different people writing a page here and there, recording the wisdom of their times in hopes that a written heritage would help us develop differently than the Shokai have. Portions of it are reproduced in many school primers.

"I want you to understand, Katrine, even though it is old and tattered and doesn't look like much, the Book of White Spells is no mean gift. It contains many treasures for those willing to search its pages. And this tome is the original. Still, I wish I had more to give you."

Closing the book, Katrine slipped it into her pocket. She took Bainu's hand between both of hers. "Yesterday, when we were at Glaine's Rest, you had a foreseeing about me, didn't you? That's why you looked at me so strangely. Please, tell me what you saw."

Bainu shook her head. "I dare not. When the time is appropriate, you'll know. Someone with more right than mine will tell you." She stroked Katrine's cheek. "Learn to have faith and patience. Now, we must go back. Renee and Sillem promised your parents you would be home before sunset."

"Thank you for the book." Katrine climbed to her feet and extended a hand to assist Bainu. "My Old Crennish isn't very good, but Father is teaching me. It'll probably take me forever to decipher it."

"Once you explore its riches, you will find it is worth the effort."

Hand in hand, they crossed back to the village.

* * *

Elnid-Kyeh waved his hand across the scrying dish and the picture vanished. He sat and pondered.

The old woman had scanty knowledge of sorcery, but the girl had demonstrated astounding potential.

First of all, she had gathered the energies with ease, even though for many novices this was the most difficult lesson to master. Multiple attempts were usually required.

Second, her hands, which were large and appeared awkward, had woven through the air as if she had been making commanding gestures all her life. Her only difficulty had been mastering the subtleties, but that would come with practice.

Third, although the spells were simple and required no great gift to memorize, still she had learned them after having heard them only once.

Her entire performance had been preposterous.

It should have been impossible.

For a few minutes, Elnid-Kyeh drummed his fingers on the table in front of him. Hollenth had obviously misjudged the girl, giving too much credence to a younger brother who was obviously jealous.

He would have to send someone else to evaluate her.

Chapter Sixteen

"Wow, Katrine," Skotlan said as he stood beside Thunder Cloud's new stall. "He sure is a beauty."

"Thanks."

"And the Glainites just gave him to you? For free?"

"It was part of the ceremony they had for me," Katrine said, repeating the half-truth she had told her parents the night before. For some reason, she couldn't bring herself to tell anyone about the Tests of Truth and her initiation into the tribe.

When she considered possible scenarios, her experiences always ended up either sounding childishly trivial or recklessly dangerous. In actuality, the process had been too personal, and in some ways too spiritual, to be shared.

As Katrine watched, Skotlan extended his hand to Thunder Cloud. When the horse lowered his head and sniffed, Skotlan grinned with delight and stroked his neck.

For a moment, Katrine lost herself in her brother's obvious pleasure.

Then, out of nowhere, she was bombarded by feelings from the rest of the household.

Even out here in the stables, she thought, wrapping her arms around herself and squeezing her eyes shut.

Since coming home from Glaine's Stand, she had been flooded by her new sensitivities. She was constantly aware of her connection with each family member and servant. Their presence and emotions reverberated like battle cries in the background of her mind.

So far, the only relief she'd had was when she had gone out on the plains this morning. But as soon as she rode back through the manor gates, there everyone was again, feeling and thinking things she couldn't ignore.

She didn't want to know how the new hired man felt about the barmaid in town or if Rosi and her husband had been quarreling.

She felt as if she were eavesdropping on people's most private moments, and she couldn't look anyone in the face.

Much of what she sensed was disturbing, like emotional garbage spewed at her from every direction.

She had always known Anton competed with her, but when she'd first ridden Thunder Cloud into the courtyard, the intensity of his anger and jealousy had hit her like a physical blow, almost toppling her from the saddle. It was as if her having a great horse took something away from him, something rightfully his, and he hated her for it. Even now she sensed him, full of spite, brooding in the house.

In Echo Hall, Kylet had implied Father was proud of her. She could feel it now, but mixed with the pride was an expectation for achievement completely out of proportion to her abilities and aspirations, which meant, ultimately, that she was going to disappoint him even more than she already had.

"You aren't listening, 'Trine," Skotlan insisted loudly. Then more quietly, he added, "You all right?"

He looked so worried that Katrine forced a reassuring smile onto her face. "Sorry. I guess part of me is still at Glaine's Stand. What were you saying?"

"I asked if you'd give me a ride on Thunder Cloud sometime. Do you think he would mind?"

"I'm sure he'd be happy to, and so would I, but I was going to suggest something different." Brushing her fingers through her brother's unruly auburn hair, Katrine feigned nonchalance. "I thought you might like to have Stubbs for your very own."

Skotlan's voice quivered with excitement. "You mean it? For keeps?"

"Sure." Grinning broadly, Katrine gave her favorite brother a hug. "Father bought Anton's pony last year, and I imagine he plans on getting you one soon. But Stubbs has been so lonely since I got Thunder Cloud. He really needs a friend. I know you'd take good care of him. What do you think?"

"Wow! Thanks, Katrine. You sure Father won't mind?"

"He gave Stubbs to me. I don't think he'll care what I do as long as Stubbs is all right. But I'll ask to be sure."

"Let's go for a ride first." Skotlan grabbed a saddle, blanket, and bridle. "You can ask Father later."

Katrine began to saddle Thunder Cloud.

All of a sudden, she was caught up in Heni's whirlpool of feelings. There was self-doubt, conceit, anxiety, resentment, and anger. In a sudden burst of insight, Katrine realized how fearful Heni was and how she ridiculed others as a way of feeling more powerful and in control.

With trembling hands, Katrine managed to get the saddle in place. As she tightened the cinch, Jaimi's presence shoved Heni's aside, inundating Katrine with her sister's attitudes. Apparently, Jaimi felt sorry for Katrine, viewing her as less than a woman because of her height and physical strength, and less than a man because of her femaleness. Her feelings bordered on pity.

Pressing her hands hard against her temples, Katrine stifled a moan. Why hadn't The Glaine or Polnu warned her about this backwash of everyone's emotions? Immediately she answered herself: it just hadn't occurred to them. The Glainites were a conservative and restrained people whose mental tones didn't echo all over the place. They probably learned while very young to keep themselves contained and, at the same time, to shield against people who were not of the tribe.

"Come on." Skotlan swung atop Stubbs and gave a little kick with his heels. "Let's go. We don't have much time till dinner."

Riding out onto the plains, Katrine drank in her younger brother's positive mood. He had always been a comfort to her, almost from the day he was born. Now she was afraid she would need his calming influence more than ever. Only his and Mother's feelings didn't overwhelm her.

She needed help.

If she had to use all her internal resources coping with other people's emotions, or running away from them, she would end up even more isolated than before.

Tomorrow or the next day, she would have to find time to go see Polnu.

* * *

Elnid-Kyeh felt a tingle at the base of his skull. One of his minions was using an amulet to make contact with him. He had left his communications amulet in the tower, so he put down his fork and reached for his half-filled wine glass. Gazing at the liquid, he made three quick passes with his hand and mumbled a few words.

The image of a woman with garish red hair floated on the wine. "It is not there, Master."

"Did you look exactly where I told you?" Elnid-Kyeh asked impatiently.

"Yes. I went over every inch of the ravine floor. I found half a dozen nails, a horseshoe, a bucket with a hole in the bottom, and a handful of coins. No other metal."

Frustrated, Elnid-Kyeh tapped the arm of his chair with his fingers.

Earlier in the summer, after using a divining spell to locate all of Kylet's magical weapons, he had sent one of his servants to the ravine south of Banur to get Kylet's spire. The search had been interrupted, and the servant, having other tasks, had returned home and then had postponed returning and completing the job.

Despite his arduous schedule, Elnid-Kyeh thought, he should have gone for the damnable weapon himself.

He flicked a breadcrumb from the tabletop to the floor. "What about the girl?" he asked.

"Nothing new," said the woman.

"Could she have the spire?"

From the way the woman's face paled, he could tell the notion had never occurred to her.

It was a remote possibility, he knew, but it had to be checked.

"I'll find out," the woman said quickly. She grinned showing teeth that protruded unattractively. "Valt serves on the Council of Elders with her father. We can do some casual snooping."

"Very well. Keep me informed." He passed his hand over the glass and the image disappeared.

Late into the night, he sat at the table, thinking.

He could not risk having Kylet's spire in any hands other than his own. If its shadow could debilitate him as much as it had in Echo Hall, how much damage could the real one accomplish?

He would have to cast his strongest divination spell to locate it now. Although it was one of the few incantations that he used which required physical and chemical aids to focus power, it never failed.

He would begin the long and complicated preparations in the morning.

* * *

A light rain sprinkled the plains.

Dressed for bed, Katrine tied back the window curtains, allowing a cool breeze to circulate through her room unencumbered.

The Glaine and Polnu had helped her learn how to moderate the effects of her new perceptions. Her days, even when brimming with people, were no longer troublesome. Now it was her nights that had become torturous.

Full of dread, she lay down.

Her eyes grew heavy. She dozed and began to dream:

She was on Thunder Cloud, galloping across a broad field. Ahead, a man dressed in black rode a speeding tornado.

She tried to reach him.

"Wait," she screamed. She urged her horse forward until they were flying across the prairie grass. Trees and hills whizzed by in a blur.

A flock of demons with an evil blue dragon at their center flew up from the ground and filled the sky between her and the man.

Grasping her bow, she loosed arrow after arrow. Whenever one struck a demon, there was a popping sound, and the demon disappeared in a puff of smoke.

Only the dragon was left.

It turned away from her and swooped and snatched at the man, raking gnarled claws across his body.

He drew a broadsword.

When he swung it, it glowed with an internal light, which was almost painful in its brightness. He fought and fought, but for every wound he gave the dragon, he received two in return.

The Spire of Kylet

The man's blood flowed into the whirlwind, transforming it into a spinning cylinder of scarlet. With no strength left, the man slumped forward.

The dragon reared back, extended its talons, and prepared to plummet down for the kill.

Terror gripped Katrine.

With fumbling fingers she nocked her last arrow and let it fly. It bounced off the dragon's scaly hide.

Kylet's ghost materialized before her.

His face was fierce with displeasure. His voice thundered. "Why do you delay? You must deliver my message, daughter. The time draws nigh."

Drenched in perspiration, Katrine woke. Her heart raced and her whole body shook with tremors. Her breath hissed past her lips in gasps. Shakily, she climbed from bed and gazed out the window at the rain.

"What am I supposed to do?" she whispered at the darkness. "I asked Mother, and she said we're not going on a trip. If there is something else I can do, tell me."

With tears streaking her cheeks, she lay down on the bed again and prayed for fatigue to overtake her long enough to grant a few hours of undisturbed rest.

Chapter Seventeen

Cool evenings and intermittent rains proclaimed summer's gradual decline.

Indoors, the air was stuffy and humid. Outdoors, it was muggy and wet. In both places, tempers tended to be short and volatile.

"Giants are a metaphor, not real people," Heni shrieked at the top of her voice, drowning out the patter of raindrops hitting the windows.

"You're crazy," Skotlan yelled back at her. "The northern mountains are full of giants."

The argument, which had begun as a discussion about the difference between history and legend, had disintegrated into a shouting match about monsters, supernatural entities, and magical creatures.

In a united front, Anton, Jaimi, and Heni took the position that all stories about enchanted beasts and beings that weren't quite human were actually allegories, parables, or fables.

Katrine, Skotlan, and Raeph insisted the stories were based on historical facts and such creatures probably still existed somewhere in the wilderness or the wastelands.

Heni seemed determined to win the debate by volume alone.

Katrine felt as if her head would burst.

Why is Father letting this drag on and on? she asked herself.

He often let the children disagree during lessons, but he usually stopped them short of bloodshed, which now seemed imminent.

Damn the Glainite awarenesses!

In general she had been doing quite well moderating them, but for the past few nights she had heard a continual, incomprehensible murmur that stirred up a variety of disturbing emotions.

The result was that she had hardly slept at all.

Today, exhausted, she felt her control slipping away.

Not only were shrill, angry voices stabbing her eardrums, but the underlying, inflamed feelings that went with the anger were battering at her soul. If it persisted much longer, she would end up screaming like a banshee just to drown them all out.

"Mer," Mother said, entering the room and slicing the bedlam into silence with her gentle tone.

Katrine jerked around.

Mother never interrupted classes. Why was she standing in the doorway looking so pale and troubled?

Father stepped quickly across the room to join her. His surprise and concern were evident. Mother whispered in his ear and then they left together.

Skotlan moved closer to Katrine. "What do you think that was about?" he asked in a hushed tone.

"Shhh." She put her finger to her lips, and for once, all the children obeyed. She could hear snatches of conversation from the hall.

"—Luren and Calli's farm—" said one voice.

"—one killed, others hurt—" said another.

"—almost everything destroyed—"

"—peacekeepers meeting in—"

The sound of scuffling feet was followed by the slam of a door.

Footsteps approached. They were Mother's. "Your father has to go into town," Mother said. "Class is over for today."

"What happened?" asked Katrine. "I heard—"

"Jaimi and Heni," Mother said, speaking over Katrine's questions, "since you are free now, you can help Rosi bottle cranifruit."

The girls groaned, and Anton started to smirk. Mother turned to him. "Anton, Brac needs your help cleaning the stables. Skotlan and Raeph, the wood box in the kitchen is almost empty. Rosi is going to be doing preserves all day, so you will need to keep it full for her."

Then it was Katrine's turn. "The irrigation water to the large vegetable garden has been running slow. You need to check the troughs to see if you can find and fix the problem."

"In the rain?" Katrine asked.

"It's just a sprinkle, and you don't shrink like a muslin petticoat," Mother said, smiling in a wan sort of way. "The rain won't be enough for us to stop irrigating. You need to figure out what's clogging the channels."

Grumbling, the children put away their books and started on their extra chores.

As Katrine removed a clump of rotting vegetation from the final trough, she wondered what was important enough to make Father leave in the middle of a lesson. He had never done that before.

She was sure some of the voices she had heard belonged to Elders, so apparently it was Council business. But that didn't make sense.

From the snatches she caught, it sounded as if there had been an accident—maybe a fire—at the Luren farm. Why would the Council bother with something like that, even if someone died? Farmers and ranchers faced tragedies all the time. Family and friends helped them out, not the Council.

When the water was flowing smoothly again, Katrine snuck out the bolthole and sat on an old tree stump to watch the grasslands ripple in the wind like a living sea.

As much as she complained, she actually enjoyed her chores, especially the ones that kept her outside. Most of all, she liked riding across the plains on days like this—when she was tired, headachy, and irritable—and letting the prairie work its healing magic on her.

She sat on the tree stump until she heard the gong announcing lunch.

By afternoon, the last of the drizzling rain had stopped.

Mother sent Katrine outside again: this time to dig up tubers and whiteroots in the garden.

Katrine was still working at it when Father returned home. He left his horse with Brac and then approached her instead of going into the house.

"Until I tell you differently," he said, "you are not to leave the manor." He turned to walk away.

Propping the shovel against the fence, Katrine moved to intercept him. Although questioning one of Father's decisions was not generally a good idea, she could tell something was very wrong. She sensed he wanted to tell her more but didn't know how. Maybe all he needed was a reason.

"Will you tell me why, Father?" Katrine asked, trying not to reveal the fright she felt at being so bold.

For a moment she thought he was simply going to ignore her and continue walking, but he stopped and turned. "The peacekeepers are looking for a band of marauders that attacked Luren and Calli's farm last night. They broke into the house and terrorized the family, stole everything of value, and destroyed what was breakable. When Luren tried to stop them, they beat him savagely. They killed his Chief Huntsman outright when he tried to intervene."

Tears formed in Katrine's eyes, and her voice cracked. "Calli and the children?"

"Unharmed, but sick with fear. They're staying in town for now. The Healers don't know if Luren will survive."

Father took hold of Katrine's arms in a tight grip and gave her a little shake. "Can I impress on you how serious this is, Katrine? It is not a time for you to be tiptoeing from the house and sneaking out the bolthole, as you did when you were younger. I need to know you are here and safe so I can concentrate on my duties as High Elder."

"Yes sir, I understand." She had never seen her father so alarmed.

"Good." He released her, and the worried look on his face eased a little. "We're hiring an exceptionally good tracker from Drena. When the outlaws have been dealt with, we'll try to get things back to normal around here. Until then, Trinnin and Urbol will take care of the herds and supervise the manor guards."

Katrine nodded.

Brac's eldest two sons were both as big as barns. They were also experts with bow, knife, and sword, as well as being the two best horsemen in Banur. Good choices for protecting herdbeasts and people.

* * *

Over the next few days, Katrine became increasingly restless and foul-tempered, as did everyone else in the household. Even Mother was developing a sharp edge to her tongue.

For the first time, Katrine heard her parents arguing.

"I have to know so I can plan," Mother said to Father, continuing a discussion at the dinner table that they must have started earlier in the afternoon.

"Well, I don't know what to tell you," answered Father.

"If you don't, who does?" snapped Mother, peevishly.

"Evi," Father said with exasperation, "I know you've planned a farewell dance for Heni two nights from now. You don't need to keep reminding me. Until the marauders are caught, the Council has ordered a twilight curfew. I can't overrule the entire Council."

"You're High Elder," Mother persisted, raising her voice in both pitch and volume. "You could convince them to make an exception if you wanted."

"You're right," Father yelled, slapping the table with his hand, "but I don't want to. I think the Council is right. Powers Above, woman, do you want our neighbors murdered on the way to a party!"

Bursting into tears, Mother covered her face with her hands and ran upstairs. Father stormed out of the house and slammed the front door behind him.

In stunned silence the children sat frozen around the table.

Then suddenly, Heni and Jaimi started wailing and rushed from the room too. Skotlan just grinned and helped himself to the candied sweet-roots on the girls' plates.

The next morning, when the children gathered in the parlor for school lessons, Father and Mother were both waiting for them.

"The peacekeepers caught the marauders on the road between Edmon and Sendig," Father said. "To prevent capture, the outlaws fought to the death." Then looking a bit self-conscious and embarrassed (probably because of the scene he and Mother had caused at the dinner table last night), he continued. "Classes are suspended today and tomorrow so we can all help Mother get things ready for Heni's dance."

Jaimi and Heni linked hands and squealed with delight.

When they had settled down, Mother took charge. "After a tragedy," she said, "people want to congregate. Not only to brighten their moods, but also to give and receive loving support. We can expect a good turnout, and we have a great deal to do to get ready."

The invitations had been written and addressed weeks ago with only the date left blank. Mother had Heni and Jaimi write that in, and then she sent Anton and Skotlan off on their ponies to deliver the envelopes by hand.

In order to prepare everything on such short notice, Mother had asked a few neighbors to help her clean the house and rearrange the furniture. She sent Katrine, Jaimi, and Heni to the kitchen to help Rosi.

When Katrine was given the task of preparing all the fruits and vegetables that were in a large tub, she had to grit her teeth to keep from throwing a fit. She hated peeling and paring.

However, when Rosi gave Jaimi and Heni the job of plucking fowl, Katrine grinned to herself, grabbed an apple and her knife, and went to work. She hated plucking even more.

All of the family's friends from Banur and Glaine's Stand were to receive invitations, and messengers began arriving with acceptances before Skotlan and Anton made it back home after delivering the last batch.

As Mother had predicted, it was going to be a very good turnout.

Chapter Eighteen

The night of the dance, Polnu came early to help Katrine style her hair in the Glainite fashion and to help with the many buttons on the back of Katrine's new lavender bodice with its matching lace overskirt.

"Hold still," Polnu said, "or I'll never get your hair right." Katrine willed herself to be motionless while Polnu coiled and looped two long braids into a sophisticated design at the back of her head.

"What do you think?" Polnu asked, giving Katrine a hand mirror so she could examine the results.

"It's so elegant. Someday you need to teach me how to do that."

Just then Mother stuck her head into the room. "Since you're all ready, Katrine, will you tend the front door? The servants are busy, and I need to get the twins dressed."

Before Katrine could answer, a duet of screeches echoed down the hall and Mother rushed off to allay the clamor. Reluctantly, Katrine left Polnu to adorn herself alone.

Soon the house began to fill with friends and neighbors, and Katrine directed them to the parlor for food and drink or to the audience hall for dancing. She almost didn't recognize an elderly man who arrived with an attractive young man, about her age, in tow. She took a closer look.

"Neyac?" she asked.

"Katrine, I'm delighted to see you again. Allow me to present Torrend of Nallee, my apprentice. Torrend, this is Katrine, Elder Mer's daughter."

"I'm most pleased to meet you," the young man said.

"The pleasure is mine, Apprentice Torrend."

"No titles tonight!" Neyac said jovially. "We're here to have fun. No robes, you see."

Running her gaze over the Recorder, Katrine forgave herself for not identifying him immediately. He looked quite different wearing stylish, formal clothing instead of his robes.

His tunic was dark blue velvet with silver threads looped in designs on the

130

collar and down the center of his sleeves. His trousers were made of the same fabric and tapered to fit smoothly into the tops of his shiny black boots. He was positively dashing.

Torrend was also fashionably dressed. He wore deep green velvet with a wide fringe of ochre lace at his neck and wrists. His eyes were brown and so was his collar-length straight hair. He had a roundish chin with a dimple in the middle and a smile full of straight white teeth.

"Let me show you around," Katrine said as she signaled Skotlan to take over door duty. "Refreshments or dancing? Where would you like to start?"

"Dancing sounds nice," Torrend answered. "Do you dance?"

"Not well, but if you're inviting me, I'm willing."

"Run along, children," Neyac told them. "This nose can always find its way to good food." He placed a finger along side his ample proboscis, turned in a circle, and pointed to the parlor. "That way!"

Just as Katrine and Torrend entered the audience chamber, the musicians began a new number.

"If you please," Torrend said with a bow.

Katrine curtsied, and when they joined the dancers, she realized Torrend was just her height.

"I thought you said you didn't dance well," Torrend commented after they had done a few turns around the floor. "We must be good. Look, everyone's watching us."

Glancing at the assembly, Katrine saw that a number of people were indeed staring at them. "I'm afraid it's you they're looking at. We don't get many strangers in Banur. When this dance is over, curious young ladies and their parents are going to swarm all over you like bees in a garden."

"I guess it's like that all over," Torrend said as he twirled Katrine. "In Nallee we paid attention to strangers too. I imagine I'll get used to it once I'm a Recorder and have more experience in the world."

Now that she had the chance to talk with an authentic Recorder's apprentice, Katrine was bursting with questions.

Just as she was ready to start asking, though, the music began a new flourish, and she had to concentrate on following Torrend's complicated steps, which were slightly different from the traditional ones she knew.

When the music ended, Katrine took Torrend's arm. "We might as well save the multitudes the trouble of seeking you out. The small, brown-haired girl over there, the one who's pretending not to stare at you, is my cousin Heni. The brazen redhead beside her, who obviously doesn't care if you know she's looking at you, is my sister Jaimi. They're unavoidable. We might as well start with them."

By the time Katrine had introduced Torrend to her sister and cousin, many other young girls had crowded around him. She left him to fend for himself and moseyed over to the parlor. It was overflowing with people, and she stood just inside the doorway and observed.

The Spire of Kylet

In a secluded corner, Polnu and Rand were engaged in serious looking conversation. Watching them thoughtfully from across the room was Rand's father, Leron.

Sal, Heni's guard, stood nearby with his lady friend, a plump woman in a red gown. Next to them, Ferrill, Heni's driver, had one arm wrapped around a cute little blond whom Katrine didn't know.

Near the food-laden table, Mother was proudly showing the twins to Polnu's parents, and behind them, four-year-old Bramt was stuffing himself with sweets. He met Katrine's eyes guiltily, but when she winked at him, he grinned, flashing teeth covered with syrupy bits of fruit and cake.

Anton, wearing his first formal tunic and trousers, strutted back and forth in front of a couple of curly-headed, flounce-decorated young girls who giggled appreciatively.

Other familiar faces advanced and dwindled like the ebbing and flowing of the tides.

Why had she come this way?

There had been a reason, she was sure, but she couldn't remember what.

Had she been looking for someone?

Yes, that was it. Since Torrend would be unavailable until Heni and Jaimi decided to let him go, she wanted to ask Neyac her questions about the apprentice qualifying examinations.

However, Neyac was nowhere to be seen.

In fact, neither he nor Father was in the parlor or the audience hall. Maybe they were together in Father's study. There wasn't any harm in wandering by and checking.

Standing outside the door, Katrine leaned forward to listen.

Although she could hear conversation, she couldn't understand the words. Still, she knew one voice was Father's. The other belonged to the Master Recorder. She was just about to leave in frustration when she heard her name.

One of Bainu's incantations leapt into Katrine's mind.

It was too simple to ignore!

"Let me hear, loud and clear, voices far, voices near." She made the gestures and focused her power on the other side of the door. The next moment, she could hear Father and Neyac as easily as if she were in the room with them.

"But something has changed her," Neyac was saying. "That wasn't the same self-conscious, uncomfortable young girl I met before."

"She has been acting different lately," Father conceded. "A bit more pensive and self-absorbed, I think, but she's at an awkward age. No longer a child, not quite an adult."

"Let her come to Pardish with me. When things happen that I don't understand, I like to take precautions."

"Now? Is it time?"

"Not yet, but Katrine is special. We both know that." A sharp note crept into the Recorder's tone. "I have never approved of your letting her spend so much time out on the plains alone. She's always in danger—and now this attack on your neighbors. I don't like it."

"Katrine has grown up strong," Father said with obvious pride. "She can fight like a man, and yet she is gentle and kind, especially with her younger brothers and sisters. She never loses control of that temper of hers."

"A good thing, too, Mer! You should've told her by now."

"No." Father was adamant. "I have allowed her as normal a childhood as I could. I don't regret it. There will be enough burdens in her future."

"Let her come with Torrend and me. All evening I've had the most unsettled feeling. Let me take her to Pardish."

Say yes, Katrine thought ecstatically. If Neyac wanted to take her to Pardish, he must want her to go to the Recorders School. This was her great chance. *Say yes, Father.*

"Give me the night to think on it, old friend. You ask a great deal of a father. It was difficult enough to let her spend a week with the Glainites. Now, if I let her go with you, who knows how long she'll be gone? She's still very young."

"She spent an entire week with the Glainites?" Neyac said sharply. "Why didn't you tell me?"

"There has hardly been time to tell you everything."

"Was it over the full moon?"

"Yes. They were having a celebration to honor—" Father's voice dwindled away. "Holy Signs! No, it can't be."

What's wrong? Katrine thought in a panic. *What does the Full Moon Celebration have to do with my going to Pardish?*

As confusion swept over Katrine, she lost control of the spell. Abruptly, the utterances ended. While she was trying to repair her concentration, Skotlan hurried around a corner and slammed into her.

"There you are," he exclaimed. "You've got to help me. Jaimi's got that awful Terina on my trail, offering to teach me to dance. Come on, you dance with me instead."

Katrine bit her lip as she thought.

It was a dilemma. She was frantic to hear the end of Father's conversation with Neyac, but Skotlan, who brought so much joy into her life, seldom asked her for anything. She hated to refuse him. Besides, Terina really was a terror. She was cute enough, but she acted exactly like Jaimi and Heni.

"I just want to show them I already know how," Skotlan said, pulling on her hand. "Come on. Please."

"Oh, all right."

As Skotlan led Katrine to the floor, he made a face at Jaimi. When the music stopped and the dance ended, he discreetly disappeared.

After that, Katrine danced with Torrend again, then with a couple of Banur youths who had never paid any attention to her before, and then with Rand.

"What am I going to do, 'Trine?" Rand asked as they glided among the other couples. "I caught my father watching Polnu and me, and I could almost hear his thoughts churning. If he can't marry me off to you, I think he'll switch to her. I feel like one of your father's herdbeasts at auction."

"You could do worse," Katrine said. "Polnu will make some man a wonderful wife."

"But someday she'll be The Glaine. I don't think the tribe would allow their leader to take a non-Glainite husband."

"I don't see why not. The Glainites are a Crennese tribe, and you're Crennese." Katrine spun away from Rand then continued speaking when she returned to his arms. "If you required official sanctioning, they could always do a Tribal Joining."

Rand shook his head, his brows pinched together. "But what would happen to Leron's family lore if I was adopted again? Father's proud of his heritage and wants it passed on. I can't risk losing it. Besides, we'd have to live at Glaine's Stand."

"I see you've given it some thought," Katrine said teasingly. "I have the feeling you wouldn't mind marrying Polnu if the details could be worked out."

Starting with his neck, Rand turned bright red until even the tips of his ears were crimson. "I've always kind of liked her. But it's been awkward. Father has been dead set on my marrying you. And I like you too, you know that," Rand said quickly, "but I like Polnu differently. Oh hell, you know what I mean."

Katrine couldn't help it. She burst into laughter at Rand's discomfort. "We've always known we were just friends, Rand. I think you and Polnu would make a great match."

"Really?" Rand said, blushing deeper reddish purple.

The musicians were playing a particularly popular number, and space on the floor became increasingly tight. Katrine and Rand edged into a less congested spot at the outer rim of the overcrowding.

"What makes you think you would lose Leron's heritage if you joined the Glainites?" asked Katrine. "You didn't lose the Crennese heritage when he adopted you. In fact, you're already carrying both lores."

Rand's eyes grew large and his grin covered his entire face. "You're right! Why didn't I think of that?"

"Of course," Katrine said with false solemnity, "you and Polnu would have to figure out how to have at least two children: a son to receive Leron's family lore and a daughter to become The Glaine." Rand's face, which had just about returned to its normal shade, reddened again. Pretending not to notice, Katrine went on. "I guess if you couldn't do it the regular way, you could adopt."

"It's not impossible," Rand said, sounding a little surprised.

"Nope," agreed Katrine.

"When did you develop all this wisdom?" Rand held her at arm's length so he could scrutinize her. "Wasn't it just yesterday that you were a scatterbrained, flighty young—?"

"I was never a scatterbrained anything," Katrine interrupted with assumed arrogance. "You must be thinking about Jaimi, and really, Rand, she's much too young for you. I'm surprised you've even noticed her."

After Rand made a suitable reply, they continued their affable banter until the music stopped. Completely forgetting to escort Katrine from the floor, Rand rushed to Polnu's side. Standing on tiptoes, Katrine watched Polnu's face as it blossomed into a glorious smile. Katrine couldn't help but match the expression.

"I hate to interrupt such private thoughts," Neyac said from Katrine's elbow, "but I'm wondering if the most enchanting young lady here would consent to dance with an old man."

"I don't know," Katrine said teasingly. "I'll go look for the enchanting girl if you'll go look for an old man."

Neyac chuckled, and then flourished a gallant bow. "May I?"

Katrine extended her hand from a deep curtsy.

As they spun with the other dancers, Katrine opened herself to Neyac's feelings, hoping to get a sense of how his conversation with Father had ended. All she got was a controlled blank. Disappointed, she realized he must have been trained to block a magical sensing. She wondered if all Recorders were taught to do that. She couldn't figure out how to ask without admitting she'd tried to read his emotions.

Despite his age, Neyac was light on his feet and danced well. The tune the musicians played was lively and cheerful, and Katrine relaxed and enjoyed herself, glancing occasionally at the assemblage along the walls as they drifted by.

With no warning, Katrine's muscles tensed.

An uncomfortable, pulsating energy flowed from one corner of the chamber. Her head began to pound and her stomach grew queasy. Her vision blurred, and a wave of weakness hit her at the same time. She stumbled, grabbing onto Neyac to keep from falling.

"Are you all right, my dear?" Neyac asked solicitously.

"Too much dancing and no dinner," she lied, saying the first thing that occurred to her. "Maybe I'd better sit down."

Holding onto Katrine's elbow, Neyac led her into the parlor and saw her seated. He brought her a glass of punch and then filled a heaping plate of edibles for her.

"Thank you," Katrine said when he presented her with the plate, "but I don't think a Master Recorder should be serving a simple herder."

"I am serving my dance partner," Neyac told her. "That's perfectly acceptable, my dear."

Katrine nibbled on a piece of sweet bread. "I feel much better now. Thank you."

"Are you sure? I dislike leaving you if you are unwell, but I've remembered an errand and—"

"Go ahead, please. I'll just sit here and rest a few minutes, then I'll try to finish this feast you brought me."

Soon, Katrine felt more like herself. She set the plate and cup on a little table and went back to watch the dancing.

When she entered the audience chamber, though, she was again hit by a series of disquieting sensations. As she fixed her attention on the far corner of the room, her vision clouded, her head began to pound, and her stomach flipped over.

What in Kareand is happening to me?

Then, she thought, maybe it wasn't her.

Maybe something bad was happening in that portion of the room. Perhaps it was some kind of magic that her Glainite perceptions were trying to identify and warn her about.

She needed help from someone who could tell her what was going on.

She squinted and searched for Skotlan. She couldn't see him, but although the world was a foggy blur, she easily spotted Jaimi. No one else had hair that brilliant shade of red. She was prattling with several youngsters her own age.

"Excuse me, Jaimi, could I talk with you a minute?"

Jaimi showed her surprise by fluttering long dark lashes over her big green eyes, but nonetheless she quickly separated from her friends. "You look awful, Katrine."

"I've got a headache."

"You're not jealous because Torrend danced with me four times and you only twice, are you? You don't own him, you know."

"No, that's not it." Once again Katrine tried to focus on the scene across the room. Yellow and red dots did pirouettes in front of her eyes, and her brain threatened to rupture. She pressed her hands against her temples to keep her head intact.

"I just wondered if you could tell me who's in the corner over there. My headache's clouding my vision, and I can't make them out."

"You mean Felda and Valt? You must remember them. They have that darling little curio shop in town."

"Of course." Without thinking, Katrine nodded, and a lightning bolt flashed through her skull. She put a hand on the wall to keep from reeling. "Last year they paid Anton to run errands for them a couple of times, didn't they?"

"That's right, while they were building the addition to the shop. A few months ago, Valt was selected to serve on the Council of Elders with Father."

"They seem different tonight," Katrine said, bluffing, trying to keep Jaimi talking until she figured out what was wrong.

"Well, Felda's changed the color of her hair, probably with a henna, and it looks dreadful. Valt is dragging his leg as if he's been in an accident."

"Anything else? Anything strange?"

"Like what?"

"I don't know. Anything."

Anything to do with the Glainites or magic, she wanted to ask. Her symptoms had to be related to the tribal initiation. She had never experienced anything like this before.

"I suppose Felda shouldn't have done that to her hair. A grown woman should have more sense, but lots of people do silly things to change their appearance. And I'm sure Valt didn't hurt his leg on purpose. They look odd, but that's their business. Now if you'll pardon me, I'd like to get back to my friends."

With her head throbbing wretchedly, Katrine stumbled to the door. When she reached it, she turned and peered at the corner one last time. Although Jaimi had only mentioned Felda and Valt, Katrine would've sworn there were four distinct outlines visible.

Chapter Nineteen

A crisp breeze played with the curtains at the sides of the window and caressed Katrine into wakefulness. It was still dark, but she felt refreshed, with no lingering signs of the previous night's headache.

From outside she heard nothing except a few early rising songbirds serenading from a nearby tree.

As she stretched and swung her legs over the edge of the bed, she reflected on the cryptic conversation she had overheard between Father and Neyac. Even the possibility, no matter how remote, of traveling to Pardish was a delightful prospect. She had dreamed and schemed about such an opportunity all her life.

Yet, something had not sounded quite right.

Father had called Neyac "old friend," but they hadn't sounded like comrades catching up on old times. They had seemed more like conspirators. Had Father possibly arranged for her to take the apprentice examinations as a surprise?

With her dressing and grooming accomplished, Katrine decided to make her way to the kitchen. No matter how quiet and inactive the rest of the house was, Rosi always got up early to bake bread, cure meats, or prepare some elaborate delicacy.

When Katrine opened her door, she almost bumped into Father. He looked as if he were just getting ready to knock.

"You're up early," he said.

"So are you."

"I haven't even been to bed." Father certainly looked weary. His green eyes, the same shade as Jaimi's, were surrounded by thin streaks of red. His sandy hair was a mess, and his clothing was rumpled. "I would like to talk with you, Katrine. Will you join me in the study?"

"Yes sir." As Katrine stepped past him, she sensed his tension and fatigue, as well as a feeling of oppression associated with being her father. It made her want to cry.

Filled with apprehension, she walked quickly through the hallway and down the stairs. Father held open the study door for her. "Sit down, Katrine."

She waited until Father was settled in his favorite chair, an old leather thing Mother often said should be tossed out. Then she got a smaller chair and pulled it opposite him. She chewed on her lower lip, not knowing what to expect.

Father gazed at her, as if he were studying each line of her face. His emotions, when Katrine opened herself to them again, seemed an incomprehensible jumble.

"Master Neyac has asked me to let you go to Pardish with him," Father said with no preamble.

Holding her breath, Katrine waited. She wanted to shriek: *What did you tell him?* But she didn't. She merely sat as still as she could, knowing Father would proceed at his own pace.

"I have spent the whole night trying to decide what to do. I know how unhappy you've been of late. Life as a herder is full of hard, tedious work, and perhaps I've given you more than your share. The reasons seemed justified at the time. Now I'm not sure."

His shoulders lifted as if he were going to shrug it off, but he never completed the gesture. He slumped deeper into his chair and looked away.

Father was never uncertain. To Katrine, it felt as if the world had slipped off center and was now spinning off in a new direction. It frightened her.

"Even though," Father said, looking at her again, "I have always known someday you would leave, I wish you had happier memories of home to take with you. I didn't know it would be like this or I might have done things differently.

"Since the attack on Luren's family, I'm frightened for you, you more than the other children. Because of your temperament, I know you won't thrive if I confine you to the manor. Yet how can I allow you to go out on the plains by yourself anymore? I'm not sure I can keep you safe here, but having you leave and travel to Pardish doesn't seem like a good option either."

He pushed out of his chair and crossed to a window. With one hand he parted the drapes, his back to her. A faint rosy streak of light was barely coloring the horizon.

"So, Katrine, I've decided to leave the decision to you. Will you go to Pardish, or will you stay at home a while longer?"

Tears surprised Katrine's eyes, and she fought to keep her voice from breaking. "Why does Master Neyac want me to go with him, Father? We've never discussed the possibility of my attending the School there. It's what I want, but— "

"I can't explain now. If you choose to accompany Neyac, maybe he'll tell you about it during your journey. However, I do know your destiny doesn't lie with the Recorders School. Not yet. There are other things you must accomplish first."

The Spire of Kylet

"But being a Recorder is all I've ever wanted," Katrine said. Teardrops rolled down her cheeks and dripped from her chin onto her tunic.

Father's voice was solemn, maybe even sad, when he spoke. "Sometimes we don't get exactly what we want, when we want it, Katrine. Sometimes we must submit to a pattern that's larger than our own designs." Father shifted his position, exposing a grim profile. "It's what I must do by letting you choose. It isn't easy."

"I don't understand. If Neyac doesn't want to take me to Pardish to become a Recorder, then why does he want me?"

Father didn't answer.

Unrelenting pressure built in Katrine's chest until she feared her heart would be crushed by it. If only Father would turn so she could read his expression, if only he would give her a hint about his wishes.

"What should I do, Father?" she said, crying. "What do you expect of me?"

Father's voice was almost inaudible. "I expect you to do what you must, to be strong and brave, and to find your destiny."

With her spine rigid, Katrine stared at her hands. She had clasped them so tightly together that her knuckles had gone white.

Why was the decision so hard? Hadn't she been plotting her escape every waking moment for months? Wasn't this what she wanted?

Why was she hesitating?

When Father said people sometimes had to submit to a pattern larger than themselves, the words had resonated in her ears and echoed in the depths of her soul until her whole body quaked in recognition of a powerful truth.

Apparently part of her destiny was to deliver Kylet's message to the Warrior. She certainly couldn't do that sitting in the safety of the manor. This must be the trip Kylet told her she would be taking. Maybe she would be allowed to study at Pardish after the communication was delivered.

Or perhaps all of this was to prepare her for something else entirely.

It was all so confusing.

No, it wasn't.

Right now, she really only had one choice.

"I know I have to leave Banur." Katrine dried her face on the hem of her tunic. "I've known for a long time. I'll go with Neyac."

"So be it," Father said softly. When he turned from the window, his face was both sorrowful and proud. He held out his arms, and she flew to him to cry anew on his shoulder.

* * *

Katrine sorted through her clothing and books, trying to decide what she could live without and what she had to take with her to be comfortable. She couldn't think too far into the future. Focusing on packing right now was enough.

Later in the afternoon, she asked Father if she could go say goodbye to her friends. Although he gave his permission, he insisted that Brac's sons, Trinnin and Urbol, accompany her.

On the way to Rand's house, she saw Anton across the lane in the company of an old man.

She had seen them together once before, she thought.

As she strained to identify the stranger, last night's headache returned, thumping at the base of her skull and behind her eyes. She nudged her horse with her heels and he took off at a gallop. She hoped the sting of the wind would clear her head. Trinnin and Urbol kept abreast of her, one riding on each side.

* * *

Anton and Hollenth ambled from the lane into the trees.

"Having her gone," Anton said, "will be a relief, but I want more. There must be some way I can turn it to my advantage with Father."

"Your biggest disadvantage," Hollenth replied, "will be your parents' tendency to forget her shortcomings in her absence. You'll have to be careful if you criticize her, or you might alienate them completely."

"But how can I show Father what a calculating, deceitful fraud she is?"

Draping an arm around Anton's shoulders, Hollenth smiled, exposing discolored crooked teeth. "We'll do some calculating of our own. I'm sure we can devise a few subtle but revealing comments, ones that will elevate you in your father's eyes and discredit her at the same time."

Anton smirked. "Good. It'll serve her right after everything she's done to make me look bad."

* * *

Sitting in the parlor at Orchard Manor, while Trinnin and Urbol waited outside, Katrine told Rand about going to Pardish.

"I'm happy for you, 'Trine," he said. "I can tell how much you want to go, but things won't be the same around here without you."

After they had reminisced for a while, Rand walked Katrine to her horse. He said casually, "My father has arranged a meeting with Polnu's parents." A sudden grin brightened his face. "If all goes well, Polnu and I will be betrothed this winter and wed next summer."

Screeching with delight, Katrine threw her arms around him. "It's about time you did something right."

Cheeks flaming, he laughed. "I was bound to, sooner or later. You'll be back by summer, won't you?"

"I don't know." She felt a cloud of worry rush over her, but she pushed it back and spoke cheerfully. "I really have no way of knowing what's going to happen, but I certainly intend to dance at your wedding."

After Orchard Manor, they went to Glaine's Stand, and once again Trinnin and Urbol waited patiently while Katrine took her time visiting.

She and Polnu gossiped and giggled about Rand, for the first time discussing him not as their mutual friend but as Polnu's sweetheart. Although redefining the relationship between her two best friends felt a little odd to Katrine, Polnu was just as radiant with happiness as Rand was, so she knew this new affiliation was as it should be.

Katrine spoke briefly to Polnu's parents, stopped to see several friends she had met during the Festival of the Full Moon, and then sought a private interview with The Glaine.

Bainu gave Brac's sons each a cup of cider and some light snacks and invited them to relax on her front porch. She and Katrine settled in a private garden at the back of her house.

The yard was well tended. Flowers in earthenware pots added splotches of color along a low fence. Bainu sat on a bench in the shade of a tree and Katrine sat on the ground by her feet. She told Bainu about Neyac and his invitation for her to accompany him to Pardish. A strange expression flitted across Bainu's face. Then it was gone.

"I feel your doubts," Bainu said as she handed Katrine a cup of cider and a plate of jemnut cakes. "Sometimes it clarifies matters to explain them to someone else."

"I wish I could." Katrine took a sip of cider and found it was just the way she liked it, tart not sweet. "Things have been changing so fast I don't have time to adjust to one situation before I'm confronted with the next. I feel like I'm just jumping from one crisis to another, hardly able to catch my breath in between them."

"That is the nature of life, child. Change is the only constant besides death."

Nodding silently, Katrine tried to absorb the day and fashion it into a memory to treasure while she was gone. Everything looked vibrant and exceptionally lovely this afternoon: Bainu's yard, the surrounding hills, the prairie, the fluffy clouds blowing in from the north, the nuts and spices in the cake she was eating.

"I'm going to miss all this," she said. "I don't know when I'll be back. I got the impression from Father that it might be quite a while." She followed the last bite of cake with a swallow of cider and then brushed crumbs off her front. "But that's not why I came. I really need to know more about the Crennese heritage. I had a very eerie experience last night at Heni's party."

As Katrine described the headache, blurry vision, and dizziness, Bainu listened attentively.

"I've never known anyone to experience those symptoms after a Tribal Joining," Bainu said. "Perhaps you'll find a clue in the Book of White Spells. Try it. I wish I had ready answers for you, but I don't."

To hide her disappointment, Katrine picked up the cup and finished her drink. "Maybe I was overly tired, though I didn't feel that way earlier in the evening. It was awful. I just hope it doesn't happen again."

"As do I," agreed Bainu. "But tell me, how do you feel about this journey with Master Recorder Neyac?" Again that strange look played across The Glaine's face, but it came and went so fast, Katrine didn't have time to analyze it.

She plucked a piece of grass and chewed on the stem. "I'm nervous, of course. I've never traveled anywhere before, but I've always wanted to. Pardish is special because I want to become a Recorder. In some ways it feels right to be going, but—I don't know—it also feels odd."

Bainu nodded. "Sometimes our paths are not of our own choosing but are merely sections of a more extensive track."

"Father told me something similar," Katrine said with mild frustration. She tossed the shredded fragment of grass aside. "It might be easier if someone would just explain to me what's going on and what my role is."

"Or it might be harder. Some things must be grown into. Boots are one. Destiny is another." Bainu smiled as she stood. "Come, you'll have to hurry if you're going to be home before dark."

As they walked through the house, Bainu held onto Katrine's hand. "I believe I know a little of what awaits you, and there is a way the tribe can help even though you'll be far from us. At each full moon until your task has been completed, we'll gather in the field outside the village and combine our powers as we did at the Tribal Joining. No matter where you are, no matter what you are doing, the strength of our unity will support and sustain you. Drink our power like a potion, and it will provide sustenance for a starving soul as well as rejuvenation for a failing body."

Chapter Twenty

Katrine decided not to take much with her: a few clothes, a hair brush, her money, the book Bainu gave her, Kylet's spire, her bow and quiver, and her painting materials. After filling her saddlebags and art satchel, she only needed to add one small carry-case to make it all fit. She collected her things together and meandered downstairs.

She stopped outside Father's study, where he, Neyac, and Sal were studying the large map of Kareand that hung on the wall behind Father's desk.

"We shouldn't have any trouble between Banur and Sendig," Sal told Father. "This time of year, the Western Caravan Route is full of farmers taking their goods to Market."

"We'll stop at an inn or hostel each evening at dusk," said Neyac.

"So if you're going to have trouble," Father said, marking a path with his finger, "this area of the Plains Trail is the most likely spot?"

"Right," said Sal. "We could go on up to Wydle and take the Central Route, but it would add weeks. We'll just have to be especially cautious between Sendig and Plains Springs. After that, the population gets denser and there are more peacekeepers on patrol."

Katrine knew her father was worried. He had suggested that the Recorders and Katrine travel with Heni as far as Branston and then complete the trip north by riverboat. Even with farmers taking their goods up the Western Caravan Route, a party of three (Katrine, Neyac, and Torrend) would be vulnerable. Traveling with Heni and her guards doubled their numbers and their security. Branston, Heni's hometown, was large enough to have its own Landorian Warriors Compound, as did most of the major cities along the Great Meriad River.

Although Katrine didn't look forward to a prolonged journey with her cousin, she understood the need.

At the last minute, much to Katrine's embarrassment, Father decided to send Trinnin, Brac's eldest son, along as Katrine's personal guard.

A solemn gathering stood outside the manor to bid the little band farewell. Rosi presented them with an enormous basket full of goodies, which Torrend stashed inside Heni's carriage, and then Rosi gave Trinnin and Katrine each a big blubbering kiss and a tight hug.

In turn, Katrine embraced each of her siblings, including Anton, who didn't even try to hide his delight at her departure. She ended with her favorite.

Skotlan had one big tear in each eye.

Brushing her fingers through his thick, unruly auburn hair, Katrine realized it would be weeks, months, maybe a year before she enjoyed this familiarity again. She had a catch in her voice as she said, "You take good care of Stubbs."

"You know I will," Skotlan croaked. "Be careful, 'Trine. Don't forget to come home." With an anguished sob, he fled to the house. He took a large chunk of Katrine's heart with him.

She had to blink back tears before she could face saying goodbye to her parents.

"Father," she said, "I'll miss your birth celebration next month. I got this for you at the trader's market. I hope you like it." She had wrapped the book in brown paper and tied a blue ribbon around it.

"Thank you, Katrine." He accepted the package and then handed her a small coin purse in return. "I've given Neyac sufficient funds to cover your expenses, but I want you to have some money just for spending. You are going to see cities larger and more elaborate than you can possibly imagine. If something strikes your fancy, I want you to be able to purchase it. May peace go with you, daughter."

"Thank you," she whispered in his ear as she embraced him.

"We'll count the days until you return," Mother said. She lifted a wisp of hair that had fallen across Katrine's cheek and smoothed it back into place, tucking the ends into the base of her braid. "Write often. Neyac can show you how to hire a runner or to find the mail caravans in each city. Oh, do be safe, Katrine."

"I will, Mother. I promise."

They held each other for a long time.

Mother finally pushed away and flung her arms around Father, muffling her sobs against his chest. He held her in his arms protectively.

Katrine leaped onto Thunder Cloud's back, waved, and called a generalized farewell. Eyes straight ahead, she rode through the manor gates and turned north.

Behind her, she heard Trinnin say goodbye to his family while Neyac shared a few last remarks with Father. Jaimi and Heni were talking so fast that the sound of their words slurred together. Torrend made a light-hearted comment to someone.

The creaking of leather stirrups taking on weight informed her when the men mounted. Soon she heard the clatter of carriage wheels and the steady clip-clop of the two plains ponies that pulled it.

Longingly, Katrine wished to turn and take one last look at the family she knew she would miss beyond imagining. She was afraid if she did, however, the tears dammed up inside would break through, and she would spin around and gallop back home again.

* * *

They spent the first night at a roadside inn just north of Drena. When Katrine swung off Thunder Cloud's back, her knees started to buckle, and she had to grab hold of the saddle to steady herself before trying to stagger forward a few steps. "I don't know what's wrong with me," she groaned to Torrend as they unhooked their saddlebags. "I've practically lived my whole life on horseback."

"It may seem like it," he said, "but I'll bet you never spent as much time continuously in the saddle as you did today. I felt the same way you do now after Neyac and I left Nallee. If it's any comfort, it gets easier."

"I'll take your word for it."

While the Master Recorder negotiated with the stable hand, Katrine leaned against a stall and flexed her legs. Torrend was right. When she had watched the herds, she also mended fences, walked along the river, practiced with her bow or spire, chased yearlings, cleared the irrigation troughs, and engaged in any number of activities that kept her limber.

Earlier in the day, as their horses plodded behind a swaying wagon pulled by four oxen, Neyac had suggested she ride in the coach with Heni and get some rest. She had opted to stay with Thunder Cloud and was now paying the price. As she walked from the stables to the inn, she tried to hold her shoulders straight and her gait steady, but her muscles cried out in protest and she ended up lumbering awkwardly.

The inn's dining hall was overflowing with farmers and ranchers and merchants, all stopping for a meal or stout drink after a day of jostling along the crowded roads. Several men played cards at one table, and in the back of the room a few couples danced to a bright tune performed by three musicians. People elbowed past each other, and occasionally an argument erupted when one person inadvertently bumped or blocked another.

When a table was cleared near the door, Neyac hustled over and claimed it for their party.

Rumors about trouble on the roads filled the hall. In addition, several versions of the attack on Luren's farm were in circulation.

At first, Katrine wondered if her father had kept grisly details from her, but when one old woman with hardly any teeth loudly insisted she knew for a fact that everyone in the Luren household had been found on the front lawn with their heads cut off, Katrine realized it was just another story growing with each telling. When she tried to assure the woman that Calli and the children were fine and the Healers even thought Luren was going to pull through, the woman told Katrine to shut up and stop spreading wild tales.

While they waited for their food, Neyac and Sal questioned a few travelers and then sat drinking ale and discussing what they'd heard, trying to sort fact from fiction. Trinnin stayed so close to Katrine, she sometimes feared that if she scratched her ear, she would bloody his nose with her elbow.

"I hate wearing a sword," Katrine heard Neyac complain between big swigs of ale, "but I suppose it is necessary under the circumstances."

All of the men in the room were armed.

Sal caught Katrine's eye. "Do you know swordsmanship?"

"Of course not, Sal," Katrine answered. "Who in Banur would teach me?"

"Too bad," the bald guard said. "You have the makings of a fine swordsman, good wrists and strong shoulders. I could show you the basics, if you'd like, and you could practice with Trinnin in the evenings. I've got an extra blade."

Katrine was flattered, but also alarmed. Their situation had to be desperate for Sal to risk arming someone as clumsy as she was.

She shook her head. "I don't think so. I'd probably cut off my foot, or worse yet, maybe yours."

Sal rewarded her with a good laugh, for which she was grateful. However, she didn't want him to think she was taking the potential danger lightly.

"I'm good with my bow," she said.

"Bows can be useful in a fight. Keep it close."

A tremor of excitement skittered up Katrine's spine, and she assured him she would.

Because of the large crowd, dinner was slow in arriving.

Heni was apparently too tired to complain. She sat next to Katrine in silence, the picture of abject misery.

Although Katrine often rotated her neck and shoulders and shifted positions, she couldn't get comfortable on the hard, backless bench. When a serving girl finally brought bowls of stew and heavy loaves of brown bread, Katrine used knife and spoon out of habit, swallowing without tasting.

The room buzzed with background noise. The air was stuffy and reeked with the smells of spilled ale, greasy food, and unwashed bodies. Exhaustion made Katrine woozy. She was dozing serenely with her head comfortably nestled on her folded arms, inches away from her empty plate, when Neyac shook her and said the innkeeper had come to lead them to sleeping chambers.

She was so tired she didn't even care that she had to share a bed with Heni.

* * *

Elnid-Kyeh held a golden chain so that the crystal dangling from it hung directly over a dot on the tower floor. He recited an incantation, and the crystal inscribed a line running true north and south. He held the bauble over the dot again, said another spell, and it marked east and west, creating a large shimmering 'X' with each arm equidistant from the center.

At the tip of each line, he set a copper saucer. Into the one denoting north, he sprinkled a few chemicals. For south, he added a handful of dirt. East held a lighted candle, and west, a dipperful of water. He began a chant, calling on the elements from all points of the continent, to summon a vision of the object he sought: Kylet's spire.

He tossed a few grains of powder into the northern saucer, which, combining with what was already there, made a puff of smoke. Air, fire, land, water, he invoked their aid. In the middle of the 'X' a picture formed.

That infernal girl had the spire casually wrapped in a rag.

He continued to chant, demanding to see where she was, what she was doing, and where the spire was kept.

The resultant image puzzled him. She was standing beside a carriage, talking to an old man. A large, fierce-looking young man stood behind her. They were in front of a rough-hewn building with horses and people milling all around them.

A tingle began at the base of Elnid-Kyeh's skull. One of his minions was calling. He ignored it, trying to get the images in the vision to become more specific.

The sensation at the back of his neck became sharper and more pronounced. His concentration wavered.

The vision faded away.

Irritated, he looked into the copper vessel holding water, cast a spell, and snapped, "What do you want?"

The face of a woman with garish red hair floated on the water's surface. "Master, I have just learned that the girl has left Banur."

"Where has she gone?"

"To Pardish. She's traveling with a Master Recorder and one of her father's hired men."

Ah, Elnid-Kyeh thought, that would explain the carriage and the men he had seen.

"When did she leave? What route is she taking?"

"They left two days ago. Her father didn't say how they were going, but I imagine they'll go straight up the Western Caravan Route. It's the most direct way. If you want to intercept her, Sendig is the best place. They should reach it tomorrow evening."

"Well done, Felda," Elnid-Kyeh said with a smile. "Very well done indeed."

Chapter Twenty-One

"It's all your fault," yelled Heni as she angrily pointed her finger at Ferrill. "How dare you leave Banur with a defective wheel on my carriage?"

"There is nothing wrong with the wheel," Ferrill answered in a calm voice. He set her bags at the end of the nearest bed in the room she would share with Katrine. "We simply lost a pin. A wheelwright can fix it in a few minutes."

"It's still your fault," Heni insisted shrilly with her arms folded across her chest. "You should have known it was loose or broken or whatever. Now we're going to lose a whole day because of your carelessness."

Torrend and Katrine stood outside the door.

"Are you sure you two are related?" Torrend asked in a whisper.

"Father swears she is his elder brother's daughter."

"It's hard to believe," murmured Torrend, shaking his head. "You're so even tempered, and she's so . . . so extreme."

It had been shortly after they had passed through the town of Edmon, when Trinnin, riding behind the carriage, noticed the wobbly wheel. They pulled off the road, and Trinnin and Sal lifted the edge of the carriage so Ferrill could resituate it. Then Ferrill pounded a wooden peg into the hole where the metal pin should have been.

"That will hold it for now," Ferrill said, "but I think we ought to go back to Edmon. I don't fancy going up and down all the hills between here and Sendig without having it repaired properly."

So they had turned around and crept back to town.

When they found the wheelwright, he agreed that it wouldn't take long to replace the pin, but he had a string of customers who were already waiting and had priority. He couldn't possibly get to it before sometime in the afternoon.

The only good luck they had was at the nearby inn. Because it was still early in the day and most people were scurrying to reach Sendig before nightfall, rooms were made available as soon as Neyac requested them.

149

The Spire of Kylet

Despite having a comfortable place to wait, Heni complained loudly and continuously. When Torrend pulled a game board and a bag of ivory tokens from one of his packs and suggested teaching Katrine how to play Racing Jackals, she agreed, leaving Heni in their room to pout alone.

They left early the next morning to make up time, but when they reached Sendig, they were stopped at the gates by a sentry.

"Unless you have business in the city," he said, "you need to move on. If you're going up the Western Caravan Route you can make it to Haley's Hostel by dark, or if you're turning off onto the Plains Trail, you're only an hour away from Dozer's Tavern. They have a few rooms, and if they're full, they'll let you sleep under the tables in the commons."

"What's the problem here?" asked Neyac. "Why are you turning us away?"

"Murder most foul," the guard replied. "Last night, a farmer and his two children, a strapping lad and a lovely young girl, were killed in their bedrolls. They had just arrived with wares for the market and were sleeping under their wagon."

The guard's voice dropped into a confidential whisper. "I have this directly from my wife's brother, who was on the way to his job at the bakery before the first peacekeepers arrived. He said the bodies were ripped to shreds. Witnesses said there were five or six men and the most vicious dog-like creature imaginable. They went straight after that poor family. The city is plumb full of peacekeepers and Landorian Warriors trying to figure out who and what and why." His voice dropped down another notch. "People are saying it was black magic, pure and simple. Conjured killers and a supernatural beast."

* * *

Elnid-Kyeh felt better than he had in a long time. The girl was dead, and his agents had her possessions.

The 'X' of the divination spell was still visible on the floor. It would last perhaps another day. He might as well use it to make sure the spire was safe.

He lighted the candle, added a little more water, replenished the chemicals, and smoothed the dirt. Then he invoked the power of the elements once again.

When the vision formed, he staggered backward.

The spire was in the girl's saddlebag. The saddlebag was on a gray horse and so was the girl! Shaking with fury, he recast the spell, this time seeking the infernal idiots who were supposed to have taken care of her.

When the vision unfolded, he grimaced with revulsion, but not with surprise. Sprawled around a dead campfire, the hired men were obviously in a drunken stupor.

Gradually, Elnid-Kyeh pushed the image back so he could identify the surrounding area. They were in a small grotto in a forest, not more than half a day's ride from Sendig.

The bunglers!

Not only had they killed the wrong girl, but they did not even have the sense to get far enough away to avoid capture. He would have to take care of them before peacekeepers or Warriors located them and questioned them under Crennese truth spells.

He wished he could teleport himself there and have the pleasure of dealing with the mercenaries in person, but representatives from his allies were due to arrive any moment. Teleportation spells took a great deal of energy and always left him fatigued, especially when covering great distances. Even projecting his image as far as the grotto would be somewhat draining.

Well, he had better get it over with quickly so he had a few minutes to rest before going into council.

With one huge mental pull, he gathered power. Bottles shattered. The dark green leaves of the trilobian plant beside the window wilted and dropped from the stalk.

He waved his hands.

A flash of lightning struck the campfire's remnants, and his image appeared in the cavern.

"You killed the wrong girl!" he yelled to make sure he could be heard through the leader's drunken haze.

"No s'r," the leader slurred. "She 'uz th' on'y tall, blon' g'rl in th'—in th'—" His voice cracked. He tried again. "in the ca—" He coughed and spat out a big wad of phlegm. "—in th' cammmmmp wi' a ol' man an' a young'un."

Elnid-Kyeh stared at the spittle that had landed a scant inch from his projected foot.

The man was an imbecile!

Again Elnid-Kyeh gathered power. Taking careful aim, he threw a spell through the vision, straight at the leader's head.

All around the shallow cave, grass wasted away, going from green to yellow to brown to dust in seconds. Birds tumbled from trees. Dried leaves rained from branches that became brittle and gnarled. The drunken men shrunk in on themselves until the skin that stretched across their bones looked like ancient leather.

* * *

After a night on the floor at Dozer's Tavern, which even with sweeping and mopping still reeked from decades of dirty boots and dining spills, Katrine was grateful to be on the road again.

Trinnin and Neyac led the way, always on alert, scrutinizing the caravans and travelers they passed. Katrine and Torrend rode behind them, and the carriage followed with Sal perched on top next to Ferrill and Heni tucked safely inside.

Journeying on the Plains Trail was more tedious and unpleasant than it had been on the Western Caravan Route. For one thing, it was boring. Before, just keeping abreast of the crowd had been distracting, and every now and then someone interesting had ridden by.

Also, there had been small towns, rustic hovels, fruit and vegetable stands, inns, ale houses, and gambling halls to look at, not to mention the fascinating people wandering in and out of the buildings.

Here, the plains seemed to stretch on forever with little to distinguish the landscape except an occasional wooded area, a few scattered farmsteads, tiny roadside hostels, and hardly any other travelers at all.

Although Neyac sometimes led the group in song or recited poems and stories, Katrine often wondered what she would be doing if she were at home. Checking the herdbeasts, visiting friends, talking with her family, studying, painting, even fighting plains cats, were all things she had taken for granted and now missed.

When they stopped in a village called Oakleaf, two drunkards battled each other with bare fists in front of the little town's combination tavern and inn. Half a dozen men and a couple of youths watched and yelled encouragement to one combatant or the other.

As Heni climbed from the carriage, Katrine looked at her with a hint of respect for her ability to endure such trips.

"Is it always like this?" she asked.

Heni glanced at the drunkards and nodded. "At least in this area, it is."

"Traveling isn't as much fun as I thought it would be," Katrine said, stretching and bending to loosen her back and shoulders. "How can you stand to do this again and again?"

"It does get tiresome," Heni said, covering a yawn with a dainty little hand. "You can ride with me if you want. I usually doze quite a bit. It helps pass the time."

"I don't think Thunder Cloud would like following the carriage on a lead rope, but thanks for offering."

As if noticing Katrine's mount for the first time, Heni said, "He surely is a beautiful horse, noble and stately."

"Thank you." Katrine caught herself starting to grin, stopped herself, and then allowed it to blossom. It was probably the first sincere smile she had ever given her cousin.

Although several people were scattered throughout the tavern, it wasn't crowded. When Neyac inquired, he learned that most of the travelers would be camping under their wagons, and the rest of the patrons were local farmers and ranchers. A small caravan that had been expected earlier in the day had failed to arrive, so Neyac was able to engage three bedchambers. They had just finished eating and were headed to their rooms when two battered and bloodied men staggered through the door.

"We were attacked east of here," one man cried. "Many are wounded. Can you help us? Anyone?"

Uneasily the people in the dining hall shifted in their seats. They glanced around as if they suspected treachery from the people at the next table or from the injured men themselves.

Neyac planted his fists on his hips and fixed a stern eye on the homespun customers. "That could have been any one of us out there. If it were, we'd have to depend on the help of others, just like these men. Come on, folks. Evil can only win when good men fail to take action."

"The Powers bless ye, sir," one man said with a sob. "We've got women out there, and children. Most of the men are dead."

When Trinnin and Sal stationed themselves behind Neyac, folding their arms so bulging biceps were visible and adding their impassioned scowls to the Recorder's, people began shoving back their chairs and offering their assistance.

Even with the combined efforts of all the tavern's customers, it was nearly midnight before the rescue mission was completed. What goods were salvageable were gathered by torchlight, the slain were buried under the sod, and a small pyre consumed the carcasses of a few beloved pets killed by the marauders for sport. The injured were transported back to the inn on a flat-bedded wagon the innkeeper provided.

After the village Healer had treated the most seriously wounded, they were given the bedchambers.

Katrine and her friends spread their bedrolls on the tavern floor like everyone else.

"I've never seen anything like it," one survivor told them. "We put up a white flag as soon as we seen them charging. We offered them all the coins we had. Didn't do no good. They attacked us anyway."

"Wasn't till we was all down," a second man continued, "dead or knocked out or too hurt to keep fighting, that they scooped up the money and began pillaging the wagons, and—and— "

"And raping the women," the first man said bitterly.

With scraped and battered hands pressed hard against his face, the other man muffled a sob.

"They laughed while they done it," the first man said, his voice cracking with emotion. "All the time, someone was laughing."

Chapter Twenty-Two

"I asked the innkeeper about a caravan," Neyac said at breakfast, his fork poised halfway to his mouth. "There isn't another one due until next week."

"Too bad," said Sal. "I hate to turn back."

"Turn back?" cried Heni. She had started spreading cranifruit jam on a small triangle of bread, but stopped. "Who said anything about turning back?"

With his gravelly voice amazingly gentle, Sal answered her. "Safety is our primary concern. Until the outlaws who attacked the caravan yesterday are caught and dealt with, the Plains Trail will be too dangerous for a small company like us."

"We could wait here for a few days," suggested Trinnin. "Maybe the peacekeepers will find them quickly."

"Staying here might be no safer than going on," Neyac said, "or going back for that matter."

"I want to go *home*," wailed Heni. "I don't want to stay, and I don't want to go back. I want to go *HOME*."

People all around the room turned and stared.

Exchanging glances, Katrine and Torrend picked up their plates and headed for the door. Trinnin was right behind them. They ate on a narrow, weathered porch that extended the width of the inn. From inside, Heni's voice continued to rise. When Katrine, Torrend, and Trinnin rejoined their companions, the discussion was over and Heni looked disgustingly smug.

They were moving on.

By midmorning, a gentle sprinkle had begun dampening hair and clothing. By mid-afternoon, the light shower had turned into a constant, irritating rain. In the distance was a tall forest and, with water trickling down her neck, Katrine was anxious to reach it so the canopy of autumn leaves could provide some shelter.

As they neared the trees, Neyac and Trinnin slowed. Ferrill stopped the carriage, and Sal hopped down.

154

"I don't like the looks of this," Neyac said. "It's a perfect hiding place for the marauders."

Sal peered in both directions. "The forest is too big to go around. We'll have to brave it eventually, unless you want to backtrack."

"No," Heni wailed, leaning out of the carriage window. "You said we were going home. You promised me. You absolutely, solemnly promised."

"Frankly," Sal muttered, "I'd rather face bandits than put up with much more of that. Let's go on."

"We could gag her," Trinnin suggested with rare humor.

Katrine started to giggle, but the seriousness on the men's faces cut her amusement short.

"Better get your bow, Katrine," Trinnin said, "just in case." Following his own advice, he got his from its case.

Neyac loosened the blade at his side, and the other men did the same. Sal pulled out a dagger and clutched it in his left hand while holding a sword in his right. After wrapping the reins around his fist, Ferrill drew his blade and laid it on the seat beside him.

Glancing about nervously, Katrine swung off her horse and retrieved her bow from the oilskin case fastened to her pack. She positioned the quiver across her back and unhooked the top closure. When she had strung her bow, she remounted and held it tight. With her elbow she felt for the knife on her belt.

As they entered the forest, everything turned preternaturally quiet. Except for the faint rustling of fallen leaves beneath the horses' hooves and the thrumming of the carriage wheels, all was silent. Not a bird chirped. Not one small animal chattered or barked or brayed.

Trees stretched above the trail, their knobby branches intertwined like skeletal hands, and hid what little light the gray sky offered. Thick brush crowded against the road on each side, making the track narrow and confining. Unidentifiable dark shapes slithered around trunks and between vines and peered from beneath moldering clumps of shrubbery.

Occasionally a drip or falling leaf caught Katrine on the face or arms, startling her with sudden fright.

As if their voices might call down disaster, the little band rode through the gloom without speaking. Even the horses seemed skittish. They stepped lightly with their ears perked and their eyes wide.

All of a sudden, a fearful foreboding washed over Katrine, crashing against her in disorienting waves. The feeling reminded her of the pulsating discomfort she'd experienced at the dance for Heni. Her head began to throb, but instead of going blurry, everything seemed to snap into crystal clarity.

Ahead, the trees were growing sparser, and for some unfathomable reason, Katrine wanted to scream "RUN" and dash for the clearing. She peered into the shadows, first on the right and then on the left, scanning for anything out of the ordinary, anything that might explain her disquieting sensations.

The Spire of Kylet

There was nothing.

Neyac or Sal would notice if anything were amiss, she told herself. *They have both traveled this road many times.*

Still, the feelings not only persisted but also intensified.

Muscles tingling, heart racing, breath coming in ragged puffs, she nudged Thunder Cloud forward.

The attack came just as she reached Neyac's side.

About two-dozen bandits, all mounted and brandishing swords, thundered out of the trees on both sides of them.

"Make for the clearing," Trinnin yelled at Katrine. Nevertheless, he didn't spur his horse forward. He reined it around.

Katrine hesitated and looked over her shoulder.

She watched Sal lean forward and slash his sword across the breasts of two men who tried to climb up beside him. On the other side of the wagon, twisted in the saddle, Trinnin forced the bandits back with a bevy of arrows.

"Come on, Katrine," Neyac shouted.

With a kick, Katrine urged Thunder Cloud forward, but her skin crawled with shivers as she imagined an arrow or knife catching her unprotected back.

Just as she cleared the woods, a scream rang out.

The carriage, pulled by stubby-legged plains ponies, was lagging behind. It was obviously the marauders' objective. They clamored around it like vultures on carrion, trying to force it to stop.

As Katrine watched helplessly, two men swung onto the carriage roof. One crawled toward Sal, and the other dangled by one hand as he tried to open the carriage door. Heni leaned out the window and pounded on his arms with dainty fists.

To prevent a third man from leaping from his horse onto one of the ponies, Sal flung a dagger at him, catching the bandit square in the heart. Then he spun around, grabbed a handful of tunic, pulled the man from the roof, and heaved him over the side into two of his outlaw companions. When all three hit the ground, the ones galloping behind trampled them without so much as a downward glance.

Trinnin, now behind the carriage, aimed an arrow at the man dangling from the door. When he missed the mark, Katrine couldn't help grinning. Trinnin never missed. She would tease him mercilessly when this was all over. Then he toppled forward, and she saw the dagger in his back.

Within her, a rage like she had never known before erupted and filled her with burning white hatred.

Without hesitation, she nocked an arrow to the bowstring and completed the shot Trinnin had missed. Then, in rapid succession, she took out another marauder and the man next to him. Their horses, without masters to guide them, bolted for the clearing in front of the clattering carriage.

Heni screamed franticly.

Two more men swung up onto the carriage. With a twang, Katrine loosed an arrow at one. He fell. Before she could get the second, he lunged forward and had Ferrill by the neck. With a quick thrust, Sal dispatched the man he was fighting, and then whirling around, he stabbed the man tussling with Heni's young driver.

Other outlaws rode behind, unable to pass because of the narrowness of the road and the swaying of the buggy.

"We've got to do something," Torrend cried out. He raised his heels to kick his mount, but Neyac snatched the reins.

"You'll just get in the way," Neyac shouted back. "When they reach the clearing, you'll have your chance to fight."

Katrine launched another arrow. It lodged in the shoulder of a man who stood in the stirrups and stretched to reach the carriage door. He lost his balance and tumbled forward. He grabbed the door handle, and his legs swung in front of the rear wheel. His grip failed. He hit the ground, and the carriage bumped over him.

Will they never stop coming? Katrine thought as she loosed another arrow. While she watched her target fall, two other men managed to board the carriage. Sal battled them both. Katrine wanted to even the odds, but she was afraid of hitting Sal if the bouncing buggy made the men suddenly shift position.

Out of nowhere, a knife caught Ferrill in the ribs. He grabbed his side, looking very young and frightened, and then he crumpled like a rag doll and fell over the side of the wagon. A man leaped onto a carriage pony, snatched up the reins, and just as the rig cleared the trees, turned it from the trail.

The sudden change of direction caused Sal and the men he fought to vanish from view. Horses carrying two bandits pounded after the wagon. The others rode straight for Katrine and the Recorders.

"Get out of here," Neyac shouted at Katrine. "You don't have a sword. Help Heni if you can."

As Katrine took off after the carriage, she heard the clang of steel against steel as Neyac and Torrend defended themselves.

Clutching her horse with her knees and gripping the reins and her bow with her left hand, Katrine tried to fit a shaft to the bowstring. She cursed under her breath as the jostling ride interfered. Finally, matching her swaying rhythm to the horse's rolling gallop, she managed to ready an arrow. The first shot went wide. She immediately nocked another. It found the back of one of the riders.

The other man swung around and charged at Katrine, sword held high over his head. As he neared her, though, he faltered. In his moment of indecision, Katrine drew her knife, ducked under his arm, and thrust upward with all her might. She heard him tumble to the ground behind her as she passed by. She didn't slow down enough to turn and look to see if he was dead.

Ahead, the carriage tossed and ricocheted along the bumpy ground. Katrine knew it would overturn any minute now. As she narrowed the distance between them, she raised her bow.

The man who was riding the carriage pony saw her coming and gaped in horror. He jumped in front of Katrine's charging horse and hit the ground with a thunk. As if this happened every day, Thunder Cloud leapt over him without so much as breaking his stride.

Pacing the ponies, Katrine reached for the harness. She missed twice before she caught it. As she reined Thunder Cloud in, the ponies began to slow.

There was a loud snap as the wagon bounced over a large rock and lurched dangerously to one side before coming to a lopsided halt.

"Are you all right?" Katrine called to her cousin.

"I—I—I think so." Heni's voice crackled with suppressed sobs. "Are we safe?"

"For now. I'm going to check on Neyac and Torrend."

As she turned and headed back toward the trail, she heard Heni shriek, "Come back. Don't leave me alone."

Chapter Twenty-Three

The picture in the scrying dish faded, and Elnid-Kyeh sat with his fingers steepled, staring into nothingness.

How had over twenty seasoned fighters been bested by a few men and a girl?

Inconceivable!

The mercenaries had been highly recommended, and he had paid them good money. His instructions to them had been simple: surround the party on an isolated track, kill them, get the spire, collect whatever other plunder they wanted, and ride away. It should have been simple.

How could they have failed so completely?

He pushed out of his chair and crossed to the eastern window so he could watch huge waves crash against the base of the cliffs. If he loved anything, he loved the raw power of the ocean. During winter, storms hurled brine almost as high as the windows in his tower. He watched the waves until twilight muted everything except the ghostly white of an occasional tall crest.

He returned to his chair and slapped the armrests.

He was sick and tired of working with idiots.

Integrating his ally's soldiers into his regular troops had become a constant battle. Each group believed it was superior to the other and wanted concessions and privileges. His military ranks were filled with contention. The mercenaries he hired were incompetent. He was about ready to start dismembering men and putting the pieces on display to encourage cooperation from the remainder.

Right now, he had to work closely with his generals to prepare for the campaign that would reclaim the monarchy for him.

At the same time, he could not ignore the spire. He rubbed his arm, remembering how Kylet had wounded him in Echo Hall with an insubstantial replica and how it had drained his powers. He could not risk having that weapon used against him once war was declared. Perhaps he ought to put the problem of the girl and the spire into the hands of a professional.

* * *

The rain had diminished to an occasional drip, and overhead a few scattered patches of deep blue were visible.

To the west, the clouds were outlined in orange and gold with long purple streaks parallel to the horizon.

In the fading light Katrine could just make out Neyac and Torrend in the distance, standing by their horses. Neyac was tying a cloth around Torrend's arm, up near the shoulder. On the ground were the bodies of several dead outlaws.

"Are you all right?" Katrine called to them.

Neyac waved as he shouted back. "We'll live. How's Heni?"

"She'll live, too."

Katrine and Thunder Cloud changed directions.

When she located the bandit who had jumped from the carriage pony, she paused. He was dead. From the unnatural angle of the body, she was sure his neck was broken, as were his legs.

She retrieved her knife from the chest of the man she'd stabbed and the arrows from the bodies of the others.

Lying where the wagon had veered off course, she found Sal's body beside the two men he had been fighting. Apparently, he'd finished them off before succumbing to his injuries. Ferrill was also dead, as were the outlaws littering the roadway.

Katrine continued up the trail until she found Trinnin. She knelt beside him. He groaned.

"Don't move," she said. "I'll get Neyac. He'll know what to do for you."

"No use," Trinnin whispered. "I'll be gone before you get back. I'm glad you're all right."

"Shhh. Don't talk." Katrine laid her fingers gently across his lips and felt them purse slightly before he choked back a cough. Blood oozed from the corner of his mouth.

"Tell my parents I died honorably." His voice was faint, and his breath was labored. "And tell your father I did my best." His body quivered, his head lolled to the side, and then he was still.

In a daze, Katrine climbed to her feet and continued to collect arrows, wiping the blood from the tips on the clothing of the dead and then placing the shafts in her quiver.

Suddenly she paused.

What was she doing?

Reality crashed down on her.

Trinnin was dead.

Sal and Ferrill were dead.

Her legs gave out. She thumped to the ground. Tears coursed down her cheeks. She hugged her legs to her chest and rested her head on her knees.

This couldn't be real. It had to be a nightmare.

Wake up, Katrine. Wake up.

But it was real.

Her friends were dead. The marauders were dead.

She, Katrine of Banur, had killed people.

Her mind couldn't wrap itself around the facts.

Somehow, though, it had felt quite natural to slay the man Trinnin had missed. In fact, she had done all her killing without much thought.

How could that be? Even when she'd had to kill a plains cat to protect her father's herds, she had felt a certain amount of trepidation. What was happening to her? Had something, somehow, hardened her heart?

All of a sudden, she felt sick. Nausea washed over her. On hands and knees, she vomited until she was almost too weak to move.

Lurching upright, she hoisted herself back into the saddle.

However, when she saw Torrend help Heni out of the carriage and could hear her hysterical sobbing, Katrine slid to the ground, unable to deal with her demanding cousin yet.

After a while, Neyac came for her. She kept her face averted, shamed and frightened and lonely. Thunder Cloud clomped along behind her, his breath warming the back of her neck.

"We'll have to spend the night here," Neyac said. "The front axle is broken, and there's no way to fix it. We'll have to abandon the carriage in the morning."

"We can't," cried Heni. "How will we get to Branston?"

"We'll manage," Neyac said soothingly. "One of your ponies can carry the supplies, and you can ride the other."

"What about Ferrill and Sal? They can't walk the whole way." Her voice took on a tone of panic as she glanced around frantically. "Where are they?"

"I'm sorry, my dear," Neyac said. "They were both killed by the bandits."

"No," Heni howled. "They can't be dead. I need them. They protect me."

"We'll take care of you now," Torrend said. "We won't let anything happen to you while we ride—"

"No, no, no," Heni shrieked. "I don't know how to ride. I've never been on a horse, and now you want me to ride a carriage pony without a saddle? I can't do it. Never. I can't. I can't."

"Maybe we can catch one of the bandits' horses for you in the morning," suggested Torrend. "They've all run off for now, but without their mast—"

Crumpling to the ground, Heni began to bawl deafeningly.

"I hate horses," she wailed. "We've got to fix the carriage. It's the only way. I can't ride. I can't. You're plotting against me. You don't care what happens to me. All of you hate me."

"Shut up, Heni," Katrine growled, glaring angrily at her cousin.

Heni pulled back in fright and shut up.

The Spire of Kylet

Appalled by her cousin's self-absorption and whining, Katrine stalked away.

* * *

"What's the matter, Heni?" Torrend asked when he saw the terror on her face. "Are you all right?"

"Did—did—did you see her eyes?" Heni croaked in a harsh whisper. "They were terrible, like they were on fire. I think she wanted to kill me. Did you see?"

Startled, Torrend looked at Katrine. All he could see was her retreating back.

"I'd better go talk with her," Neyac said quietly to Torrend. "You stay and take care of Heni."

Nodding, Torrend sat on the ground next to Heni and slipped his arm around her shoulders.

"The twilight often makes things look strange," he said soothingly. "Don't worry. I won't let anything hurt you."

* * *

Katrine whistled for Thunder Cloud, and he stopped grazing to join her. She removed his saddle, blanket, and bridle and wiped him down with some cloths from her bag.

While she worked, she thought of home.

Father had given her the tack shortly after her stay at Glaine's Stand, and Mother had woven the blue and black saddle blanket on a small loom she had set up in the parlor.

What would they think of her when they found out about tonight? Would they be repulsed by her violence? She was.

Would they blame her for Trinnin's death?

Would Brac and his wife?

They should. It was her fault.

She could have warned everyone. They could have been prepared.

"It might help to talk about it," Neyac said from behind her.

"I don't think so."

"You fought well, like a soldier or a guard."

"More like a lunatic, you mean."

"We'd be dead if we hadn't fought. Are you sorry we won?"

"No, that's not it." Katrine slumped against Thunder Cloud, letting him support her weight as she looked over his back into the night. "It's my fault we were caught off guard. I thought something was wrong. I had a really bad feeling, but I didn't say anything. Then it was too late."

Neyac moved closer and put his arm around her. "It's possible you saw or heard something that Sal and I missed," he said, "but even if you did, how could you guess what it meant? This is your first journey away from home. I imagine most of what you've experienced seems strange to you. Don't blame yourself."

"But that's not all," Katrine said. She felt just as she had at Glaine's Rest when Bainu confronted her about Kylet's spire, as if she had to make a full confession. Usually, she was slow to admit her failings to adults, but Neyac had the same quiet authority that The Glaine had. She couldn't stop herself from telling him everything.

"No matter what you say, I know it's my fault that we were surprised by the robbers. But the worst part is the way I felt while I was lobbing arrows at them as fast as I could. I was killing men, and I felt good about it. It felt right, as if that's what I was supposed to do. I didn't try to wound anyone. I didn't try to knock anyone from his saddle. I didn't try to scare them away or anything like that. I was trying as hard as I could to kill them—on purpose."

"I don't see that you had any other choice. You were defending yourself and your comrades."

"But some of them might have families, wives and children, who love them and are waiting for them to come home." She balled up her fists and squeezed them hard to keep from crying.

"Mourn your friends, Katrine, but not the bandits. They wouldn't have felt sorry for us if they had won. Nor would they have robbed us and left us unharmed. They might have killed the men outright, but not you and Heni. Not two beautiful young women. They wouldn't have killed the two of you until they tired of all the vile sports they would have enjoyed at your expense. Don't waste a moment feeling bad for them."

Katrine whirled around to face the Recorder.

He flinched and took a step back.

"That's just it, Neyac," Katrine cried. "I don't. Not one bit."

"You want to?"

"Shouldn't I? People aren't supposed to kill people."

"In an ideal world, that's true," Neyac said, "but we don't live in an ideal world. Here, we must always strive against evil or else evil will win."

Nuzzling Thunder Cloud's neck, Katrine ran her fingers through his mane. "I'm sure you're right. I just need a little time to think."

"Before it gets any darker, we need to set up camp. Why don't you build a fire while you're thinking?"

"All right, I will."

Katrine cleared a shallow circular pit and lined its sides with stones.

She used her flint to set fire to a small pyramid of rotted wood and dry leaves she had pulled from a hollow log. Much of the deadfall under the trees was damp from the rain. She added twigs gradually to make sure she didn't snuff out the laboring flames.

Heni sat by the broken carriage, dabbing her eyes with a handkerchief.

The Spire of Kylet

Off to the side of the trail, Neyac and Torrend buried Sal, Ferrill, and Trinnin. Then they gathered the bodies of the marauders for a pyre out on the plains.

By the time they got it burning and had returned, Katrine had vegetables and dried meat simmering in a pot of water over the campfire.

The wind changed and brought with it a foul, charred-flesh smell. Katrine's stomach turned over, and she staggered quickly away from camp before she started retching again.

When she returned, Neyac told her to get her bedroll and to lie down a while.

Then he collected ingredients from the carriage and set about making flat bread. He shaped the dough into patties and dropped them onto an iron sheet he had propped over coals scraped from the fire.

With her blanket wrapped around her shoulders, Katrine watched the Recorder work.

While the bread browned, Neyac pulled one of his bags from the carriage, removed several little packets of spices, and sprinkled bits of them into the soup. "Recorders have to develop a multitude of talents," he said, talking to no one in particular. "Cooking is one of the most practical ones. You hungry?" he asked, peering over at Katrine.

"A little."

On the other side of the fire, Torrend sat down beside Heni, and she clung to his arm as if she were a swimmer and he her only hope of not drowning. Every time Heni looked in Katrine's direction, she cringed and a fearful expression flashed across her face.

"I'm sorry I yelled at you, Heni," Katrine said. "I was upset, but not at you."

Heni shivered and her voice squeaked. "You scared me."

"I didn't mean to. I'm sorry." Changing the subject so she wouldn't end up apologizing to her cousin all night, Katrine turned her attention to Torrend. "How's your arm?"

"It's sore. Neyac bound it, but I hope we'll get to Plains Springs early enough tomorrow that I can find a Healer. No offense intended, Master Recorder."

"None taken," Neyac answered with a smile. "If I were you, I'd want a Healer too."

"I know a little Glainite healing," Katrine said. "Renee, one of the tribal Masters, gave me a medicine pouch as a going-away present." Suddenly embarrassed, she ducked her head, fearing her offer sounded arrogant. "I really don't know much, but maybe I can ease the pain and help prevent festering."

Neyac stared at her quizzically, but when she met his gaze, he began stirring the soup with a big wooden spoon.

"I'll appreciate anything you can do," Torrend said. "It really hurts."

Before fishing the medicine pouch from her saddlebags, Katrine set a cup of water by the fire to heat. Carefully, she removed Torrend's bandage. The laceration was just below the shoulder, a long gash but not too deep. She poured him some wine and stirred in a spoonful of leiti.

"Drink this," Katrine told him. "I'm going to mix an antiseptic, and I'll warn you right off, it stings. The leiti will take the sharp edge off."

After gulping down one big swallow, Torrend looked at her trustingly.

She palpated the area around the wound and quietly recited a couple of healing spells.

"What're you mumbling?" asked Torrend.

"Just some old chants my father taught me."

"I think your water is hot," Neyac said. "Better hurry up with your doctoring. The bread's done and so is the soup."

While the powders dissolved, Katrine tore a swatch of clean cloth from one of her spare tunics. She soaked the fabric in the antiseptic, placed it over the wound with only a slight groan from Torrend, and then tied it into place with another long strip.

"Thank you." Torrend opened his mouth for a huge yawn. "Now that the pain's gone, suddenly I'm quite drowsy."

"That's one of the effects of leiti," Katrine said. "You'd better eat fast because soon you're going to sleep whether you want to or not."

When Neyac dished out the soup, he handed Torrend the first bowl and a large chunk of flat bread.

After Katrine accepted her serving, she dipped the bread into the broth and was happy to discover how quickly it settled her stomach.

Stars peered out of the black sky, and a gibbous moon glowed hazily through a gauze-like strand of clouds.

From the forest, an animal shrieked.

Heni shuddered and looked around warily. "I've never been in the open at night before," she said in a quaking voice. "What if something comes out of the woods and attacks us?"

"The animals will stay away from the fire," Neyac said, "and there probably aren't any other bandits in the area. They tend to be territorial." Muttering under his breath, he added, "If that's what they were."

Katrine's head jerked up. "What do you mean?"

"Of course they were bandits," Heni said quickly. "What else could they have been?" Before Neyac could respond, she answered herself. "Nothing. They saw my fine carriage and thought we had lots of money. They couldn't have been anything else."

"You're probably right," said Neyac with a shrug. "I was just thinking out loud because the attack seemed strange. Why would so large a force bother with one carriage and a few riders? Looking at us, I wouldn't have thought we'd be worth the trouble. Of course, they didn't know we had an expert archer with us," he gave Katrine a wink, "or that all the men were skilled fighters. Still—"

"Are you trying to scare us, Master Recorder?" asked Heni nervously. "If you are, you can stop. I'm already terrified."

"I'm sorry, my dear," Neyac said with real contrition. "Forgive me."

"But I'm really frightened," Heni said. "Maybe you could divert us with a song or story, something light and cheerful."

"Well, now," Neyac replied, stroking his short gray beard thoughtfully, "that's an invitation a Recorder can't resist." Humming softly to himself, he fetched a leather case from among his packs. Opening it, he removed a mandolin. He fiddled with the tuning pegs and then, plucking the strings, began to sing in a bright tenor.

The song he chose was a lighthearted ballad about a cross-eyed, bowlegged young man who tried to woo a beautiful lady by having a Crennese wizard put a spell on him to change his appearance. The girls were delighted with the song, and they both laughed at the ending, which revealed, after describing the wedding, that the beautiful lady was also under a spell and was really old and homely.

The final phrase was "The perfect pair!" Neyac punctuated the words with a flourish along the strings.

"That was lovely," Heni said, patting a yawn with her hand. "Thank you. I guess I'll go lie down in the carriage, though I doubt I'll sleep a wink. Oh, I do wish I could have a hot bath and a soft bed—and maybe a tall fortress with a full militia." She sighed, stood and stretched, then climbed into the coach.

For some time Katrine and Neyac sat listening to the crackling fire. Torrend, with his head on his saddle, was sound asleep, and despite Heni's prediction, her soft, rhythmic breathing quickly joined Torrend's in a quiet, sleepy duet.

Neyac tossed a few branches onto the flames. Sparks glittered upward like hundreds of twinkling newborn stars.

"Why do you avoid talking about the Glainite adoption, Katrine?" asked Neyac in a low-pitched tone.

She gaped at him, and he grinned back at her.

"I could tell you a lot of lies about how I found out," Neyac said, "but the simple truth is I was guessing. Of course, your reaction proves me right. Why don't you want to talk about it? Or are you going to try to convince me I'm wrong?"

After a long pause, Katrine shrugged. "I just think it's private. That's all."

"Your father told me about your saving The Glaine's life. He showed me the cat's hide she presented to him. That was a very big animal. It must have taken a great deal of courage to tackle it."

"Only instinct," she said, realizing Neyac wasn't going to just drop the topic. "I reacted without thinking. I've been at war with the plains cats for as long as I can remember."

"So the Glainites invited you into the tribe. Did you have to pass the Tests of Truth?"

Again Katrine gawked. "How do you know about the Tests?"

"I'm a Recorder, Katrine. We're called Recorders because we gather and record the history of Kareand. Sometimes we do it in songs, sometimes in verses or prose, and sometimes in pictures. Regardless of the medium, we always record. Everything. We study what everyone else has recorded, too. It's our job. I'd like the story of the Tests of Truth and your initiation into the tribe."

"But then you'd tell people." With determination, Katrine shook her head. "I don't want anyone to know."

"Why not?"

"Because some things happened I'm not supposed to discuss. I told The Glaine, and she wouldn't even tell the Masters. She said my life would be in danger if people found out, maybe the Glainites, too. So I won't tell anyone—except for one part if the right person shows up. But that's all."

"Who is the right person?"

"I won't tell." She drew her lips into a tight line. "I don't dare."

Chapter Twenty-Four

When dawn brightened the eastern sky, Katrine climbed to her feet and rekindled the fire.

Neyac had stood the first watch, waking her after the major portion of the night had passed, and only then because he could no longer keep his eyes open.

She had used her time on sentry duty to make markers for the three graves they would leave behind today. Using the point of her dagger, she had etched each name on a separate fragment of wood she'd pried from the damaged carriage: Trinnin of Banur, Sal of Branston, and Ferrill of Yallon.

Mindful of her sleeping companions, she'd planted the tokens as quietly as possible and braced the bottoms with rocks.

She gently shook Torrend.

"I'm going to take Thunder Cloud and see if there are any game animals in the forest," she told him quietly. "Our provisions are in terrible shape. Containers are broken and the contents spilled all over the floor of the carriage."

Torrend untangled himself from his blanket and sat up.

"All right, I'll stand watch here." He reached out and briefly clasped Katrine's hand. "By the way, whatever you did to my arm helped a lot. It feels much better."

"Good. We'll do it again when I get back."

She grabbed a handful of Thunder Cloud's mane, swung up bareback, and rode into the woods with her bow in hand and her quiver across her back. A short time later, she returned with a small wild pig slung across her lap. Together, she and Torrend cleaned the carcass and constructed a spit from green wood.

Soon thereafter, an enticing aroma tickled the air.

"Tell me about yourself," Torrend said. He sat on the ground, close enough to the fire to turn the roasting meat.

"Not much to tell, I'm afraid." While she talked, Katrine retrieved her medicine pouch and set a cup of water near the flames to heat. "I'm the first of eight children. My father is High Elder of Banur. And this is the first time I've ever been far from home." She considered a moment, and then sighed. "Mostly all I've ever done is work on my father's ranch. What about you?"

"I guess my life's been about as exciting as yours. I've got an elder sister, and I certainly hope you've been nicer to your younger siblings than my sister was to me. She was always bossing and pushing me around. Of course that stopped as soon as I was bigger than her." Torrend grinned wickedly at the memory. "You should've seen her face the first time she told me to do something and I told her to try and make me."

Katrine laughed. "Must've been quite a surprise."

"Felt good, too."

Steam rose off the heating water, and Katrine stirred in some powders. "What does your father do?"

"He has an apothecary in Nallee. Mostly he sells concoctions made from herbs for sick farm animals, but he also grows and cures some rare plants used in sorcery. Every now and then, he makes a potion for someone, things to change the color of their hair or make their skin softer. Stuff like that. In addition, he often mixes medications for the local Healers."

The laceration on Torrend's arm was nearly closed.

Katrine mumbled another healing spell as she applied the antiseptic and bound up the wound again.

"I'm not going to give you any leiti today," she said. "You'd have too much trouble staying in the saddle. If you're reasonably careful, you won't need anything for the pain." She moved to a nearby rock and sat with her legs stretched out in front of her.

"Apothecary? You're Crennese then?"

"My father is," Torrend told her. "He grew up in a village in the Verdant Mountains where my grandfather was magician to the High Elder and my grandmother was the town Healer. There weren't many other Crennese around, and no girls my father's age, so he left the area to look for a wife of the wizard blood. He found my mother instead. She's Nistarian."

"I'm a half-breed myself. Nistarian and Boradid." Katrine's brow furrowed with concentration as she studied Torrend's features. "You must come from a line different from the Glainites, or did you get your brown hair and eyes from your mother?"

"My parents have similar coloring. Not all Crennese are dark like the Glainites, you know. Jallyna, one of the Sister Wives, was Crennese and had auburn hair and a fair complexion."

"I remember reading about her in my history text," Katrine said, which was true enough, and meeting the Sister Wives at Echo Hall had confirmed it. Glaine had been dark, Jallyna fair skinned with auburn hair, and Terishe in between.

Katrine was so used to the Glainites with their bronze skin and black hair that she tended to think of all Crennese that way. She would have to remember not to make snap judgments now that she was out in the world.

"What was it like being Crennese in Nallee?" Katrine asked. "I have a friend named Rand who's Crennese. He says people are afraid of him."

"Some of them probably are. It's because of the magical battles during the Second Great Uprising. People don't understand our powers, so they fear them. Once, when I was quite young, a woman wouldn't let her son play with me because she was afraid I'd give him warts or something if the game didn't go my way. However, most people accepted us because my father helped to keep them, their families, and their animals healthy."

Torrend turned the spit and dribbled a little wine over the pig.

"Of course," he continued, "I imagine the real problems will come when I seek a wife. Although my sister married a Nistarian man, I think most fathers are more protective of their daughters than they are of their sons. Maybe I'll find a nice Crennese girl when I'm a Recorder."

Rubbing the bandage on his arm, Torrend looked at Katrine quizzically. "Did your friend teach you the healing lore?"

"Rand? No, it was the mother of another friend. You danced with Polnu at Heni's farewell party. Her parents were there, too."

"Oh, yes, I remember them. Heni introduced us."

"Really?" Katrine couldn't think of a single reason for her cousin to introduce Torrend to the Glainites. Heni was actually quite prejudiced. She had probably made some snide remark about the wizard blood without realizing Torrend was Crennese too. Torrend, being a gentleman, must have ignored the comment and forgotten it.

"Polnu's mother is a Master Healer," Katrine said. "When I told her I was going on a trip, she offered to teach me a little about tending injuries. As she packed the medicine pouch, she told me what each medication was and how to use it. I'm sure she was thinking about how clumsy I am, but she was kind enough not to say it outright."

"Healing is a useful skill to have," Neyac interposed.

Katrine and Torrend jerked around.

The Master Recorder yawned and awkwardly clambered to a standing position. He stretched and twisted as if his muscles and joints had stiffened from the night on the ground. He shuffled over to the fire and sniffed the roasting pig. "Smells good enough to eat. How long has it been cooking?"

"Not long enough," answered Torrend.

"Too bad. I'm hungry and we need to be— "

A small screech interrupted him.

Katrine sprang to her feet as a disheveled Heni burst from the carriage, waving her arms wildly.

"There are bees in the coach!" Heni shrieked. "One stung me!"

Forcing down an urge to laugh, Katrine took a few steps forward and reached out her hand. "Let me take a look. I might be able to help."

Heni's face turned a brilliant scarlet. "It got up my skirt." She pointed to an area near her left knee. "About there."

"I've got a powder that makes a fine poultice, but I'll need to see if the stinger is—"

"Katrine," Heni yelped, "there are men present. A lady does not expose her limbs in mixed company."

"Oh, Heni, don't be stupid," Katrine snapped with exasperation. "We're not children. I'm sure Neyac and Torrend have seen a woman's leg before."

As Torrend quickly turned away, face reddening, Katrine thought: *Well, maybe not him.*

"You're so uncouth, Katrine. You have absolutely no sense of propriety. Look, you've embarrassed Torrend. If you had any shame, you'd be embarrassed yourself."

This was one too many criticisms for Katrine. She was tired from the rough night of trying to sleep on the ground. Her body ached from hours and hours on horseback. And her emotions had been worn raw by the previous day's life-threatening violence. Anger burst out of her mouth.

"You ungrateful snob!" she shouted. "I was only trying to help."

"Well," Heni screamed back, "being vulgar isn't helpful!"

"Fine!" Katrine hollered. "I don't give a damn about your stupid old bee sting. Take care of it yourself!"

"Now, now, children," Neyac said mildly. "Let's not quarrel. There's a little stream just inside the woods."

"I know," Katrine snapped, her bad humor now targeting Neyac.

"Why don't you show Heni where it is and let her freshen up a bit? She has to change into trousers to ride anyway, and you could check her sting at the same time."

"I don't *own* any trousers," Heni said, sticking her nose in the air and speaking in an arrogant tone. "As I told you last night, we must fix the carriage. I can't ride."

"Hmmm," Neyac said as he stroked his beard. "Since we have no way of repairing the carriage, I suppose you'll either have to learn to ride or else walk all the way to Branston. Of course the choice is up to you, my dear, but either way a skirt will be cumbersome. Katrine, do you have any britches she can borrow?"

"I guess so," she grumbled. "They'll be too long, but we can fold up the bottoms." She dug through her meager belongings until she produced a pair of sturdy brown trousers and a pale yellow shirt. She draped them over her arm and picked up her medicine pouch. "All right, let's go, Heni. You might want to bring a comb or brush, too."

"This is a waste of time," Heni whined. "We've got to fix the carriage. You don't understand, any of you. It's irrational to expect me to ride a horse. It really is."

Without a word, Neyac began rolling up his blanket. Torrend splashed wine on the pig. Heni stared at them, one after the other.

No one looked at her or spoke.

When Katrine headed for the woods, Heni called, "Wait for me." Katrine paused while her cousin grabbed a carry-case from the coach and then walked on. Heni hurried to catch up.

When they emerged from the trees a half hour later, Heni was dressed in Katrine's clothes. The shirtsleeves and trouser bottoms had been rolled up. A bright sash of green silk accented Heni's slender waist. Her rich brown hair hung in two long braids entwined with ribbons. And she was smiling.

"Really," Heni said cheerfully, "I never knew how much freedom of movement the rest of you have." She tossed her bundled clothing onto the ground near the carriage. "Skirts are so inhibiting." Perching on a large rock, she kicked her legs. "I wonder what it would feel like to wear trousers that actually fit properly."

Torrend stared appreciatively at Heni's petite figure. Katrine caught his eye and grinned knowingly at him, and he quickly looked away.

"That's much better," Neyac said, assessing Heni's changed wardrobe, "much more practical for traveling. Now, let's eat. I've warmed some leftover bread, and I think the meat's done." He pulled out his knife and began hacking off chunks. "Yes," he muttered, "it's perfect."

After breakfast, Katrine and Heni hauled things out of the carriage and sorted through them while Neyac and Torrend cleaned up the dishes.

"Look," Heni said, pointing at the edge of the forest. "There are some horses hiding in those trees."

"Nicely saddled and bridled," remarked Torrend.

"Must have belonged to the bandits," Neyac said. He eyed the pile of things the girls had stacked on the ground. "It seems we have more to transport than I originally thought. A couple of extra pack animals might come in handy."

Katrine had just pulled her art satchel out of the carriage. Dropping it, she whistled for Thunder Cloud. "Let's go," she said to Torrend.

Several horses and a few plains ponies were huddled together. Among them was Trinnin's horse, and Katrine's eyes grew moist when she remembered how hard he'd worked to buy it. He had hired out to do heavy labor in the evenings after he finished his regular workday for her father. For two years he had hardly gotten any sleep. He had gone all the way to Sendig to attend one of the few horse auctions held west of the Great Meriad River. He'd been so proud when he returned and rode his new mount into the courtyard.

"Not much of a herd," Torrend said, "but my father always told me horses are sociable animals and don't like being alone. They must feel lost without their owners."

"I'm glad they found us. At least we can get those saddles off before their hides get chafed too badly."

Upon returning to camp, Katrine unsaddled a roan mare.

"Hey there, young lady," Neyac exclaimed, "we're supposed to be leaving."

"I know, but look, there's no saddle blanket. That's got to hurt." She inspected a large, oozing raw spot on the horse's back. "No one is going to be riding this horse for a while."

Neyac heaved a resigned sigh. He and Torrend began unfastening cinches.

"I should have some salve," Katrine mumbled to herself as she rummaged in the medicine pouch. "Renee said it was for minor cuts and scrapes." She pulled out a small jar. "Here it is." She spread a gooey, yellowish substance on the ulceration.

"Are you going to doctor them all?" Neyac asked as he tossed another saddle onto the growing heap.

"No," answered Katrine seriously, "just the ones that need it." She knelt by a white pony that reminded her of Stubbs and examined its legs.

"What now?" Torrend asked. "Do we take them with us or let them go?"

"We could sell them in Plains Springs," suggested Heni. "Horses always bring good prices, even little ponies."

"I think we should set them free," Katrine said, washing away dried blood and spreading salve on a narrow cut. "We only need one or two. The others would have a comfortable life here. There is plenty of water and good grazing."

"I'm inclined to agree," said Neyac. "We have enough to worry about just taking care of ourselves." While Katrine patched up the next patient, he dug through the pile of discarded tack. From the uninjured mounts, he selected a small brown plains pony and saddled and bridled it.

"Your ponies aren't used to being ridden," he told Heni, "so they can carry the luggage and supplies. You'll ride this one."

"I'm not getting on that!" cried Heni. "You can't make me."

"Your choice," said Neyac.

Katrine ran her hand across the flank of Trinnin's horse, a dappled mare, and then down the shoulder. A front leg had been injured in the fighting, and she bound it, hoping it would heal with time. She knew that, like its master, the horse would have to be left behind. But maybe it would breed. Someday there might be of whole herd of dappled horses in this area.

When all the doctoring was completed, Katrine helped Neyac and Torrend load the remaining provisions and Heni's luggage onto the two carriage ponies.

"We'll take along the one great horse that's not hurt," Neyac said. "We might need it later."

Patiently, Torrend explained the rudiments of riding to Heni, but she kept silently shaking her head. Her eyes opened wide with horror when he finally lifted her up and set her in the saddle.

When Katrine, Torrend, and Neyac slowly rode away with the pack ponies and extra horse trailing behind on lead ropes, Heni tearfully begged them to stay and help her fix the carriage.

They kept going.

She yelled and screeched and howled and threatened and sobbed.

She called them all kinds of names.

Katrine was shocked to discover Heni even knew some of those words. She had never heard them spoken except by the roughest of her Father's hired men.

The three riders kept going.

Katrine used her Glainite senses to stay in touch with Heni's mind.

She could feel her cousin fighting to push back her panic.

She was aware of the exact moment when Heni nudged the pony with her heels, and clutching its mane in terror, began bouncing along behind the others.

Chapter Twenty-Five

By late afternoon, Neyac had directed his little band to a large, clean hostel on the western fringes of Plains Springs.

"I think we all deserve a little comfort," he said. "Why don't we clean up and go out for an especially nice dinner? I know several dining establishments that have entertainment as well as good food."

"I'm all bruised and battered," groaned Heni. "Maybe after a long soak, I'll be able to eat. Right now, I just want to feel solid ground under my feet."

Quickly dismounting, Katrine positioned herself to be handy when Heni swung off the pony. As she expected, Heni's legs buckled and she almost tipped over. Katrine steadied her with an arm around her waist.

"Torrend, if you'll stay with the animals, I'll arrange for rooms then help you unload the luggage and see to the horses."

The apprentice nodded.

Supporting her wobbly cousin, Katrine followed Neyac through a wide doorway and into the inn. Almost as soon as they entered the spacious lobby, the innkeeper, a slightly built and jolly fellow, rushed from behind a long desk, grabbed the Master Recorder, and gave him an enormous bear hug.

"Neyac, you old vagabond, it's about time you came home."

"Randel, it's good to see you," Neyac said, returning the embrace. "We need rooms and baths if possible."

"Ho, ho," Randel said, eyes all a-twinkle, "who are these lovely young ladies. You must introduce us first."

"Katrine of Banur and Heni of Branston. Ladies, this is my younger brother, Randel."

"Brother?" gasped Heni and Katrine together.

How can someone as old as Neyac have a brother this young? Katrine wondered. *Randel doesn't appear to be too much older than Father. Neyac looks at least twenty years older than that.*

"Yes, I'm his brother," Randel said, "but don't hold it against me. I'm really a very nice fellow. Not a bit like this old wanderer."

The Spire of Kylet

Looking from one man to the other, Katrine spotted the family resemblance in the large hooked noses, the full, amused mouths, and the slightly shorter than average stature. Neyac had such a powerful personality that Katrine often forgot that he was shorter than she was.

For a moment, she puzzled once again over the age difference, but then it occurred to her that she was fourteen years older than her twin sisters and her mother was still young enough to have another couple of babies if she and Father decided that was what they wanted.

"Now," Randel said, "you need a room with two feather beds for the ladies and a single one for yourself, right?"

"I have an apprentice with me, too," Neyac told him. "He's out front with the horses and luggage."

"Why didn't you say so?" Randel swiveled and called loudly. "Kert, I need you."

Immediately a towheaded boy of about ten years stuck his head through a curtained doorway at the rear of the lobby. "Yes, Father."

"Go show—" Randel paused and looked at Neyac.

"Torrend. His name is Torrend."

"Go show Torrend where to stable the horses. Then help him bring in the bags." The boy nodded and started for the door.

"Oh, Kert," the Master Recorder called.

"Yes, Uncle Neyac."

"Torrend hurt his arm yesterday. He shouldn't lift anything too heavy. I'll come out later and help you carry in the bags."

"Don't be ridiculous, Neyac," Randel protested. "I have more than one son. Kert, Chaz should be outside somewhere. Have him help you." Randel hooked a thumb in Neyac's direction and rolled his eyes up. "I don't want this worthless, decrepit, older brother of mine to have a heart seizure and die from doing any real work."

"Yes, Father," Kert said, grinning at what appeared to be a frequent family jest. He hurried out through the door.

"He's grown," Neyac said in a wistful tone. "I didn't realize it had been so long."

"Only a year or so, but they grow fast at this age." Randel crossed to a small, rectangular door built into the wall behind the desk. He opened it, revealing a shallow cupboard, and pulled out two keys. "Let me show you to your rooms, but if you sneak out of town without spending some time with me and the family, I'll hunt you down and string you up by your thumbs."

"No need to worry." Neyac clasped his brother on the shoulder and climbed the stairs next to him, as if he couldn't abide letting go. "I went to Banur by the western route, so I missed Plains Springs on my trip out of Pardish. Now that I'm here, I don't know how I can bear to leave at all."

Right after Chaz and Kert brought up the bags, Randel stopped by to show the girls how to work the new indoor latrine and bath chamber, which was behind a partition in the corner.

"We keep a large cistern of heated water behind the inn," Randel said. "You just need to pump like this to fill the tub. When you're done, you lift this plug and the dirty water drains away. Usually we ask our guests to keep the water below the red line, but the hostel's not full, so you can use whatever you need."

Bowing graciously, he closed the door behind him.

"I'm first," Heni cried and started working the pump.

"I'll do that while you get out your clean clothes and undress," Katrine said. "I'm anxious to bathe, too."

When Heni finally climbed out of the tub, Katrine hopped in.

"You're not going to use the same dirty water, are you?"

"I don't have the energy to pump anymore. Besides, I've shared dirtier bath water than this at home in the winter when it was too cold to go out and use the bath house."

As Heni rubbed her hair with a towel, she mumbled to herself, "I always knew there were advantages to being an only child."

Katrine was cleaned, dried, dressed, and refreshed when a light tapping sounded at the portal. Heni jumped up to answer it, so Katrine continued combing the tangles out of her damp hair. Torrend and Neyac looked dashing with their fresh grooming and garbing.

"Let's go eat," said Neyac. "I'm half starved."

Swiftly finishing her hair by catching it at the nape of her neck with a ribbon, Katrine stood and brushed her hand across the faint wrinkles in her rose colored skirt. "So am I."

As Neyac herded the group down the stairs, he told them, "The food here at the inn is good, but it's simple. I'm in the mood for something extravagant. Also, a little entertainment would be nice after our tedious journey, so I thought we would go—"

"Won't your brother be offended if we don't dine here?" asked Katrine.

"Of course not," answered Neyac. "Besides, I've already told him. He understands. He knows we'll breakfast here. Many of the locals even come to the inn for their morning meals. Randel's wife does all the baking, and there is not a cook in Kareand who makes better breakfast breads. The dining hall will be crowded in the morning, but for dinner, Plains Springs has other delights to offer."

The establishment Neyac chose was called The Fighting Boar. When Katrine saw the sign out front with its engraving of a fierce pig's head, she feared the Master Recorder had delivered them to some scruffy enterprise in spite of his comments about wanting a fancy dinner.

She was pleasantly surprised when they entered and she discovered an elegantly furnished hall with sparkling chandeliers, dazzling white tablecloths and napkins, and glimmering plates, glasses, and flatware.

"This is more like it," Heni said.

The Spire of Kylet

After a servant showed them to a vacant table near a small stage, Neyac ordered for them all. More than half the tables were already filled with customers, and delectable aromas drifted from the various serving dishes scattered around the room.

To distract herself from her rumbling stomach, Katrine watched and listened to the people seated nearby. Great varieties of clothing, hairdos, accents, and dialects were in evidence, and she was shocked to realize how sheltered her life had been.

When a server brought steaming soup, hot bread, and cold juice to the table, Katrine happily turned her attention to staving off starvation. "This is as good as Rosi's cooking," she said between bites.

"I'm glad you like it," Neyac said, "but don't stuff yourself. We still have several more courses to enjoy before dessert. And let me tell you, the cherry trifle here is beyond description."

While they ate, Katrine turned to the Recorder with a question that had been bothering her. "Why hasn't Regent Laria called peacekeepers to patrol the Plains Trail? It seems quite dangerous and unprotected to me."

"Regent Laria's authority is limited," Neyac said after swallowing a spoonful of soup. "She's not Kareand's ruler in the same sense as a king or queen would be, and her responsibilities are specific. Like all the Regents before her, she provides minimal leadership."

"Only until the real king returns," Heni said dreamily. "The seers say a descendant of Danied-Ohln and Terishe will someday rebuild Shanree Palace. I would love to see that. Can you imagine? A real king and queen. Royal courts and formal balls. Courtiers."

"Until that happens," Neyac replied, "the Regent is authorized to collect taxes and to decide how to use the revenue to provide services that affect the entire realm, such as funding the Recorders School and the Landorian Warrior Compounds. She appoints the Headmaster and the Warlord, assures that they fulfill their responsibilities, decides when they should retire, and selects their successors. She constructs and maintains the caravan routes, helps establish Councils of Elders, and is the final authority in times of crisis. The only exception is in the case of war, either civil or foreign. Then the Warlord's authority supersedes hers."

"I know all that," Katrine said, her voice full of impatience. "So, why isn't she protecting travelers on the Plains Trail?"

Neyac used his napkin to dab at a bit of soup that had dripped from his spoon onto his beard. "Town Elders are responsible for enforcing the laws in their areas of authority. Usually, they organize volunteers to act as peacekeepers, or they impose taxes so they can hire professionals. The farmers along the Plains Trail don't have time to volunteer, and their incomes fluctuate with the seasons, so imposing a peacekeeper tax is impractical. Trained watchers on the Plains Trail are notoriously scanty."

Torrend broke off a chunk of bread and dipped it in his soup. "Then why doesn't the Warlord do something?"

"It's a tricky situation," Neyac said. "Regent Laria is responsible for ensuring the safety of travelers on the major caravan routes, and she has delegated the task to the Warlord. He assigns Warriors to do regular patrols. Councils of Elders can request help from the local Landorian Compound, but they often hesitate because they're afraid to give up their authority, even temporarily, for fear of losing it permanently.

"The Regent and Warlord walk a delicate line between being supportive of local governance and taking over too much control."

"Even so," Torrend said, "someone has to do something or commerce between towns will stop. The farmers won't be able to get their wares to market, and city-dwellers won't be able to buy food or other goods."

"I hope that's not a foreseeing." Neyac flicked his fingers toward the east to ward off bad luck.

Katrine didn't believe for a second that he was superstitious. She grinned at him to let him know he wasn't fooling her, and he winked back.

"I've already sent word about our attack to the peacekeepers here," Neyac continued, "and I'll talk to the Landorian Captain at Branston as soon as we get there. In the meantime, children, let's eat before all of this gets cold."

Just as the server was clearing away the soup bowls, a small band of musicians mounted the stage. While they played, a beautiful woman with golden hair and a voice like a nightingale sang love songs to the crowd. Katrine and her companions finished dinner and lingered over the trifle, which Katrine admitted was even better than Rosi's, because they were reluctant to leave before the end of the stirring performance.

When the singer let the last note fade away, the audience clapped wildly. As the clamor dwindled and the performers exited, a single voice could be heard from the back of the room.

"You're making a mistake, friend."

Chapter Twenty-Six

Katrine craned her neck to see who was causing the commotion.

After some searching, she spied a tall, muscular man dressed all in black. He was holding a smaller man by the scruff of the neck.

"Someone as clumsy as you shouldn't try thieving as a livelihood," the larger man said as he shook the other soundly. "Now return my money pouch, and I'll let you go in peace."

"Let me down," the small man squeaked. "I don't have your money. I've never seen you before."

"Let me introduce myself. I'm Captain Asher of Landor, and if that doesn't mean anything to you, simply think of me as the man who's going to hurt you if you don't return my wallet." To emphasize his words, he gave the little fellow another rough shake. "Now!"

Icy fingers played up and down Katrine's spine. Captain Asher was the Warrior Kylet had told her about in Echo Hall—but he was terrifying. Approaching him for any reason didn't seem like a very good idea. He appeared completely capable, both physically and intentionally, of ripping his poor captive to pieces.

Every inch of the little man quaked. The expression on his face looked as if he had reached the same conclusion Katrine had.

"Your pardon," he said meekly. With trembling fingers, he pulled a money pouch from the front of his jerkin and held it out. "Is this yours?"

Asher loosened his grip on the man's neck and dropped him in a heap on the floor as he snatched back his wallet. "Now get out of here before I call a peacekeeper and have you thrown into the town dungeon."

Scrambling to his feet, the thief rushed from the hall.

Asher motioned to a server, counted out several coins, and then sauntered toward the door.

"Come along, children," Neyac said. "We have business to attend to." He tossed some money on the table and quickly stepped away, but Katrine loitered, forcing herself to think.

Although Kylet's ghost had said she and Asher would cross paths, he hadn't told her how to make contact. Even if she could force herself to speak to the Captain without stuttering, which was doubtful, how was she supposed to find him later so they could talk privately?

Maybe she could sneak out of the inn later and ask around until she discovered where he was staying. People would surely remember someone as big and distinctive as he was.

Maybe by the time she located him, he would have calmed down enough not to scare her to death.

Wrapped up in her own thoughts, she lost sight of Neyac. When she caught a glimpse of him again, she could hardly believe her eyes.

"Asher, my boy," beamed Neyac, "what are you doing in Plains Springs?"

The Warrior spun around. When he saw the Master Recorder, the scowl on his face was replaced by a radiant smile.

It took Katrine's breath away.

"I'm running errands for the Warlord, as usual," the big Warrior answered.

A few seconds earlier, Katrine had not found Asher the least bit attractive. His long, wavy black hair framed a broad forehead, chiseled cheekbones, and a strong, stubborn jaw. His dark eyes were deep-set and brooding. His nose had obviously been broken, and his mouth, although well shaped, had a harshness that was almost cruel.

But that was before he smiled.

When he smiled, all the perceived defects switched into assets, and he was incredibly handsome. Katrine had never seen anyone like him before, and she hurried to catch up with the others so she could be introduced.

"This is Katrine of Banur," Neyac said as she joined them.

When Katrine curtsied, Asher extended his palm and she placed her fingers in his hand as she rose.

When she looked up, their eyes met.

The intensity of his gaze was so strong, Katrine felt as if he were trying to peer into her soul. Nervously she glanced away. She felt her cheeks burn with embarrassment. When Asher lifted her hand to his lips for a light kiss, Katrine looked up again. The intensity was gone.

"I'm pleased to meet you, Katrine," rumbled Asher in a voice pitched slightly lower than a thunderclap. His dark eyes danced with humor, and his lips curled up at the corners.

"The honor is mine, sir," said Katrine.

Even though she knew the Warrior was amused either by her blush or her awkward curtsy—and she usually hated being laughed at—there was something so infectious about his smile that she couldn't be offended and had to smile back.

"Oh, enough formalities," Neyac snapped impatiently. "Come on, boy, tell us the news. What are you doing so far away from Landor? Are you aware of the trouble between here and Sendig? Where are you staying? Are you going to be here long?"

"I'm just stopping for the night," Asher said, answering the last question and ignoring the others. "Tomorrow I'm heading eastward."

"So are we," Neyac said. They moved out of the doorway and onto the wooden walkway in front of the hall. "Any particular reason you're going that way?"

"There's been an increase of violence in the area."

"We had some trouble ourselves on the way here from Banur," Neyac said. "We lost three members of our party to an ambush yesterday."

"We'll need to talk. Regent Laria and Warlord Leeds think the outlaw movement is organizing along the Meriad."

Heni grabbed hold of the Warrior's sleeve. "Is Branston in any danger?" she asked anxiously. "That's where we're going. I live there."

"I don't know, miss," Asher said. "Branston is a large city and has its own Landorian Compound. I suppose it depends on how daring the renegades get as their numbers increase." He looked back at Neyac. "Perhaps we should travel together for a while. We might benefit from each other's counsel."

"Excellent. We're staying at the Springside Inn. Why don't you join us there? I don't know if the inn's full, but the proprietor is my brother, and I'm sure he'll make room for you regardless."

"It's not full," Katrine said, surprising herself by speaking up. "Randel mentioned it when he showed us how to use the bath."

"All right," Asher said. "I'll get my gear and meet you later tonight."

As he strode away, Katrine was struck by the way the Fates sometimes simply took control of events. If Asher was going to travel with them, she would have ample opportunities to speak with him alone. Kylet's message must be even more important than she realized if the Powers were taking such an active role in getting it delivered.

"The night is still young," Neyac said. "Do you ladies want to do any shopping while we're here? This is the largest town we'll stop in until Branston."

"What about Yallon?" asked Heni.

"Too far off the trail. We would miss a full day's travel going there."

"Ferrill always insisted we stop at Yallon," Heni said, her eyes misting over and her lower lip quivering. "His parents live there. Someone needs to let them know he's never coming back." She blotted her cheeks with her handkerchief. "I suppose I need to write to Sal's lady friend in Banur and tell her too."

"I'm sorry, my dear, I didn't understand." Neyac patted her shoulder sympathetically. "If you feel you need to stop and see your driver's people, of course, we'll make the time."

"But what will I tell them? I'm not very good at this kind of thing." She looked pleadingly at Katrine. "Will you go with me? I don't think I could stand going alone, and you always know what to say and do."

"Of course, I will," Katrine said, although she could hardly believe anyone thought she knew what to say when tact and diplomacy were required. Yet, in this situation, she would have an advantage over her cousin because her feelings weren't so deeply involved.

She understood Heni's apprehension, too, because of Trinnin. Katrine had already written to his parents, and it had been a very difficult and unpleasant task.

"We'll do whatever we have to when we get to Yallon," Katrine said in order to stave off a flood of tears—her own and Heni's. "However, right now, we're in Plains Springs, and I think we ought to see about buying you some britches and shirts. I only brought three pairs of trousers. If you don't buy your own, one of us will have to ride all the way to Branston without changing clothes."

Abruptly Heni's mood brightened. "Yes, let's do that. Do you know where we should look, Neyac?"

"Follow me, ladies."

By the time Heni, Katrine, Neyac, and Torrend returned to the inn, they were laden with parcels and night had fallen. Heni had purchased four pairs of britches: dark brown, forest green, black, and gray. She'd bought six bright shirts, a couple of sashes, and a pair of sturdy riding boots. Through Heni's encouragement, Katrine had finally indulged herself by buying a colorful shirt, black trousers, and a couple of sashes also. It took nearly half the money her father had given her, but she was excited about having something new to wear.

When they returned to their room, Katrine filled the bathtub with hot water, and she and Heni washed all of their dirty clothing. There was a small balcony outside their window, and they spread their laundry out on it so the items could dry in the night air.

Then the two girls flopped wearily into their beds.

Katrine slept soundly for the first time since leaving home. When a knocking sound interrupted her dreams, she resented it and rolled over, covering her head with her pillow.

"Let me try," a booming voice said. The resultant pounding shook the room.

"Come on, girls," called Neyac. "It's time to get up and start moving unless you want to begin the day without breakfast."

Katrine battled past pillow and blanket.

On her way to the door she grabbed one of Heni's feet and gave it a rough shake. "Time to get up," she mumbled to her cousin.

Opening the door a crack, Katrine saw Neyac and Asher in the hall. "Give us a few minutes," she said, stifling a yawn. "I guess we overslept."

"I guess you did," agreed Neyac. "We're going to the dining hall and order breakfast. If you don't get down by the time we finish eating, we'll eat your share as well."

"There goes our primping time," complained Heni.

The two girls dressed in new outfits and packed in a hurry, barely taking time to fold the clothing they'd left out on the balcony to dry.

When they got to the dining hall, it was full of customers, just as Neyac had predicted.

Katrine was struck by how large, bright, and cheerful the room was, so different from the smoky, awful-smelling, eating rooms of the sleazy establishments they had stayed at earlier. She hoped Neyac would direct the group to places like this for the remainder of the journey.

Standing in the doorway, the girls scanned the room for the Recorder and the Warrior.

* * *

"She doesn't know?" Asher asked.

"Not yet," answered Neyac. "Her father left it to me to decide when to tell her. But not now, here they come." Standing and waving his hand, Neyac caught the girls' attention and motioned them over.

* * *

"Where's Torrend?" Heni asked as she sat down across from the men and began filling a plate from a large platter that was centered on the table. When she had taken her share, she passed the tray to Katrine, who had already helped herself to a hot sticky bun from a basket of sweet breads.

"This is heavenly," Katrine said. She licked her fingers and wiped them on a napkin before taking the tray from Heni.

"Torrend had his breakfast long ago," Neyac said in answer to Heni's question. "He and Randel's boys are saddling the horses. Did you get your things packed?"

"Yes," Heni and Katrine answered together.

"Good. I told Torrend to get the luggage loaded as soon as possible. Our new provisions should already be in place."

"Have you given any consideration to my suggestion of purchasing a carriage?" Heni inquired sweetly. "I know my father would reimburse you once we reach Branston, and I would personally be extremely grateful."

"As a matter of fact, I did give it some thought."

Before Neyac got any further, Asher interrupted. "It's not practical. If we're going through outlaw country, a person's life can depend on a swift horse. Buggies are too damned slow, and if they overturn, you're in one hell of a mess."

"I'm sure you're right," Heni said, batting her eyes and trying to look appealing. "But for someone like me, a carriage is certainly more practical than a horse in an emergency. I'm a very poor rider, and if my horse broke into a gallop, I would surely tumble off. At least in a coach I would have some hope of escape."

"As I mentioned earlier," Neyac put in, "we have already lost one carriage to an attack. Yesterday was Heni's first attempt at horseback riding."

Two deep creases appeared between Asher's thick black eyebrows. He forked a bite of sausage into his mouth and pondered as he chewed. After he swallowed, he said, "The way I see it, we have two choices. We can all agree to abandon you if we're attacked, whether you're on horseback or in a carriage, and leave you to your fate. Or we can tie you to the saddle, and one of us can control your horse with a lead rope."

Heni gawked at him with an open mouth.

"I would recommend the latter." Asher sounded indifferent, but a bit of mischief played across his face. "You'd stand a better chance of survival staying with the rest of us, no matter how bruised and battered your body or your pride became."

"You—you can't be serious," sputtered Heni. "I won't be tied to the saddle like a slab of meat! That's absurd. And," she added primly, "I don't believe the others would agree to desert me, either."

"Well?" Asher scowled at Neyac and then at Katrine. "Are you willing to let this spoiled child risk all our lives?" His expression stated clearly that it was time someone dealt with Heni's imperiousness.

Katrine agreed with him, but Asher didn't know how close Heni was to having a tantrum right there in front of everyone.

Katrine glanced at Neyac questioningly, hoping he would come up with a way to deal with Heni before she embarrassed them all, but he just hitched his shoulders in a noncommittal shrug. With a sigh she hoped wasn't audible, Katrine twisted on the bench so she had Heni full-faced.

"Katrine!" Heni shrieked. "You're not siding with him!"

"I'm sure the Captain knows more about this situation than the rest of us do," Katrine said with her pulse racing, praying she wouldn't botch this by saying the wrong things. "I know I would hate to desert you, but I don't know that I'd let myself be captured, raped, tormented, or tortured for you. If the area is as dangerous as Captain Asher implies, I think we need to take all the precautions we can."

"I should have known I couldn't depend on you," Heni said sniffling. As she tried to rise, Katrine put a hand on her shoulder to prevent it. When Neyac and Asher still didn't offer any assistance, Katrine sighed again.

"You're not thinking, Heni," Katrine reproached her gently. "I know we've never been close, but I'd hate to see evil men get their hands on you. You're petite, and you're pretty, and you're feisty. You would keep coarse men entertained for quite a while before they got bored enough to kill you.

"Your riding was much improved by the end of the day yesterday. If you allow the Captain to secure you to the saddle for now, just in case of an emergency, as soon as your skill level has increased adequately, I'm sure he'll let you ride normally.

"Of course, there is an option he didn't consider," Katrine said, and for some reason she was pleased by the startled expression on Asher's face. "You probably have enough money to stay in Plains Springs until the Landorian Warriors or the local peacekeepers have dealt with the renegades. I could explain to your parents, and they could send for you when traveling is safer."

"An excellent suggestion," Neyac exclaimed. "I'm sure Randel and his family would love to have you here."

"Would you stay, too, Katrine?" Heni asked apprehensively.

"I can't. My father gave me over to Neyac's care, and wherever he goes, I'll go too."

"All right," Heni said. She wiped her nose and eyes on her napkin. Holding her head up high as she looked straight at Asher, she said, "You may bind me to the saddle. If Katrine is leaving then so am I."

Chapter Twenty-Seven

"All set," Torrend said as he joined his friends in the dining hall. "Kert helped me balance the loads. Everything is ready."

"Did you do as I instructed?" asked Asher.

Fidgeting nervously, Torrend nodded without looking at either Heni or Katrine.

"Good," Asher said. "We'd better get started."

As the group crossed the lobby, they halted long enough to say goodbye to Randel and to thank him for his hospitality. Randel bowed gallantly, then surprised them all by giving Katrine and Heni each a hug. Neyac shooed them toward the door and lagged behind for a private word with his brother. He rejoined the group just as they were stepping outside.

Five mighty horses stood in front of the hostel, saddled and waiting. Heni's carriage ponies were beside them, provisions and luggage tied on their backs. The little brown pony that Neyac had selected for Heni from among the bandits' mounts was missing.

"Where's my pony?" Heni asked Torrend. When the young apprentice opened his mouth, no words came out, and he looked at Heni pleadingly for a moment, and then glanced at Asher.

"Not fast enough," the Warrior said brusquely. Then his tone gentled. "If we had to, we could abandon the pack animals, but we can't afford to lose you. You can't match our pace on a plains pony, so you'll have to ride a real horse."

"No," cried Heni. "I can't."

"Up you go, miss." Without asking for permission, Asher picked Heni up and deposited her in the saddle. He tied a rope around her waist, passed it under the horse's barrel and up over her legs twice, then looped it around the cantle in back and the saddlebow in front. He finished by knotting the ends together and slicing off the excess.

Throughout the operation, Heni's indignation escalated.

When Asher handed her the reins and fastened the rest of the rope to the bridle, she was purple from shouting. He merely ignored her and swung astride his own tall mount.

"Give the lead rope to Katrine," Heni screeched at the top of her voice. "I wouldn't trust a bully like you with my worst enemy."

Nodding solemnly, Asher passed Katrine the rope. When his back was to Heni, though, he gave Katrine a quick wink and a grin. She had to fight against the urge to giggle. If she laughed, she was sure Heni would have convulsions.

With Neyac and Asher leading the way, the others fell in behind. As they rode through town, Katrine let out as much rope as she could in order to give Heni a sense of freedom. She wrapped the cord around her hand and held it with her reins.

Since Randel's inn was near the western border, Katrine hadn't seen much of Plains Springs when they had entered town. Even when they'd gone shopping, they had stayed in the same general area.

Now that they were traversing the city proper, Katrine understood what her father had meant when he told her she would see cities beyond imagination.

The streets were paved with stone, similar to the cobbles in the courtyard at home, but ten times the size and much smoother. The streets were so wide that several large wagons could pass each other with room to spare.

There were buildings four and five stories tall, many with ornate designs around windows and doors. Bright banners and flags flapped crisply in the breeze from rooftops and steeples. Every now and then, they passed a yard or porch bedecked with earthenware pots overflowing with vines or flowers.

Katrine could hardly believe that Yallon, Branston, Pardish, and many cities along the Great Meriad were even bigger than this.

And there were people everywhere. She had never seen so many serious looking individuals rushing around and behaving as if everything in their lives was of the utmost importance.

Behind her, Katrine heard Torrend ride up beside Heni.

"I'm sorry," he said quietly. "There wasn't anything I could do, you know. Asher told me to saddle the extra horse."

"I'm not speaking to you," Heni said in a tone obviously meant to freeze Torrend like a summer flower in a winter storm. "Not ever again."

"Come on, be fair. I'd like to hear you say no to something that behemoth told you to do."

"I did. I told him no all the time he was tying me up."

"Didn't do you much good, did it?" Torrend asked dryly.

"Well," Heni replied petulantly, "I guess not. But at least you could've warned me so I wasn't caught completely off-guard."

"And then what?"

Although Heni dropped her voice low, Katrine could still hear what she said. It astonished her.

"I would have let Katrine talk me into it, of course. She can be very persuasive."

"Wouldn't it be nice if you two became friends by the end of our journey?"

"We have years of animosity between us," Heni said. "Friends might be a bit too much to hope for. Still, I don't think we actually hate each other anymore." They rode in silence a moment. "By the way," Heni said, "what happened to the pony? We didn't just leave it behind, did we?"

"Neyac gave it to his nephews, Kert and Chaz, for being so helpful with the luggage and animals. They were delighted."

As the day progressed and the company passed from the city to the plains, clouds scudded across the sky, tantalizing them with the promise of a refreshing rain. But not a drop of water fell to earth. The air became increasingly muggy. Heni slumped in the saddle, drooping like a delicate blossom wilting in the noonday sun.

Frequently, Asher ranged in advance of the others then came back to consult with Neyac. As midday approached, he suggested they veer off the road and rest for a while behind a clump of trees.

"The foliage is thick enough to provide us a measure of camouflage while we're at our ease," Asher added.

"Do you suspect trouble?" asked Neyac.

"There is a small party coming this way. They could be legitimate travelers like us, or they could be outlaws. Since we're alone on the road right now, I don't think it hurts to be cautious. We need to take a break so we can eat and stretch our legs, but we'll be vulnerable after we dismount. I would just as soon let this company pass by before we reappear in the open."

At Neyac's nod, Asher led the others to the back of the thicket where there was a slender opening. After passing single file through the gap, they discovered an oval clearing among the trees with plenty of room for the horses to graze and a trickling stream to provide water.

As soon as Katrine swung off of Thunder Cloud, she began the task of unraveling her cousin's bindings. Neyac and Torrend rummaged through the supply packs and pulled out provisions for the noon meal.

When Heni slid from her horse's back, she crumpled into a little heap. Katrine helped her over to the stream. Then she got a rag from her saddlebags, dampened it, and washed Heni's face and neck for her. Suddenly she realized why Heni was having a worse time than anyone else. She, who never set foot outside if she could help it, had gotten terribly sunburned despite the overcast weather.

Katrine fetched her medicine pouch and gently rubbed salve all over Heni's face, arms, and hands. She gave her a drink of water and told her to lie in the shade. When Heni did so without arguing, Katrine knew how unwell her cousin was feeling.

"Neyac," Asher said, "I'd like to get a closer look at this other party as it passes. While you're getting lunch ready, I wonder if you could spare

189

Katrine. I'd like to have her watch with me."

Katrine's head jerked around, and she stared at Asher in bewilderment. "Me?"

"A good choice," Neyac said while he unwrapped and examined a large block of yellow cheese. "Katrine worked many years on her father's ranch, and Mer told me once that her eyes miss nothing. If you're looking for something out of the ordinary, Katrine just might be able to spot if for you. Go ahead. We can manage without you both."

"Do you mind?" Asher asked Katrine. "A fresh outlook is often beneficial."

"All right, if you think I can help."

Asher preceded Katrine though the undergrowth, holding back bushes and branches to clear a path for her. After he found a concealed spot that still permitted a good view of the trail, he began talking in a soft lulling voice.

"What I would like you to do is close your eyes, take several slow, deep breaths, and relax your muscles. Clear you mind and think of nothing. When the travelers come into view, observe them casually, almost without giving them any notice. Keep your breathing regular and your thoughts free, and then just describe whatever you see. All right?"

"Why?"

"Please, just try. Relax, breathe deep, and let your mind drift."

Even though Katrine thought Asher's request was peculiar, if not completely mad, as he continued crooning in a mellow drone, she automatically began to follow his instructions. She closed her eyes, slowly breathed in and out, and let her muscles become fluid and loose. Her mind wandered aimlessly, and she felt if she relaxed much more, she would doze off.

"Good," Asher whispered. "Keep it up."

Before long, Katrine heard approaching hooves and wagon wheels, sounds that seemed far away and inconsequential. Her chest rose and fell, and her mind floated peacefully. She felt dissociated, but the sensation was not unpleasant.

"Now," Asher said, "open your eyes and look."

Suspended languidly in a nebulous state between sleep and wakefulness, Katrine lifted her eyelids with some difficulty. Her words formed dreamily.

"I see a wagon drawn by four plains ponies. On the seat at the front, a fair-haired man holds the reins. Next to him sits a woman in a blue dress. Her outline is blurry. She almost looks like a man in disguise. Maybe I can—" Katrine squinted and crinkled her brow to hone her concentration, but a dull throb began to rap at the base of her skull.

"No," Asher said softly. "Don't focus on her. Just let your mind glide. Take another slow breath and relax. Is it a man or a woman?"

Inhaling deeply, Katrine looked at the figure through half-closed eyes. The pain in her head disappeared. "It's a man, but he's wearing a dress and bonnet. That can't be right."

"Ignore it. Stay relaxed. What else do you see?"

"Two men on plains ponies are riding behind the wagon. One has a hunting beast on a leash. No. Something is wrong with the animal. It's blurry like the woman. It has the face of a man." Katrine shook her head, trying to chase away the nonsensical images. "How can an animal pretend to be a man? I don't understand."

"Is there anything else peculiar about the beast?"

"Four toes. Should only have three."

"What else?"

Katrine's body tensed. "Feelings. Anger. Fear. Hatred." As she spoke, her voice lost its musing quality and began to increase in volume. She started to rise. "Evil."

Asher clamped his hand across her mouth and pushed her to the ground.

"Quiet," he murmured. "Shhh, it's all right. Hush, now. Hush."

After a moment, Katrine felt her head clear, and she grappled with the Warrior's large fingers, trying to pry them from her face.

"I'll remove my hand if you're sure you're under control," he said in an undertone. When Katrine ceased struggling, Asher loosened his grip.

"Why did you do that?" Katrine sputtered in an indignant whisper.

"Sorry, but you were getting a little loud. I was afraid they might hear you."

"How did you make me have those strange visions?" Katrine demanded as forcefully as she could without raising her voice. "It was like being in a trance, wasn't it? Like priests in the Temple of the Sun or the Crennese seers?"

"Not quite." Asher peered over the bushes briefly then sat down beside Katrine. "I don't think they heard you. They're continuing on their way."

"Tell me what you did to me," Katrine insisted. "Why did I see those things?"

"It's something I learned at Landor. Not everyone can do it. I just had a hunch that you might have the right characteristics. I'm sorry if it distressed you."

"That's no answer," Katrine said. "What happened to me?"

"Maybe you were right before. The easiest thing to compare it with is a trance, a special kind of trance."

Asher got to his feet and brushed dust and bits of grass and dried leaves from his black trousers. "Let's go back. Neyac must have lunch ready by now."

Frustrated, Katrine got stubborn.

She didn't move.

"First it's not like a trance, and then it is like a trance. Make up your mind." She folded her arms across her chest and scowled. "You did something to me to make me see those strange things. You'd better explain, right now."

Asher didn't even try to hide his amusement. "Or what?"

"Or maybe I'll scream," Katrine threatened and was delighted at his angry grimace. "Maybe those people who just went by can explain it to me."

* * *

Dropping to the ground, once again Asher muzzled Katrine by putting his hand over her mouth. He glared at her, feeling out of control.

He wasn't used to dealing with civilian girls.

He had lived his entire life at the Landorian Warriors Training Compound, where his father had been an officer as far back as he could remember.

Asher had become a Neophyte at age ten, the youngest person ever accepted for Warrior's training. The only girls he had ever known had all been in training, too.

If he and Katrine were at Landor right now, he would know exactly how to handle the situation. But they weren't. He didn't even have the experience of dealing with sisters to help him. He only had four brothers.

"Damn it," Asher mumbled to himself. "Is this what it's going to be like the whole fraggin' way?"

In a fierce undertone he asked her, "Do you promise to be quiet while I tell you what I can?"

Katrine couldn't actually nod, not with one of his hands at the back of her head and the other clamped hard across her face, but from the pressure on his fingers, he assumed she was agreeing.

"I mean, silent," he reiterated. "Not one sound. Not a single word. I'm surprised those people went on by. You've already made enough noise to alert a deaf man. Silence, understand?" Again he interpreted the pressure on his hands to mean assent.

"Is what going to be like what?" Katrine asked immediately after he released her, but she kept her voice low.

"Is traveling with adolescent girls going to be a constant pain in the a—a constant pain?"

"Oh, I should think so," Katrine whispered back with sweet sarcasm. "I imagine it's a lot like traveling with a Landorian Warrior. Now, you said you'd explain."

Not letting his smile show, Asher had to admire her spirit. Looking at it from her perspective, she certainly had the right to be upset. He was a stranger to her, and he had asked her to do something she hadn't known she could do and at which she had been surprisingly effective.

Then he had manhandled her twice.

He owed her something.

"What I asked you to do is hard to describe," Asher said, running his fingers through his thick black hair and pushing it away from his eyes. "It's a non-Crennese form of farseeing, and the talent for it is rather rare.

Personally, I don't have it, and I wasn't sure you did. I'm sorry I didn't warn you, but I honestly didn't know what was going to happen. I won't ask you to do it again if you found the experience too distressing."

"What did the vision mean?"

"I don't know. I still have to figure that part out. Do you mind if we go now? I'm famished, and I've told you everything I know."

"Why did you think I had this rare talent?"

"I just had a feeling." He helped her to her feet and held back a branch for her. "I'm sorry I was rough back there. I was worried about our safety. I hope you'll forgive me."

"I suppose I owe you an apology too," she said, looking up at him shyly. "I should've saved my questions until the wagon and riders were beyond hearing distance. I'll forgive you if you'll forgive me."

"Done," said Asher.

* * *

When they returned to the grove, Katrine sat alone with her thoughts, picking at the luncheon Neyac had prepared.

The incident with Asher had reminded her of the strange experience earlier in the summer when she was going into the ravine with Rand and Polnu to bury a plains cat. A pulsating heat, somehow associated with evil, had overwhelmed her. Immediately after the first occurrence, she hadn't been able to remember the details, but the affair today brought it all back.

Then there was the episode at Heni's party, and the one right before the attack in the woods. She assumed the latter two originated with the Glainite Joining, which had changed her greatly, but the one in the ravine had been prior to her initiation.

Katrine rubbed her temples and the back of her neck.

She wondered if she could be losing her mind. Some people believed it was madness that gave the priests and seers their powers. Maybe that was what Asher had sensed in her, the beginnings of insanity. Maybe that was why she had gone into the trance so easily.

"We had better get moving," Asher said after everyone had finished eating and the supplies had been repacked. He hefted Heni onto her horse and secured her as he had previously.

Disturbed and preoccupied, Katrine mounted Thunder Cloud and followed as the Warrior led them back to the trail.

Chapter Twenty-Eight

As the day progressed, they met fewer and fewer people along the track. At one point, they came upon a small caravan, and Asher led them a distance off the trail until it had passed. Later, a small band detoured warily around them.

That night, Neyac conducted them to the home of some friends of his. Their impromptu hosts welcomed them and graciously invited them to share dinner with the family. During the meal, the Master Recorder regaled everyone with amusing stories, and Katrine's dark mood dissipated in laughter.

After they all helped clean up the dishes, Neyac arranged for them to sleep in the barn.

"I'm sorry I can't offer you beds," their elderly host said while he guided them across the yard with a lighted lamp, "but with the grandchildren visiting—"

"Not to worry, old friend," said Neyac. "We'll be comfortable in the hay loft. Thank you for the meal and your kind generosity."

"Yes, thank you," the others echoed.

Katrine showed Heni how to make a little nest in the musty smelling hay and then fashioned one for herself. She lay on the edge of her blanket with the other side folded back and ready to pull over her as the temperature dropped. Straightaway she drifted to sleep and dreamed of Echo Hall.

Kylet's ghost floated before her.

"Daughter," the Wolkarean Warlord said, "you must rise and deliver my message to Asher. He is puzzled and will not find the answers he seeks without the information I have given you. Wake now, and do as I bid."

"But I'm so sleepy," she mumbled.

"All will be well," Kylet told her. "Tonight is a full moon, and even now your adopted family is gathering to send you strength. You do not travel alone, daughter, for many are united behind you without knowing why. The

Sisters send their love, and together we watch over you. Now, awaken. Asher waits for you outside the barn, although he knows it not. Farewell."

Even though wakefulness tried to elude her, Katrine gritted her teeth and forced herself up. She pulled on her boots, tucked in her shirt, and patted at her hair, hooking a few wisps behind her ears. Carefully, she made her way to the ladder and down. Silhouetted in the doorway of the barn, she could see the outline of the huge Warrior.

"Trouble sleeping?" Katrine asked.

* * *

Asher spun, dropped into a crouch, and reached for the smallsword sheathed on his belt.

"Don't sneak up on me like that," he growled as he straightened and dropped his hand.

As soon as the words were out of his mouth, he chastised himself. He shouldn't snarl at her. It wasn't her fault he was preoccupied. The Warriors under his command were used to his moods, and around them he didn't have to watch his every word. But he wasn't with his Warriors.

He'd have to be more careful now that he was traveling with civilians.

Briefly, the image of his mother's face flashed through his mind. She was always telling him he'd never marry if he didn't learn to interact with girls differently than he interacted with Warriors. She was probably right, but why had that popped into his head right now?

"Sorry," said Katrine. "Could we take a walk? I have something I need to tell you."

"Certainly." Asher gestured with his hand for her to go before him. "The moon is full tonight. There's plenty of light for us to follow the path around the garden."

* * *

As they strolled with the soft moonlight bathing them, Katrine suddenly felt all her weariness drop from her body and her fears flee from her mind. She looked up at the lunar globe, and a sense of wholeness, fellowship, and composure engulfed her. She knew that somewhere to the southwest the Glainites were united on her behalf.

A modest stone wall surrounded the garden, its few late-ripening vegetables still waiting to be harvested, and Katrine pulled herself up and perched on top.

"I have a message for you," said Katrine, "but I'm afraid you won't believe me unless I tell you how I got it. Are you awake enough to listen to a long story?"

The Spire of Kylet

"I'm awake enough," he answered with a grin that almost made Katrine's heart stop beating.

When she began her tale, she stared up at the twinkling stars instead of at Asher's face. "You might recall that Master Neyac mentioned I'm from a little town called Banur. It's situated toward the southern end of the Ildec Minor River. Even farther south is a Crennese village inhabited by the descendants of the first Glaine."

"I'm familiar with Glaine's Stand," Asher said. "If it helps with your story to know it, I've even been through Banur a few times."

"It helps. Are you also familiar with Echo Hall?"

"Yes. I once spent a night there." Asher raised his eyebrows and twitched his broad shoulders as he gave her a wry smile. "The experience was interesting."

"I spent a night there, too. That's where I got the message. It's from Kylet, the last Wolkarean Warlord."

In the shadowy light, Katrine saw Asher's body go stiff and his face go blank. His hands clenched and unclenched. Although he said nothing, muscles at the sides of his jaw and neck jerked fitfully.

Involuntarily Katrine shrank back.

"I'm sorry," Asher told her at last, his voice betraying none of the passion his body had disclosed. "My journey to Echo Hall was for the purpose of making contact with the spirit of Kylet. He did not present himself to me. I shouldn't be angry that he chose to communicate with you instead. I can guess his reasons. I only wish he hadn't waited so long."

"I don't understand." Feeling guilty, Katrine placed her hand on Asher's arm. "Why would he ask me to give you a message if he'd had the chance to do it himself?"

"That's not important right now." Asher reached over and patted her hand, the one resting on his arm. "However, I would like to know what you were doing in Echo Hall, what Kylet's message is, and why you decided to tell me now instead of earlier. Not necessarily in that order."

Katrine chewed on her lip for a moment. "I guess I didn't tell you before because I couldn't figure out how. I have trouble believing what happened, and I was there. How can I expect someone else, a total stranger, to believe me?"

She took a stray strand of hair and twisted it nervously around her finger until she realized she was mimicking one of Jaimi's habits. She folded her hands in her lap.

"Kylet came to me in my dreams tonight," she continued, "and he said I had to tell you now. So here I am."

"What were you doing in Echo Hall overnight? It is a place where few Nistarian men would willingly visit during the darkness. I can hardly imagine a young girl going there."

"I don't think that matters."

"I'm older than you, Katrine," Asher insisted forcefully. "You might not know what's important in this instance."

As Katrine gazed at Asher in the moonlight, she thought he looked younger than he usually did. Maybe it was his self-confident demeanor, his brusque speech, and his commanding behaviors that made her originally place him near his thirtieth year.

Looking at him tonight, she would guess he was five, no more than ten, years older than she was. That would make him twenty-five or younger. She smiled then stopped. Why was that such a comforting thought? Asher frowned at her as he waited for her to continue speaking. She was forced to rethink her estimate again. Ageless, she decided.

"I'd like to hear why you were in Echo Hall," he said, looking and sounding stern, "the whole story. Then I can make up my own mind about what is important and what is not."

Chewing on her lip again, Katrine wondered if she could stare him down. She hadn't intended to tell him more than Kylet's message, but with him looking at her with those piercing dark eyes, everything was suddenly different.

She realized she wanted him to like her.

Of all the people she'd ever met, he came the closest to matching her imagined picture of the Warrior of Four Bloods with his rugged good looks, his muscular physique, and his aura of authority. She caught herself studying his features, looking for the unknown mark of Zeroon and thinking perhaps he really was the prophesied Warrior, but then she remembered Kylet said no Wolkareans had yet returned to Landor.

She sighed.

"Well, have you decided whether or not to trust me?"

"It's not really a matter of trust," Katrine said. "It's just that the whole story is complicated. I'm not comfortable with parts of it, and if I tell you, I want you to promise you won't tell anyone else." She paused a moment. "Except—I guess you'll have to tell the Warlord. Kylet said you needed to give the information to him."

She didn't look at Asher while she talked.

Because of the way his face changed with his moods, she wanted only to say things that made him smile.

"Do you promise?" she asked, glancing at him. He lowered his eyes and shrugged. She assumed that meant yes.

Focusing on a big apple tree next to the house, she said, "It all started when my father asked me to gather some herdbeasts for market."

Asher listened patiently as she recounted how she had saved Bainu's life and was invited to join the Glainite tribe if she could complete the Tests of Truth. As he smiled encouragement at her, she began taking pride in her accomplishments.

When she described using the scarf to strain the water in her well, he exclaimed, "Very clever."

When she told him about her and her horse smelling each other's breath in order the become friends, he shook his head in wonder and mumbled, "Amazing."

Then she detailed her night at Echo Hall.

When she came to the part where Kylet told her that Elnid-Kyeh was a changeling, Asher jerked with a start, undergoing one of his rapid mood changes.

"By the Coils!" he swore, pounding the palm of one hand with the fist of the other. "Now it makes sense." He paced back and forth a few minutes, occasionally smacking the stone wall with his hand and shaking his head.

His sudden intensity made Katrine nervous, and she pulled back every time he neared her.

As quickly as before, his mood switched. "Your pardon," he said gently as if he had never had a temper outburst in his life. He cupped Katrine's hands in his and gave them a reassuring squeeze.

"I didn't mean to frighten you again. I think best when I'm moving. You must know my anger is with Elnid-Kyeh, not with you. Please continue."

But Katrine was distracted by the Warrior's touch. Her heart pounded so loudly in her ears, it was all she could hear. She couldn't think. Nor could she break the spell that kept her eyes fastened on his hands enclosing hers.

Abruptly, Asher released her and stepped away. "Please continue your tale."

Once she regained her wits, she finished her account of Echo Hall, and then ended with her initiation at the Festival of the Full Moon. Despite his brief outburst of emotion, Asher was a good listener, attentive and polite with few interruptions.

"What has it been like for you since joining the tribe?" Asher asked. "Have you used your new heritage?"

"When we were attacked by bandits, Torrend was wounded. I said some healing spells on his arm. I don't know enough about the Crennese lore to do much else."

Katrine became thoughtful. "I've learned to shield myself from other people's feelings—that part was really hard in the beginning—but I've had some strange physical reactions. I've had headaches and blurred vision and dizziness."

"What was happening around you when you felt that way?"

So Katrine told him about the dance for Heni, the occurrence in the ravine, and even the premonition before the bandits attacked. She expected him to chide her for making a fuss over nothing, spoiling the rapport they had developed, but instead he nodded his head.

"You know what they are," Katrine crowed with delight. "Tell me."

"It's hard to explain," Asher said, "but you might say a magic spell is involved. People who can do the kind of trance you did on the trail are particularly sensitive to this enchantment. If it happens again, do what you did today. Relax your mind and body and just let any images flow over you. Concentrating, peering, and probing only make the symptoms worse."

"But—"

Asher held up his hand and shook his head. "Another time. Right now, you must get some sleep and so must I. Dawn isn't that far off, and we have a long day's travel ahead of us. Come."

He extended his hand, and Katrine allowed him to help her down from the wall. As she gained her footing, she thought he held onto her hand a second or two longer than necessary to assure her safety. Her heart missed a beat.

Silently they walked back to the barn.

The warmth of Asher's touch lingered in Katrine's mind as she settled down on her blanket. His huge hands, hard and strong, had held hers so gently.

On the other side of the loft, she heard him move around a moment before he lay down.

An owl hooted. Crickets chirped. Heni sighed. Neyac snored. Torrend rolled over and rustled the hay.

Carefully, Katrine filtered out all the other night sounds so she could listen to Asher's breathing as he relaxed into sleep.

Chapter Twenty-Nine

Katrine woke with straw in her mouth. She spat it out, and as she untangled herself from her blanket, she realized she had straw in her hair and clothing as well.

"I've got to take a bath," she muttered to herself. She shook out her blanket, grabbed up her boots and saddlebags, and headed for the ladder.

"Is it morning?" moaned Heni. "I don't think I slept a wink all night. How can animals stand to live in barns? They're awful." She stretched and yawned, and then sat up. "Where are you going?"

"First I'm going to see where everyone else went," Katrine said, waving her hand at the loft, which was vacant except for the two girls, "and then I'm going to find out where I can get a bath."

"Wait for me," Heni cried, stumbling to her feet and gathering her things. "I need a bath, too."

The girls made their way down the ladder and through the barn, but they slowed when they neared the door because they could hear hushed voices. Of one opinion, they tiptoed nearer, spied through a crack in the wall, and listened.

"Can you do it?" Asher asked very quietly.

"Sure," Torrend said. "Just make sure you tie the message securely to my leg. If it comes loose, I don't know what I'll do. You did explain about me in the note, didn't you? I'd hate for Warlord Leeds to cage me."

"Of course. Rejoin us as quickly as possible. By the time you get to Landor, we should be on our way up the Great Meriad. Seek us."

"I will."

"How long will it take you to change?"

"A few minutes."

"You had best be about it then," Neyac told him. "I'd like you on your way before the young ladies wake up."

Without another word, Torrend crouched on the ground and a metamorphosis began. His neck disappeared into his shoulders, his legs shortened and became spindly, his body shrank and changed shape, his face shifted and grew a beak, and his skin sprouted a fine covering of brown feathers. Within a very short span, the young man was gone and a large brown hawk stood in his place.

Katrine and Heni both gasped. Asher spun toward the barn. He made a quick gesture with one hand, turned his attention back to the hawk, and swiftly fastened a note wrapped in oilcloth to the bird's leg.

"Go safely," Asher said.

The bird bobbed its head and took flight.

Katrine and Heni were so dumbfounded by the scene they'd witnessed, they didn't pay any attention to the barn door when it opened or to the Master Recorder when he entered.

"Damn," said Neyac.

"Damn," said Asher when he joined Neyac in the doorway.

"What happened?" Heni asked incredulously as soon as she sighted the two men. "Torrend flew away?"

"Is Torrend a Shokai then?" Katrine demanded, almost beside herself with rage. "Have I traveled this far to deliver my message to traitors?"

"Traitors? How dare you!" roared Asher. His face turned red and his neck muscles twitched. "And what are you? Spies?"

"Easy, boy," Neyac said, resting his hand on Asher's shoulder. "You must look at it from their viewpoints. We didn't tell them what we were planning, and Torrend didn't share his secret with them. They're not mind readers or seers. It must seem very confusing and rather suspicious."

"Even so, I will not have anyone accuse me of treason," Asher snarled, "especially not some ignorant adolescent female, who was spying on something that was none of her business."

"Gently, Asher," Neyac said, his tone soothing but also commanding. "Some words are hard to take back, and in this instance we are in the wrong. If we didn't want the ladies to know what we were doing, we should have chosen a more private spot and ensured against discovery. Now, all we can do is explain and try to restore their faith in us."

* * *

Asher turned his back on the cousins and locked gazes with Neyac. He had begun to calm down, but he still had responsibilities that he could not surrender to the Master Recorder.

"Until Warlord Leeds gives us permission," Asher said, "we aren't free to explain much. These girls are neither Warriors nor Recorders."

"I understand," Neyac said with a nod, "but we must tell them something. We still have quite a journey ahead of us, and—"

"Stop talking about us as if we're not here," Katrine said angrily. "If there are others who can change shape besides Shokai, then just tell us." She continued sarcastically, "Even though I'm just an ignorant adolescent female, I assure you I'm as trustworthy as a Warrior or a Recorder. Now, I'm waiting for an explanation if you have one."

"Good," Neyac said. "Why don't we all find a comfortable bit of hay and sit down?"

Asher stood off to the side while Katrine sat on the floor with Heni right beside her. Neyac looked around, pulled up an empty wooden crate, and straddled it.

Let Neyac handle this, Asher told himself.

He walked over to the barn door, leaned on the frame, and stared at the sunrise.

What was it about that girl that could turn him into a raving maniac with just a few words? She called him names, so he retaliated by insulting her?

He could hardly believe it.

She, at least, had the excuse of being young. He was supposed to be an adult. He shook his head at his own stupidity. He ran his fingers through his hair and pushed it back from his forehead. Taking slow deep breaths, he listened to the Recorder begin.

"Torrend is Crennese," Neyac said.

"He is?" Heni asked, astounded. "He has magician's blood? I never suspected. He seems so normal."

"He told me," Katrine said. "So what?"

"One of Torrend's sorcerous gifts is shapeshifting."

"Obviously," Katrine said. "Even I could see that."

"If you keep interrupting me, Katrine, I'll never get through the telling," Neyac said with exasperation.

"Go on," Katrine mumbled sourly.

"Thank you. When Manderig created the races and bestowed their heritages on them, he gave the Crennese the full range of wizard powers. That includes shapeshifting, true shapeshifting. Even though the demon taught Haldrid how to change shape, demon powers are different from human ones. When a Shokai changes shape, there is always a defect of some kind."

Neyac reached down, picked up a handful of straw, and twisted it into a knot, as if he needed to do something with his hands while he thought. He tossed the wad aside before he continued speaking.

"When a true sorcerer reshapes himself, as Torrend did, his change is perfect. The bird Torrend became can still think like a man, but its body is a hawk's body. Torrend will eat what a hawk eats and sleep where a hawk sleeps until he takes on his own form again. You saw, ladies. It was a real hawk, not a caricature, and that's how you can tell Torrend isn't a Shokai."

"Assuming you're telling the truth," Katrine said, clearly dubious about the whole affair, "why did Torrend turn into a bird and fly away? If he was going to do it, why didn't he do it yesterday or tomorrow or some other day? Why this morning?"

Turning to address Asher, Neyac asked, "Well?"

"It's your story. You decide. Just be careful with information the Warlord might consider confidential."

Neyac nodded. "Last night, Katrine, you gave Asher information imperative to the defense of Kareand."

Jumping to her feet, Katrine shrieked at Asher with clenched fists. "You told? How could you? You promised."

Asher shrugged his shoulders and didn't comment.

He had done what was expedient.

Neyac knew a great many people all over Kareand, and Asher had needed advice on the fastest way to send the Warlord a message. He could have gone himself, but he didn't think it was safe to leave Neyac alone on the road with three youngsters in tow.

When Neyac told him about Torrend's talent, Asher thought it was a perfect solution. Torrend could cover the distance much faster than Asher could ride, even taking advantage of his Captain's status and demanding a fresh horse at each Landorian Compound.

Naturally, he confided the whole story to Neyac. There were only a few people in all of Kareand that Asher trusted as much as he trusted the Master Recorder. Still, he felt a certain amount of shame because he had not honored Katrine's wishes, and feeling that way made him angry.

Damn it to hell and back, he thought. *I don't have to justify my behaviors or decisions to anyone other than the Warlord. I certainly don't need to explain myself to a teenage girl.*

"What did you tell him, Katrine?" Heni asked. "Surely, you don't have any military information."

"What Katrine told Asher is private," Neyac told Heni in a tone that brooked no contradiction. "But it was essential that the information be taken to Warlord Leeds as fast as possible. We still have a long journey to Pardish, and Torrend agreed to fly to Landor and deliver the message to save time."

"All right, Neyac," Katrine said, "I suppose we have to accept your story. My father has faith in you, and I guess I do too. However, some people obviously have trouble respecting what is told to them in confidence. I don't think a person like that is honorable or trustworthy."

When Asher pivoted to face her, Katrine met his gaze with a glower.

"Katrine," he said mildly, "it was necessary. Try to understand."

"I suppose we need to get moving," Katrine said coldly, ignoring Asher and directing her comments to Neyac. "Is there someplace Heni and I can bathe before we leave? We've both got hay all through us. Probably fleas as well."

"Not fleas," squawked Heni.

"I itch enough to have fleas."

"There's a bathhouse," Neyac said. "I'll show you where, but don't take too long. We need to eat some breakfast and take to the trail as quickly as possible."

* * *

At Serpent's Head, Elnid-Kyeh took a break from his military council to meet with the assassin his Captain of the Guard had selected.

In this instance, Elnid-Kyeh had acquiesced to the Captain's wisdom. Since the girl was now traveling in the company of a Landorian Warrior, he had agreed to employ an assassin rather than a thief to obtain the spire.

"This is the girl," Elnid-Kyeh said, moving aside so the hired man could see into the scrying dish.

"Any particular instructions? Do I need to go to the trouble of making it look like an accident?"

"Not at all. Use whatever method is best for you. Just don't fail. What I want is the weapon she carries in her saddlebags. Dispatch her any way you want, just get me the weapon."

"Where is she?"

"Almost to Yallon."

"That's a month's travel from here," the man said. "I hope you're not in any hurry."

"But I am." Elnid-Kyeh started chanting and gesturing with his hands.

"What are you doing?" the man sputtered.

"I am sending you there."

"Nooooooo!" The man's voice faded away as Elnid-Kyeh made the last gesture and cast the spell.

* * *

The rest of the trip to Yallon was tense.

No matter what Asher said, Katrine could not bring herself to forgive him. As they rode in silence, she often relived their interactions.

After a while, she began to feel foolish. Still, he shouldn't have told anyone her secret. *Her secret?* No, she reminded herself again and again, only part of it was hers.

Kylet must have had a sound reason for choosing Asher as the recipient of his message, and Asher probably had just as good a one for sharing it with Neyac. Besides that, Neyac already knew about the Tests of Truth and her initiation, all he had lacked were the details.

Finally, she acknowledged to herself, although it stung to the core of her being, she had overreacted and behaved abominably. As the miles passed and Yallon's rooftops became visible amid the hills and trees, she ached to tell Asher she was sorry. But each time she looked at his formidable countenance, the words froze on her tongue.

When they entered the city, Asher left to go on business of his own, telling them he would meet them later that afternoon.

Neyac tried pointing out the local wonders, but Katrine's foul mood would not let her enjoy anything. Once again, Neyac guided them to a nice inn.

"We all need a good rest for our bodies—and our temperaments," Neyac told Katrine and Heni as they followed the innkeeper to their rooms. "After you ladies have completed your business with Ferrill's family, I would suggest that you take time to enjoy the entertainments and amusements Yallon has to offer. This negative atmosphere is beginning to jangle my nerves."

The innkeeper opened the door to the girls' room, and after letting Heni precede him, he deposited the luggage on the floor.

Katrine stayed with Neyac in the hall.

"I'm sorry." She scraped her boot along the bright, multicolored rug that covered the floor and then stared at the scuffmarks. "I know I've been acting childish and making the trip miserable for everyone. I was stupid. I wanted Kylet's message to be our secret."

"You like Asher, don't you?" Neyac asked astutely.

She nodded. "Probably more than I should. If I didn't, it wouldn't have hurt so much. I thought he sort of liked me too, at least a little, but he yelled at me and called me names and told you and Torrend what I said." Leaning against the wall, she closed her eyes tight and bit down on her lower lip so she wouldn't start bawling like a baby. "I want to tell him I'm sorry," she said after a moment, "but when I look at him, I get so nervous I just can't."

"Growing up is difficult and often painful." Neyac patted her cheek affectionately and then wiped away her tears. "Maybe Asher shouldn't have told me what you said without asking you first, but he's a Captain in the Landorian Warriors, and his responsibilities are great. He did what he had to, and I think his frustration was because he expected you to understand. That might not have been fair, but I think it shows he has a special feeling for you, too."

"But he doesn't even talk to me anymore. I don't know what to do. I've been really mean to him, and I don't know how to fix it."

"If you can't bring yourself to approach him, the next time he apologizes to you, accept it graciously. That's all it'll take."

"Are you sure?" Katrine said, still sniffling.

"Yes, I'm sure."

Feeling unbelievably relieved, Katrine hugged Neyac and gave him a quick kiss on the cheek. When she joined Heni in their room, she was smiling for the first time in days.

"Before we go see Ferrill's family," Heni said, "I've got to take a nap. Right now I'm just not up to it." She stretched out on the bed, but Katrine paced between the window and the door and back again. Heni sat up abruptly. "Stop that immediately. I'll never get to sleep with you tromping around. Why don't you go shopping or something? Come back later."

"Fine, I will." Taking up the leather satchel containing her art materials, Katrine paused at the door. "I'll be downstairs in the parlor. Come get me when you're ready."

After Katrine closed the door on her cousin, she realized she really wasn't in the mood to draw anything.

Briefly, she stood outside Neyac and Asher's door.

Yallon was the biggest city they had seen so far, and she wanted to go exploring. Maybe Neyac would go with her. She raised her hand to knock and then let it drop. If Asher was back, he might answer, and she wasn't ready to face him yet. Turning around, she walked away.

She selected a little out-of-the-way corner in the parlor between a settee and a tall potted plant. She opened her satchel and pulled out a board, parchment, and charcoal. She clipped the parchment in place, and chose a brownish charcoal stick.

Inspiration was slow in coming.

A steady stream of people pulsated in and out of the little room. The ventilation was wretched, and the afternoon heat collected and refused to dissipate.

Soon Katrine felt groggy. She wished she'd stayed upstairs with Heni and tried to sleep, but she was too drowsy to return now. She watched for an unusual face or an interesting costume that might spark her interest.

Through drooping eyelids, she noticed a strange, yet familiar, figure enter the room. It was a woman, or rather a man dressed like a woman, similar to the one she and Asher had seen on the trail. Maintaining her relaxed state and keeping her breathing smooth, she began to sketch both faces she saw, surrealistically and superimposed on top of each other.

When she finished, she got out her little blowpipe and blew sealant over the picture. Then, leaning the board against the wall so the picture could dry, she decided to close her eyes for just a moment. After a short rest, she might have enough energy to go back to the room and take a nap.

"Katrine," a voice boomed in her dream. "Why are you sleeping in the lobby? Is something wrong with your room? Katrine, wake up."

The voice belonged to Asher, and she tried to pull herself from sleep's deep quagmire so she could apologize, but the voice dwindled into the distance. Katrine allowed her consciousness to drift away also. If this was a dream, she could just as easily apologize to him in her sleep.

Cold water splashed against her face, and instantly Katrine was awake, on her feet, and furious. "What are you doing?"

"I'm sorry," Asher said, "but I couldn't rouse you. This isn't a safe place for a young lady to take a nap. Let me escort you to your room. I'll go away when you're secure."

"It's so kind of you to be concerned." The words came out sarcastic and rude, which wasn't what she intended at all.

For the briefest of seconds, the expression on Asher's face looked vulnerable, maybe even a little hurt. Then the fierce Warrior was back. He started to say something, decided against it, set the empty cup on the floor, and turned to leave.

Biting her lip, Katrine watched him until he was almost to the door. "Asher," she called. "Don't go. I'm sorry I've been so mean. I'd like you to escort me to my room, really I would."

He waited patiently while she gathered her things together and stuffed them into her bag. Then he extended his forearm, and she lightly placed her fingertips on it.

"Are we friends again?" he asked.

"Friends," she said.

"About time," he murmured. Then he smiled his glorious smile.

Katrine forgot how to breathe.

I could learn to like arguing with Asher, she thought, *if he always gave me such a wondrous gift when we made up.*

Entering her room, Katrine found Heni sitting on the edge of the bed, elbows on knees, face cupped in her hands.

"I can't go see Ferrill's family on an empty stomach," Heni said. "I just can't. Isn't it about dinnertime? We could go after that. I'm sure that would work out better. Once his people get the news, they won't feel like eating. It's not fair to spring something like this on someone when they haven't even had their dinner. I'm certain we ought to wait until later this evening. Don't you think so?"

After the girls had enjoyed a pleasant meal with Neyac and Asher, the first in several days, Heni said, "Maybe it's too late. They're working people and probably go to bed early. If we go now, we'll disturb their sleep. Maybe I ought to just write them a note and send it by messenger tomorrow."

"I think we all ought to accompany you, Heni," said Neyac. "I'll arrange for a carriage. You ladies look so lovely tonight it would be a shame for you to change out of your fine skirts for a horseback ride."

"But—"

"It's always best to get unpleasantness done and out of the way," Katrine said soothingly. "We'll go with you and see you through this, Heni. You don't have to do it alone."

* * *

The assassin had recovered from being transported to Yallon and was wandering down a busy street when he caught sight of the girl just as she left a building and climbed into a carriage.

He ran down the road, trying to locate a rig-for-hire along the way, but the coach rounded a corner and disappeared into the night.

He headed back to the dining hall where he had first seen her. Someone would remember a girl that attractive. They might even know where she was staying.

* * *

Ferrill's parents handled the news about their son's death better than Heni did. She cried and carried on and embraced the members of Ferrill's family repeatedly. They looked sad and slightly dazed when Katrine led her cousin back to the carriage.

"You were very brave," Katrine told Heni. "Now you can have a good cry. It won't bring Ferrill back, but you'll begin to heal sooner if you let the pain come out."

Heni laid her head on Katrine's shoulder and sobbed all the way back to the inn.

* * *

Asher watched Katrine from the other side of the carriage.

She was a complicated young thing.

Although she had a nasty temper—and Asher smiled inside when he realized it was quite a bit like his own—still, she was basically a kind, compassionate person.

Sometimes he wished she were just a few years older, closer to his own age. Immediately he pushed the thought aside.

She was a child, and he needed to keep that fact firmly in mind.

Chapter Thirty

As they made their way toward Branston, Asher was constantly on alert. Several times he left the girls and Neyac, along with the pack animals and Torrend's horse, in some concealed spot as he scouted along the trail.

When they neared the city, he turned to the Master Recorder and said, "I don't understand it. In a few places, I've found all the signs of large encampments: discarded tack and broken weapons, used targets, remnants of campfires, plus foot and hoofprints of many men and horses. But all the camps were deserted. Where could they have gone?"

"I don't know," Neyac answered with a shake of his head. "If they're planning insurrection, Landor or Pardish seem the logical targets."

Asher pushed back a strand of hair from his face. "I'll be glad when Torrend returns. Maybe Leeds knows what's going on."

"We're almost there," Heni cried with delight. "I can hardly wait to get home and sleep in my own bed and see my parents and my friends. Let's hurry. I wouldn't even mind trying to gallop."

It had been quite a while since Asher had tied Heni to the saddle. He had stopped doing it when they came to more populous areas that afforded greater safety. She had never offered to go at more than at a trot before.

"Fine," Asher said. "The horses could use a good run."

The horses took off at a brisk clip as soon as they were given their heads, but before long they were forced to slow down. People straggled up the road, at first just a few, then in increasing numbers. Men, women, and children carried bags thrown over their shoulders. Wagons loaded with household goods clanked among them, some pulled by plains ponies and some by the people themselves.

Hazy smoke hung in the air.

When Asher signaled a halt at the top of a rise and they could finally see Branston, they just stared. The city gates dangled askew. Crudely bandaged individuals wandered aimlessly, calling out names, and every now and then a young child could be heard wailing.

The Spire of Kylet

"What's happened?" Heni called loudly to some passersby. "Where is everyone going?"

No one answered.

For a few moments she watched in shocked horror, and then a look of panic swept across her face.

"Mother! Father!" She gave her mount a mighty kick.

The others had to whip their horses to keep up with her.

Inside the city walls, burnt houses smoldered and the number of injured multiplied. Hacked, mutilated bodies sprawled in doorways and hung from balconies. Whole sides of buildings had fallen, and lifeless arms and legs poked through the rubble.

Volunteer bands, directed by peacekeepers wearing the orange and yellow seal of Branston, sifted through the wreckage, looking for survivors and collecting the dead.

Over the thudding of horses' hooves, Asher called to Neyac, "This is why the marauders' camps were empty."

"I'm afraid so," Neyac agreed solemnly.

* * *

Katrine held her quivering cousin around the waist.

They stood together in front of a once elegant house. Like all those around it, it had been sacked and burned.

"Katrine, you stay with Heni," Asher told her. "Neyac and I will go see if anyone is here."

Katrine nodded at him and tightened her grasp. Every now and then Heni shivered, and Katrine stroked her hair or patted her back until the tremors subsided. While they waited, Katrine wondered about her own family who were so far away. She prayed for their safety.

After quite some time, Asher returned.

"Would you describe the members of your household?" Asher asked Heni in a gentle tone. "No one is left alive, but we don't know if your parents are among the dead."

"I want to see," Heni croaked in an odd sounding whisper. She swallowed hard a couple of times, fighting back tears, and straightened her spine in an attitude of resolve. "Even if my parents are dead, I want to see them one last time."

"Please," Asher said, "believe me. You don't want to see this. If you'll just describe—"

"No!" Heni shouted.

In a flash, she disengaged herself from Katrine's embrace, dashed around the Warrior, and darted into the ruined building. Asher and Katrine sprinted after her, following the sound of her rapidly falling footsteps.

When they caught up with her, Heni was positioned cross-legged on the floor in the middle of a devastated sitting room, surrounded by splintered furniture, ripped cushions and drapes, and slashed paintings.

Cradled on her lap was the torso of an attractive woman whose frame was battered and bloody. Tenderly, Heni was running her fingers through the long chestnut hair with its occasional strand of gray, lifting it away from the woman's face. She swayed gently back and forth as if rocking a child to sleep.

"Mother," whispered Heni. "Oh, Mother."

Much of the woman's clothing was torn and tattered, as if she'd fought hard against her attackers. Long ugly slashes and purplish bruises were visible through the gaps, but for some reason her face had been left undamaged. The woman's features were peaceful in death.

Katrine hadn't seen her Aunt Rulina for several years and had forgotten how beautiful she was and how much her daughter resembled her.

Although Heni gazed at her mother warmly, Katrine could tell she was a seething volcano of hatred and fury beneath her calm exterior. Her sense of loss was devastating and wrenched at Katrine's heart, but her desire to return violence with violence was so profound it was frightening.

As the moments passed, the intensity of Heni's agony increased until it became more than Katrine could bear. Frantically, she struggled to erect the impenetrable emotional shields that Polnu had taught her. When she finally had them in place, she shook with exhaustion. She stretched her arms out imploringly. "Come, Heni. Let's go outside."

"No," Heni said, softly but firmly. "There is a small garden my mother loved at the back of the house. I'll leave after I've seen my parents buried there, not before. The man in the hall whose throat was cut is my father. If you won't help me, I'll dig their graves myself with bare hands and fingernails if I must, but I won't go until it's done."

"Of course, we'll help you, my dear," Neyac said. He entered the room through a portion of buckled wall, his clothing smudged with soot and dirt, a spade in his hand. "I've already begun a grave for those slain here. If it's not in the garden you spoke of, we'll prepare a new spot. Come, help us find something to use as shrouds."

Heni led them through the sleeping quarters until they found a few blankets in the least damaged bedchambers. She chose a pink floral quilt for her mother.

"They took her jewelry," Heni said flatly.

She rearranged her mother's clothing so it covered the body more modestly, and then she kissed her mother's cheek and closed the blanket over her.

As they placed her father's body on a dark geometric patterned blanket that Heni said he'd always fancied, she took a moment to stroke his hand.

"Look, Katrine," she said, "they cut off his finger to remove my great-grandfather's ring. You remember it, don't you? It was gold and fashioned like a dragon with two tiny rubies for eyes. My great-grandmother designed and commissioned it for their betrothal. It was my family's most treasured heirloom."

"I remember," Katrine told her. Then Katrine gently lifted her cousin's fingers away and laid her uncle's hands across his chest, the mutilated one below the whole, and pulled up the sides of the blanket to cover the body. Neyac and Asher carried the shrouded forms from the house.

They buried Heni's parents in one grave in the little garden her mother had loved behind the ruined house in the once great city of Branston.

As Neyac and Asher hollowed another plot for the servants, Heni searched the grounds for late blooming flowers. Most of the manor's decorative gardens had been buffeted and trampled by the marauders during their looting, but Heni found a few undamaged plants and plucked all of the colorful blossoms. She arranged them on her parents' grave. Then, taking a small knife she had found in the kitchen, she cut off a long lock of her lustrous brown hair and wove it in-and-out among the flowers.

"It's all I have to leave you," Heni said in a choked whisper, kneeling beside the fresh mound. "I'll always love you, and oh, how I'll miss you. Goodbye, Mother. Goodbye, Father. Some day we'll meet again in the realm of spirits."

For quite a while, Heni remained motionless and silent, as if praying. Neyac and Asher finished burying the servants and cleaned their hands in a small pool of water that remained puddled at the bottom of a half-demolished fountain.

"You'll kill them for me, won't you, Katrine?" Heni asked in a dull passionless tone.

"What?" Katrine gasped.

"The evil men who did this to my parents, you'll kill them for me, won't you? Their deaths must be avenged, and it should be at the hand of one of our bloodline. The grandparents are all too old or already gone to their graves, and the aunts and uncles are too involved with their own homes and families. Of the cousins, only you and I are old enough, and I'm not suited physically. That leaves you."

"Heni, I'm going to Pardish to become a Recorder, not to Landor to become a Warrior."

"She's in shock," Neyac said quietly in Katrine's ear. "She doesn't know what she's saying."

"When you do it," Heni continued as if no one else had spoken, "you must be sure to retrieve my father's ring. My parents always intended it for my husband, then later for my first child. I know my father's spirit won't rest easy until the ring is returned. My mother gave it to him on their wedding day, and he never took it off. You must kill them all, but especially the one who has the dragon ring. It's the only one like it anywhere."

"Please, Heni," Katrine pled, "let's get away from here. We can talk about it later."

Slowly and deliberately, Heni rose to her feet, her brown eyes locked on Katrine's pale ones. "You will kill them, Katrine. I feel it all the way through my body to my very soul. I saw your fierceness when the bandits attacked us. Evil men will quake at your coming and lie dead at your passing. You will avenge my parent's deaths, but you must not forget the ring."

"All right, Heni." Katrine took her cousin's hand and pulled her away from the garden. "If it happens as you say, I'll remember to get your father's ring for you."

After they mounted their horses, which Asher had tethered to a lopsided pillar, they made their way through debris-cluttered streets. Everywhere they glanced, they saw another horrendous panorama of death and devastation, pain and suffering.

The shield Katrine had built to protect herself from Heni's distress wasn't strong enough to shelter her from the incredible anguish of the people. She wanted to do something to help, like lob a few hundred arrows into the people responsible for this misery, but right now she was powerless.

She distracted herself by picturing in her mind how the city must have looked before the assault. Where partial buildings and walls were still intact, elaborate engravings, brightly painted murals, or designs in relief were visible.

Many courtyards held smashed fountains and broken statuary, but even the remnants of these damaged artifacts conveyed a sense of beauty and grace. Trees, shrubs, and flowers, all dressed in autumn's yellows and reds and orangey golds, were abundant along the streets and in private gardens.

The city was so large it seemed to stretch on forever.

"I'm no stranger to the aftermath of violence," Katrine heard Asher say to Neyac, "but this," he waved his hand broadly, "this looks more like the work of an army than a band of desperadoes."

"Maybe it was," Neyac replied in somber tones. "I hope the Commander at the Compound has some answers for us."

* * *

Two young Warriors stood guard at either side of the gates at the Landorian Compound. Both had bandages around various parts of their bodies, and one leaned on a crutch. They saluted Asher as he rode up to them.

"Powers Above, men," Asher roared, "you should be in the infirmary."

"We're among the least wounded, sir," said the youth with a bloody cloth tied around his head. "The infirmary is reserved for those too severely injured for duty."

"Carry on, then," Asher said as he urged his horse forward. The young men saluted again as he passed by.

Asher leaned toward Neyac and said in an undertone, "This is worse than

I thought. It's beyond unbelievable, it's unimaginable."

Once through the gates, Asher discovered that the large central square had been converted into a temporary hospital.

Row after row of tents and other crude shelters, some no more than blankets propped up by sticks, were lined up on the eastern side. On the west, many people—civilians as well as Warriors—lay on pallets or sat huddled in blankets, waiting to be seen by the Healers.

Volunteer helpers and healing apprentices rushed back and forth from one side of the courtyard to the other, carrying linens and blankets, water skins and cups, and what looked like kettles of soup and baskets of bread.

Like all Landorian Compounds, the primary buildings were arranged in a horseshoe shape and consisted of the infirmary and armory on the left, the officers' and Warriors' dining halls on the right, and the administrative building in the middle. Housing units, barracks, and stables were spread out behind the other structures. All visible buildings had sustained damage.

As Asher cautiously led his group through the chaos, he noticed people on stretchers being carried into the central buildings, and he assumed the Healers were taking the most seriously injured inside before the temperature dropped with the setting sun.

Suddenly, Katrine reined to a stop and swung off her horse.

"Go ahead without me," she said. "There aren't enough Healers for this many wounded. Maybe I can help."

"I'll help too," offered Heni.

Katrine gave her a quizzical look, but Heni slid from the saddle and stared back. Her expression was a blend of pleading and resolve. "I don't want to be alone. Just tell me what to do, and I'll do it."

"All right." Katrine groped around in her saddlebags until she found a leather pouch, which she tied to her belt. Then she handed the reins of her and Heni's horses to Asher. "Will you take care of our mounts?"

"Certainly," Asher said. "After Neyac and I stable the horses and unload the pack animals, we'll be in there." He pointed directly ahead. "That's the Regulatory Building. When you tire and want to rest, come and find us. I'll make sleeping arrangements for you somewhere."

As Asher rode off, he wondered if he would be able to make good on that offer. A visiting Captain was usually offered generous hospitality, but with this much devastation and this many injured, there might not be any accommodations left.

* * *

For several days, the assassin searched for the girl.

Although people in the dining hall had remembered her and her party, no one had any idea where they were staying or for how long. Rather than waste time wandering the streets aimlessly, he had immediately begun inquiring at the inns, starting with those nearest to where he had seen her.

Today he had found it, but she and her companions had left after only one night.

Of all the fraggin' luck!

The innkeeper's daughter thought she had heard one of the girls say they were traveling to Branston, but she wasn't sure.

The assassin was furious.

That damned fool of a magician had transported him here without supplies or necessities—and apparently without considering the possibility that the girl might move on before he located her.

As soon as it was dark enough, he would have to steal a horse so he could follow.

Chapter Thirty-One

It took Katrine and Heni quite a while to find the Master Healer who was in charge and to offer their aid. The Healer was an elderly man, white haired and wrinkly, who was nearly as old as Bainu. He looked as if he would soon need a Healer himself if he didn't get some rest.

"Do you have any experience?" the weary man asked. "Of course, we can always use unskilled help for changing and washing bedding and for feeding those who can't feed themselves, but what I really need are some more adept Healers."

"I'm afraid I don't have much training—" began Katrine.

"More's the pity," the Master Healer mumbled.

"—but I've been adopted by the Glainites and therefore share the Crennese heritage." Heni gasped, but Katrine ignored her. "I've been instructed in a few healing spells and some herbal and medicinal lore. I also have a medicine pouch prepared for me by a Master Healer."

"Blessed Signs," the old man exclaimed. "We're so nearly out of medications. Do you have antiseptic powders? We ran out yesterday, and our Healers are trying to combat infections with spells alone."

"Yes," Katrine answered, untying the bag on her belt and handing it over. The Master Healer grabbed it like a greedy child who had been offered sweets.

"Use anything you need," Katrine said. "Now, please put us to work. We'll help in any way we can, but we need to stay together."

"Come along," the Healer said without moving. His head was almost stuck inside the pouch. When he located the antiseptic powders, he heaved an enormous sigh of relief. He addressed the girls with renewed vigor. "I'll introduce you to some of the others. They can tell you where you're needed the most."

For the rest of the day Katrine and Heni worked wherever they were told, crossing and re-crossing the Compound until the area had to be lighted by torches and small bonfires.

At first a Healer always stayed nearby to give instructions and to watch, but as their confidence in the girls grew, their supervision became less and less.

Katrine bound injuries, said healing spells, and occasionally put the sleep on those in extreme pain. Heni followed behind, giving the wounded sips of water or broth and sometimes straightening blankets or running to fetch another one. She was never idle, yet whenever Katrine reached for a clean bandage or a cup of water for mixing potions, Heni was on hand with what she needed.

* * *

Asher took a few minutes to rest and think. He ran his fingers through his thick hair and pushed it out of his eyes.

When he and Neyac had entered the Regulatory Building, he had planned on offering his support and assistance to Captain Fernan. He hadn't expected to find that the Captain, his Arms Master, and all the senior officers had been slain during the fighting and that a newly promoted Section Leader had taken charge. He had spent the entire day interviewing the surviving Warriors and going through the slain Captain's reports.

According to Section Leader Denman, as soon as the marauders attacked the city gates, Captain Fernan had dispatched a runner with a message to Captain Piper at the Compound in Lolloc, asking for reinforcements. The runner had used a secret passageway through the city wall, but no reinforcements came. Everyone assumed the runner had been caught and killed.

Asher dispatched another runner at once with a report on the situation in Branston. In his letter to Captain Piper he requested additional troops, particularly some senior officers. He also sent a separate communiqué, which he asked to be forwarded to Warlord Leeds at Landor.

Until reinforcements arrived or he received new orders from the Warlord, Asher had no choice but to stay here. There was no way he could leave an inexperienced Section Leader in charge of this mess.

* * *

As the frenzy of the day slowed with the coming of night, Master Healer Gillian sought out Katrine and Heni and suggested they get some sleep. Tired and spent, they made their way to the building Asher had shown them eons ago. Shortly thereafter, wrapped in the blankets from their packs, they were settled on the floor behind a screen in the room Asher and Neyac were using as a command center.

Before Katrine drifted to sleep, she thought she heard Asher talking about Shokai disguised as travelers infiltrating the countryside. Once, she heard something about the Wolkareans returning at last.

She wanted to stay awake and listen to the rest of it, but she was too exhausted to keep her eyes open for another second.

* * *

Elnid-Kyeh swept his hand across the scrying dish. The picture of the sleeping girl faded into the water.

If he had not scried Branston to enjoy the aftermath of its destruction, he would not have discovered that the infernal assassin had missed the girl at Yallon.

Did he have to watch these stupid Kareandeen mercenaries every minute to make sure they did their jobs?

If he did, what good were they to him?

At least the banquet he held for his generals was a success. Now that it was over, the men were happily drunk and asleep, or maybe they were happily drunk and amusing themselves in the bed of some servant. He did not care which.

He only wanted a few moments to relax, but there was something he had to do first.

He cast another scrying spell.

A picture of the assassin on horseback, pounding through the darkness, formed on the water in the bowl.

Weaving his hands through the air, Elnid-Kyeh chanted the words to another incantation. There was a flash of light, and his projected image appeared in the middle of the road.

The assassin's horse reared in fright and dumped its rider to the ground. Then it ran off.

"You raging fool," the assassin yelled as he climbed to his feet. "I was on my way to Branston to kill the girl and get the weapon you want, and now you've scared off my horse."

"I told you not to fail," said Elnid-Kyeh.

The assassin dusted off his clothing. "It's not my fault I couldn't find her. Yallon is a big city. You said you were sending me to her, but by the time I found out where she was staying, she had already gone."

"Incompetence."

"Incompetence?" bellowed the assassin. "You're the one who sent me to a city so big you could hide an army in it. If you think you can find someone better than me, go right ahead. I didn't want this fraggin' job anyway. I only agreed as a favor to my good friend, Lairnus."

"You wish to resign the commission?" asked Elnid-Kyeh.

"You're fraggin' right I do."

At Serpent's Head, Elnid-Kyeh made a quick gesture and mumbled a few words. A moment later, a bolt of lightning struck the assassin in the chest

and slammed him to the ground, dead.
  "Resignation accepted."

                              * * *

As more and more people found their way to the Landorian Compound, the courtyard overflowed with wounded. As a result, sanitation became a problem. Latrines were dug at the outskirts of camp and were often sprinkled with lye. Large pots of water were kept boiling to sterilize bandages and bedding. Volunteers patrolled the perimeter to kill rats and other vermin.

The whole area reeked of blood, excrement, sickness, sweat, and death.

Yet despite this, Heni accompanied Katrine every morning to assist the Healers. She worked as hard as anyone, and she never complained, no matter how tired she became. Helping others lessened the pain of her losses and made her grief bearable.

As time progressed, her services became more useful. She had always been a good student, and she quickly picked up information and skills by watching, listening, and asking questions.

She began mixing potions and steeping powders for Katrine and the Healers. Twice, following detailed instructions, she helped set and splint bones. Once she even assisted with the delivery of a baby, an experience that brought tears of joy to her eyes as she witnessed the renewal and resiliency of life.

Because she could follow complicated directions, the Healers came to depend on her and to specifically request her presence. Soon she was venturing all over the camp with tasks of her own, no longer an appendage to Katrine.

She had never had to work before, and she was surprised to discover that it wasn't nearly as awful as she had always feared. The injured people she helped were so grateful, and the Healers so appreciative, she experienced a new sense of pride, pride that came from accomplishing rather than just having or belonging or being.

For most of her life she had built her self-concept on having the right possessions, or belonging to the most prestigious social groups, or being petite, well dressed, and pretty.

Late at night, lying on her bedroll, she often felt pangs of regret that she had waited so long to begin developing her inner self.

Wherever her parents were, she hoped they were proud of her and the person she was striving to become.

                              * * *

After Katrine had been working with Master Healer Gillian one day, he said, "I've heard many good things about your skills. Now I see they are true. You have the instincts of a Healer. I have no children of my own, and I would be honored if you would allow me to share my heritage with you."

Katrine couldn't find the words to express how humble and gratified she felt by his faith in her. She wanted to say something profound, but all she could think of to say was "I would be the one who is honored, sir."

They chose a time when Heni was engaged elsewhere and then slipped away to a quiet area behind one of the barracks. Gillian held Katrine's hands in his and spoke the Crennese chants of sharing.

"The bestowal won't be as strong as if we were able to do the complete ritual by moonlight and with tribal support, but it will make you sensitive to my teachings and facilitate your learning."

Thereafter, Gillian allowed Katrine to assist him in several surgeries, and while he operated, he explained the procedures to her. He demonstrated bone setting, the detection of internal injuries, and the diagnosing of infections and diseases. He also taught her more healing spells, some of which were complicated and could only be used for specific ailments. As she learned, she used her skills to ease pain and suffering.

But regardless of what she had been doing, her favorite part of each day was sharing the evening meal with Asher, Neyac, and Heni, talking over what they had each accomplished and the things they had observed.

Asher had assumed command since there were no other high-ranking officers available. At first he made humorous references to similar experiences in his past. But as the days went by, those comments grew less and less frequent.

From remarks she overheard, she knew the Warriors and Healers thought Asher was doing a phenomenal job. She had seen him with Gillian a few times, reviewing the needs of the hospital camp, and the Master Healer was full of praise for him. Neyac was usually at his side, taking notes, keeping records, forwarding instructions, and easing Asher's load in any way that he could.

* * *

Inside the Regulatory Building, Asher broke the wax seal on the letter he just received from Captain Piper at Lolloc. In response to the request for reinforcements, Captain Piper wrote that he was too shorthanded to provide any.

His letter said if it were a crisis, of course, it would be different, but Branston's emergency had come and gone. At this time, he had two large companies out because of other marauder attacks. The good news was that a boatload of Warriors from Landor would arrive soon. Also, he had forwarded Asher's request for senior officers to District Commandant Adrian at Botul.

When Asher finished reading the letter, he was so angry he wadded it up and threw it across the room while he went through his entire repertoire of profanity. When he realized he was beginning to repeat his curses, he picked up the letter, smoothed it out, and handed it to Master Recorder Neyac so he could read it too.

* * *

One evening, as Katrine and Heni were having dinner with Asher and Neyac in the large dining hall, the Recorder told the girls they were leaving.

Asher heaved a lusty sigh. "The reinforcements have finally arrived," he told them, "as well as the Compound's newly appointed Captain."

His smile of relief said a great deal about his opinion of being an administrator, and Katrine laughed at him. His smile grew even brighter, and he said, "There isn't any reason for us to stay here."

"I've arranged our passage on a riverboat," Neyac said. "Asher and I had hoped Torrend would bring word from Warlord Leeds before we left, but obviously the boy's been detained. We need to get on with our journey."

"How soon do we leave?" asked Katrine. "I can't go without explaining to Gillian and saying goodbye to some of the people I've worked with."

Nodding her head, Heni agreed. "I've also made some friends I'll want to see before we go."

"Do you want to come with us, Heni?" Asher asked. "I thought you would prefer to stay and help rebuild your home."

Heni's face went so pale that Katrine slipped an arm around her for fear she might pass out.

"I have no home in Branston now," Heni said with a quiver in her voice, "and I never will again. I want to go to Pardish with Katrine and then back to Banur. She's the closest family I have left. It would be cruel to separate us." Tears started dripping down Heni's cheeks. "You can't possibly expect me to stay here all alone."

"Of course not, my dear." Neyac reached across the table to pat her hand. "I was presumptuous and booked passage for you already. Asher was just checking to make sure you wanted to accompany us since I didn't consult you before making our plans. We leave early tomorrow morning."

Later, as they left the dining hall, Katrine pulled Neyac aside.

"I've written a letter to my parents to tell them about my aunt and uncle and to assure them Heni and I are safe. I should have done it sooner, but I kept putting it off because I didn't know what to say. They'll be so sad and so worried." She shivered involuntarily. "The last letter I sent was from Yallon. Before we leave, I've got to see this one on its way."

"There is a caravan taking some of the injured to relatives in the west. Warriors will be traveling with them to provide protection. I'm sure they'll be carrying the mail. We can make arrangements for your letter with them."

"Thank you."

Then Katrine and Heni threaded their way through the hospital camp to say their goodbyes.

The Spire of Kylet

Gillian embraced Katrine. "Your assistance will be sorely missed, but the worst is over. The apothecaries have united behind our efforts and are mixing powders and preparing healing herbs for us. I've replaced most of the medicines that we used from your supplies. I hope you know that many lives were saved through your generosity."

"Thanks for all you've taught me," Katrine said.

Gillian took her hand and kissed it. "If you ever need an old man's aid," he said, giving her the newly refilled medicine pouch, "send for me, and I'll come."

* * *

From Serpent's Head, Elnid-Kyeh watched as Katrine and her companions boarded the riverboat at Branston. He was greatly relieved.

Not knowing where the girl was going with Kylet's spire was becoming a drain on his energy. She had begun to intrude on his thoughts when he should have been attending to the plans he and his allies were making.

He had been unable to get his spies near her in the hospital camp. She was too busy rushing around. Then in the evenings, she was always with the Warrior and the Recorder.

Having her on the riverboat would be almost as good as having her in his dungeon. He would know where she was, and he could surely position one of his new assassins nearby.

Chapter Thirty-Two

After the hectic journey on horseback, followed by the equally frenzied demands of the hospital camp, Katrine had trouble adjusting to idleness on the riverboat.

At first, she was fascinated since she had never traveled by water before.

She inundated Neyac with questions, and he explained what he could.

The Great Meriad was a wide, meandering river with murky, yellowish water. Neyac said the color was caused by the spring runoff from the northern mountains. As the tributaries rushed to the Meriad, they picked up dirt and sand and silt, mostly saffron and ginger in color, and carried it with them.

He told her they were on a flat-bottomed craft designed to float in waters many times shallower than the depths required by oceangoing ships. Above deck was a structure much like a two-storied inn with cabins for passengers and a dining hall for meals. The below deck was divided into areas for rowers, storage, cargo, and animals.

Later, when Katrine asked a crewmember to take her to see Thunder Cloud, the man told her that passengers were not allowed down there.

After familiarizing herself with the vessel, Katrine found the voyage monotonous and tiresome. For hours she simply stood at the stern and watched the waves created by the rowers diminish in size as they rippled toward shore.

From the instant Heni boarded the boat, she complained of motion sickness. Katrine couldn't understand it, since she hardly felt any movement at all.

Nevertheless, Heni did nothing but lie on a bunk in their cabin. Whenever Katrine offered conversation or medication, Heni moaned and threatened to die. After listening to her cousin for a while, Katrine felt like jumping overboard. Or, better yet, tossing Heni over.

She had hoped Heni had outgrown this kind of behavior in Branston.

Of course, Katrine had to admit, the idleness and stuffy quarters weren't doing *her* mood any good either.

The Spire of Kylet

Unable to stand any more of Heni's whining, Katrine went outside and claimed an empty deck bench. She opened the Book of White Spells that Bainu had given her and sat pondering the Old Crennish writing, wishing she understood it.

"Interesting reading?" asked Neyac, suddenly dropping down beside her and stretching his short legs straight out in front.

"Might be for a scholar," Katrine said. She passed him the tome to inspect. "It's written in Old Crennish, and although my father would have a great time with it, my ability to translate has never been very good."

"Where did you get this?"

"The Glaine gave it to me before I left Banur. She thought it might prove helpful sometime. Maybe it would if I could read the stupid thing."

"Hmmm," Neyac murmured softly. "Asher told me about the experience you had when you spied on those travelers."

Katrine growled with annoyance. "Of course he did. The man is totally incapable of keeping a secret."

"Now, now, dearie," said Neyac. "I thought you were over being angry with Asher."

"It comes back now and then, especially when I'm losing my mind with boredom."

"Well, try to control it. We still have a long way to go. Now, as I started to say, not everyone can do the kind of seeing you did that day. Perhaps the same technique would work here. I rather suspect it will since The Glaine gave you the book, and her insight and wisdom are legendary. I doubt she would have given it to you unless she was fairly certain you could read it.

"Instead of trying to figure out the meaning of each sentence, why don't you just relax and open your mind? See what comes to you? For those with the skill, it's a trick that can prove helpful in many situations."

"You mean I shouldn't try to understand the words?"

"Exactly. Words are just symbols that stand for something else. If you understand the meaning, the result is the same."

"That's impossible. You can't know the meaning without knowing the words."

"Well, consider this. If I draw a picture of an apple, everyone who sees it and has also seen a real apple will know what I mean. It won't matter if they all speak different languages and have different words for that specific fruit. That's why Recorders often chronicle important events with illustrations. Pictures are one method of overcoming language barriers. Understanding is what's important, not words."

"And you think something like that might work here?"

"It's a guess, but it's the only way I can make sense of Bainu's giving you this instead of a Nistarian translation."

"I suppose I might as well try." Katrine opened the book to the first page. Remembering the instructions Asher had given her, she relaxed her body, made her breathing even, and let her thoughts float away. When she felt she had achieved the appropriate level of mindlessness, she looked down through lowered lashes.

At first, all she saw were the odd, angular characters of Old Crennish writing. Then slowly the markings were replaced by pictures, which moved through a revealing sequence of events. Katrine described them to Neyac.

"I see an old woman sitting high on a hill, remembering her flight from Shokareen as a child. She is thinking that someone should write a history about the settlement of Kareand before it is forgotten. Manderig recently went into the mountains and has not returned. She fears he has died and now the new order will fail. She has seen signs of it already as Nistarians and Crennese openly covet the wealth of the Boradids. She decides to record what she can remember. Her name is Miri."

Katrine stared at the book.

Was it bewitched or had it in some way bewitched her?

"How can I know all that without reading it?" Katrine demanded. "How does this strange trick of Asher's work?"

"Later, Katrine," Neyac said. "When we get to Pardish, I'll explain it all to you. For now, just accept it. If you don't mind, while you interpret, I'd like to take down the translation for the Recorders."

"Why?"

"I'd like to compare it with existing versions. I don't think any of the others were done using this technique. Who knows? You might come up with some new and enlightening insights. Will it make you nervous if I write down what you say?"

"I don't think so, but I'd like to read it when you're finished."

"Excellent. If I miss something, you might catch it."

They spent the rest of the day with Katrine describing what she saw in the book and Neyac taking it down in his quick, compact handwriting. Occasionally he asked her to pause and sketch a particularly interesting item or incident. He didn't call a stop until the waterfront town of Lolloc came into view.

"We won't be here long," Neyac told Katrine. "Just long enough to pick up passengers and provisions and mail. Even so, there should be time for you to take Heni down to the dock and walk her around a bit. Asher and I are going over to the Landorian Compound. Don't stray from sight of the boat. We'll be back as quickly as possible."

"All right," Katrine said.

Although Heni protested, Katrine finally got her out of bed and onto the pier. After strolling the length a couple of times, Heni admitted that she felt better and was even hungry.

They had passed a food vendor's cart, so they went back and purchased warm sticky buns at the price of two buns per copper. They each bought two and then sat on a couple of crates to eat, licking the honey off their fingers between bites.

Every now and then when the wind changed, the air grew pungent from half a dozen fishing boats docked upstream. As the men cleaned the fish, they threw the discarded parts into the water.

Clamoring raucously, a flock of birds swooped down and quarreled over the tidbits.

When Katrine spied Neyac and Asher threading their way between the stevedores who were busily hauling freight to and from the various vessels, she poked Heni and pointed. Sighing loudly, Heni got to her feet. Reluctantly the two girls started back toward the boat.

Abruptly Katrine stopped, suddenly aware of that peculiar combination of heat and fear and hatred that she'd felt in the past. She spun around, eyes wide and unblinking. She searched the shadows for something—something she couldn't identify.

She knew it was there. She knew it was dangerous.

Deliberately she drew her knife and stood half-crouched.

"What is it?" cried Heni. "What's the matter?"

Katrine said nothing. She didn't dare interrupt her concentration. Her gaze swept the surrounding buildings, the boats, the people.

Her survival, her very life, depended on her finding the threat before it found her.

"Neyac, Asher," Heni called. "Come quick. Something's wrong with Katrine. Hurry."

* * *

"What is it?" Asher asked Katrine. When she didn't respond, he moved directly in front of her. "What do you sense? Tell me."

Although Katrine worked her mouth for a moment, she made no sound. Her pale eyes darted everywhere.

He gripped her chin and forced her face up. "Tell me," he repeated forcefully. "Tell me what you sense."

She whispered through tight lips, "Evil. But I can't find it."

"Take them aboard," Asher told Neyac. "I'll look around."

"No," Katrine cried out. "I will look around!"

"Katrine," Asher boomed, "get back on board. I'll tell you what I find."

Without another word, Katrine twisted free of his grasp and tried to shoulder her away around him.

"What's that?" Asher called and pointed.

When Katrine spun around to look, he clipped her neatly on the jaw, slung her over his shoulder, bent to pick up her knife, which had clattered to the ground, and carried her to her cabin. Neyac and Heni followed close behind.

"Watch her," Asher ordered as he deposited Katrine on a bunk. "Don't let her out of here, even if you have to tie her up. I'll return as quickly as I can."

Asher sprinted back to the pier. He talked with the food vendors and several dockworkers, but no one had seen anyone following the girls or paying them any special attention. He spoke with the captain of the riverboat, but was unable to discover anything amiss. Uneasy, but with no other recourse, he returned to the cabin to learn what he could from Katrine.

"Why'd you do that?" Katrine grumbled as she sat up on her bunk and rubbed her jaw.

"You were about to do something foolish, and I didn't have time to argue."

"Well, did you have to hit me so hard?"

Asher felt the blood rush to his face. *Damn.* Something about her always made him defensive, even when he knew he was right.

"I'm sorry," he said. "I didn't want to hurt you, but I was worried about your safety. It was the quickest solution I could think of."

"Unless part of the solution is to suffocate me to death, could we please get out of here? You're crowding me so tight I can't catch my breath."

With Neyac, Heni, and himself all pressed around her, Asher could understand why she might feel claustrophobic. Still, he hesitated. "I have to know why you acted the way you did out there, Katrine."

"Fine, but do we have to talk in here? The air is so stale I can't even breathe, much less think."

Running his hand through his hair, Asher exhaled noisily.

He wasn't all that comfortable in these little cabins himself, but could he keep her safe on deck?

Yes.

The riverboat wasn't very big. If someone tried to hurt her, the only place he could go to escape Asher would be overboard.

"All right, but stay between Neyac and me."

"What?" yelped Katrine. "I can take care of myself. You don't have to treat me like a baby."

"Then don't act like one," he snapped. "Until we know what happened on the pier, we need to be cautious." He fixed her with an icy glare. "You either do it my way or no way."

He saw the defiance flash across her face, and he prepared himself for a battle, but she just stared at him a moment and then backed down.

"All right," Katrine grumbled. "I'll do anything to get some fresh air."

"Heni," Asher said, "do you mind waiting here while Neyac and I talk with Katrine?"

Although Heni was clearly curious, she glanced at Katrine, who was scowling thoughtfully, and shook her head. "I don't mind."

"Good. Bolt the door when we leave. Katrine, you might want to get your cloak." She glared at him but grabbed her wrap off a peg beside the door anyway.

Asher and Neyac emerged on deck with a sulky Katrine between them.

It was already dark, and the nearly full moon had scaled halfway up the evening sky.

"Well," Asher said as soon as Katrine had perched on a deck bench. "What happened?"

"I don't know." Katrine tried to sound indifferent, but Asher didn't believe it. He didn't know her well enough to understand what the undertones in her voice meant, but he certainly recognized that they were there.

"I felt like someone wanted to hurt me," she said, "and I wanted to get to him first. Before I could track him down, though." she pointed an accusatory finger at Asher, "you hit me."

"I doubt it's that simple," Asher said. When she frowned defensively and took a deep breath, he held up his hand to stop her before she could launch into a tirade. "Don't bother getting huffy, and don't pretend it doesn't matter. My patience is in short supply tonight. There is more going on here than you're telling me."

"I don't know what you mean," Katrine said in a haughty tone. "If you think I'm hiding something, you're wrong."

A man and woman seated themselves on a bench toward the stern and looked out over the water. Their soft voices could be heard as they murmured romantically to each other.

"Let's go forward," Asher said, taking Katrine's elbow and steering her to the left. "I don't think we should risk being overheard. I'll tell you some things, and then maybe you'll decide you have more to share."

As Katrine leaned on the railing at the boat's prow, Asher stood on her right and Neyac on her left. A faint trace of moonlight reflected on the dark water, and overhead the stars twinkled like a billion tiny fireflies. The air was brisk, and an occasional breeze carried the tangy scent of foliage growing along the banks.

"It is such a lovely night," Katrine said, sighing softly. "Do you have to spoil it? Can't we talk about this tomorrow?"

"No," Asher said, "this can't wait. Things are moving too fast. The Shokai have already started infiltrating Kareand."

"Careful, boy," Neyac said. "Timing."

"How do you know that?" Katrine asked, her words overlapping with the Recorder's.

"Some Shokai have been spotted by Warriors and Recorders. Remember when Neyac told you that their shape changing is imperfect? Observant eyes can sometimes spot the flaws."

"And the Wolkareans," Katrine asked with excitement. "I heard you mention them one night. I was almost asleep, but I know I heard that."

"Yes," said Asher. "A few Shokai were identified by the one Wolkarean who has been summoned to Landor."

"Summoned to Landor?" Katrine's eyes sparkled like the stars above her. "Are the Wolkareans returning then?"

"Not yet, but soon the gathering will begin."

Suspiciously, Katrine eyed Asher. "Why are you telling me this? What has it got to do with me?"

Asher took time to study the moonlight dancing on the water before answering. "We think one of the reasons the Shokai are penetrating Kareand at this time, before the arrival of their main force, is to find the enchanted weapons Kylet made. The burning heat and sense of evil you've described are sometimes experienced by people the Shokai are focusing their attention on."

Other than the infrequent call of a night bird, the lapping of the waves at the sides of the boat was the only sound for quite some time. When it became apparent that Katrine was not going to comment, Asher continued.

"You told me about feeling heat and a sense of evil in the ravine near your home, and the headaches and blurred vision at Heni's party. You also described some eerie sensations in the forest before the bandits attacked you." Asher paused, and Katrine nodded with her brows pulled together and her lower lip firmly between her teeth. "They are all variations of the same thing, Katrine. The Shokai are watching you."

"But why would the Shokai want Kylet's magical weapons? They can't make them work, can they?"

"I don't know," Asher said, "but even if they can't, if they have them, we can't use them either. But I don't think it's safe to assume the shapeshifters can't control the weapons. The Shokai have cultivated great sorcerers in the past, and they might be strong enough to turn Kylet's wizardry against us."

For what seemed like an eternity, Katrine chewed on her lower lip. Asher waited impatiently, resisting the urge to take her by the shoulders and give her a rough shake. At last she met Asher's eyes, and her rebellion was as clear as if she shouted it.

"If I tell you, you must understand you can't take it from me. Bainu said no one had the right to take it, and I won't give it up."

Asher and Neyac stared at each other in puzzlement.

"What in Kareand are you talking about, girl?" asked Neyac.

"Kylet's spire," Katrine answered as if she thought he should have known. "That must be what the Shokai want."

"Holy Signs!" Neyac exclaimed in surprise. "Just when I think I've got everything sorted out, Katrine, you surprise me again. You had better tell us the whole story."

Asher shook his head in astonishment while he listened to her explain.

After Katrine told them about finding the spire, she described showing it to The Glaine and her identifying it as Kylet's.

"If that awful burning sensation comes from the Shokai," Katrine said, "they must have been looking for the spire in the ravine after I found it. But I don't care if they are chasing me, I won't give it up. Bainu said I didn't have to."

"By the Coils, girl," Asher swore, "how have you stayed alive?"

The Spire of Kylet

Before Katrine could answer him, they heard an erratic flapping of wings above them. With that as the only warning, a large gray owl dropped out of the sky and sprawled inelegantly on the deck at their feet.

Slowly it dissolved and reformed into Torrend. He panted heavily, and on his face and chest were crimson streaks.

"I'm glad I found you," he gasped. "Warlord Leeds sent me to Serpent's Head, and then he gave me your new orders." His voice trailed off as he lost consciousness.

"I'll get my medicine pouch," Katrine said, spinning on her toes and dashing for the cabin.

As Asher bent to pick up the boy, Neyac asked him softly, "How did you think to draw her out with the story about the enchanted weapons? Did you actually suspect it?"

"No, but it was the only truth I dared tell her," Asher said as he carried Torrend toward their cabin. "I had to warn her that the Shokai are after her. I never suspected she had Kylet's spire. People have been searching for it ever since Renath fell."

"For it to turn up in Katrine's possession," Neyac said, "makes a certain amount of sense."

"And that's frightening."

They were just about to start up the stairs when Katrine came bounding down. She spun around and preceded Neyac and Asher back up.

Chapter Thirty-Three

After putting Torrend on a bunk, Asher stood aside so Katrine could clean and bandage the injuries. Before the boy passed out, he had said he brought new orders from Warlord Leeds. Asher had to clamp down on his impulse to search the boy's pockets for them.

When Torrend fluttered his eyelids, Neyac lifted his head to give him a sip or two of water.

"How are you feeling?" the Master Recorder asked.

"Much better now, thank you." Torrend looked anxiously in Katrine's direction and flushed with embarrassment. "Neyac, I'm sorry about transforming in front of Katrine. I know you didn't want the girls to know, but I just couldn't hold it any longer."

"It's all right," said Neyac with a comforting smile. "She and Heni were spying on us when you changed the first time. They both already knew. Tell us what happened."

"Warlord Leeds had me fly to Serpent's Head, and I guess I was spotted somehow and followed back to Landor."

"How is that possible?" Asher asked Neyac.

"I'm not sure. Maybe Elnid-Kyeh has some kind of magical ward to ensure shapechangers can't sneak into his realm."

"That's probably wise," Asher said with a nod, "if you're working with dark forces. Unfortunately, it's inconvenient for us. I'm sorry for interrupting you, Torrend. Please go on with your tale."

Torrend grimaced as he shifted position. "When I left Landor to come find you, four shapechangers chased me in the guise of other hawks. They caught me a couple of times and really slashed me up with their talons."

"How'd you get away?" asked Katrine.

"I flew through a cluster of trees and changed into an owl while I was moving. When I came out the other side, they didn't pay attention to me." He shuddered slightly. "I never want to do anything like that again. Flying is hard enough, but changing shape while you're flying is worse."

"A very clever maneuver, though," Neyac said, clasping Torrend's shoulder, "one that probably saved your life."

"What news do you bring?" Asher asked, unable to control his impatience any longer.

"Warlord Leeds wants you and your whole party to meet him near Alume." Torrend gestured for his shirt, which had been removed so his injuries could be tended. Katrine handed it to him, and he pulled a piece of folded and sealed parchment from a pocket. "He explains in here."

As Asher started reading, he saw Torrend out of the corner of his eye looking at Neyac with chagrin. "I realized after I was halfway to Landor that if I carried Asher's note inside my shirt, it would be assimilated in the change just like my clothes are. I've never carried anything extra when I transformed before, so it didn't occur to me earlier. Sorry."

Several times Asher turned to pace and then realized it was impossible in the cramped quarters. He scowled and tried to stand still. Finally he leaned on the wall opposite the cabin's door to finish reading the letter.

"It's as he says." Asher refolded the parchment and stuck it in his shirtfront. "When we get to Botul, instead of taking another vessel to Pardish, we'll continue on to Rock Falls. That's the ultimate destination of this boat, isn't it, Neyac?"

"I believe so. We can check in the morning."

"We'll have to climb the path beside the Falls," Asher said. "When we get to the top, Leeds will have a boat waiting to take us to Alume. Neyac, why don't we go back on deck for a while? There are some things I'd like to discuss with you, and Torrend probably needs to get some sleep." He narrowed his eyes as he looked at Katrine. "You, young lady, had best get to bed, too. And try to stay out of trouble."

Asher could see Katrine's mind churning and expected a spate of arguing. Instead, she bent over and kissed Torrend's cheek. "I'm glad you got back safely," she said. She swirled around on one foot like a dancer and then crossed to the door.

Torrend lay back on the bunk, a smile quirking the corners of his mouth and a rosy glow coloring his cheeks.

The cool look Katrine tossed Asher probably caused his face to go red too, he thought, but if it did, it wasn't from pleasure.

The boat passed Bilmont during the early hours, but since there was no signal flag indicating the need to stop, it floated on by. Around noon the next day, they docked at Jeneff.

Asher forbade the little party to disembark.

"We'll be here a very short time," he told Katrine and Heni when they expressed the desire to stroll along the pier. "I've talked with the captain, and we're not picking up passengers. We're just stopping for provisions and water. Everything should be ready and waiting. As soon as it's loaded, we'll be moving again."

"We just want to go for a walk," Katrine persisted. "We'll stay close and come aboard as soon as the departure bell rings."

"I can't imagine what I've said to give you the impression this is open for discussion," Asher said dryly. "You are not going ashore. The topic is closed."

Her face white with fury, Katrine clenched her fists, turned, and walked away, leaving Asher frustrated and confused.

Without a doubt, Katrine brought out the very worst in him.

Every time he thought they were becoming comfortable around each other, something new happened, and she challenged him again. In response to her rebellion, he became authoritarian and defensive.

Damn it.

Until the Warlord gave him permission to explain what was happening, he had no idea how to make things go smoother between them.

* * *

Feeling sulky, Heni crossed to where Torrend sat on a deck bench.

"He is such a bully," she said as she sat down beside him.

"Who?" asked Torrend. "Asher?"

"Yes. He's always bossing us around. Who put him in charge, anyway?"

"Warlord Leeds, I think. I got the impression, although no one said it exactly, that Asher has an important position with the Warlord. I don't understand the military hierarchy, but whatever it is, Asher is near the top. The Warlord gives him all the assignments that have to be handled in just the right manner."

"I don't believe it," she said, taking a moment to scrutinize Asher while he stood chatting with the boat's captain. Even though the graying captain was clearly twenty or thirty years the older, if Heni had to choose who projected the stronger sense of authority, she would have to choose Asher. "All right, maybe I believe it, but I don't have to like it."

"No, you don't," Torrend agreed with a laugh.

Heni smiled back at him. "How are you doing? You look a lot better than I expected from what Katrine told me."

"I'm fine. I was more tired than hurt. I had needed a good sleep for several days, and last night I got it." Torrend watched a seagull glide overhead, and Heni looked up so she could watch too.

"Being a bird is a rough life," Torrend said, shaking his head a little. "You have to eat a great deal to keep up your strength, but if you eat too much, you get bogged down, which makes flying hard. It feels really good to be myself again."

Heni studied the toe of her boot, afraid to look directly at Torrend.

She had something to say, and it wasn't easy for her.

"I'm afraid when we first met, I made some foolish comments about people with the wizard blood. I'm sorry. I did it out of ignorance not spite. I would like to understand. Can you—would you mind—telling me what it is like being Crennese?"

Taking Heni's hand in his own, causing butterflies to flutter in her stomach, Torrend said, "I wasn't offended. But I'm glad you're willing to learn."

* * *

Katrine was too angry to be around people. She stormed back to the tiny cabin she and Heni shared, and after slamming things around, kicking the bunks, and cursing enthusiastically for a while, she felt a little better.

It wasn't just Asher's attitude that put her in a bad mood, she realized. It was the cramped quarters, the idleness, and even some homesickness.

Having worked that out in her mind, she pulled out her art satchel. Now that she was calmer, she could do some drawing.

When she returned to the deck, she sat near the railing facing the Jeneff docks. She got out her board, parchment, and charcoals.

Quite a few people meandered around the pier, some moving crates, some toting merchandise to vendors' stalls, and some just strolling.

An old hunchbacked man limped one slow step after another, leaning on a cane for balance. He caught Katrine's attention because, when she looked at him, his image blurred.

By now the occurrence was familiar to her. She relaxed and let the images flow. When she could clearly see the second face within the first, she picked up her charcoal and began to sketch.

* * *

Trying to be unobtrusive, Asher watched Katrine in profile from a position near the bow. She settled on a deck bench and started drawing. The pinched expression on her face faded. With each stroke she made on the paper, her body relaxed more. She began to smile.

When she started blowing something through a little pipe onto the picture, he decided it was a good time to have a chat.

"I guess it's my destiny to be at odds with you, Katrine," Asher said, sitting down beside her. "There is much you don't understand that I'm not free to explain. I'm responsible for your safety, and you haven't been cooperating."

Katrine put the pipe away, and then packed the charcoal she'd used in a leather box that held similar pieces in slightly different shades. "If anyone other than me is responsible for my safety, it's Neyac," Katrine said. She wiped charcoal off her fingers with a rag and then stowed it and the box of charcoals in her large satchel. "My father authorized him to oversee my well-being until I return home."

Not wanting to begin another argument, Asher leaned over to peer at the completed picture.

He was impressed.

"That's a fascinating sketch. How did you come up with a concept like that? Two faces in one?"

"You taught me. Now whenever I see someone with a blurry outline, I just relax. This is a representation of what I see." She reached into her bag and pulled out another picture. "I did this one in the parlor of the inn where I fell asleep." Asher waited for her to make some sarcastic comment about his waking her by throwing water in her face, but she didn't. "And this one," she indicated the drawing she had just finished, "is that old man down there."

"Holy Signs!" Asher groaned. "How the hell will I keep you alive? Get to your cabin, now!"

* * *

Katrine was frightened by Asher's tone.

She jumped to her feet and stuffed her pictures into the satchel at the same time. Almost simultaneously, she was beset by the pulsating heat and sense of evil that she now understood to be caused by Shokai concentration.

For the briefest of moments, she paused and looked over the railing.

Suddenly, a fiery pain struck below her right shoulder.

As her legs gave out beneath her, she saw something protruding from her chest. She looked at it dumbly, trying to make its size and shape conform to a known mundane object.

It was a dagger.

* * *

"Neyac, Torrend," bellowed Asher. "Get Katrine to her cabin and see if there's a Healer on board."

As they obeyed, he sprang from the boat.

Running in the direction Katrine had pointed, Asher searched everywhere for the old man he had seen in Katrine's drawing.

He talked to longshoremen as they hauled crates and barrels to and from the riverboat. He talked to nearby vendors. No one had seen who had thrown the knife. No one had noticed an old man hobbling around the pier.

Not daring to dally because of the short time the riverboat was to be docked, Asher gave up and returned to talk to the captain. The captain told Asher that Jeneff's Healer had died last week, and he doubted a new one had been found yet. The nearest Master Healer was in Botul, two days away. Asher had no idea if Katrine could last that long.

Worried and frustrated, he went to Katrine's cabin to see how badly she had been hurt.

* * *

"I'll do it," Heni insisted with full confidence. "Neither of you has any training, and I assisted Katrine and Master Healers for many days at Branston. Now get out of my way and do what I tell you."

Obediently, Asher and Neyac moved aside as Heni bent over Katrine's body.

With quivering hands, Heni handed Asher a thick pad she'd made from her favorite muslin petticoat.

"As soon as I pull out the knife," she said, "you must slap the bandage over the wound, hard, and hold it tight or the chest cavity will collapse. You must be swift and sure, or we'll lose her. Are you ready?"

* * *

"Ready," Asher said with a crackle in his voice.

His mouth was dry with nervousness, but he wasn't about to let Heni know, not if he could help it. She had set herself up with a burden that was heavy enough. She didn't need to carry his fear as well.

He positioned the pad near Katrine's chest. Consciously, he willed his hand to remain steady rather than trembling like it wanted to.

Katrine's eyelids were fluttering faintly as Heni grasped the dagger. When she swiftly pulled it out and Asher slapped the bandage into place, Katrine arched her back and screamed.

Then she fell back on the cot, unconscious.

Chapter Thirty-Four

When the boat docked at Botul, Katrine was vaguely aware of a change in momentum. She grappled with her mind to regain full consciousness. Mumbling and thrashing, she cursed out of frustration because her thoughts wouldn't coalesce into sentences.

Strong hands held her while different ones touched her brow. A voice chanted words she should understand. A cup was pressed against her lips. She swallowed something that burned her throat all the way down to her stomach. Before she could identify the taste or the sounds, she slipped off the edge of the world into an eternity of grogginess, pain, and nasty tasting drinks.

She became aware of a spot of light in a dark sea, and she swam toward it. In the air above her, she heard Asher and Heni's voices.

"I'll stay with her," Asher said. "I've passed this way many times, and it's a sight worth seeing."

"I don't know." Heni sounded full of conflicting emotions. "I hate to leave her, but I've always wanted to see Shanree Palace."

Katrine made her lips move. "Are we near Renath?"

"Yes," Heni said. "We'll be passing it soon." A cool hand rested on Katrine's forehead. "You still have a fever. How do you feel?"

"I feel like I want to see the palace, too," she whispered in gulps. "Let's all go out and look."

"You're in no condition to go anywhere," Asher said. "Heni, maybe you'd better get Torrend to put her back to sleep."

"Has he been putting the sleep on me?" Katrine asked weakly, prying her eyes open so she could see her cousin. When Heni nodded, Katrine tried to sound menacing. "Well, if he does it again, I'll slap him from here to Serpent's Head and back." She paused, and her voice dropped into a whisper, "As soon as I'm strong enough."

A soft knock came at the door, and before Heni could take a step in that direction, Neyac and Torrend entered.

The Spire of Kylet

"Don't you ever put the sleep on me again, Torrend," Katrine said, managing a faint growl. "Now I want to see Renath Island. I am accepting volunteers to help me with the stairs."

"Woke up grumpy, did she?" Neyac mused. "Oh well, if you don't mind carrying her, Asher, a bit of fresh air might improve her disposition."

"Really, Neyac," Heni said, planting her fists on her hips, "she's still feverish. She needs to stay in bed."

"Now, now, my dear," the Recorder chided, "I don't think a few minutes will hurt, and if we don't take her outside and let her see the island, she is likely to have fits. That won't help her fever or her wound."

"All right," Heni said, "but she has to take her medicine first." She poured water into a cup, added a spoonful of green liquid from a silver flask, stirred, and handed it to Katrine.

"Medicine?" She sniffed the concoction dubiously. "What is this?"

"We got it from a Healer in Botul," said Neyac. "He checked you over, but Heni already had everything under control. Drink up, my dear."

"It'll help your fever go down," Heni said.

Katrine took a deep breath then drank the potion down quickly. The bitter aftertaste made her quake all over. Heni handed her a cup of plain water, and Katrine took a gulp and swished it around in her mouth before swallowing. She shivered again.

"Shall we go?" Neyac asked.

When Asher lifted Katrine, he cautioned her. "You'd better lie quietly. There's no Healer on board, and Heni had a demon's own time getting the bleeding to stop. If it starts again, she'll pitch us all into the river."

After they reached the prow, Katrine tried leaning forward, but a stab of pain made her slump back. She let her head nestle against Asher's chest. Neyac stood on her left, and Torrend, holding Heni's hand, stood on the right. Other passengers lined the railings. All gazed forward.

In the distance, an enormous rock, like a mountain with its upper half chopped off, thrust out of the water. It was Renath Island, and the Eastern and Western Meriads flowed out of the northern mountains and converged at its base. One tremendous river, the Great Meriad, then flowed down the lower two-thirds of Kareand on a quest for the sea.

Many centuries ago, Renath City had been built on the high plateau.

Standing tall in its center was Shanree Palace, constructed of pure white granite. Many turrets and towers jutted from the sides of the elegant structure and stretched up toward heaven. As the sun set, the western walls sparkled with yellows and golds.

Thick vegetation had smothered most of the city's buildings, making the town look like a series of green hummocks. Tendrils of vines and ribbons of weeds dribbled down from the top of the butte like icing dripping down the sides of a cake.

Once there had been four beautifully wrought bridges that connected

Renath Island with the mainland. Legend said that when Kylet, dying and heartsick, left the capital city, he pronounced a curse against Elnid-Kyeh that was so potent it shattered all four bridges at the same time. Jagged remnants still dangled precariously from the rims.

When the riverboat began its journey up the Eastern Meriad, it passed through deep shadows. Heni touched Asher's arm. "I think you'd better take her back to our cabin. It's starting to get chilly now that the sun has set. In her weakened condition, she could develop any number of illnesses."

"Please, Heni," Katrine begged. "I hate that stuffy cabin. Let me stay out in the fresh air a little while longer."

"I don't think that's a good idea. You've been seriously injured. We don't have a Healer to help you if you develop pneumonia."

"I'll make a bargain with you," Katrine said, and then had to catch her breath before continuing. "Gillian taught me a great spell for warding off chest colds. If you let me stay out here, I promise I'll use it. Besides, everyone knows spells work best if they're cast in the open air."

"Really?" Heni asked with surprise. "Is that why the hospital camp at Branston was in the courtyard?"

Nodding slightly, Katrine managed to keep a straight face.

"Oh, all right," Heni said, "but I'm going to get you an extra blanket."

As she trotted out of sight, Asher sat on a deck bench with Katrine on his lap. "You're a frightful liar," he said. "Healing spells don't have to be said outside."

"I know." Katrine started to giggle, but the pain in her chest stopped her. "I just couldn't stand the thought of going back inside so soon."

Wheezing weakly, she had difficulty catching her breath. She let her head loll to the side, resting it on Asher's shoulder while she concentrated on inhaling and exhaling. Suddenly she was aware of the warm arms that were wrapped around her.

Her heart sped up, and she became very self-conscious.

"Uhm," she said, "if you'd care to put me down, I'm sure I'm capable of sitting by myself."

"I might be willing to let you stay out here for a while," Asher said, "but I'm not the least bit convinced that you're doing as well as you pretend to be." His tone lightened. "You might slip between the rails and fall into the river. Then what would I do when Heni came back?" He paused a moment before he continued broodingly. "You've almost been killed once while I was standing right next to you. At least this way, if nothing else, I could shield you with my body."

A snappy comeback popped onto Katrine's tongue, but she swallowed it. She had a tendency to get sarcastic when she was nervous, and Asher's holding her was definitely making her nervous. But she really didn't want him to put her down, maybe because she felt so safe, so protected. It wasn't a sensation she was used to. She liked it very much.

Then the meaning of Asher's words hit her.

He was prepared to shield her with his body?

What?

Was he willing to sacrifice his life for her? It sounded like it. But why?

She might have a crush on him—she did have a crush on him—but she didn't flatter herself into thinking he had any romantic feelings for her. Someone as mature and powerful and important as Asher was not likely to be attracted to someone like her: an awkward, insignificant girl from nowhere.

But if not for love, what?

She tried to puzzle it out. There had to be a reason. But her mind was fuzzy from fatigue, fever, and probably the medication. She would have to save that question for later.

"Asher," she asked, "what happened back at Jeneff? I saw a dagger in my chest, but I couldn't believe it. You said the Shokai wanted the spire, but since the knife was thrown from the pier, they couldn't get to it. Why try to kill me?"

"Strange things are happening in Kareand, many of which we don't understand. I tried to find someone who saw what happened, but I couldn't."

"Are you sure they were aiming at me? You were there too. Maybe you were the target."

"That's certainly an idea worth considering," Asher said, "but I really don't think so. Assassins don't miss. If you hadn't moved just as he tossed the blade, he would've gotten you straight in the heart."

She shivered at the thought, and Asher's arms tightened around her comfortingly.

"I'm sorry," he said. "That wasn't very sensitive of me. I shouldn't have been so blunt."

"It's all right," Katrine said, not wanting him to think she was a coward even though, in truth, she was very frightened. Someone had tried to kill her!

She was glad to see Neyac and Torrend ambling toward them. She hoped they would provide a distraction. After they sat down, she asked Torrend, "Do you know the healing arts? I feel like someone's been saying curative spells over me."

"It's been a joint venture," Neyac said. "I looked up some of the simpler spells in your copy of the White Book and did the translations. Because of Torrend's Crennese heritage, he was able to collect the powers necessary to make them work. Of course, the Healer at Botul used several spells on you too."

"Well," Katrine smiled weakly, "thank you both for your efforts." She was exhausted, but she didn't want to show it. If she did, Asher would probably haul her off to bed. "I guess I ought to say some healing spells on my own behalf. I promised Heni I would."

Right on cue, Heni returned with a blanket, which she draped around

Katrine. Asher loosened his hold long enough to tuck in the edges.

Katrine closed her eyes, but before she could decide which spell to recite first, she dozed off.

Although she slept fitfully for the next few days, Torrend didn't return to put the sleep on her.

* * *

One night after most of the passengers and crew had gone to bed, Asher woke Heni by rapping quietly on the door. She looked exhausted, rumpled, and ill-tempered when she answered.

"Don't you ever sleep?" she grumbled.

"Not so you'd notice," he mumbled back. "I'm sorry to disturb you, but I need to take Katrine out on deck."

"You're insane!" Heni cried out. Katrine moaned in her sleep, and Heni lowered her voice. "As we travel farther north, the weather is getting chillier. It's cool enough during the day, but it's really cold at night. Come back tomorrow afternoon after it warms up."

Asher shook his aching head.

He hadn't slept well since Katrine had been injured.

Torrend had transformed and carried a message to Warlord Leeds, informing him of the incident at Jeneff. Even though, when the Warlord replied, he didn't find fault with Asher, it made no difference whatsoever. Asher knew he was to blame. He should have been more watchful.

Filling his lungs with air and blowing it out noisily, Asher kept tight reins on his temper. His patience tended to run thin when he was this tired.

"It has to be now," he said with careful control, "by the light of the full moon. We reach Rock Falls day after tomorrow, and I don't know how she'll make the climb unless her condition improves drastically. This is supposed to help."

"But she might—"

"Don't argue with me, Heni. Whatever magic is at play tonight will make her stronger. Trust me. I have it on good authority."

"Well, all right, if you're sure." Heni grabbed the clothes tossed over the end of her bunk. "I'll go with you."

"No," Asher said. "I don't even know if I'll be allowed to stay. She'll be safe, though. I know that much."

Not giving Heni the opportunity to disagree with him again, Asher slipped his arms under Katrine's sleeping form and lifted her, blanket and all. "I don't know if she needs to be awake," he said, talking more to himself than to Heni, "but the forces calling her can wake her if they need to."

When Asher started for the door, Heni stepped in front of him and adjusted the blanket. "Take good care of her," she whispered, her lower lip trembling emotionally.

"I will."

The moon was full and high when Asher carried Katrine onto the deck. He sat on a bench, cradling her against his chest as tenderly as if she were a newborn babe. The moonlight bathed her in a silver glimmer.

"Is there something else I should do?" Asher asked the black, star-filled sky. No answer came.

A moment later, Katrine shuddered and took several quick breaths. When she opened her eyes, she was looking directly at the moon. She smiled. Then she inhaled very slowly, as if savoring a pleasant and stimulating aroma. Each breath seemed to come easier and to be deeper.

Her hand moved to her wound. She closed her eyes, took an enormous breath, and chanted softly in an undertone. Asher couldn't understand what she said, but he recognized the words as Crennish.

Then time stopped, and with it all sights and sounds and smells and tastes, as if the world hesitated in its rotation.

The moment passed.

"That's better," Katrine said as she snuggled against Asher, looping one arm around his neck. "If you can stand to hold me a bit longer, soon I'll be able to sit up without any help. My Glainite family has kept its promise and sent me their strength." She added, sleepily, "I wonder if Bainu knew how badly I'd need it."

She dozed off, and her breathing became as smooth and even as if she'd never been hurt.

When Asher looked down at Katrine in his arms, a smile tugged at the corners of his mouth.

She was so innocent. So trusting. So lovely.

Without thinking, he laid his lips lightly on her forehead and kissed her.

When he realized what he had done, he had a moment of panic.

It was true that a few times she had aroused his male instincts, but he had quickly suppressed them, establishing clearly defined boundaries.

She was too young.

He could not be thinking about her in *that* way.

Then he relaxed.

Of course not.

The impulse had been no more than the one he always had to kiss his sleeping niece and nephew whenever he visited his elder brother's home.

Chapter Thirty-Five

Katrine woke feeling much better.

Heni tried to keep her in bed, but Katrine was adamant about getting up. When she showed Heni the scar, the last vestige of the wound, Heni sat down on her cot, looking stunned.

"Why? If you had the power to heal yourself, why didn't you do it sooner and save us all a lot of grief?"

"Until Asher took me out in the moonlight, I was too weak. The Glainites have a ceremony that unites them and makes them strong. Before we left Banur, Bainu promised they would do it on my behalf each full moon until I return home. It was their strength that powered the spell, and it was their combined focus that caused the wound to heal in a single night. I couldn't have done it alone."

Heni's eyes welled up and her lips began to quiver.

Thinking that Heni must feel as if her efforts had been for nothing, Katrine quickly added, "If you hadn't patched me up and watched over me, I would have died before the tribe could fortify me. I know I owe you my life."

"Oh, Katrine," Heni burst into tears, "you have so many people who care about you—not just your family, but a whole tribe. I'm all alone. I don't have anyone"

Sitting down next to Heni, Katrine enfolded her cousin in her arms.

"You have me, Heni, and Torrend and Neyac and Asher. And all my family back in Banur. And Uncle Brenden and his family in Tremmerton. And all your aunts, uncles, and cousins on your mother's side. Plus all of those people you helped in Branston."

Sniffling, Heni mumbled, "But I hardly know them."

Katrine lifted Heni's face until their eyes met. "I know you miss your parents, Heni, and I know that no one can ever fill the empty place they've left in your heart. But you don't need to feel alone. Wherever you go, you'll be loved. Over the past weeks, you've demonstrated depths I never guessed at before. From now on, you'll have me, no matter what happens."

The Spire of Kylet

Heni threw her arms around Katrine, buried her head on her shoulder, and finally let all the pain and loss come out.

* * *

The riverboat docked at Rock Falls below the gushing waters that gave the town its name.

Before disembarking, Asher and Neyac took Katrine out on deck and asked her to check the crowded pier for anyone with the blurry outline she had seen before.

"No," Katrine assured them. "I don't see any of those double-image people down there."

"Good," Asher said, "but they could be hidden. Neyac had a suggestion last night, and I think it's worth trying."

"I remembered seeing in the Book of White Spells a charm of concealment that could render several people invisible," Neyac told her. "As we climb the narrow trail beside the falls, we'll be exposed unless you can use the spell to shield us."

The Recorder opened the book Katrine had lent him and pointed to a paragraph he'd marked. "You'd better let the book teach you the spell. It's complex. I could translate, but if I chose a Nistarian word that didn't quite match the Old Crennish one, the magic could go wrong. I've no idea what the consequences of that might be. Are you willing to try it?"

"I suppose so, but why?"

"By the Coils, Katrine," Asher bellowed, apparently forgetting there were other people on deck, "someone tried to kill you."

When passengers turned to stare, Asher took a deep breath and lowered the volume, although his voice still shook with passion. "Think, girl! The Shokai are looking for you. You've felt their burning hatred more than once. Do you want to die?"

Katrine was so taken aback by Asher's fervor that she shook her head rapidly. "No," she gasped.

"I'm fraggin' glad to hear that because I certainly can't tell by your behaviors. The hike to the top of the falls takes quite a while, and there are outcroppings of rocks and clumps of brush all the way up. An arrow could catch you, and we wouldn't even know an assassin was around until we saw the shaft in your back."

"We're worried about your safety," Neyac put in, using a gentler tone, "and since we've been traveling together, your enemies probably have us marked as well. Will you study the spell?"

"I already said I would." Katrine knew she sounded peevish, but Neyac's phrase *your enemies* had struck her like an icicle through the heart. She acknowledged that someone had tried to kill her, but she hadn't made the association with the word *enemy*.

She had always tried to be good and fair in her dealings with people.

Even when she had been the angriest at Heni, she had never caused her cousin any harm.

Her skin prickled to think someone hated her enough to want her dead.

She had an enemy.

Why? What had she done?

Before she could work herself into a panic, she glanced over the spell. Neyac was right. It was complicated. "This'll take some time. I don't want to make any mistakes."

"If you need privacy, why don't you use our cabin?" Asher said. "We're all packed, and Torrend and I are going to make arrangements for the horses to be taken up."

Katrine heard Asher's words in the back of her mind, but she wasn't really listening.

When she had first come out on deck, she'd been aware of a thundering sound in the background. But Neyac and Asher had hustled her over to the railing, pushing her through the crowd, so she could check the dock. Then Neyac had shoved the Book of White Spells into her hands.

She hadn't taken a good look at Rock Falls before, and now she was mesmerized.

Water gushed over the lip of a high cliff and pounded into the river below, churning up a cauldron of fountains and mists. As light shone through the vapor, it created a rainbow that arced across the rocks. It was a magical scene for a girl who had spent her entire life on the prairie.

"Katrine," Asher said loudly, trying to get her attention, "I said Torrend and I are going to see to the horses. You can use our cabin." His voice sharpened. "You're ignoring me."

After taking a moment to flash Asher a glance, Katrine again peered at the waterfalls in amazement. "I've never seen anything like this before. It's unbelievably beautiful."

She struggled to find a better descriptive word but threw up her hands in surrender. "It's just too beautiful."

Then she noticed the path winding among the outcrops on the left side of the spewing waters. "The trail looks too narrow and steep for horses. How do you get them to the top?"

Asher pointed upward at a configuration of wood and ropes that hung out over the edge of the bluff. "See that tall contraption? It supports an intricate array of counterweights and pulleys, as well as a winch. They use it to lift supplies and animals. The platform swivels, so after a load goes up, the whole thing makes a half turn, and the crates and animals are lowered to the ground in back of the mechanism."

"Sounds like magic," said Katrine. "Did the Crennese design and build it?"

Asher chuckled as he shrugged. "I don't know. Do you, Neyac?"

The Spire of Kylet

"Well," Neyac said, stroking his short gray beard, "I wouldn't be surprised if Katrine's guess is correct. The device has been here a very long time. It's called Banyan's Hoist, and it's mentioned in several old manuscripts. No one remembers who Banyan was, but the Crennese once lived in these mountains. They might have built the lift to improve commerce with other communities. If there was some spell weaving in its creation, that might explain how it's remained functional for all these centuries."

"I'll bet the horses don't like it," said Katrine.

"Horses are blindfolded and placed in a sling," Asher said. "Usually they hang there, frozen. But every so often, one panics and works its way free, only to die on the rocks below. Torrend is going to put the sleep on our horses so they'll be safe."

"But if no one's there to wake them, won't they topple over when they're lowered to their feet?"

"Torrend will weave a special modification into the spell to take care of that," Neyac said. "As soon as their hooves touch the ground, the horses will wake up on their own."

"I didn't know you could do that." Then Katrine remembered something vaguely. "Well, maybe I did. I think Bainu mentioned something about being able to adjust spells to fit specific circumstances, but I don't know how it's done."

"There's much you don't know," Neyac said with a hint of criticism that made Katrine uncomfortable. "You need to find time to finish reading the White Book."

"Maybe when we get to Pardish," she said.

She would never be a scholar like her father. She hated translating too much. But she knew she would eventually read the Book of White Spells, if for no other reason than to tell Bainu she had done it.

Just then a load of crates was attached to a cable and hoisted upward.

"Wow!" Katrine exclaimed. "What a ride that would be. Why don't they do the same thing for people and save them a long hike?"

"I understand it was tried once," Neyac said. "Someone built a cage to use in place of the sling. Everyone thought it was a great idea, but the first people to ride in it became terrified about half way up. They started screaming and shaking the bars. The cable snapped or the cage came loose, I'm not sure which, but all the people were killed."

"I'll walk, thank you," mumbled Katrine while goose flesh popped up on her arms. "I guess I'd better go study this spell. I don't want to accidentally turn us all into toads."

First, though, Katrine had something more important to do. She hadn't realized that she would be separated from her saddlebags. Now that she thought about it, though, it made sense for personal possessions to go with the horses and supplies rather than carrying them while hiking up that steep trail. She had just finished retrieving her spire and money pouch and had slipped them into her shirtfront when Torrend came by for the bags.

With that accomplished, Katrine sat down with the Book of White Spells, gazed at the page Neyac had shown her, and let the book teach her the incantation and gestures for the concealment spell.

Remarkable, she thought when she had finished memorizing the words and gestures.

Neyac and Bainu were both right. This book was worth getting to know.

After the horses and travelers' packs had been sent to the top of the ridge, Asher gathered the group behind some tall foliage so Katrine could recite the shielding spell.

"We have to stay close together," Katrine told them. "It'll take a lot of concentration to maintain the spell, and the more distance there is between us, the harder it'll be for me to hold it. Once I say the guidewords and release the power, it will seem like we're walking in a shadow. If everything suddenly goes bright, you'll know you've left the magic's sphere of influence or I've lost control. Whichever, it means you're no longer concealed. Ready?"

"Just a minute, Katrine," interrupted Torrend. "Isn't there a way I can help you? I'm Crennese, too."

"I don't know. I'm new at this." She looked inquiringly at Neyac. "Do you know?"

"I seem to remember reading something about more than one person feeding energy into a spell, but I'm not sure." He tapped his head with a finger. "Getting old, you know. But if you'll loan me your book, maybe I can find it."

Katrine pulled the Book of White Spells from her tunic pocket and handed it to him. He flipped pages a moment and then began bobbing his head. "Here it is," he said, "maybe I'm not quite senile yet."

He motioned for Torrend to put his hand on Katrine's shoulder. "You need to be touching. If you gather and release the power at the same time, you'll both be able to support the spell."

"All right, Torrend," Katrine said. "These are the gestures. Have your forces ready, and when I make the last move, let them fly. Ready?"

"Ready."

As Katrine chanted the words, she gathered the necessary powers and could feel Torrend doing the same. With the final gesture, they animated the spell. The world around them darkened to twilight.

"Since we can't be seen," Asher said, "let's maintain the illusion by not being heard as well. We'll go slowly so we can watch for loose rocks and other hazards. No conversation unless absolutely necessary, and then only in whispers. Understood?"

"Understood," came the soft response of the others.

* * *

The Spire of Kylet

Weary, Elnid-Kyeh collapsed onto a soft chair in his bedchamber.

He had just teleported the last Shokai priest back to Shokareen.

Happily, he would have a couple of days to rest before he had to convey himself to the site where his troops would soon be engaged in war games. One of the Shokai priests had suggested the practice battles, and Elnid-Kyeh had agreed.

His own efforts at uniting his troops with those of his allies had been a dismal failure. He thought having them implement a series of raids, starting small and working up to the destruction of Branston, would be enough to ensure their cooperation.

Instead, the two groups had ended up fighting over the plunder, resulting in several injuries and even a few deaths.

This same priest had also suggested bringing a Shokai senior novitiate to Serpent's Head to work as Elnid-Kyeh's assistant. So far, Rylinjer had proven extremely useful. He had taken over many of the more mundane tasks, like scrying the names on the list Elnid-Kyeh had procured in the spring and locating those who had moved to new areas.

Elnid-Kyeh wished he had a dozen workers who knew sorcery. He could keep them all busy and then would not need to work so hard himself.

He massaged his temples and neck in hopes of conquering his headache.

He had already assimilated the life forces of three captives today, but it hadn't rejuvenated him. He was going to have to eat and sleep for a while to rebuild the strength he had expended while the Shokai priests were here. They had demanded his time in never-ending shifts.

A knock at the door sounded. An old crone entered with his dinner tray. Elnid-Kyeh did not smile outwardly, but he could not help being amused. The younger servants had begun avoiding him, sending only the elderly to attend to his needs, men and women whose hold on life was so tenuous and weak that they were not good candidates for soul draining.

The woman set the tray on a round table, poured him a cup of wine, removed covers from the dishes, and backed out, never taking her eyes from him. He waited until she was gone then moved to the straight-backed chair he preferred while eating.

He had received word that his new assassin had misunderstood his instructions. Instead of resorting to violence only if he could not acquire the spire any other way, he had tried to kill the girl at Jeneff. Even that he had botched.

Elnid-Kyeh had been so involved with other matters that he did not have time to deal with the bumbling idiot himself. He had been forced to let Rylinjer send Lairnus, his Captain of the Guard, to Jeneff to kill the man. Tomorrow, Rylinjer would have to cast a spell to bring Lairnus back.

Picking up the wineglass, Elnid-Kyeh looked at his reflection floating on the ruby liquid.

He had not scried the girl for quite a while. He wondered if she had reached Pardish yet.

He did not have the energy to go to his tower for his silver scrying dish and thrice-sanctified oil. Possibly he could use a simpler spell to locate her. He was so familiar with her now that he should not have to rely on special implements.

For a moment he argued with himself.

Over the past months, he had become obsessed with the girl and the spire she had so mysteriously obtained. It had actually been a relief while the Shokai priest had been here and the press of business prevented him from thinking about her.

Maybe he should ignore the urge to scry her now.

Yet, he would enjoy his meal more if he knew where she was.

Surrendering to curiosity, he cast the spell.

No image formed on the wine.

He cast the spell again. Still, nothing.

Could she be dead? he wondered. Could she be shielded? Or was this spell not strong enough?

Maybe he was too fatigued to cast the spell adequately. He did not know, nor really care.

In a few days, when he felt better, he would try again.

There was no place she could hide from him for long.

Chapter Thirty-Six

By the time Katrine and her party reached the trail at the base of the cliff, all other climbers were a goodly distance ahead. With Asher in the lead, the others followed in pairs, walking slowly and watching for pitfalls that might betray their position.

They stayed in a close knot, halting every now and then for rest and water and a few words of encouragement, particularly for Heni, who was near collapse before they had gone halfway.

"I can't do it," she gasped when they stopped for the fourth time. "Go on without me. I'll rest and meet you later." She looked up and down the trail. "No one is close enough to harm me if you leave."

"If we move away," Asher said, "you'll suddenly become visible. If the enemy notices, they'll know we're using magic to shield ourselves."

"What enemy?" Heni whined. "I don't even know why we're doing this."

"The enemy who tried to kill Katrine," Asher said harshly. "It wasn't that long ago. Have you forgotten how hard you worked to keep her alive?"

"But that was at Jeneff. You're not saying someone wants her dead badly enough to have followed us here, are you?"

"I think it's possible, but this is a hell of a place to talk about it. There's another group behind us. We've got to get moving."

"I can't," cried Heni. "I really can't."

"Hold onto the back of my belt. That'll help. Come on, girl, you can do it."

Reluctantly, Heni got to her feet and grasped the wide black belt as instructed. When Asher began walking, she was propelled along behind him.

Before they reached the top, Asher was supporting Heni with his right arm and Neyac with his left. Katrine and Torrend lurched together at the rear, bracing each other.

The trail led straight to the back of Banyan's Hoist, where workers rushed around unloading crates and stacking them in neat rows.

As Katrine and her companions stumbled past them, she found it incomprehensible that no one seemed to hear their gasping breaths and loudly thumping hearts. But not one person so much as turned to glance in their direction.

Asher led the little group into the forest, where they all sprawled on the grass in exhaustion.

The world brightened considerably.

"Oh, my aching head," Katrine moaned. She dampened her handkerchief with water from the leather skin she carried and swiped it across her face and neck. When it didn't cool her quickly enough, she poured water into her hand and splashed herself with it.

"I didn't think we could hold it," Torrend said.

"One of us couldn't have done it alone. Too much concentration for too long a time."

"And too long a walk for stiff old joints," complained Neyac. He pulled off his boots and stockings and began rubbing his bright red, swollen feet.

"Or even young ones," Heni groaned from where she'd fallen.

"While you rest," Asher said after a moment, "I'll go see if our boat's ready."

As Katrine watched him stride away, she whispered softly to Neyac. "Doesn't he ever get tired? He moves as if he just completed a casual stroll instead of that grueling climb. How does he do it?"

"They train them hard at Landor," said Neyac. "Compared to some of the things Asher's done, that climb probably felt like a casual stroll." Then he made a pillow of his arms, closed his eyes, and was soon snoring.

Relaxing on a cushion of autumn leaves, Katrine found the sounds of the moving water soothing. Although she felt drained, she couldn't doze like the others were. She lay on her back and watched the gathering clouds slowly eliminate the patches of blue that showed among the scatterings of yellow and brown leaves overhead.

A few evergreens towered above the other trees, and Katrine rolled onto her side and sketched them in the dirt with a stick. The only evergreens she had seen before were illustrations in books. She was getting restless when she heard Asher and someone else approaching.

"I assume Leeds briefed you on our guests." Asher's deep voice carried, although he was obviously trying to keep it quiet.

"Yes sir." The answer was pitched so low, Katrine had to strain to hear it.

"I don't want one hint of surprise or recognition on your face. Do you understand?"

"Yes sir."

After Asher roused Neyac and the others, he introduced the young man with him. "This is Bryand. He has arranged our passage to Alume for Warlord Leeds."

Bryand hardly looked old enough to be out of his teens. He had a plain broad face and auburn hair, which reminded Katrine of Skotlan. Quickly, she pushed thoughts of her favorite brother from her mind. Since seeing the devastation at Branston, she couldn't think about her family without worrying, so she tried not to think about them at all.

The young Warrior was dressed much like Asher, all in black, but his shirt lacked the four silver studs that formed a square on Asher's collar.

Gesturing to each member of the party in turn, Asher gave Bryand their names. Katrine watched carefully to see if, despite Asher's orders, the young Warrior's face would reveal a hint of what Asher had warned him against. His eyes stayed on Heni a bit longer than the others, a common reaction, but otherwise his responses were polite and impartial.

Irrationally, Katrine wanted to slap Asher's face for presenting her with a mystery without a resolution.

"Before we can board the boat," Bryand told them, "we have to go upriver a ways. The currents near the falls are strong, and we don't want to risk being washed over. Your horses are waiting. Most people prefer to ride after the long climb."

The murmurs of agreement indicated this group would be no exception.

The barge to which Bryand directed them was a much smaller version of the flat-bottomed boat they had traveled on coming up the Great Meriad. There was no below-deck area for animals or rowers, and the horses were corralled in a fenced area at the stern.

In the middle of the deck, a boxlike structure contained the galley and four small cabins. There were rowlocks along the side railings, and despite the chill in the air, bare-chested rowers were already in place. A single bench was provided for the passengers to use.

Bryand waved to the captain as soon as they had boarded. The lines were cast off, and the rowers bent into the oars and dug a path through the water.

When the boat reached Alume, it continued on until the town was out of sight, then the crew swung it as close to the eastern bank as possible.

"Sorry about not docking back there," said Bryand, "but Warlord Leeds didn't want you to be seen."

A ramp was lowered into the water, and the companions, holding their horses' reins, sloshed their way to dry land. Bryand paused and gave the riverboat captain a salute before leading the party into a tall pine forest.

Katrine was glad they had a guide. The trees were thick and hid the position of the sun. After a while, she was sure they were riding around in circles, despite Bryand's reassurance that he knew exactly where they were.

Eventually they came to a large clearing that contained many tents and horses and Warriors in black uniforms.

"This way," Bryand said, guiding them to a large tent near the middle of camp. "You can dismount now."

Several young people, dressed in brown instead of black, rushed forward, made a pile of the travelers' packs and supplies, and led the horses to a makeshift corral among the trees.

The flap at the front of the tent was pushed back and out stepped a tall, middle-aged man with a well-worn, tanned face, a square jaw, and wavy dark hair sprinkled with gray. He was dressed similarly to Asher and Bryand, but there were six silver studs arranged in a circle on his collar.

From behind him emerged an elderly gentleman clothed in a maroon robe with gold trim on the collar and cuffs. His scanty hair, thin eyebrows, and bushy beard were all snowy white.

"Asher, my boy," the tall man boomed. "Welcome."

"Neyac," the elderly man said, "I could hardly believe it when I learned you were traveling with Captain Asher. Good fortune, old friend."

Asher and Neyac stepped forward and clasped hands with the men who had addressed them. Then both started to introduce the others.

"One at a time," the elderly man chided good-naturedly. "These old ears can't understand a word you're saying."

Neyac looked at Asher. "Well, boy, I guess we're in your domain. You do the introductions."

Asher nodded.

"Warlord Leeds, Headmaster Miksel, this is Katrine of Banur and her cousin, Heni of Branston. Apprentice Torrend, of course, you've already met. Ladies, this is Warlord Leeds of Landor and Headmaster Miksel of Pardish."

For the first time in many months, Katrine found herself speechless. She stared first at the Warlord and then at the Headmaster, feeling overwhelmed at meeting the two most important men in Kareand at the same time. Only meeting Regent Laria could have equaled the awesome nature of the moment. She would have silently berated herself for her childish reaction if she hadn't seen from the corner of her eye that Heni was similarly impressed.

"What did you do, Asher?" Warlord Leeds thundered affably. "Scare them to death on the way here?"

"Ha," Asher replied in kind. "The presence of the two of you together could take the spine out of a tree."

Warlord Leeds guffawed, but Headmaster Miksel approached Katrine and took her hand.

"I've looked forward to meeting you, Katrine. I was very impressed with your rendering of the great golden hawk. It's excellently done and hangs on my office wall."

"I'm honored," she said, recovering a bit of her composure. "I'm pleased to know the package reached you. I've never sent anything by caravan before, and I wasn't sure it was reliable."

Then Headmaster Miksel offered his hand to Heni. "You're Katrine's cousin. Warlord Leeds let me read Captain Asher's report about Branston. I was sorry to hear about your parents. I met your father a few times when he came to Pardish with special goods for the Recorders School. Charel was a fine man, as I'm sure your mother was a fine woman. Their loss is a loss to us all."

Anguish flashed briefly across Heni's face, but then she visibly pulled her emotions back inside. She managed a courteous smile. "Thank you, sir, for your kind words." He patted her hand gently.

After that, the old man clapped Torrend on the back and gave him a mischievous grin. "Tired of flying yet?"

"Quite. I'd like to keep my own form for a while if I may."

"Now that you're all here safely, the Warlord won't need you to carry messages to the Captain anymore. However, we might still need to use your talent again sometime. For now, rest and relax."

"We're just getting ready for lunch," Leeds said, throwing his arm across Asher's shoulders. He pulled back and frowned at the soggy condition of his uniform.

"You didn't let us dock at Alume, sir," Asher said. "We had to wade to shore."

"Well, you had better get into something dry before you eat. It gets chilly up here." The Warlord called loudly, "Jana." A short, trim female Warrior rushed forward. "Katrine and Heni will be sharing your tent. Show them where it is so they can change."

"Yes sir."

"You three," he told Torrend, Asher, and Neyac, "can use my tent. We'll decide where to put you up for the night later."

As the travelers reclaimed their packs, Katrine stepped alongside Torrend and whispered, "So the real reason we haven't seen you much since Botul is you've been carrying messages between Asher and the Warlord. Neyac told us you were under the weather and sleeping a great deal."

"Asher didn't want you to know," Torrend divulged in an undertone. "He was afraid it would make you and Heni nervous."

"He was right. What's going on? Why are we here?"

"Sorry," Torrend said as he tossed his saddlebags across his shoulder. "You'll have to ask Asher."

Chapter Thirty-Seven

Dressed in dry clothing, Katrine sat alone after she finished eating, her back against one of the towering pines. The forest had a different look and feel from the woods back home, where grass and wildflowers proliferated from the prairie all the way to the tree trunks. Here, the ground was covered with pine needles, an occasional weed, and a few brambly bushes.

With nothing else to do, she watched the activity in the camp, fascinated by its foreignness.

Apparently many of the Warriors were Asher's friends. As soon as he emerged after changing his uniform, people flocked around him. Three, who approached together, seemed particularly meaningful to him.

His face did one of its rapid, unexpected changes when he saw them.

Although a certain tension had left him when he first greeted the Warlord, now, since joyously clasping hands with his three friends, he appeared as carefree as a child who knows he is surrounded by love and protection.

The first man was as tall as Asher, with golden brown hair and facial features so handsome he could break the hearts of the angels. He had a slightly lopsided smile, which was the only thing that kept him from absolute perfection, and when he moved it was with the grace of a plains cat. Two tiny crossed swords glistened on his collar instead of silver studs.

The second man's head, which was covered with straight, blond, straw-like hair, didn't even come up to Asher's shoulder. He wore a quiver and bow case across his back, and his body rippled with sinewy strength. Although the mischief of a joker and a trickster danced across his face, there was also a sadness about him. Deep lines radiated from the corners of his eyes, and Katrine guessed either he was approaching middle age or he'd had a very hard life.

Jana, the female Warrior that Warlord Leeds had assigned to share her tent with the cousins, was Asher's third special friend. She was petite, not quite as tall as the straw-haired man, but like him her wiry muscles were well defined. Also like him, she wore her hair, which was a rich brown like

The Spire of Kylet

Heni's, cropped short. Her eyes were big, and her mouth and chin rather small, giving her a wispy, pixie-ish look.

Asher and the three sat together, talking and laughing, off to the side of the camp. Watching them, Katrine felt a wave of homesickness and, under that, a bit of envy. She had often felt like an outsider, observing but not actually being part of things, even with her family much of the time. Now, everything she was connected to was hundreds of miles away.

No, not quite everything, she realized.

She had Heni, and her cousin's situation was even more dreadful than Katrine's. When this journey was over, Heni had no home or parents to return to.

While they changed their clothes, Heni had wheedled Katrine into helping her braid red and yellow ribbons into her hair. She'd then put on a bright red shirt with her forest green britches and tied a yellow sash around her waist. It was an eye-catching combination, and Katrine was pleased to see it was producing the results her cousin wanted. Several young Warriors were clustered around, flirting with her. She looked happier and livelier than she had in a long time.

A few feet away, Torrend was scowling jealously, which, Katrine thought, might have been Heni's intention.

"May I join you?" Asher asked.

Katrine jerked around, startled, not having noticed him come this way. She nodded and patted the ground beside her.

Asher sat and leaned against the tree trunk with his shoulders barely touching hers. One long leg stretched out in front of him, and the other was bent at the knee with the sole of his boot flat on the ground.

"How're you feeling?" he asked.

"Quite well, now that I'm dry and fed." Asher seemed on the verge of saying something else, so Katrine hurried on before he could. "I'm sure you're not here to inquire about my health, and I have a question for you. I've tried to bring it up several times, but something always seems to interrupt. Will you answer it now, before you tell me what you want?"

"Ask," Asher said with a grin, "and then we'll see."

"How did you know to take me on deck that night in the moonlight? I never told you or Neyac about Bainu's promise."

Pursing his lips, Asher stared into the distance and took several slow breaths. He was silent for so long, Katrine began to wonder, as she studied his profile, if she had offended him.

"I had a vision, or maybe a dream," he said at last, "in which Kylet finally appeared to me. That probably sounds strange, as if I thought I had the right to expect the last Wolkarean Warlord to materialize right in front of me. But I've anticipated it ever since I was a child. I should've known, as soon as I met you, that if he ever did visit me, it would be because of you."

"What do I have to do with it?"

"A great deal." When Katrine opened her mouth to ask another question, he forestalled her with an upraised palm. "Kylet told me your welfare depended on my getting you where the moon glow could reach you. He said the Glainites were assembling to send you strength. Obviously their magic worked, or we wouldn't be here now."

"What did you mean when you said you should've known, if Kylet visited you, it would be because of me?"

"Later."

"It's always later. You and Neyac both say that. Neither of you ever tells me anything."

"You were right when you implied I came with a purpose," Asher said. "Warlord Leeds wants you and me to accompany him and the Recorders on a little junket. There's something he wants you to see."

"What?" she asked suspiciously.

Asher shook his head, stood, and taking her hand, pulled her up after him. "One of the Neophytes has already saddled your horse."

"But what does he want me to see?"

"You'll have to ask Leeds. I'm only the errand boy."

Frowning, Katrine poked Asher on the chest. "You once called me a frightful liar. What does that make you?"

He just rolled his eyes up and clamped his lips tight.

Clearly, he wasn't going to answer her questions. She would like to get stubborn and refuse to go with him, just to see what he'd do, but she decided she had better not. Asher was in his element here, and he just might pick her up, toss her over his shoulder, and haul her off to Warlord Leeds, kicking and screaming. Although in other circumstances that might be kind of fun, this didn't seem to be the right time or place.

Feeling grumpy, she followed Asher to where Thunder Cloud waited. She swung up into the saddle.

No trail existed where Warlord Leeds led them.

They had to duck under limbs and weave in and out of foliage. Irritated, Katrine batted away branches that grabbed at her hair and clothing. For some reason, that reminded her of the baby plains cat she had watched swatting puff weeds, and the memory made her smile, ruining her perfectly good, bad mood.

After a while, Leeds signaled a stop. Silently, they waited in a copse of trees until a Warrior appeared out of nowhere.

"Sir," the Warrior said, saluting Leeds, "the perimeter guard just went by. He'll be back in a little over an hour. There are no wards in the area you asked about, but five paces farther there is something magical. I'm not sure what."

"Did you mark it?"

"Yes sir."

"Good. Return to your post. Alert us if the sentry shows up early."

"Yes sir."

In awe, Katrine watched the Warrior turn around and blend back into the shadows.

"We need to go the rest of the way on foot," Leeds said. They left the horses behind and stole forward in a half crouch. As they neared the crest of a hill, Leeds dropped to his hands and knees and crept forward. The last few feet, he flattened completely and belly-crawled.

That looks unpleasant, Katrine thought with displeasure.

But Headmaster Miksel and Neyac, now wearing simple homespuns and not their Recorder's robes, crawled right behind him.

Well, Katrine thought, *if they're willing to creep through the underbrush and slither like snakes, I guess I have no right to grumble.*

She got on her knees and followed.

Before she reached the summit, Asher intercepted her and whispered directly into her ear. "I want you to do what I taught you on the trail. Prepare yourself by relaxing your mind and your muscles. Warlord Leeds needs to know if you see any of those double-imaged people in the valley. If you do, he wants to know about how many. Will you do it?"

"Since I'm here, I might as well," she whispered back at him. "But with a whole camp full of Warriors, it seems to me he must have someone else who can do this trick of yours."

"He doesn't, not here and now." Asher shifted his position so they had direct eye contact. "It's important, no matter what happens, that you do not lose control. If your feelings threaten to overpower you, lie down, close your eyes, and let your mind float away. Do not, I repeat, do not draw attention to us."

"I guess if I start to lose control," she said half teasing, half serious, "you can always slug me and knock me out again."

"I assure you," Asher said dryly, "Warlord Leeds would not find that amusing. Are you ready?"

"Give me a minute." There was no sense asking Asher what to expect, or why she was doing this. Right now, it was enough that he had asked her and she wanted to please him by doing her best. She shut her eyes, slowed her breathing, and willed herself to relax.

After a moment, she told him, "I'm ready."

Until they topped the rise, she kept her gaze lowered, focused on nothing, trusting Asher to lead her.

"Now, Katrine."

She raised her head and looked over the knoll. Below her, camped on both sides of a deep crescent-shaped chasm, were hundreds of soldiers wearing blue, orange-trimmed uniforms. Tents were pitched everywhere. Strange beasts milled about the area, growling and snapping at each other but turning submissive when swatted by their masters.

Many soldiers sharpened or practiced with weapons.

A wooden plank bridge, supported by stout ropes, spanned the rift, and a few individuals carefully worked their way across it.

"How many have the hazy outline?" Asher asked quietly.

Rolling over onto her back, Katrine clenched her fists and closed her eyes tight. She wrapped her arms around her head and clamped her teeth on her lower lip. With all her might, she fought to keep her screaming inside.

A bead of moisture formed in the corner of her mouth, and when she touched it with her tongue, she discovered it was blood.

"Katrine," came Asher's urgent whisper, "what is it?" He blotted her mouth with a cloth. "Catch your breath. Breathe in and out. Slowly."

Obediently, she inhaled, exhaled, inhaled again. The hammering of her heart echoed in her head.

She opened her eyes, fumbled for one of Asher's hands, and clung to it, squeezing until her fingers went numb. Searching his face, she sought a safe port in which to anchor herself.

He lightly stroked her forehead with his free hand.

"Tell me," he said with gentle firmness.

"It's awful," she moaned at last. "So much hatred and greed and misery, I can't bear it."

"Take your time. Breathe some more. Relax and let your mind drift. Just like on the trail, remember?"

Accepting his comfort, Katrine let herself dissociate. Her mind floated somewhere above her. Gradually her knotted back and shoulder muscles loosened.

Asher brushed his fingers gently down her cheek and tapped her on the chin. She looked up at him, and he smiled.

In that moment, nothing existed but his smile. Here was safety.

"That's better," he said softly. "Now, how many down there carry the double image?"

"At least half, but that's not the worst part."

"What else?"

Momentarily, the feelings crashed down on her again, and she felt like a piece of driftwood dashed against the rocks in a storm, drowning and splintering and spinning out of control.

Then something new swept over her: a profound and frightening desire to rush into the camp below and destroy the source of this horrific evil. Rain fire on them and burn them up. Slash, stab, jab them. Wrap fingers around necks and slowly squeeze out the life, just like wringing out the laundry. She could do it easily, she knew. She could kill them all.

Kill them all.

Kill them.

Someone grabbed her shoulders and shook her hard.

Chapter Thirty-Eight

With enormous effort, Katrine yanked her attention away from her violent visions.

Asher's hands crushed the flesh on her upper arms. "Are you all right?" he demanded in a hushed but determined tone.

She managed a nod, and he released his bruising grip and took her hand instead.

"What happened?"

Tears leaked down her cheeks. "It's consuming me, Asher. I've got to get away from here. I can't hold out much longer."

"Besides the double-image people, what's down there?"

Keeping her eyes on his face, letting him be her anchorage in this emotional gale, she forced out the syllables: "Elnid-Kyeh."

"Are you sure?" Warlord Leeds asked in a rough undertone. "How do you know?"

Shuddering in remembered terror, she clung all the harder to Asher. "He tried to snatch me out of Echo Hall one night. He's on this side of the cleft by the largest fire. He's fanning their bloodlust into a frenzy." The sounds below took on a sinister and menacing quality. "Please," she begged, "if you don't want me to go berserk, you've got to get me out of here."

Asher pried her fingers from his hand. "You've done well. Start inching backward. We're all coming with you."

When they returned to camp, the sun was low in the sky. Warlord Leeds and Headmaster Miksel retired to the Warlord's tent to talk over what Katrine had told them and to consult one of the Recorder's books of prophecy.

With Asher and Neyac flanking her, Katrine sat on the ground at the forest's edge. They didn't speak. Every now and then she shuddered, and Neyac or Asher patted her back or squeezed her hand comfortingly.

"I'm sorry," Asher said. "I didn't know it would be so hard on you."

"I know." She felt numb and washed out inside. Just speaking took more energy than she could spare. She had to rest a moment before she could go on. "I felt your concern. I knew you wanted to help, but you couldn't. No one could."

Once again silence enveloped them.

After a while, Katrine spoke again. Even she could hear how tired and hopeless her voice sounded. "Someday, one of you is going to have to trust me enough to explain what's going on. I know something is happening to me. It started with the Glainite initiation. Bainu understood, but she said she had no right to tell me. Eventually, someone has to."

When the Recorder and Warrior protested, Katrine shushed them. "It's no use. You forget my Crennese lore. I haven't had it long, and I don't use it well, but it's still there. I sense the awful secret you struggle to keep from me." She paused to give them time to answer, but neither said anything.

"Bainu taught me an incantation for going into someone else's mind. I haven't tried it yet. I don't know how you sort through a person's thoughts and daydreams so you can separate them from their memories or how you can tell a fleeting reaction from a deeper conviction. So I've resisted the temptation to take the information from you, but that means I have to wait until one of you speaks. Please make it soon. I don't know how much longer I can bear having this, whatever it is, hanging over me."

Laboriously, she heaved herself to her feet. "I'm weary and heart-sore. I'm going to lie down for a while. If anything happens you think I should know, feel free to wake me."

* * *

Asher watched Katrine until she disappeared within the jumble of tents. "She's right, you know."

"I suppose so," said Neyac. "It must have been easier in olden times when this was openly recognized and a path set at birth. But even that wouldn't have prepared her for the rest of it. With this battle facing us, I don't know if it's better to tell her now or to wait until it's over."

"There will never be an ideal time. She's apt to be upset, no matter what the circumstances."

"You're probably right," Neyac said, rising. "Let's go see what the Warlord and Headmaster have found out."

* * *

Katrine woke to the sound of Asher's voice. She rubbed her eyes sleepily as she sat up.

"Leeds wants us to attend a meeting he's having with some of the officers," Asher said.

"All right. Give me a minute to pull myself together."

"I'll wait outside."

The Spire of Kylet

Hastily, Katrine took a cloth and swept the day's dust from her tunic, trousers, and boots. She brushed her hair, wishing she'd braided it that morning. There wasn't time now. Instead she tied it with a thong at the nape of her neck.

When she stepped out of the tent, she saw that twilight had passed and the darkness of night had settled over camp.

"You slept through supper," Asher said, handing Katrine a hard roll with meat inside. "I asked one of my men to entertain Heni. I don't know how long this'll last, and I didn't want her to become alarmed if she couldn't find you."

"That was thoughtful. Thank you."

Just before they reached the Warlord's tent, Katrine caught sight of her cousin. The man with her was the handsome one with the tiny crossed swords on his collar. He and Heni were already having fun. He was doing a card trick, and she was laughing. After the meeting, Katrine thought, she should remember to ask Asher what the little swords meant.

Holding back the tent flap, Asher motioned for Katrine to enter.

The Warlord's tent was sparsely furnished. A bedroll was spread out on a cot that was pushed to one side. There was a collapsible table and a few similarly constructed chairs at the back. Half a dozen small trunks were stacked in a corner. A solitary lamp dangled from a cord attached to a crossbeam, and smoke from the wick drifted in slow curls and faded into the shadows at the tent's peak.

Warlord Leeds and the two Recorders each occupied a chair. Torrend was seated at Neyac's feet. A dozen Warriors were scrunched together on the ground facing them, legs either crossed or pulled up to accommodate the crowded quarters. Those already present slid in even tighter to make room for Asher and Katrine, who sat side by side—almost, but not quite, touching.

"Many of you know why we're here," Leeds said, keeping his voice lowered, "but I want to recapitulate for the benefit of those who don't." He swept a glance across his audience, and a few heads nodded.

As the Warlord spoke, Headmaster Miksel took notes, and Neyac, using an art board balanced on his knees, appeared to be making a sketch of the gathering. The tip of Torrend's tongue protruded slightly from the corner of his mouth as he also labored over a piece of parchment.

Briefly Katrine felt a lump of envy lodge in her throat. She should be sitting with them, adding her talent to theirs.

When Leeds began talking again, she forced herself to listen.

"A few years ago, we at Landor received reports of strange creatures swimming across the Great Meriad. They roamed around villages and towns, usually spending the majority of their time at one particular home. After a few days, they would leave.

"If homeowners tried chasing them away, the animals went without a fight, but they always came back. After a while, people got used to them. A few even offered them food and shelter, considering them pets. The result was that, soon, these creatures had access to whole communities.

"Toward the beginning of last winter, new reports reached us. People were disappearing. Some returned later, seeming different to family and friends. Others were never seen again. Then several bodies were discovered, bodies that had been mangled by some kind of beast the Healers couldn't identify. This caused some of us to wonder if the appearance of the creatures and the disappearance of the people were connected.

"Teams made of Warriors and Recorders traveled to all the towns that had reported either creatures or disappearances. Although not all of the villages that had been visited by beasts had anyone vanish, each of the towns that reported disappearances had been visited by strange animals not long before. We stationed some of our best trackers in the towns still hosting the creatures and gave them instructions to follow the animals if they left.

"Jana, since you were one of the successful trackers, why don't you take over? Describe your experiences with the beast and what you ultimately discovered."

Since Jana was one of Asher's special friends, Katrine paid careful attention to her. She decided Jana was probably nearing her mid-twenties, and although she wasn't pretty in the same way Heni was, she was still attractive, in a strong, self-confident, Warrior-ish sort of way. She had two silver studs on her collar.

"I found the creature at Perlithe, a small farming community just west of the riverport town of Jeneff. In appearance it was much like the hunting nestinas the northern wanderers use to chase down mountain bears, except this animal had a more barreled chest and longer legs. Unlike nestinas, it wasn't at all interested in the farm animals.

"The creature had taken up residence at the home of one of the local Council members. When I arrived, it had been with them off and on for about a month. I stayed with the Councilman's family until three days later when, shortly after sunset, the beast crept away.

"It proceeded north up the Meriad, looking behind itself often. About half way between Jeneff and Botul, it swam across the river. Then I was afraid I'd lose it. Although I'm a good swimmer, the Meriad is wide, and I had to stay downriver and well behind the animal to keep from being spotted.

"After journeying north along the Eastern Meriad for two days, the beast started trailing a band of men. I assumed it was stalking them, and I was torn between remaining unseen and warning those I thought were its intended prey."

"It's a good thing you stayed focused on your assignment," Leeds interjected.

"Yes sir," Jana said with a quick bob of her head before she continued with her report.

"Then, incredibly, right before my eyes, the animal changed into a man.

The Spire of Kylet

When the other men saw him, they welcomed him with a lot of laughter and backslapping and the passing around of a skin of wine. Over the course of several days, I watched similar creatures make similar transformations as they joined the group. They led me to Marlett's Cleft.

"I scouted around for a while, listening to the soldiers banter. They talked about other encampments with which they were allied and with whom they would soon engage in war games.

"They also bragged about destroying Branston as—" her voice cracked, and she paused a moment before continuing, "—as a training exercise. A brawl broke out as two groups disagreed over who had gathered the most plunder.

"After Branston, they divided their forces and set up camps in several locations to drill and prepare for the upcoming battle simulations." She stopped, as if her story was complete, and then raised her hand to reclaim the floor. "I discovered the beasts had been sent to the villages to learn Kareand's strengths and weaknesses and, in some instances, to identify key individuals to be replaced by shapechanger look-alikes. I raced back to Landor and reported to Warlord Leeds."

Eager attention switched to the Warlord, and he settled deeper into his chair before he spoke. "Two other trackers reported similar experiences, although Jana garnered the most information." Leeds paused dramatically and gave each of the people in the tent a significant and serious look.

"I'm afraid what Manderig feared in ancient times has come to pass. The creatures infiltrating the villages and the individuals replacing the missing townspeople can only be Shokai shapeshifters. Our ancient enemies have found Kareand."

Chapter Thirty-Nine

A hush fell.

Finally Katrine could not stand the silence any longer. She said what she thought everyone else was thinking. "Does that mean the Wolkareans are ready to return?"

"Yes," Warlord Leeds said, "and soon the gathering will begin. But so far, only one Wolkarean has been called to service, and that is not enough for an army. Therefore, this fight is ours. We must push the Shokai and their Kareandeen allies back across Marlett's Cleft before their numbers grow any larger."

"But sir," Katrine said, raising her hand like a schoolgirl, "what about the Warrior of Four Bloods? Where is he? Doesn't he have to come forward so he can lead the Wolkareans into battle?"

"That's what the prophecies say, but we don't know who or where he is. I'm afraid we can't wait for him. Any other questions?"

Suddenly embarrassed, Katrine shook her head. She shouldn't have said anything. A few Warriors snickered quietly, but Leeds apparently heard them and silenced them with a scowl. Katrine felt like casting Bainu's invisibility spell and disappearing.

"Officers," Leeds said, "I want weapons and gear ready for inspection by tomorrow noon. We'll attack at first light the following day. Dismissed."

As the tent emptied, Katrine heard Leeds tell the Recorders, "I'll leave half a Section behind to guard the camp. You'll be safe here with the Neophytes and non-Warrior staff."

Once outside, Asher told Katrine he had assignments. He left her feeling confused and uncomfortable. She could see no reason for having been invited to the meeting in the Warlord's tent, and she'd made a fool of herself with her questions.

She wandered listlessly. It was too early to go to bed, and she was much too agitated to sleep anyway.

By the light of partially shuttered lanterns, the camp bustled with activity.

265

The Spire of Kylet

Warriors sat on the ground sharpening their swords and knives. Others fletched arrows.

Even though Katrine wasn't part of the Landorian Company, as she watched the Warriors prepare for battle, she felt as if she should get ready also. Borrowing a whetstone, she ran her knife over it until the edge was keen. Then she sheathed it and went back to Jana's tent to check her quiver. It was only half full.

She offered to help the fletchers in exchange for enough arrows to replenish her supply. At first the Warriors were dubious, but when they saw she had skill and training, they accepted her assistance.

While Katrine worked, she noticed Asher talking with Jana and their straw-haired friend near the middle of camp. After a few minutes, Asher's two friends nodded at something he said and then went off together. Asher crossed to the man with Heni. After a few quick words, Heni got up and walked one direction while Asher and his gorgeous friend went another.

As soon as Katrine finished her work with the fletchers, she joined some Warriors who were repairing tack. Again she offered to help. Leatherwork was a job she had done many times on her father's ranch.

It didn't occur to her to go to bed until the Warriors started turning in.

Heni was already in her bedroll when Katrine pulled off her boots and lay down, fully clothed, on her mat.

Since the meeting in the Warlord's tent—no, since looking at the camp along both sides of Marlett's Cleft—Katrine had been trying to understand herself.

She was almost overcome with conflicting feelings.

A pervasive sense of responsibility had settled on her shoulders, but she couldn't understand why. It made her feel strange and unfamiliar with herself. At the same time, she was excited at the thought of recapturing the savage rightness she'd felt when battling the bandits outside of Plains Springs.

But why?

She wanted to fight Elnid-Kyeh, yet how could she reconcile that with her lifelong desire of becoming a Recorder? The two were incompatible. Recorders used intellect and reason, not physical strength and courage. Strangely, Katrine was beginning to identify more with Asher than Neyac.

Ever since peering over the ridge at the enemy, she'd felt dirty, as if she had been contaminated by exposure to all that hatred, greed, and bloodlust.

Now she felt driven to destroy the people associated with it.

When had she become a violent person?

Was she turning into a monster?

The whine of Heni's voice startled her out of her contemplations.

"It's not fair," Heni said, rolling over and sitting up. "I was just getting to know Stephin, one of the better looking Warriors, when Asher came along and told him to get busy. When I asked why, Asher told me to go to bed. Just like that! No explanations. No apologies. Nothing. Just *go to bed*. You'd think at this time of night the chores would be done and the Warriors could relax."

"Not when they're preparing for battle." Katrine tried to make the situation real by saying the words aloud. It would be so much easier to pretend she had imagined it all.

"Battle?" Heni exclaimed in disbelief. "With whom? We're in the middle of nowhere."

"Back in the hills there is a whole camp full of soldiers, and some of them are Shokai shapechangers."

Heni was silent for a moment. Then, with a knowing grin, she shook her finger at Katrine. "You're teasing me again."

"No, I'm not. It's true. We move out at dawn, day after tomorrow."

Heni's face blanched and all the levity disappeared. "You're not going!"

"Yes, I am. No one has said I could, but I intend to anyway." Suddenly noticing Heni's fear, she reached over and squeezed her cousin's hand reassuringly. "You'll be safe here. I heard Warlord Leeds say he's leaving some Warriors to protect the camp. The fight will be over by Marlett's Cleft, which is quite some distance away. Don't worry."

"Do you think I'm worried about myself?" Heni demanded. Her voice became husky with suppressed emotion. She twisted the edge of her blanket as if she were trying to strangle it. "What if something happens to you? What would I tell your parents?"

"I don't know," Katrine said. She was sobered at the thought of being injured or killed, but her resolve remained firm. "It doesn't matter. I've still got to go. The forces out there are evil, truly and completely evil. Even if it costs my life, I have to try to destroy them."

Tears trickled down Heni's cheeks.

Katrine scooted over beside her cousin and wiped the wetness away with her fingertips. "Don't worry, Heni. It'll be all right."

"How can you say that? You don't know it's going to be all right. No one does. After the horrors at Branston, I didn't think anything could ever frighten me again. But the thought of losing you, after we've finally become friends, is terrifying. I don't think I could bear it."

"You mean a great deal to me, too. We've both grown up because of what we've experienced since leaving Banur. You're stronger than you realize. No matter what happens, you'll be all right."

For a few minutes, Katrine and Heni sat with their arms around each other. "You're really going?" Heni asked.

Katrine nodded, "I don't know why, but I have to."

"I'm not very brave, Katrine, but I'll try not to embarrass you by making a scene." Heni sniffled a moment then ventured a little grin. "But I won't promise not to cry and try to make you feel as guilty as possible."

Katrine chuckled and moved back to her own bedroll. "Good. I don't want you to change so much that I can't recognize you anymore."

Sliding back down under the covers, Heni rolled onto her side and faced Katrine. "We could've been friends years ago if we had ever bothered to get acquainted. I'm sorry we wasted so much time hating each other."

Katrine reached across the distance between their mats and took Heni's hand. "Maybe our friendship means more to us now than it would have if we had always cared. Now, we should both try to get some sleep."

"Good night, Katrine."

"Good night, Heni."

Although Katrine tried to embrace slumber, it was elusive and fled from her grasp. She lay flat on her back with her hands clasped over her heart and listened to the night sounds. She heard the perimeter guards making their rounds, a gentle wind whistling through the pine trees, an occasional hoot of an owl or cry of some timber animal, and the hum of the camp, slowing down after the activity of the day.

These strange, alien sounds were very different from the ones she'd heard outside her window at home. She caught herself straining to hear the chirping of crickets, the whispering of tall prairie grass in the wind, or the far-off cry of a plains cat.

Jana entered, stripped, and without saying a word, settled in her bedroll on the other side of the tent. Katrine wanted to ask her how Warriors managed to sleep in the face of combat, but before she could find the words, the woman's rhythmic breathing indicated that she was already asleep.

With her thoughts spiraling and racing wildly, Katrine realized her life had been turned topsy-turvy within the space of a few months. Images darted through her memory: the ravine, Polnu and Rand, the Glainites, Bainu, the Tests of Truth, Echo Hall, the journey, bandits, Asher, Neyac, Heni, Branston.

Home.

Tears welled up in Katrine's eyes and then dripped from the corners, wetting the hair around her ears. She whisked the dampness away with the palms of her hands.

She began counting backward from one hundred. That had successfully put her to sleep in the past.

Not tonight.

Skotlan's face suddenly appeared before her closed eyelids, followed by Mother, Father, and the other children.

Did any of them really know how much she loved them?

Had she ever told them?

Before leaving Banur, she should have comforted Father by telling him she had many happy and loving memories of her family to carry with her.

The Sister Wives, Kylet, Bainu, even Father, had hinted that she had a destiny to fulfill. Now for the first time, she feared they were right. She felt an inexplicable something rushing toward her, and she knew it was beyond her power to avoid it.

Yet, she was not afraid. It all seemed appropriate somehow.

Even if she should die on the battlefield, far from home and surrounded by strangers, she would die contented, knowing she was doing what was necessary. The only tragedy would be if she lost her life before telling her family how much they meant to her.

Slipping from her bedroll and fumbling in the dark, she located her art satchel. Then she crept from the tent in search of a lantern so she could write her parents a letter.

* * *

Elnid-Kyeh stared at a dark corner of his tent.

This regiment was not ready for the scheduled trial skirmishes. The Kareandeen and Shokai soldiers were still hostile toward each other and refused to take orders from the other group's officers.

His presence in the field had not had the calming effect he had expected, but he had solved that.

In a general assembly, he had given the troops two days to drill together and show they could work cooperatively, or he would start executing men at random until coordinated efforts were achieved.

Tonight there had been no arguments among the men after the evening meal: a very good sign.

* * *

As the first rays of daylight filtered through the trees, Neyac watched Katrine and Asher glare at each other with their hands clenched into fists.

Standing beside him, Miksel observed the scene with interest too.

"If you say that to me one more time," Katrine snarled at Asher, "I'm going to smack you right across the face."

"You are the most exasperating person I've ever met," Asher snapped back at her. "You are not going with us tomorrow, and that's final. You might as well accept it. If you don't, I just might have to knock you out and tie you up."

"You just try hitting me again, you big bully. I'm ready for you this time, and you'll get more than you bargained for."

"Again?" Miksel said, giving Neyac a startled look.

"It's a long story," Neyac answered.

Since Neyac and Miksel were both early risers, they had gone for a stroll to watch the sun come up. They met Katrine while she was checking on Thunder Cloud. A few moments later Asher joined her. Within seconds they were arguing.

"Bully? Me, a bully?" Asher exclaimed. "You're the one who's trying to browbeat me into letting you have your own way, even if what you want is stupid and irresponsible."

"Now you're calling me stupid?" Katrine yelled.

"All right, children," Neyac said firmly, clapping his hands like a schoolmaster calling his class to order. "Enough of this silliness."

Katrine and Asher spun toward him, and both started yapping at once.

"Enough," Neyac repeated even louder than before. "You're making a spectacle of yourselves, squabbling like a couple of spoiled toddlers."

"Then you tell her she can't go tomorrow," Asher said, flexing his hands in agitation. "Maybe she'll listen to you."

"I don't care if you are acting as my guardian," Katrine declared. "You can't keep me here either. This ridiculous barbarian is ignoring the fact that he's the one who made me go look at the enemy camp yesterday. Now he expects me to sit here like a good little girl and pretend it didn't happen while the grownups go fight. Well, I won't. Kareand is my land too. If the Warriors are going to face our enemies, then I am too. I don't know why, but I have to."

"You can't—"

Neyac cut Asher's comment short. "She has a point."

Asher scowled. "She'll be more useful after she learns how to defend herself. She could get killed out there tomorrow."

"Do you really think so?"

Asher slowly unknotted his fists. "Maybe not. She's managed to stay alive this long through some unfathomable miracle. Maybe she could survive the battle, but there is no way to be sure. No fight is predictable."

"True," Neyac said, "but you both seem to have forgotten something. This decision is not yours, Asher. Or yours, Katrine. It is the Warlord's."

"What's going on?" Leeds boomed. When he had come out of his tent, he had glanced around and apparently recognized there was a problem. He'd headed straight for them.

Asher started to answer, but Neyac was faster. "We're having a small controversy about whether or not Katrine should join your forces in the morning."

Snapping to attention, Asher said, "Sir, I've tried explaining to her that she could put herself and others in danger because of her lack of training and experience, but she refuses to listen. She is inordinately stubborn."

"And you're merely tenacious, is that it?" the Warlord asked, a touch of humor in his tone. Asher scowled but didn't reply. "You, Master Neyac, disagree with the Captain's judgment?"

"I can't say I disagree exactly. It is true Katrine is inexperienced, but her instincts are good. She also has some unusual skills that might prove beneficial."

Warlord Leeds narrowed his eyes and studied Katrine openly.

She seemed to be looking at the top button on his uniform, Neyac judged.

If she could stand up to Leeds without sagging, it would be a good test of her determination.

She assumed a posture that was as stiff as a board.

"I understand Asher's concern for you," the Warlord said. "Yesterday you had an overpowering reaction just looking at our enemies. If this happens every time you face a fight, how do you expect to accomplish anything?"

* * *

Katrine's impulse was to make a quick, sarcastic remark.

She was angry with Asher, and she didn't like being scrutinized by the Warlord. She knew, however, if she wanted Leeds to take her seriously, she would have to express herself with respect and logic. The first time she tried to answer, her voice came out a squeak. She swallowed, took a few deep breaths, and tried again.

"Part of the problem last night came from being unprepared for what I was going to experience. Now I'm forewarned. Also, tomorrow I could actually do something practical. The need to act was extremely strong. It still is."

Leeds acknowledged her comments with a slight nod. "Formal instruction can teach you to control the compulsion you describe. Without it, you might put yourself in more danger than needful. It might be wiser for you to wait to fight until after you've been trained, not just in weapons and tactics, but also in dealing with this type of stimulation. Tomorrow's fight won't be the last. You'll have ample opportunities to defend Kareand in the future."

"I won't beg you to let me go with you—"

"Good," Asher mumbled under his breath.

"Captain," Leeds snapped, "you forget yourself."

"Yes sir," Asher answered.

"—but," Katrine continued, "I also won't stay here."

Leeds didn't say anything.

Asher's face went purple with fury.

"You can put guards around me if you want to, but I know a spell for invisibility, so I don't think it'll do much good."

* * *

Asher could feel the blood rushing to his face, but he said nothing. He had already forgotten his boundaries with the Warlord once. He certainly didn't intend to give Leeds the opportunity to chastise him twice. Still, he knew a couple of things Leeds didn't, and it made keeping silent difficult.

"I'm not one of your Warriors you can boss around," Katrine said matter-of-factly. "I'm sorry, but I'll do whatever I want."

With one eyebrow cocked and his eyelids narrowed, Warlord Leeds locked gazes with Katrine. For several seconds they stood immobile, just staring at each other. Suddenly, the Warlord broke the match with a chuckle. "You've got courage, I'll grant you that. I've wilted full-grown men with that look."

"You're not going to let her go?" Asher blurted out. Quickly he pulled himself together. "My apologies, sir, I spoke without thinking."

"Oh, relax, Asher," the Warlord said. "I didn't mean to muzzle you permanently." He turned to Katrine and pinned her with his forefinger. "You, young lady, present a real problem. I need time to think."

"You might also need a bit more information," Neyac said, scratching his short gray beard.

"That's possible," Leeds said. "Do you have any?"

"Could we meet in your tent? There are some things we should discuss before this goes any further. The secrecy has gone on long enough."

Asher glanced at Leeds and then at the Master Recorder.

"Now?" the Warlord asked. "You think this is the right time?"

"It has to be before tomorrow's battle. You don't have the whole story, and Katrine doesn't have any of it."

"Come then," Leeds said. He turned and strode off toward his tent, leaving the others to follow.

Chapter Forty

As soon as they entered the Warlord's tent, Neyac gestured to one of the chairs. "Please sit down, Katrine."

Unwilling to make any concessions until she knew what was going on, Katrine refused. "I'll stand, thank you, and I won't stay if I don't want to."

"Fine, but stand by the chair in case you need to sit later."

Katrine faced Neyac like a pugilist before a match of fisticuffs. She didn't actually feel hostile, but she was on edge, ready to duck if a blow came out of nowhere.

"Do you mind if I do this my way?" Neyac asked the Warlord.

"It's your show," Leeds said, "but I hope you know what you're doing." He sat on his cot and crossed his legs.

"So do I," Neyac said.

Miksel got comfortable in one of the collapsible chairs, and Asher paced around the back of the tent.

Neyac pulled a small book from his pocket and tapped it on his hand thoughtfully. Then with the air of a man who was risking his entire purse on one toss of knucklebones, he handed it to Katrine and pulled up a chair next to Miksel.

"That is Headmaster Miksel's Nistarian translation of the Book of White Spells. He lent it to me to compare with the one you and I started on the riverboat. I'm sorry we never finished. It would have answered a great many of your questions."

Narrowing her eyes, Katrine tried to give Neyac the look her father used when he wanted to convey the message *your story needs work*. Her questions had nothing to do with the historical past. They were here in the present.

"If you remember, the part we read together was written by a woman named Miri. But she wasn't the only author. The book was passed from generation to generation, and everyone who wrote in it included his or her own interests and experiences.

"I've marked a page, and I would like you to start reading there. This

273

section was written by a man named Devlyn."

Katrine ran her eyes along the words.

"Aloud, please," Neyac said.

Katrine couldn't imagine what this had to do with whether or not she got to fight Shokai tomorrow, but with four powerful men all staring at her, she thought she might as well get it over with. Then maybe they could get back to the real issues.

She began reading:

I write this because I fear no one will bother to remember the Wolkarean lore. Manderig decreed that the Wolkareans should be born to each of the other three races so their bonds would be with all people rather than to parentage or clan. Therefore, the Wolkareans are a strange breed with neither true kin nor lands of their own.

When Kareand was settled, the Boradids claimed the eastern coast, the Crennese the northern mountains, and the Nistarians the great prairie. But the Wolkareans were wanderers who had to go where they are needed. Only the city of Landor has provided them a home. However, they cannot stay there long because their duties carry them to and fro across the land.

Still, I do not regret my heritage even though it is both a blessing and a curse. My gifted vision allows me to see what others miss: the motivation behind the deeds of my countrymen. When I am confronted with evil in people, I am driven to dispel it by either helping them correct their ways or by helping our society punish their misdeeds.

It is a valuable service I perform, and I will always be grateful that I was born with the mark of Zeroon. I know the paleness of my eyes has caused many to tremble.

Katrine paused. "The paleness of his eyes? That was the mark of Zeroon?"

"Yes," Neyac said, "pale, nearly colorless eyes."

Katrine bit her lip but then reasoned she had no cause for this knot in her stomach. Neyac wasn't serious.

"That's silly," she said. "Anyone can have pale eyes."

"Why don't you read a little farther?" Neyac suggested. "It might help you understand."

I know the paleness of my eyes has caused many to tremble. And when my orbs burn with righteous anger, evil men quake in their terror for they know their punishment is at hand.

"There," Neyac said.

"There what?" asked Katrine, marking the place with her finger.

"After the battle with the bandits," Neyac said, "do you remember Heni saying your eyes looked as if they were on fire?"

"Yes," Katrine said hesitantly.

"It took a long time for that blaze to die down. It was still there when we talked while you cared for your horse."

"This is absurd," Katrine said, feeling almost faint. "You're implying I'm a Wolkarean."

"Not implying, telling," Neyac said. "Last night Warlord Leeds said one Wolkarean has been called to service. That one is you, Katrine. You're the first."

"Don't be ridiculous," she said sharply. "I'm a simple herder from Banur."

"No, Katrine," Warlord Leeds said, leaning forward intently. His tone was perfectly serious, and the expression on his face was grave. "Neyac is right. Your parents have known you were a Wolkarean since the day you were born. Your father left his position at Landor to devote himself to your upbringing since at that time you were the only known Wolkarean to have been born in many generations."

Shaking her head, Katrine tried to dislodge the bee buzzing between her ears. "My father was never at Landor. He grew up at Sindell then migrated across the plains after he met my mother. He's a rancher not a Warrior."

"A man raised in a seaport town suddenly decides to move inland?" asked Leeds. He shook his head. "No, Katrine, your father left Sindell for Landor. He met your mother while she was at Pardish studying to become a Recorder. After you were born, they decided a herder's life would provide many strengthening experiences for a developing Wolkarean. They didn't want you growing up at Landor. They were afraid you would be considered an oddity and isolated from the other children if you were the only Wolkarean there. They took you to Banur where your true heritage wouldn't be recognized."

"I don't understand. Now you're telling me I don't even know my own parents."

"How much can any of us know about our parents," Leeds asked, glancing briefly at Asher and smiling. "Parents live and grow up and plan their futures before their children are born, and youngsters are seldom interested in the past. Someday, if you ask, maybe your parents will tell you their story. Right now, though, I am the Warlord of Kareand. I have called you here as a Wolkarean. Will you accept the charge and come to Landor to be trained?"

"But I don't want to be a Wolkarean," Katrine said, pleadingly. "I want to go to Pardish and become a Recorder. It's all I've ever wanted."

Headmaster Miksel went over to Katrine and put his arm around her. "I'm sorry, child," he said. "Some things can't be chosen. Many can be Recorders, but right now, you are the only one here who can be a Wolkarean. With war on the horizon, we are facing grave times. If the Shokai are victorious, someday there will be no Pardish, no Recorders, and nothing left that we love."

Trapped and frightened, Katrine searched the faces around her. When her eyes reached Asher, they stayed. "They're playing games with me, aren't they?"

Asher shook his head. "No, Katrine. It's all true. As Warriors travel, we try to identify Wolkareans so they can be added to the rolls and someday be called into service. The Recorders help us. We have lists of young people and the villages or cities they live in. Now that the time of need has arrived, they will all be summoned to Landor by Warlord Leeds. Your name is at the top of the list."

Like a stampede of herdbeasts, Katrine's thoughts tore through her head, making the world turn inside out and crosswise.

"And that little trick you taught me?" she asked him. "Relaxing my mind so I can see things?"

"That is the first step in teaching you to use the gifted vision of the Wolkareans," Asher said. "That's why no one else could look at the camp by Marlett's Cleft and know how many Shokai were there. The double-image people you see are all shapeshifters. To the rest of us they look like ordinary people. But Manderig gave the Wolkareans special talents to see behind many masks."

Katrine had assumed that seeing the double-images was a side effect of the Glainite Joining. She thought it indicated some weakness that kept her from accepting their full heritage.

How could she be a Wolkarean?

She wasn't anything like the Wolkareans she had studied about in the histories. She wasn't particularly strong, or intelligent, or brave, or wise, or self-sacrificing, or fair.

Right now, she was just confused and overwhelmed.

"The headaches and blurred vision," she asked Asher, "what are they?"

"According to writings at Landor," Asher said, "you get those symptoms when you try to use mundane vision to see something that can only be seen with your Wolkarean senses. The harder you try, the worse it gets. The relaxation exercise I taught you is one of the ways to move beyond that."

All of a sudden, an icy fist hammered inside Katrine's chest as a terrible realization hit her.

"The first time I got headaches from concentrating was in my own home at a dance for Heni. I told you about Felda and Valt. Are you saying there were Shokai in my house?"

Neyac patted the air with his palm to interrupt her. "As soon as Asher told me about your conversation, I wrote your father. Obviously this Felda and Valt have been replaced by shapeshifters. Your father has been warned."

The tension in her chest eased, and Katrine nodded her thanks. It was bad enough to worry about marauders threatening her family, but the thought of Shokai in quiet little Banur was horrifying.

"Why didn't you tell me before?" Katrine asked Neyac. "If my parents knew, why didn't they tell me?" She felt a sudden flare of anger. "And if my father used to be a Warrior, why didn't he ever teach me to fight? To use a sword?"

"Your father wanted to give you as normal a childhood as he could," Neyac said soothingly. "He wanted to spare you this if possible."

"Well, Master Recorder," Leeds said brusquely, "I assume you have a point to make. None of this is news to anyone except Katrine. I don't see how her knowing is going to affect my decision about tomorrow."

A quiet chuckle escaped Neyac.

"There is more," he said. "I know I shouldn't have kept it from you, but you were so excited about our bringing you a real live Wolkarean, I didn't want to overburden you. Of course, Asher knows too, so if you're going to be angry, you'll have to get mad at both of us."

Warlord Leeds squinted ominously at Neyac, who looked as if he might break into a little jig of excitement.

"What in Kareand are you talking about?" demanded Leeds. "Do you have a whole community of these young people hidden away somewhere?"

"No, nothing like that. You have had all kinds of hints. If you haven't figured it out, it's not my fault. Katrine, please tell the Warlord your heritage."

"My heritage? Why?"

"Just humor me. Please tell him."

"All right." Her feelings were too jumbled up and bewildering for her to argue. She needed to finish this interview so she could get away and think things through. "My father is Nistarian, and my mother is Boradid."

"Go on," Neyac said. "That's not all. Tell them about the initiation."

"That's private!" Katrine all but yelled.

Why couldn't they just leave her alone for a while?

"Come on," Neyac said, encouragingly. "We're going to have lots to talk about. We might as well get everything out in the open."

"All right," she said, giving in because she couldn't handle much more. She was starting to go numb. "During the summer, I was adopted into the Glainite tribe through the Tests of Truth. Is that what you wanted?"

"Remember," Neyac crowed, "she told you she knew an invisibility spell."

"By the Coils," Warlord Leeds swore, "of course." He aimed an angry and accusatory finger at Asher. "You knew all this time and didn't tell me?"

"Yes sir," Asher said with a completely blank face.

"I ought to have you flogged," Leeds bellowed, "for not informing me immediately. In fact, I still might when I get my wits back."

"It makes perfect sense," Headmaster Miksel said, talking more to himself than anyone else. "If she had been born this way, Elnid-Kyeh would have killed her in her infancy. He surely knows the prophecies as well as anyone."

Bewildered, Katrine looked from Warlord Leeds to Neyac, from Headmaster Miksel to Asher. "What are you talking about? If I had been born what way?"

Asher, who had stayed near her throughout the discussion, cupped

Katrine's chin in his hand and tipped her head up until she was looking into his eyes. Then he took hold of both her hands. "Nistarian from your father. Boradid from your mother. Crennese through the Glainites. Wolkarean by birth."

Jerking away as if she had been burned, she sank weakly into the chair Neyac had proffered earlier.

"No," she whimpered.

"Yes, Katrine," Neyac said. "You are obviously the Warrior of Four Bloods."

In stunned silence, Katrine grappled with the horror of Neyac's words.

Biting down on her fist, she jumped up, ran from the tent, and plunged into the forest.

Chapter Forty-One

Katrine sat with her knees drawn up to her chest and her arms wrapped around them.

In the distance she could hear the faint sounds of the Landorian camp, enough to guide her when she decided to go back.

If she decided to go back.

Right now, she was too numb to decide anything.

She couldn't cry.

She couldn't think.

She could hardly breathe.

With just a few words spaced over a few minutes, Neyac had destroyed her world.

Nothing would ever be the same for her.

Ever.

Why hadn't her parents prepared her?

How could they have known even part of the truth and have kept it from her? If she had grown up knowing she would someday need to go to Landor to become a Warrior, she would never have built her dreams on becoming a Recorder. She wouldn't have wasted hundreds of hours learning to paint, a useless skill now, and she could have focused on learning to fight. If she'd had any preparation at all, maybe she wouldn't feel so devastated.

Abruptly she had gone from herder to Wolkarean to Warrior of Four Bloods. Tomorrow would be her first battle. She didn't doubt for a moment that Leeds would let her fight, but now she realized how pitifully little she knew.

She didn't know swordplay. She didn't know strategy or tactics. She didn't even know the hierarchy and the ranking of the Warriors.

She had been cocky and unrealistic when she told Asher she planned to join the fight. Despite the compulsion she felt, she really hadn't expected to do much, maybe lob a few arrows.

Now everything was different.

The Spire of Kylet

This morning she had been a girl hoping to become a Recorder.

Now she was the fulfillment of prophecy.

How was she supposed to cope with that?

Already, she knew, the news was spreading throughout camp. When she went back, everyone would treat her differently.

Some would be suspicious or doubtful. Others would be curious. A few might be pleased or excited like Neyac.

But their expectations!

They might not know what to expect, but they would all expect something from her.

Every mistake, every foolish choice, every clumsy move she made from now on would be discussed, argued, and dissected. No one would just see her, Katrine of Banur, ever again.

What about her family? Her friends? How would they react?

Mother and Skotlan, Bainu, Rand and Polnu, they would understand it was not her choice. They would do what they could to support her without adding to her stress, but the others?

Father would be proud, she was sure of that, but now his expectations would be greater than ever. She had disappointed him constantly in the past. He would probably be even more difficult to please in the future.

Anton would hate her. He had always acted as if any accomplishment of hers diminished him. Now he would think she became the Warrior of Four Bloods just to show him up.

Of course, Jaimi would be mortified that her sister had reached this pinnacle of masculine notoriety, demonstrating once and for all that Katrine had no sense of feminine decency.

And the people of Banur? They would probably think it was a lie, a hoax, a fraud.

It was hopeless.

"May I join you?" Asher asked as he sat down beside her. "I thought you might need someone to talk to."

"There is nothing left to say."

They sat silently, Katrine chewing on her lower lip with Asher watching her. Then she blurted out, "Oh Asher, why didn't you tell me? How could you and Neyac know what was happening to me and not speak up?"

"It was a difficult decision," Asher answered. "We talked about it many times. We thought if we could just get you to Landor, somehow your natural instincts would take over. We didn't expect to end up here. We didn't expect a battle to intervene. I'm sorry."

When she didn't respond, he went on. "I understand a little of what you're going through."

"Not likely," Katrine said with bitterness. "No one can."

"I think I do. Right now you're probably feeling vulnerable and exposed. You think everyone will be watching you, judging everything you do. You think they'll be jealous or skeptical or expecting too much. And you think no matter what you do, it won't be enough. There will always be someone to criticize. So in the end you're afraid you'll fail. Right?"

Katrine gaped at him in astonishment. "That is exactly what I was feeling. How did you know?"

"It was the way I felt when Regent Laria called my father to be Warlord, as if I would never be seen for myself again, as if I would always live in his shadow. Of course, it's different for you. You have to live in the shadow of a prophecy."

"That's right. How can I— Just a minute! Regent Laria made your father the Warlord?"

Asher thumped himself on the forehead with his palm. "Sometimes I forget you're not from Landor. You're a Wolkarean, and we've spent so much time together, it simply slips my mind that all of this is new to you. Everyone at Landor knows Leeds is my father."

"Warlord Leeds is your father?" Katrine repeated incredulously.

Rolling his eyes heavenward, Asher chuckled. "Everyone reacts like that when they first find out. Yes, indeed, Warlord Leeds is my father. I was in my second year as a Neophyte, and he was a Captain when Regent Laria called him. I thought my life had ended. I was young and ambitious. I was afraid that from then on, no matter what I accomplished, the officers and my peers would think it was based on favoritism, and I was right."

"What did you do?" Katrine asked.

"For quite a while I worked twice as hard as everyone else. I wanted to make sure people knew I earned whatever I got. But it didn't help. There were still those who said I got the finest opportunities and the best assignments because I was the Warlord's son. Eventually I did what we all have to do in the end. I stopped caring about what other people thought. It's hard, Katrine, but it's the only way. You'll have to do it too. Regardless of what anyone says, all you can be is yourself, and all you can do is your best."

Katrine hid her face in her hands. "I didn't want any of this. I just wanted to be a Recorder."

"I know," Asher said sympathetically.

He slid over closer and slipped his arm around her shoulders.

Unable to keep her feelings buried any longer, Katrine nestled against Asher's chest, and her body began to shake with sobs.

* * *

For the next several minutes, Asher held Katrine in his arms while she cried, sobbing as if a lifetime of hurts had to be washed away.

All the while, he stroked her hair and murmured softly to her.

"It's not fair. Life never is. But it'll be all right. You'll see. You'll make it all right."

The Spire of Kylet

He hadn't told her, but he'd wept like this when he learned his father was going to be the next Warlord. He knew all his dreams of achievement as a Warrior would be ruined.

He hadn't believed the pain and disappointment would ever go away, nor did he imagine a time when he would be proud to be the Warlord's son. Yet the pain had faded and the pride had developed. They would for Katrine, too. But he knew that at fifteen, tragedies felt as if they would go on forever.

At last, Katrine's sobs gave way to hiccupping sniffles, and she sat up and wiped her face with the handkerchief he had ready for her.

"I'm sorry," she said. "It's just been too much, too fast. I'll be all right."

"I know you will."

Giving a rueful laugh, Katrine's tone became ironic. "I'll bet that's the first time you've ever had one of your Warriors crying in your arms like a baby."

"Well," Asher said with a grin, "it's certainly the first time I've been in that position with someone who outranks me."

"Outranks you? Who me?"

"You're the Warrior of Four Bloods, Katrine. You outrank everyone, including the Warlord."

When she pulled back in shock with her lower lip trembling, Asher laughed at her. He gave her a brotherly squeeze. Then he took his arms from around her, tapped her playfully on the nose, and clasped his hands around his bent knee.

"Don't worry," he said, "Leeds isn't going to turn over command to you. At least not until you've learned a hell of a lot more than you know right now."

Color drained from Katrine's face, and Asher chuckled again.

"Turn over command to me?" she said. "Holy Signs, what a horrible idea!"

"The prophecies say the people will follow the Warrior of Four Bloods. The Warlord will be there, doing his share no doubt, but you'll be the one in charge."

"No. I can't do it," Katrine said, breathing heavily. She twisted Asher's handkerchief into knots. "I'll never be able to."

"Not any time soon, anyway," Asher said. "But someday, when you've had time to mature in your skills, you'll be surprised at what you can accomplish."

For several minutes Katrine gazed off into the distance, silent and brooding. Then without looking at him, she asked, "How old are you, Asher?"

"Me? Why do you ask?"

"Will you tell me?"

"Possibly, but first I'd like to know why you're curious."

"It's just sometimes you seem so old and wise. And when you're upset, you get this fierce, intense expression around your eyes and mouth. Then I think you must be nearly as old as my father. Other times, you're gentle or funny or relaxed, and then you look almost as young as I do."

"That young?" Asher said, laughing heartily.

"Like now," Katrine said with a sense of awe creeping into her voice. "When you laugh and when you smile, the years just fall off your face."

"Then I definitely need to start smiling more."

"And laughing, too. You have a very nice laugh. Now tell me. How old are you?"

"Twenty-one," Asher said. "I'll turn twenty-two right before Midwinter Festival. Is it too old or too young, do you think?"

Katrine turned and stared at him for a moment, her lips pursed and her brow wrinkled.

"It seems kind of young for a Captain. You've got four studs on your collar. That's only two less than the Warlord. Most people with only one or two studs look lots older than you. I've been watching, but I haven't seen anyone else in camp with four studs, and no one at all with five."

"You're observant," he told her, pleased that she was interested enough to watch the Warriors and try to figure things out for herself. "But I assure you there are plenty of other Captains around Landor and in the Landorian Compounds. And there are only four District Commandants at any given time. They're the ones with five studs."

"What's a District Commandant?"

"When Kareand was first settled, Zeroon divided the land into three districts. The northern mountains, the eastern seacoast, and the great plains. A District Commandant is assigned to each area and is in charge of the Warriors and Neophytes who are serving there. The fourth Commandant is responsible for administering the Training Compound at Landor."

"And the other ranks?"

"We can talk about that later, Katrine. I promise I'll answer all of your questions the first chance that I get. But right now, if you're up to it, you probably ought to report back to Leeds. He's worried because you took the news about being the Warrior of Four Bloods so hard. Neyac and Miksel are concerned, too."

Katrine sighed and looked down as if studying the backs of her hands. "I'll have to face them eventually, won't I?"

"I'm afraid so."

Asher sprang to his feet, and Katrine clambered slowly to hers.

She extended her hand to him trustingly, the way a child who faced a busy street might reach for a parent or older sibling. "Will you go with me?"

Taking her hand in his, he answered, "Always."

* * *

As Katrine sat facing the Warlord in his tent, Asher stood beside her, his hand resting on the back of her chair.

He was so close, even though he wasn't touching her, she could feel his body warmth through her clothes.

She had reluctantly dropped his hand when they entered camp, afraid that the familiarity might be misconstrued. Now she clasped her hands tightly together in her lap to keep from reaching for him again.

Neyac and Miksel sat at right angles to the Warlord.

"I have considered the situation thoroughly, Katrine," Leeds said, "and I've decided to allow you to accompany us tomorrow."

No big surprise there, Katrine thought to herself. *I don't know if I should be happy or horrified.*

Leeds glanced around at the others, but no one said anything.

When he began speaking again, he kept his eyes on Katrine as if she were the only person in the tent with him. "I know you're untrained and inexperienced. I also know I'm putting you at risk. If this were going to be a normal fight, steel against steel, I would never do it. Never. But Elnid-Kyeh is here.

"I don't know what he might throw at us. If he's as powerful as the legends say, it could be almost anything. We have surprise on our side, but I think we'll need every advantage we can muster.

"The records at Landor imply that combining the four bloods in one person is magical all by itself. I hope that means you'll be protected and can help if Elnid-Kyeh hits us with something extraordinary."

Leeds paused a moment then said, "Comments?"

"Sir," Asher began, "since she doesn't know swordsmanship or hand-to-hand combat, could I recommend that she not be included in the vanguard? She is trained with a bow and could join Unit Leader Eltin's archers."

"But I want—"

"Katrine," Leeds snapped at her, his voice sharp like the crack of a whip, "I am the Warlord. I expect you to remember that."

Astounded by the Warlord's demeanor, which was so different from his earlier casual camaraderie, Katrine clamped her jaws tight and sat mutely staring at her feet.

She heard, rather than saw, when Leeds turned to the Recorders. "You've probably studied the Crennese prophecies more thoroughly than any other two men in Kareand. Is there anything, anywhere, that indicates it would be unwise to have Katrine on the battlefield this soon after coming into her power?"

"Actually," Miksel said, "there are passages that might support your decision. The seer Katrel wrote: *The newly sprouted seedling will be carried by winds from its nurturing soil to face floods and fires, and turn them, despite the tenderness of its leaves and the softness of its bark.* As you are aware, I'm sure, all of the prophecies about The Great War are vague and subject to interpretation."

Neyac scratched his short beard and nodded agreement. "Nesme wrote:

The fledgling that saves the world will fly out of the nest to fight wind and rain on unformed wings."

"Both of those passages," Miksel said, "could refer to Katrine's having to meet the challenges of her calling without adequate training."

"All right," Leeds said, "it's done. Captain Asher, I want you to spend the rest of the day preparing Katrine.

"Make sure she knows enough about protocol, hand signals, and her Unit to be effective tomorrow. Take her to Unit Leader Eltin. Stay with her and make sure she understands his orders. Katrine, you'll join the archers under the command of Unit Leader Eltin. You will report to him in the morning at the time and place he designates. You're dismissed."

Chapter Forty-Two

Asher led Katrine outside.

As they walked, she noticed that Warriors stopped talking and doing their chores, or whatever Warrior assignments were called, in order to watch them. She felt herself getting angry. She wanted to yell at everyone to get back to work. Since she couldn't do that with Asher right there, she simply stopped and glared.

Most of the Warriors immediately resumed what they had been doing, looking a little embarrassed. Some, however, continued to stare, and their glances were not friendly.

It's as if they think if there was no Warrior of Four Bloods then there wouldn't be any war, she thought.

"Let's go this way," Asher said, taking her elbow and steering her into the forest. "What did you think of your first orders from the Warlord?"

"Holy fraggin' Signs," Katrine exclaimed. "He scared the breath clear out of me. You didn't even argue with him about my going tomorrow. In fact you told him what to do with me."

"Lesson number one," Asher said. "When the Warlord starts a sentence with 'I've decided,' there is no more discussion and no argument. When he asks for comments, he only wants suggestions on how to make his decision work."

Katrine already felt as if she had been thrust into a world of unknown rules and unfathomable prospects. Now she felt like there was another obstacle planted in her way to make her stumble and fall.

"Well, that's just great," she said sarcastically. "How am I supposed to know when to speak and when to shut up if you all talk in code?"

"That's part of what Leeds wants me to teach you today. If you had come to Landor as a Neophyte, you would have learned most of this before you ever saw the Warlord, certainly before you exchanged a hello with him. He knows this is going to be difficult for both of you."

"You mean it'll be difficult for me because I don't know what's going on.

But him? I don't believe it'll be hard for him. He already knows everything, and he's in charge. He's just like my father."

Pine needles crunched beneath their feet as they walked.

A couple of small rodents ran from under a bush and scurried up a tree, chittering loudly as if scolding the humans for intruding into their habitat. Katrine would have laughed under other circumstances. At this time, it only served to reinforce how out of place she was here in the north, far from the prairie and home.

"I think you were right when you said Neyac or I should have told you the truth in the beginning," Asher said. "I apologize for that. We have wasted a lot of time that could have been spent explaining things to you, things about Landor and the Warlord and his job."

Asher paused long enough to hold back a branch for Katrine, and then he continued speaking.

"Over the past ten years, Leeds has been the highest military authority in Kareand. His word is law at Landor. Even though he takes counsel from the District Commandants and even us lowly Captains, he doesn't have to. He has no one to answer to except Regent Laria. In case of war, he doesn't even answer to her.

"Now here comes a fifteen year old girl into his life, into his camp, into his battles. She doesn't know anything about being a Warrior, but he's got to help her learn what she needs to know in order to take over his job. That's not an easy situation for a man."

"It sounds awful when you say it like that." Katrine kicked a pile of fallen leaves. A moldy scent drifted after them as they scattered, making her sneeze. "I don't want his job."

"I'm afraid it isn't optional, Katrine. You are what you are. Nothing is going to change that."

They came to a stream speckled with large rocks. Asher stepped from one stone to another. About midway, one wobbled beneath his foot, but he shifted his weight and maintained his balance. Before he moved on, he extended his hand to assist Katrine. He did not let go of her until they were both safely on the other bank.

"For the Warriors to trust you enough to follow you," Asher said as they continued their walk, "you must be disciplined and restrained in front of them. You must also be skilled in weaponry, leadership, tactics, and strategy. Although you need to be personable, you must also maintain strict boundaries. You need to know when to seek counsel and when to give orders. Watch Leeds every chance you get. He's an expert at balancing all of that."

Katrine shook her head and said nothing.

All of this had to be a mistake.

Even if she had the right bloodlines, she was probably just a decoy. She could distract everyone until the real Warrior of Four Bloods showed up. In the meantime, Elnid-Kyeh could use her for target practice.

That would just be her luck.

Right now, she would be happy to go back home and be a herder for the rest of her life.

Yet, Neyac and Asher were so sure that this was her destiny, and so were Leeds and Miksel.

What if it were true?

Part of her felt like it might be. That would certainly explain some of her past experiences: having Kylet's spire, meeting him and the Sister Wives in Echo Hall, succeeding at the Tests of Truth, successfully battling the bandits outside of Plains Springs. Those things made sense if she was the Warrior of Four Bloods. So did throwing the spire to kill a plains cat when she didn't even know how.

Blessed Signs, she thought, if she really was the prophesied Warrior, if she was the best the Powers could find, the people of Kareand were in seriously deep trouble.

Pointing to a fallen tree nearby, Asher suggested they sit on the trunk.

After Katrine was seated, Asher straddled the log as if it were a horse. She studied the ground, digging into the dirt and undergrowth with the toe of her boot. She sighed.

"I need you to pay attention," Asher said. "Do you think you can stop feeling sorry for yourself and concentrate for a while?"

"I'm not feeling sorry for myself," Katrine said, snapping her head up and glowering at him.

He cocked an eyebrow at her, and her glower melted as hot blood rush to her face.

The Warrior of Four Bloods blushes? Katrine thought. *That's just another inconsistency between the image of the "big-strong-save-the-world-Warrior-of-Four-Bloods" and the "stupid-never-been-anywhere-or-done-anything-weak-girl."*

"All right," Katrine admitted, "I'm feeling a little sorry for myself."

"Can you move beyond it?" Asher asked, not critically, but like he would help her deal with it if she needed him to.

"I'll try."

"Good. Now I have a question for you." He picked up a twig and twirled it slowly in his hands. "If I hadn't warned you to be still when you looked at the enemy camp, what would you have done?"

The question surprised her, and her response came automatically. "I'd have rushed down there and killed as many of those evil soldiers as possible."

"How?"

"What?"

"How would you have killed them? You didn't have any weapons except your small belt knife, did you?"

Without thinking, Katrine rested her hand on the spire tucked inside her tunic, but she knew it wasn't a weapon she would have used. She hadn't even tried to throw it since she had shown it to Rand.

Asher repeated his question. "How would you have killed them?"

"I don't know," she admitted in frustration. "I just felt like that was what I was supposed to do."

Nodding, Asher said, "Lesson number two: rushing blindly into combat is an effective way of getting killed. If you want to live to be an old Warrior, you have to learn never to go knowingly into danger without a plan, no matter how you feel."

"I remember this," Katrine said. "I learned the verse in one of my first primers. *There are old Warriors, and there are bold Warriors, but there are no old, bold Warriors.*"

"Right. A hot head never leads to a rational decision. Lesson number three: follow your orders. When we meet with Unit Leader Eltin, he'll tell you what the assignment is for the archers. Sometimes only the Warlord knows the entire plan, and that's why following orders is so important. You might only have access to one piece of the puzzle, but without that piece, the puzzle can't be completed."

"But I'm not like other people. I'm still trying to figure out who and what I am. Will Eltin's orders take into account that I have these peculiar compulsions I don't understand?"

"No," Asher said bluntly. "Completing the assignment is up to him. Controlling yourself is up to you."

"But I don't know how."

"I'll teach you. I know a great deal about the Wolkareans. I've spent most of my life, even before I became a Neophyte, reading, studying, and analyzing their records at Landor. By evening you'll be able to bring many of your Wolkarean senses under conscious control. Automatic control takes practice. Now, lesson number four—"

Asher talked and Katrine listened.

As if a Healer were removing a long bandage from across her eyes, letting flickers of light creep in slowly, Katrine caught the first rays of understanding, the first glimmers of belief.

* * *

When twilight fell, Elnid-Kyeh entered his tent and lay down on his bedroll. Today the troops had done better. Unfortunately, he had needed to execute a dozen men to promote the necessary level of cooperation.

Perhaps he could return to Serpent's Head within a day or two. He did not like being so long away from his tower and the sea. As the camp quieted, he relaxed. Sleep was near.

The amulet at his throat twitched.

Not bothering to get up, Elnid-Kyeh touched the crystal.

Hollenth's face floated in the air in front of him. He was the only one of

The Spire of Kylet

Elnid-Kyeh's servants who could communicate without the aid of an amulet of his own.

"Milord," Hollenth said. "Your servant Valt has just told me a most upsetting rumor."

By the time Hollenth had finished reporting, Elnid-Kyeh was on his feet and pacing the length his tent, going from one end to the other and then back again.

Curse that infernal girl.

The last time he had attempted to scry her, trying to keep track of Kylet's spire, she had blocked him somehow. Now, if Hollenth's information was correct, she was prophecy's heir: the Warrior of Four Bloods.

That would certainly explain why she had that damnable weapon.

He did not have his scrying dish with him, nor his thrice-sanctified oil. He would have to return to Serpent's Head to discover the truth about her.

But he had war games to supervise tomorrow. If he did not stay, his troops would merely revert to their previous level of hostilities. Then he would have to execute more of them to restore order.

If teleportation spells did not require so much energy, he could go to Serpent's Head, scry the girl to find out if what Hollenth discovered was correct, and then come back again.

But such a venture would be too tiring.

He could not risk it. Tomorrow was much more important.

Another few days would not matter.

She was a child after all, and it would take time for her to mature and to be adequately trained before she became a threat.

For now she could wait.

Chapter Forty-Three

Nervousness woke Katrine.

As she lay on her mat, she could hear soft movements in the camp and smell faint cooking odors. Jana and Heni were still sleeping, but she knew the call to assembly would come soon.

Quietly she crept to the corner where she had placed the uniform she'd been issued last night. It was black like Asher's, but of course it had no collar studs. Her hands shook so badly when she put it on that she had to try several times to get the buttons fastened.

She was crossing to the tent flap when someone struck a light chime just outside. "Assembly in a quarter hour," a small voice said.

Immediately Jana roused and began dressing.

As instructed, Katrine grabbed her bow and two quivers and went to the area indicated by Unit Leader Eltin. She took her designated spot. She waited silently while other archers joined her. She wondered if Asher had suggested she be assigned to this unit because its leader was one of his friends.

When he introduced her to Eltin last night, she recognized him as the short, straw-haired man whom Asher had greeted so warmly when they first arrived here.

At the quarter hour, Eltin walked up and down among the archers. When he came to Katrine, he asked to see her bow. He examined it closely.

"It's made of sinella wood, isn't it?"

"Yes sir." The words felt strange on her tongue.

"Bows like this are rare, but they are supposed to be the finest ever made. Where did you get it?"

"It was a gift from the friend who taught me to use it, sir," said Katrine.

"Crennese?"

"Yes sir." She wanted to ask how he had guessed, but Asher told her to answer only direct questions and not to initiate anything. She remained silent.

"I would like to discuss it with you sometime," Eltin said, and then moved on down the line.

The Spire of Kylet

After his inspection was completed, Eltin stood at the front while Jana, who was another of Asher's friends, walked by with an officer that Katrine didn't remember seeing before.

"Everything ready?" the unknown officer asked.

"Yes sir," Eltin said.

"Dismiss them for breakfast," Jana told him.

"Yes ma'am."

Eltin turned to his troops. "Fall out for breakfast. Reassemble in half an hour."

Katrine went with the unit, picked up her meal, and followed them to a long table. When they finished eating, they scraped their plates and left them and the utensils in big tubs.

She was following the others back to the assembly area when Eltin approached. "Master Neyac would like a word with you. Make it quick."

"Yes sir." It was easier to say with each repetition.

She spied Neyac over by Warlord Leeds's tent. The Recorder was standing with his arm around Heni, who wept quietly.

"Heni was afraid you would go without saying goodbye," Neyac said. "So was I."

"I'm sorry. I didn't know it was an option. Asher's orders were very strict."

"Do be careful." Heni threw her arms around Katrine's waist. "Neyac's been explaining everything to me, and I'm trying to understand. I truly am. But I couldn't bear to lose you."

Returning the embrace, Katrine whispered, "I'll come back. I promise." Then she turned to Neyac. "Did Jana give you the letter to my parents?"

He patted a pocket of his Recorder's robe. "I've got it right here."

Grabbing Katrine's arm, Heni cried out, "You are afraid something's going to happen to you, aren't you?"

"No, I'm not." Katrine gave Heni's shoulder a squeeze then lifted her cousin's fingers away from her arm. She tried to sound confident and reassuring. "I don't know how long this will take or what my next orders will be. I'm just covering contingencies. That's all. Please, don't worry."

She gave Neyac a quick hug. "I'm sorry I got so upset yesterday," she whispered in his ear. "I wish we'd had time to talk. When I get back? All right?"

"When you get back," he said, putting his arm around Heni again.

Rejoining her unit, Katrine found Thunder Cloud saddled and waiting for her. All around, Warriors gathered up weapons, and when the signal was given, they swung onto their steeds. The dull clanging of gear and an occasional whinny were the only sounds Katrine heard. There was no talking, no whispering, and no joking among the troops.

Once she was on Thunder Cloud, Katrine checked the quiver on her back to make sure it was positioned correctly. The extra one hanging from her belt had two cords at the bottom, which she tied around her thigh so it wouldn't bounce as she rode. She had already strung her bow and held it in her left hand with her reins.

The spire, inside her shirtfront, was warm against her skin.

Eltin's hand flashed the 'move out' signal, and she fell in line and followed.

Although Asher had told her to keep her eyes on Eltin, she furtively searched for the Captain within the shadows of the trees. She knew he commanded the vanguard. Even if they couldn't speak, she wanted a glimpse of him before the battle for luck, for comfort, for reassurance, for something. As her unit rode deeper into the forest, she realized she wasn't going to see him, and she stopped looking.

To prepare for the upcoming conflict, just as Asher had taught her, Katrine took several deep breaths, centered her inner being, and then carefully began constructing a mental wall. The technique was similar to the one Polnu had taught her to protect herself from other people's emotions. However, instead of using a cushion of thought, she built layer upon layer of rock hard determination, creating a fortress that would shield her from the evil and bloodlust of Elnid-Kyeh's army.

South of the enemy camp, Eltin positioned the archers among the trees. Their job was to shoot flaming arrows at the wooden bridge and set it ablaze. If it wouldn't burn, and some feared Elnid-Kyeh might have ensorcelled it, they were to prevent reinforcements from using it to join the fighting on this side of the Cleft.

Once their location was established, they waited.

Katrine hated waiting. She had always hated waiting. And this morning was the absolute worst. Asher told her that physical activity helped protect Wolkareans from the fatigue caused by their mental shields. Already she was developing a headache from concentrating. She needed action.

To the east, the sky shone pink around some low dark clouds that clung to the horizon. A crisp breeze fanned the air.

The lilting song of a bird brightened the silence. Eltin made a few quick moves with his left hand, and the sound was repeated by one of the archers. It then echoed twice from different locations. It was surely a signal, but Asher hadn't explained what kind. For all Katrine knew, it might mean *Pretty sunrise, isn't it?* Obviously it wasn't something she needed to know.

She hoped it meant the fighting would start soon.

All of a sudden, a small band of mounted Warriors led by Asher plunged over the crest of the hill in the west. Shouting ferociously, they whirled into camp like a cyclone, stirring up confusion, knocking over tents.

Soldiers rushed around bumping into each other and tripping over their own feet. Some were only half dressed and pulled on articles of clothing with one hand while they grappled with weapons in the other.

The enemies' horses were corralled, and several soldiers tried to saddle their mounts amid the onslaught. Some of the more daring clambered up bareback and took off after the Landorians.

"Now," said Eltin, and his voice called Katrine's attention back to her unit and their assignment.

She thrust her specially prepared arrow into the torch Eltin held and sent it flying toward the bridge. It hit and stuck midpoint in a plank. Other lighted arrows followed, and soon the bridge was in flames.

"Katrine, Zack, Brollin—" Eltin barked out several more names, "cover the Captain's retreat."

"Retreat?" mumbled Katrine under her breath.

Sure enough, a bellow from Asher recalled his forces, and they turned and fled up the hill. Enemy soldiers were in close pursuit.

Frantically, Katrine nocked and loosed arrow after arrow. Why was Asher retreating so soon? What had gone wrong? With blinding fury, she tried to empty the quiver on her back. Shokai soldiers tumbled from their horses.

Asher's Warriors disappeared successfully over the hill. Katrine heaved a sigh of relief. It was short-lived.

The foe turned to confront the archers.

Suddenly, Asher reappeared with reinforcements. From the north and south, Warriors poured into the area. They had the enemy surrounded on three sides with the Cleft on the fourth. Soon the field was packed with men and women battling with swords.

"Yield," shouted Eltin. He made two quick gestures, right and left, and his unit spread out ten paces apart.

When Eltin briefed her last night, he said that after the armies met, the archers' job would change. They were responsible for keeping the enemy from sneaking around the edges of the battlefield, either to escape or to launch a rear attack.

More waiting, Katrine thought resentfully. She didn't want to watch the action, doing nothing but warming Thunder Cloud's back with her rear-end. Besides, Asher told her to keep her body moving. How was she supposed to do that and follow Eltin's orders at the same time?

As she took her position, her gaze was drawn to a movement across the Cleft. Several men crouched on the ground and began transforming. Soldiers who had been there one moment were replaced by a flock of winged beasts. They were atrocious parodies of eagles and hawks and griffins and other creatures out of myth and legend, all with oddly shaped wings and razor sharp beaks or teeth.

Katrine kicked her horse and galloped over to Eltin.

"Who said you could leave your position?" he snapped.

Pointing her finger, she cried out, "Shapeshifters, sir. They're crossing the gap."

Straight away Eltin ordered the archers to target the fliers. A volley of arrows filled the sky. When they struck a target, human-sounding cries erupted from beaks and muzzles. One creature reshaped as a man in a scarlet robe and faded from sight before he hit the ground. Katrine was so startled when he disappeared that she muffed her next shot, missing the mark by several inches.

"Some are bewitched," Katrine heard one of the Crennese archers say. "But I can't tell if the spell conceals, fetches, or teleports them."

"Enough jabber," barked Eltin. "Focus."

"Yes sir." The Crennese Warrior readied his bow.

A hideous eagle dove for Asher, and Katrine nocked an arrow as fast as she could. Before she could pull back the string, Asher sliced the bird's head from its body with a single stroke and then continued fighting with a Shokai soldier.

As quickly as the archers killed one flying shapechanger, another underwent the metamorphosis. Again and again, the archers launched their missiles. Katrine's arms felt heavy, and a burning ache in her shoulders worked its way down her back. Despite the continuous barrage, always a few creatures reached the Warriors, ripping flesh from faces and hands and bodies.

"Sir," Katrine said, "if we could only keep them from completing the transformations—"

"Good idea." Dividing his unit, Eltin had part leave their horses and creep through the underbrush to the Cleft's edge. There they could reach targets on the other side of the divide without trees and foliage getting in the way. Katrine and those left behind continued bringing down ones already in the air.

"It's working." Eltin gave Katrine a wink and still managed to launch an arrow that pierced the neck of an approaching griffin.

A ball of blue mist appeared in the middle of the camp. It oozed outward like colored smoke being poured from a bottle. A shapeless form bobbed and twisted in its center. Gradually it took shape, pulling the blue vapor inward until the whole mass congealed into a winged dragon.

An earsplitting shriek drowned the clanging of swords.

The dragon grabbed a Warrior and ripped him in half with a violent twist of its claws. Blood and gore splattered those nearby. Lashing its tail, the creature smashed men and horses without distinguishing friend from foe.

Warriors fled in panic. Enemy soldiers gave chase.

New flying creatures swooped across the cleft after undergoing the change, unseen, behind a cluster of boulders. The archers tried to stop them with another dynamic volley of arrows, but there were too many.

The battlefield was in chaos.

Katrine lobbed arrows as if her body had been created solely for that function: grab an arrow, nock it to the string, pull back, release, grab an arrow, nock it—endlessly.

A winged lizard, like a miniature dragon, latched onto the back of an archer near Katrine and began gnawing on the man's neck. The Warrior screamed, dropped his bow, and swung his arms behind him. He was unable to dislodge the beast.

Nudging Thunder Cloud with her heels, Katrine rode closer, drew her dagger, and stabbed the little creature.

The injured man tumbled from his horse.

Quickly vaulting from Thunder Cloud's back, Katrine grabbed some rags from her saddlebags, made a pad, and fastened it around the Warrior's neck. She hoped to slow the bleeding until a Healer could take care of him.

It only took a few seconds, but as she remounted, she remembered Asher telling her not to get distracted by the wounded. He said the urge to help often caused novice fighters to get killed. She wondered if she would get into trouble when all this was over.

She smiled to herself. This wasn't trouble enough already?

She reached into her quiver and realized her arrows were running low. She couldn't remember what she was supposed to do if she emptied her backup supply. As she tried to dredge up the memory, she heard a screech and glanced up to see a monstrous raven diving for her, talons stretched forward. As if she had never held a bow before, her fingers became so clumsy she couldn't fit the arrow to the string.

It gave out a loud squawk and dropped, a bit of fletching visible in its breast. Katrine's eyes darted left, and Eltin gave her a nod and pointed to the attacking flocks.

"Focus," he said, taking his next shot.

A brief lull followed.

Katrine surveyed the battlefield. The enemy camp had been obliterated. There were no tents, no corral, and no campfires, only bodies crumpled on the ground or fighting.

In the middle of the field, the blue dragon began to pump its wings, generating clouds of dust. Leaves and pine needles swirled in little cyclonic designs. Fighters threw arms across their faces to protect their eyes. Some tumbled from their horses. Others lost their footing, staggered, and fell.

The dragon flexed its leg muscles and sprang into the air.

While Katrine watched with dread and fascination, the dragon's outline blurred. Beneath its features was Elnid-Kyeh's face, full of wanton cruelty and greedy for power and dominance.

Higher and higher, the dragon climbed.

As it circled above the combatants, it swung its head from side to side, its red eyes scanning the tree line.

In her heart, Katrine knew it was searching for her.

Chapter Forty-Four

Suspended in the air, the dragon shrieked triumphantly when it saw Katrine. As if drawn by a magical thread, she nudged Thunder Cloud forward.

Piercing hatred struck her like a fist, almost toppling her with its malice. Her head spun, and her stomach heaved. If her shields were protecting her, how much stronger would the blow have been without them?

Spreading its bat-like wings, the dragon glided toward her.

"Katrine," Eltin shouted, "into the trees."

Hearing the words, Katrine tried to obey. She struggled with every ounce of strength she had, but she was frozen in place by a power she couldn't even imagine. Only her eyes could move, and they were fastened on the dragon, tracking its slightest twitch as it flapped nearer.

Help me, Kylet, she prayed silently. *Tell me what to do.*

Like a sudden light in darkness, Bainu's invisibility spell burst into Katrine's mind. She pulled energy into herself, past headache and dizziness. She forced her lips into the right sequence of sounds. As if she were slogging through rock, she pushed against the magic that held her in place. Making the tiniest of wiggles with the tips of her index fingers, she performed the commanding gestures.

Perspiration sprouted on her forehead and dripped into her eyes. The dragon began a backward stroke to slow its momentum. The hind legs swung forward to grab her.

Deep within, she found a hidden reservoir of power, and with a great push she uttered the last syllable and achieved the final gesture of the spell. When she disappeared, she was freed from whatever enchantment had held her.

Clamping her heels to her horse, she guided him to a new position.

The dragon screeched in rage and disappointment.

Arrows zipped through the air, struck, and then bounced from the dragon's armored scales. They were followed by more. Despite the ineffectiveness of the shots, the archers persisted. Katrine realized Eltin was trying to distract

Elnid-Kyeh and give her a chance to escape.

Katrine slipped her bow over her head and shoulder so it hung across her back alongside her quiver.

Although mundane arrows apparently could not pierce the dragon's hide, perhaps a magical weapon could. She reached inside her tunic front and pulled out Kylet's spire.

Before she could throw the weapon, her brain exploded into a raging forest fire. The pain was so agonizing she expected her skin to crackle and burst into flames. She fell forward and clutched at Thunder Cloud's neck, almost afraid her touch would char him and turn him to ash.

Elnid-Kyeh had ripped apart her invisibility spell and knocked down her mental barriers as easily as if they had been a house built of straw and dried leaves.

What the fraggin' hell was she doing? She was an immature herder, and he was a trained sorcerer. She must have been insane to try and face him.

* * *

At the dragon's deafening roar of victory, the combatants on the field froze.

All eyes turned.

In horror, Asher watched Katrine cling lopsidedly to her horse. She looked nearly unconscious. The dragon dropped down toward her with sharp, evil claws extended.

Gradually, as if she struggled to lift a mountain through sheer willpower, Katrine pulled herself erect in the saddle. Her hand came up, holding something metallic and shiny.

She raised her head.

Asher blinked and squinted against the brightness.

Her eyes glowed like twin suns.

The dragon jerked to a halt. It flapped its wings awkwardly as it tried to turn and flee.

* * *

"Now, daughter," Kylet's deep voice resonated in Katrine's ears. As he and the Three Sister Wives enveloped her in their protection, her fears disappeared and her energy retuned.

With a flick, she let the spire fly. At first it looked as if it would catch the dragon just below the neck, a deathblow, but then the weapon dipped and swayed.

At least, she told the spire silently, *slow the dragon down. Wound it. Hurt it. Make it leave.*

When the spire reached the target, it slashed upward from lower abdomen to chest, and then grazed one wing. Purplish blood oozed from the cuts.

But the devil did not fall.

An audible moan reverberated from the throats of the Landorian Warriors.

Katrine grabbed the spire when it returned to her, never taking her eyes from the dragon.

The wounded wing faltered.

The dragon dropped.

Off balance, it flew in a bobbing pattern back toward the Cleft, changing shapes, blurring from one form into another, getting smaller and smaller.

As if they had been released from a spell, the Warriors and enemy soldiers rushed at each other, and the clashing of swords once again shattered the day.

* * *

As Elnid-Kyeh strove to reach safety, he cursed feverishly. The girl had used that damnable spire against him, and it had sapped his strength.

He could no longer maintain the massive form he had assumed.

With his energy draining away, he had to take the shape of smaller and smaller creatures in hopes of making it across the Cleft before his muscles gave out completely.

* * *

Taking heart, the archers filled the air with arrows. But other winged creatures intervened, clustering around Elnid-Kyeh, now the size of a sparrow, shielding him and intercepting the shafts with their bodies. When he reached the other side of the crevice, one of his minions darted from behind a boulder, caught the tiny bird, and spirited it from sight.

With the dragon gone, the Landorians rallied and took on the battle anew. A wall of Warriors formed and pushed the enemy closer and closer to the Cleft.

As the enemy found their numbers dwindling and their backs approaching the deep rift, they dropped their swords and lifted their hands high above their heads.

Warlord Leeds rode to the front to explain the conditions of surrender.

He stopped when several hideous screams were heard.

With a thick line of blood arcing across his shirtfront and down his left arm, Elnid-Kyeh staggered from behind the rocks.

"Warlord!" he shrieked, his voice trembling. "Coward! You attacked us without warning, and I was not prepared. You will not be so lucky next time. Do you hear me? Next time we meet, I will crush you. And do not expect much from that inconsequential girl you call the Warrior of Four Bloods. Her powers are weak, and she will not live long enough to develop them."

Warlord Leeds yelled back, "Today was her first battle, and she gave you a pretty little souvenir. Quite a feat for a weak girl."

A few anonymous chuckles tickled the afternoon air, and Elnid-Kyeh's face grimaced with fury. He waved his hands, murmured some words, and an orange light flashed from his fingertips.

The Landorian Warriors dropped to the ground, held their breaths, and waited for death. But the sounds of torment rose from the surrounded foe, who began falling and writhing.

"You'll take no prisoners, Warlord," Elnid-Kyeh called with a vile laugh. "This is how I reward failure."

Then the Shokai prince disappeared.

* * *

Huge funeral pyres were built for the fallen among both the Landorian and enemy troops. Overhead, dark clouds hung, as if even the heavens were somber in the wake of such devastation. The day was bleak and heavy as evening approached.

Warriors checked the bodies of the slain to see if Elnid-Kyeh had miscalculated and left even one of his soldiers injured but alive. He had not.

Warlord Leeds refused to leave any of his Warriors near the battleground overnight, and he ordered a return to camp, even though it meant traveling in the dwindling light.

The severely wounded were carried on stretchers made from tree branches and the cloaks of the dead. Warriors rotated the task of carrying them, those riding on horseback trading places with those who trudged along bearing the litters on foot.

Travel was slow through the woods, especially for those who walked, for no trails existed, and the Warriors had to duck beneath low hanging branches and fight their way through the underbrush. Finally the Warlord ordered several men to blaze a trail with their swords.

When the wind changed and blew from the east, the air was filled with a foul smelling smoke, thick with the stench of charred flesh.

Although injuries had been treated on site with bandages, medications, and spells, Healers walked beside the stretchers. Katrine joined them, trying to alleviate pain and fortify the wounded in hopes that all would survive the arduous, jostling trek back to camp.

While they marched, one of the Warriors voiced a question that had been puzzling Katrine.

"Why didn't Elnid-Kyeh use his spell to kill us?" a stocky young man asked. "He had the power. Why did he kill his own troops and let us go free?"

One of the Crennese Warrior-Healers answered. "There are many ways to work magic," the woman said. "If a spell is simple, one needs only to say the words, collect the energies, and make the gestures. However, if it is complicated, one needs time to prepare. Often a sorcerer will pronounce the spell beforehand, leaving out a key phrase. Then, when he needs it, all he has to do is say the phrase and make the final gesture while he gathers and releases his power. Elnid-Kyeh must have prepared a spell against his own forces in case of trouble. He had no spell in readiness for us because he didn't know we were coming."

"If he can use magic that strong against us," an injured man asked, "how can we win?"

"That'll be up to the Warrior of Four Bloods," the Crennese woman answered.

No one else said anything, but Katrine felt many eyes on her.

And so the expectations begin, she thought.

Chapter Forty-Five

A weary band finally stumbled into camp well after night had spread its inky cloak over the forest. Heni flung herself into Katrine's arms and insisted on checking her over to make sure she was uninjured.

Headmaster Miksel and Neyac had both learned a great deal about medicinal herbs and treating injuries during their travels. They assisted the Healers, and so did Katrine and Heni, as did many Warriors who had nothing to offer but willing hands.

The day after the battle, the Healers worked in shifts, some getting much needed sleep or food while the others labored, only to switch before any felt truly refreshed.

Several of the injured did not live through the day, and they were laid to rest in a clearing among the trees. The atmosphere in camp was solemn, and those who spoke talked only in whispers.

* * *

Nearly two weeks passed before Warlord Leeds commanded the Warriors to break camp. By then, all of the wounded had either responded to the ministrations of the Healers or had been buried.

The remaining troops were anxious to be away from the mountains before the snows started. Frost sparkled on the ground in the mornings, and the nights were cold. Once the order was given, the Warriors quickly took down tents, bundled supplies, and loaded the pack animals.

While Katrine was finishing the tasks assigned to her, a familiar hawk, large and brown, landed in front of Warlord Leeds. Torrend transformed back into himself.

"Message delivered, sir," Torrend reported smartly. "In return, District Commandant Edmon said to tell you he looks forward to having you back where you belong."

"He's not the only one," Leeds boomed. He clasped Torrend on the shoulder. "We're moving out. I guess I should have let you stay at Landor rather than making you fly one way and ride back the other. But I may still need your services."

"My pleasure, sir," Torrend replied. "I've gotten quite comfortable with flying now. I don't mind a bit."

"Good lad," Leeds said. "Mount up."

Leeds and Asher rode at the front of the company.

"Move out," Asher roared. The Warriors lined up behind their leaders and began the long journey west.

Now that the battle was over, Katrine was no longer assigned to Eltin's unit. She rode behind Leeds and Asher, alongside Heni, Torrend, and the two Master Recorders.

"I've decided to give this horse a name," Heni said with pride. "Neyac said since she's not branded or marked, there's no way of locating the rightful owners. The bandits probably stole her, but she's mine now."

"That's right," Neyac asserted. "No one else has any claim to her that I can tell."

"What are you going to call her?" Katrine asked.

"I'm afraid it will sound dumb." Heni blushed and ran her fingers lightly down the horse's chestnut neck. "Her coloring reminds me of my mother's hair. Do you think it would be disrespectful if I named her Rulina? Even though I never learned to ride before this, my mother rode all the time. She loved animals, especially horses. I think she would be pleased to have my mount named after her."

"That's a splendid tribute, Heni," Katrine said. "Your mother was a beautiful woman, and your horse is a beautiful animal."

"My father always called my mother 'Ruli,' so that's what I'll call my horse for short, but her real name will be Rulina."

"It's lovely," Torrend assured her.

Leaning forward, Heni nuzzled her face in her horse's deep mane. "Ruli," she said, "my very own Ruli."

Warlord Leeds was worried about the possibility of more Shokai lingering in the desolate hills. He assigned outriders to range ahead of the company to search for other enemy encampments. Asher and Katrine were often paired and assigned scouting duty.

"How are you doing?" Asher asked her one afternoon while they patrolled the area north of the trail. "You've been quiet all day."

"I'm fine," Katrine answered. She ran her fingers through a lock of hair that had escaped her braid, flipped it behind her ear, and then pulled the hood of her cloak tighter around her face. "No, I lied," she said, reining in her horse. "I'm not fine."

"What's bothering you?" Asher halted his mount next to hers. "Maybe I can help."

Conflicting feelings wrangled in Katrine's chest. She and Asher hadn't argued since before the battle. She hated to risk quarreling now. Still, she had to know if what she heard had been the truth. She gave up trying to find a diplomatic approach.

"Oh, snakespit," she swore. "I don't know how to word this, so I'm just going to ask." She paused and Asher raised his eyebrows expectantly. "This morning," she told him, "when I was using the—uh—the trenches, I heard two women talking. They said you beat up a couple of Warriors who complained because I didn't kill Elnid-Kyeh and who said I was worse than useless. The women said Warlord Leeds reprimanded you and promised you would be punished when we get to Landor. Is it true?"

"Damn it," Asher said. "I didn't realize it had become so public that it was being discussed at the latrines." Meeting Katrine's eyes, he said, "Yes, it's true."

"Why, Asher?" she wailed. "It's bad enough to have them talking about me all the time. Now, if your reputation is damaged or you lose rank and privileges because of me, I just don't know how I'll bear it."

"Slow down, girl," Asher said, flashing the hand signal for stop at the same time. "My reputation and rank and privileges are my business. The females you heard talking obviously didn't know the whole story."

"But, Asher—"

"If you think I got chastised, you should have heard what Leeds gave those men when I reported what they had said. No Warrior is allowed to say about a comrade what they said about you. It was malicious, it was false, and it was born of envy. Leeds doesn't allow that kind of sewage because it divides and demoralizes the troops."

"But—"

"If," Asher said loudly, scowling at her, refusing to let her interrupt him, "if I had reported what I heard without losing my temper, Leeds would have had those men flogged. Instead, I allowed myself to get angry, and I trounced them. That was a breach of my trust as an officer. I'm a Captain, and I have no right to manhandle the men. I got what I deserved, and I'll take whatever's coming."

By the time Asher stopped for breath, Katrine's mouth had fallen open and hit her collarbone. "Holy Powers," she breathed, "it must have been awful."

"It was offensive."

Katrine shuddered. She tried to push her feelings back to prevent her dismay from showing, but she couldn't.

"I hate this," she said. "I thought Landorian Warriors were supposed to know all about the Warrior of Four Bloods, and they should surely know about battles. This was my first one, and I wasn't prepared. They must know I didn't miss on purpose. I tried. If they act like this, how can I expect anyone in Kareand to support me?"

"You can't let two dimwits like those get you down. They wanted a miracle. Failing to get that, they wanted someone to blame for the war that's coming. Most of the Warriors feel it was an honor to witness your first confrontation with Elnid-Kyeh. You wounded him, and he didn't mark you. That was a great accomplishment."

Katrine felt herself blush, but it was accompanied by a happy grin too.

"In addition," Asher continued, "Eltin has spread the word that you were the first to spot the shapechangers. He has also told everyone that even under pressure and knowing who you are, you followed the chain of command and reported to him, accepting his authority and letting him give the orders. That has earned you the respect of every officer in the company and most of the troops. The Warlord and I lead the way."

"Really, Asher? I did all right?"

"By the Coils! You were splendid, Katrine, absolutely splendid. I thought you knew."

"You never told me."

"I'm a dunce!" Asher said, smacking his forehead in frustration. "I should have told you a dozen times. Leeds should have, too. I've been so proud of you I could burst. Not just the way you handled yourself during the fight, but everything you do. You've helped the injured when you should have been eating and sleeping. You've accepted every assignment, even the menial ones, with dignity. You never take offense, even when someone tries to goad you. You treat everyone with courtesy and respect. You show promise of becoming a fine leader. Have you been worrying about your performance ever since the battle?"

"A little," she admitted. "Then this morning, when I heard those women, I thought," she couldn't look at him, "I thought maybe you defended me because what they said was true—that I'm useless."

Asher cleared his throat and spat, as if he was getting rid of a foul taste. "I should have those she-devils flogged for trying to stir up trouble."

"Oh no," Katrine cried, "please, don't. They did me a favor. If I hadn't overheard them, I wouldn't have asked you about it. And you might never have told me you were proud of me. I'm grateful to them."

Reaching out a gloved hand, Asher squeezed Katrine's arm and gave her one of his glorious smiles. "Feeling better now?"

"Yes," Katrine said, basking in the warmth of her feelings for this man. How she loved his smile! If she could, she would dedicate her life to making him smile, even if it meant giving up every hope, every goal, every dream she had ever had.

"Come on," he said, "we need to hurry." He prodded his horse gently. "I hope by the time we're finished, they've set up camp for the night. I'm getting hungry."

"Me too."

The trek through the northern hills seemed to take forever. Provisions ran low, and travel slowed as the Warriors took time to hunt and forage. The nights were bitter with cold, and the days weren't much better.

The Spire of Kylet

A light snow dusted the ground early one morning when an outrider galloped up to the Warlord.

"We've checked both sides of the trail," she reported. "It's clear all the way to Pardish."

"Mount up," Leeds bellowed. "We're almost there."

Katrine and her friends halted their horses at the pinnacle of the trail.

Below them, spread out over a series of hills, was the elegantly walled city of Pardish. Standing side by side, the Recorders School and Regency were massive complexes built of white and gray stone. Wide, straight streets were lined with trees whose bare branches formed a latticework around businesses, homes, and parks. Many domes and steeples and turrets poked above rooftops, and colorful flags and banners flapped in the brisk, winter breeze.

A mixture of feelings washed over Katrine.

All her life she had dreamed of traveling to Pardish—Kareand's repository of knowledge, wisdom, and artistic excellence—so she could become a Recorder. Now, because that path was closed to her, seeing the fabled city was a bittersweet experience.

"That's Landor, across the river," Asher said, pointing beyond Pardish to another enormous city. "There in the center, behind the second wall, is the Training Compound. Landor may not look as dignified as its sister city, but it has its own appeal."

"They're both very big," Katrine commented.

"That's an understatement," Asher said with a laugh. His eyes shone brightly, and his lips curled up at the corners.

Katrine gazed at him in silence and considered the past few months.

Since their first encounter in Plains Springs, he had yelled at her, made her angry, hurt her feelings, irritated her, and sometimes frightened her. He had also taught, comforted, praised, and protected her.

He had helped her accept her destiny.

If Asher was going to Landor, there was nowhere else she would rather be.

"Come on," he urged. "It's been a long trip. Let's go home."

EPILOGUE

Elnid-Kyeh sat alone and fumed while gigantic waves battered the base of the cliffs below his bedchamber's window. He was still healing and regaining his strength after his most recent contact with Kylet's cursed spire. The bewitched weapon had debilitated him so thoroughly he had barely made it back across Marlett's Cleft to safety.

If he had not drained the life forces from several of his servants to fortify himself, he would not have been strong enough to confront the Warlord.

Then, instead of preserving his men and taking them home with him, he had been forced to cast the annihilation spell and destroy them all so he could absorb the energy created by their death throes. Otherwise, he would not have been able to rejuvenate adequately to teleport himself all the way back to Serpent's Head.

His lips curled into a smile. At least the annihilation spell had provided an impressive demonstration of his power for the Warlord and the girl.

Slowly his smile faded.

Now he would need to send one of his servants to Shokareen with a report on the battle. Shokai priests regularly checked on him, using their own scrying implements, and it would be better if he told his side of the story before they started drawing their own conclusions. In frustration he slapped the arms of his chair. That would mean admitting defeat.

What if his allies lost faith in him and withdrew their support?

He could not allow that to happen.

He would have to word his communiqué very carefully.

He needed to convince the Most High that this had been an unprovoked attack by a vicious and bloodthirsty Warlord. It was a blessing that he had not had all of his Shokai soldiers with him. At least he would not have to request reinforcements.

What he needed was a plan for destroying the girl before she learned to control her powers. He could not let her mature enough to become a hindrance to his plans. Nor could he let her gather the Wolkareans and conduct them to Landor for training.

His best course, he was sure, was to keep Kareand's leaders so busy they had no time to organize. Using renegades to kill and plunder, making the roads unsafe for travel and promoting fear in the citizenry, had been the first step. Now he needed a clever second one.

Thoughtfully, he drummed his fingertips on the table at his side. He must accelerate and advance his plans while the Landorians were basking in their ill-earned battle pride.

Suddenly, he chuckled.

He could recall Hollenth from Banur.

Of all his minions, Hollenth was the most devious and the least bothered by conscience or principles. Hollenth could use his creativity to provoke the populace, confound the leadership, and prevent the gathering of the Wolkareans.

Then Elnid-Kyeh could devote his time and attention to destroying the Warrior of Four Bloods.

Connie A. Walker was born in Blackfoot, ID, attended elementary school in Kansas City, KS, and graduated high school in Fairbanks, AK. She has been an insatiable reader and a compulsive writer since childhood.

She is the author of the prize-winning plays *The Light Still Burns* and *Nearly a Woman*, as well as the prize-winning children's book *Timmy and the K'nick K'nocker Ring.*

Ms. Walker has a B.A. in theatre/playwriting from Brigham Young University, plus a B.S. in psychology and an MSW from the University of Utah. She has worked as a graphic artist, a technical writer, a foster care worker, a clinical social worker, and a mental health programs manager.

Now retired, she prefers to spend her days tapping away on her computer. When not writing, she enjoys painting with watercolors, quilting, and watching classic black-and-white science fiction movies.

www.ingramcontent.com/pod-product-compliance
Lightning Source LLC
Chambersburg PA
CBHW061541170626
46811CB00001B/35